Contemporary Basque
DETECTIVE and CRIME FICTION

Basque Literature Series #16

Contemporary Basque Detective and Crime Fiction

Edited by
José Manuel López-Gaseni

CENTER FOR BASQUE STUDIES
UNIVERSITY OF NEVADA, RENO
2023

This book was published with generous financial support from the Basque Government.

This is an authorized translation from the original Basque language edition Egungo euskal krimen-literatura published in 2021 by UPV/EHU Press.

This book is part of the functions of the Research Group LAIDA (Literature and Identity) (IT 1572/22; GIC 21/118), which is part of the network of official Research Groups appointed by the Basque Government and approved by the University of the Basque Country.

Center for Basque Studies
University of Nevada, Reno
1664 North Virginia St,
Reno, Nevada 89557 usa
http://basque.unr.edu

Copyright © 2023 by the Center for Basque Studies and the University of Nevada, Reno
ISBN-13: 978-1-949805-78-9
Epub ISBN: 978-1-949805-79-6
All rights reserved.

Library of Congress Cataloging-in-Publication Data

Names: Lopez Gaseni, José Manuel, editor.
Title: Contemporary Basque detective and crime fiction / edited by José Manuel López-Gaseni.
Description: Reno : Center for Basque Studies, University of Nevada, Reno, 2023. | Series: Basque literature series; #16 | Includes bibliographical references. | Summary: "The study of Basque crime and detective fiction, as with that of any other culture, implies addressing a supposedly peripheral genre that has nonetheless been remarkably vibrant throughout its history. Within the topic of contemporary Basque literature, there is a place for some more humble genres outside the main literary currents, such as short stories, children's, and young adult literature, and even comics. Here, though, we will concentrate on crime fiction. In order to do so, this introduction will follow a classic pattern. In other words, we will first survey the broader history of the genre and conclude by exploring the emergence of crime fiction in the Basque Country"-- Provided by publisher.
Identifiers: LCCN 2023039349 | ISBN 9781949805789 (paperback) | ISBN 9781949805796 (epub)
Subjects: LCSH: Detective and mystery stories, Basque--History and criticism.
Classification: LCC PH5292.F5 C66 2023 | DDC 899/.923087209--dc23/eng/20231012
LC record available at https://lccn.loc.gov/2023039349

Printed in the United States of America

Contents

Introduction: Some Notes to Describe the Detective and Crime Literary System *by José Manuel López-Gaseni* 7

Chapter 1: 110. *street-eko geltokia* (110th Street Station)(1986): A Basque's Harsh Exile or Homesickness in the City *by Jon Martin Etxebeste* 50

Chapter 2: Aingeru Epaltza's Three Intrigue Novels: *Sasiak ere begiak baditik* (Even Brush Has Eyes, 1986), *Ur uherrak* (Muddy Waters, 1993), and *Rock'n'Roll* (2000) *by Asier Barandiaran* 69

Chapter 3: Bernardo Atxaga's *Gizona bere bakardadean* (The Lone Man) (1993) *by Xabier Etxaniz Erle* 92

Chapter 4: Itxaro Borda's Detective Cycle: The World of Amaia Ezpeldoi *by Ur Apalategi* 104

Chapter 5: Constructing Harkaitz Cano's Literary Universe: The Influence of the United States *by Aiora Sampedro Alegria* 123

Chapter 6: Taking the Genre to the Limit: On Jon Alonso's Novel *Zintzoen saldoan* (In the Group of the Righteous) *by Javier Rojo Cobos* 135

Chapter 7: The Gaze of the Other: Jon Arretxe's Noir Fiction *by Javier Rojo Cobos* 143

Chapter 8: Ramon Saizarbitoria's *Lili eta biok* (Lili and Me, 2015): The Spanish Civil War and the Investigative Novel *by Miren Billelabeitia and Jon Kortazar* 152

Chapter 9: The Police Novel in Basque Children's and Young Adult Literature *by Xabier Etxaniz Erle and Karla Fernández de Gamboa Vázquez* 177

Chapter 10: Ramiro Pinilla's Police Novels: Contesting the Lack of Memory *by Santiago Pérez Isasi* 195

Chapter 11: Dolores Redondo's *El guardián invisible* (*The Invisible Guardian*, 2013) *by Maite Aperribay-Bermejo* 207

Chapter 12: Unveiling the Cover: The Front Covers of Basque Detective Novels *by Susana Jodra Llorente and José Antonio Morlesín Mellado* 224

Chapter 13: Basque Crime Fiction and World Literature Studies *by Stewart King*..244

Index 255

About the Authors 276

Introduction

Some Notes to Describe the Detective and Crime Literary System

José Manuel López-Gaseni

The study of Basque crime and detective fiction, as with that of any other culture, implies addressing a supposedly peripheral genre that has nonetheless been remarkably vibrant throughout its history. Within the topic of contemporary Basque literature, there is a place for some more humble genres outside the main literary currents, such as short stories, children's, and young adult literature, and even comics. Here, though, we will concentrate on crime fiction.

In order to do so, this introduction will follow a classic pattern. In other words, we will first survey the broader history of the genre and conclude by exploring the emergence of crime fiction in the Basque Country.

The Name and Essence of the Genre: Blurred Boundaries

There has been long and extensive discussion about the boundaries and essence of this genre. There is no agreement either on a definition of what constitutes crime fiction or its boundaries. In 1928, the American writer S. S. Van Dine claimed that twenty rules had to be fulfilled to write a crime novel while Raymond Chandler gave ten, and Thomas Narcejac noted four laws with which the genre had to comply. Of these definitions, few have been followed down to the present.

As Tzvetan Todorov (1971) says, there are two stories in crime fiction: the story of the crime and the story of the investigation of that crime. Whatever the case, in order to differentiate itself from other genres that employ a similar theme, the crime must take a central place.

Regarding the crime, in most cases there is a murder. Among the exceptions, one could cite *The Moonstone* by Wilkie Collins, in which the crime is the theft of a diamond. Furthermore, the crime may be simulated, as in the case of Arthur Conan Doyle's *The Hunchback*. As mentioned before, crime is necessary and it must be central to the story.

There are also many types of characters that head the investigation of the crime. Looking at the history of the genre, this is typically a police detective (hence the term for the genre in the European tradition: the *police novel*). The second most common type of main character is the private investigator, whether assigned professionally to the task or not. Nevertheless, there can be other types of investigators, such as a journalist (many crime stories are presented in the form of a *chronicle*) or a man of the church (Father Brown in Chesterton's novels, William of Baskerville in Umberto Eco's books).

The central component of the crime is more consolidated than the type of investigator. Because of this, following Vázquez de Parga (1993) and Valles Calatrava (1991), we prefer to use the terms *crime novel* or *crime story* rather than *police novel*, although this latter term will also be employed in this work. Moreover, there is an opportunity for greater diversity within this "crime story" term and that will be very useful in the Basque versions of the genre.

Because of this diversity, however, it is difficult to give a precise definition of the genre. There have been a lot of interesting attempts, but in essence we always go back to the initial binary scheme. As such, crime fiction is made up of stories about a crime and the investigation of that crime. Valles Calatrava defines it thus:

> We will thus use the term "crime novel" to allude to the narrative form known as "police novel," which incorporates a set of stories characterized mainly but not exclusively (. . .) by their use as a basic theme a criminal event conceived as a confrontation between justice/crime and their representatives. (Valles Calatrava 1991: 22)

All the variants that have existed throughout the history of the genre are included without much difficulty in this denomination, yet two main developments stand out: the *mystery novel*, pioneered by Edgar Allan Poe, whose main exponents are Arthur Conan Doyle and Agatha Christie; and all sorts of *hard-boiled* or *noir fiction* works, which have been described in terms of a shift toward realism, whose essential pillars are Dashiell Hammett and Raymond Chandler. Todorov proposes a third facet alongside some of his interesting explanations of adaptations of the genre. In his view, a mystery—the essential element in the first group of novels—disappears in noir fiction, or at most is moved to a secondary level. Hence, its centrality in the evolution of research on the theme is also diminished:

> There is no story to be guessed; and there is no mystery, in the sense that it was present in the whodunit. But the reader's interest is not thereby diminished; we realize here that two entirely different forms of interest exist. The first can be called curiosity; it proceeds from effect to cause: starting from a certain effect (a corpse and certain clues) we must find its cause (the culprit and his motive). The second form is suspense, and here the movement is from cause to effect: we are first shown the causes, the initial givens (gangsters preparing a heist), and our interest is sustained by the expectation of what will happen, that is, certain effects (corpses, crimes, fights). (Todorov 1971: 60)

Thus, a change in the point of interest occurs and a new element appears: *suspense*. With that shift, a third variant of the genre appears, as will be seen in the next section.

Todorov's perspective is structural. He understands crime fiction as a "popular" genre (*mainstream* in the sense of its broad appeal), and he ignores other important issues, such as topic, intent, and speech. The experts that followed Todorov in studying successful genres like this include John G. Cawelti and Gary C. Hoppenstand (Colmeiro 1994: 46–64).

Cawelti's main concept is "formula": "Formulas are ways in which specific cultural themes and stereotypes become embodied in more universal story archetypes" (Cawelti 1976: 6). In his view, each genre creates its own specific formula. He divides mainstream literature into three main genres (mystery, adventure, and romance), with crime fiction being part of the first of these.

Hoppenstand bases his approach on Cawelti's arguments, not without some harsh critiques, to propose a new classification: Mystery, Fantasy, and Romance/Adventure. For him (Hoppenstand 1987: 15), literary forms are expressions of myth (in the sense of myth as an expression of society). Myth at the root of crime fiction is that of a crisis stemming from death and mortality. In Hoppenstand's classification, as in that of Cawelti, detective fiction is part of

Mystery, at the rational end of the irrational-rational spectrum. Therein, he distinguishes a number of sub-formulas, depending on the type of detective: the classic sub-formula (life and death as puzzle), including the use of an amateur sleuth; the detective sub-formula (classic noir fiction), which presents a professional police officer leading the investigation; the hardboiled detective sub-formula, based on an honorable private detective; and the avenger detective sub-formula, in which the detective is an upstanding vigilante who possesses extraordinary talents (resembling the spy subgenre).

The Origins and Evolution of the Genre

As to the origins of the genre, one might say that it emerged as a hybrid of several previous trends. Even-Zohar (1990) observes that literary innovations are often complemented by borrowings from non-canonized systems. Many kinds of models and repertoires make up the crime genre. In Poe's early crime narratives ("The Murders in the Rue Morgue," 1841; "The Mystery of Marie Rogêt," 1842; and "The Purloined Letter," 1844), which mark the beginning of the genre, the integration of supernatural literary models from Romanticism stands out. They also reveal several changes of function, especially in relation to the so-called Gothic novel and more specifically those taken from Mary Shelley's and E.T.A. Hoffmann's narratives. The "mystery" component that Poe borrowed from them, which would become crucial in his work, had up to that moment been considered irrational and inexplicable. Thereafter, however, it would be explained from the perspective of logic and reason. Early crime fiction also borrowed from crime adventure published in serial form. These serials were basically adventure stories starring a criminal, but without any mystery. Certain social conditions were also essential. These included the importance of positivism and rationalist thinking in understanding the investigation as a scientific process; and the arrival of industrialization, urban development, rising crime rates, and, as a result of this, the creation of the police force institution (Valles Calatrava 1991: 47).

Initially, as the genre was completely new, Poe's stories were received poorly by both cultured and the popular readers, as has happened with many new literary creations. Nevertheless, translation came to the rescue. As he had done with Poe's poetry, Baudelaire translated the stories into French, under the title *Histoires extraordinaires* and that "source-oriented" (to use Toury's terminology; 1980: 112–121) translation was decisive in spreading and gaining recognition for the work among European intellectuals (Fernández Colmeiro 1994: 32). In this way, the genre also reached a wide readership and thus gained the approval of two different audiences. In fact, in Even-Zohar's words, writers who were able to create a new genre by integrating models, "clearly were conscious of the fact that their readers were often consumers of both systems, so that all kinds of manipulations could be meaningfully grasped by them just like any kind of literary 'allusions'" (Even-Zohar 1978: 18). Some years later, another member of the same school, Zohar Shavit, approached this very subject by adapting Lotman's (1977) concept of "ambivalence" to synchronous events:

> Unlike Lotman, I propose a reduction of the scope and the range of the notion of ambivalence in order to apply it to one specific case only: texts that sychronically (yet dynamically, not statically) maintain an ambivalent status in the literary polysystem. These texts belong simultaneously to more than one system and consequently are read differently (though concurrently), by at least two groups of readers. Those groups of readers diverge in their expctations, as well as in their norms and habits of readling. Hence, their realization of the same text will be greatly different. (Shavit 1986: 66).

This way, Shavit establishes that in order for two different readerships to accept the same text, the structure of this ambivalent text combines two models: one more established and the other newer. The former is more conventional, and aimed at a readership which is accustomed to popular readings. The latter, on the contrary, is more sophisticated and, often created as a result of adapting and renovating a previous model, is aimed at a cultured readership. This is what Poe did when he integrated the aforementioned models and, thus, located his stories in two different systems at the same time. This approach would be a constant throughout the history of the genre down to the present, in both its main and hybrid works.

Poe's innovation, through the filter of positivism and the scientific method, led to Arthur Conan Doyle's model. Where Dupin used reasoning, Sherlock Holmes would apply science. From then on, mystery fiction became formulaic and, therefore, as peripheral as it was successful. Exceptions to this were, as Martín Cerezo (2006: 209) points out, Agatha Christie, S. S. Van Dine, and Dorothy L. Sayers in the 1920s and 1930s.

From the 1920s on, however, the genre made a narrower impression through the realist variant. Then some other repertoires from the past were revived and brought into play, such as chivalric, adventure, and even picaresque literature. Montalbán talks about all this in an interview with Colmeiro in which he refers to:

the hero that is in reality an antihero and that in general has a romantic attitude towards commitment, towards relationships with others, sympathy with the vicitim, with the loser, which was already in the literary tradition since the Renaissance, not in the chivalric novel but in its origins, in Arthurian legend. That is that codification of the hero as a man who feels a commitment to the victim. (Fernández Colmeiro 1988: 15).

The intrigue of the aforementioned repertoire also replaced the "mystery" of the previous model. The action and subject matter became more dynamic and shifted to the big city streets, and hence the term "realist police novel" that Chandler uses when discussing Hammett's work and his often-quoted statement: "Hammett took murder out of the Venetian vase and dropped it into the alley" (Chandler 1950). Such realism is distinctive, and realist novels reflect the socioeconomic atmosphere of the time in which they are developed. Regarding the language they use, however, although they seek to reflect the language of lowlife characters, in general there is a tendency toward the stylized and hyperbolic speech of intradiegetic narrators (irony, sharp humor, surprising comparisons, and so on; and these features of tentative realism have been, additionally, the most imitated).

Furthermore, one can differentiate two chief currents within the realist police novel, according to who the main character is: fiction in which this character investigates a crime and that in which the criminal is the main protagonist. In the former, that of the investigator, as the epitome of justice and morality, he or she goes after the criminal in numerous ways (*The Maltese Falcon*, *The Big Sleep*, *The Glass Key*, for example). In the latter, the criminal protagonist appears in three roles: as a representative of social chaos (W. H. Burnett's *Little Caesar*; D. H. Clarke's *Louis Beretti*); the unexpected criminal who confesses their crime (*The Postman Always Rings Twice*, *Pop. 1280*, Tom Ripley himself); and the righteous criminal who seeks some kind of justice (whose forerunner can be examined in the models of Arsène Lupin and Simon Templar), such as Richard Stark's (Donald Westlake) Parker (Valles Calatrava 1991: 50–51).

The third subgenre, which Colmeiro dubs the psychological or costumbrista police novel, developed primarily in Europe. The clearest example of this is found in Georges Simenon's Maigret police novels. Herein, the realist elements are more obvious, there is a more profound exploration of the psychology of the characters, a sharp critique of society and the police component is not so important. The European tradition of police (and crime) fiction that is so identifiable today was shaped on the basis of this model, with its own nuances developed in many different countries.

Besides the above, suspense took on an autonomous dimension until the creation of the *suspense novel*, likewise within crime fiction. Suspense and spy fiction fit more comfortably into the general crime model than their police counterpart, although not all experts agree on this. However, we have also made some room for spy literature here, as it has been produced in Basque. It retains the element of mystery from the mystery novel. What is more, investigative stories take up most of the account, and suspense is added in order to find out what will happen to the protagonist and the other characters. In other words, there is a longing to know how the spies or secret agents will overcome the obstacles they encounter along the way, with numerous ups and downs in between. Graham Greene and John Le Carré are prominent representatives of spy literature. Taking into account this fourth direction, several examples of the Basque variant of the genre will be included here much more easily.

The Position of Crime Fiction in the Literary System

The aim of this section is to locate crime fiction in the literary system. Following the hierarchical metaphor of the polysystem theory, canonized works and repertoires are located in the center of the system, while non-canonized works are on the periphery. Although crime novels emerged in the English-language model of two countries, the United Kingdom and the United States, nowadays works in this genre are written and published all over the world. In this regard, when it comes to establishing the abovementioned position, we should look at the world literary system.

Even-Zohar wanted to make it clear that canonization is a matter of the tastes of the numerous opinion groups that make up the "Institution" (Even-Zohar 1990, 31) at a given moment and, though indirectly, that it has nothing to do with the literary value of the works themselves. However, some commentators in the contemporary "Institution," taking Harold Bloom as a reference, established and universalized the western canon. Several voices, of course, challenged this canon, above all in the field of what has been termed cursorily cultural studies. These voices, however, have not proposed any alternative canon and, in its place, they advocate a multiple centered system or, put more bluntly, they suggest an opposition between central and peripheral cultures. This position is consistent with Polysystem theory. In fact, as Even-Zohar notes, as a "system of systems," it is a multi-layered whole, in which center-periphery relations act as a kind of field of opposition. He adds, "This actually allows for hypothesizing more than one 'center', although in many historical cases, centers are stratified in such a way that chiefly one eventually succeeds in dominating the whole" (1990, 88).

Leaving aside the discussion of canonized works and repertoires that take center stage, it is clear that what is known as "genre literature" (that is, one which deals with a subgenre or addresses a particular audience) is located on the periphery of the literary system: the western, the romance novel, the historical novel, the comic, children's and young adult literature . . . and crime fiction too. Such types of literature are perceived as being written according to closed schemes which are familiar to the reader (and hence their success), without bringing about any other innovation. This is generally the case with crime novels.

Curiously, however, many writers in the center of the system are interested in the potential that the crime genre may have for other purposes. Umberto Eco was not the first writer that has sought to overcome the notion of such fiction as mere pastime and make use of the crime plot for higher purposes. Indeed, as Colmeiro says, "one of the characteristics of contemporary postmodern art consists of the inter-fertilization of highbrow and popular art, as one can note in the work of John Barth, Umberto Eco, Manuel Puig, and Manuel Vázquez Montalbán" (Fernández Colmeiro 1994, 27).

Many canonical international writers have used elements of crime fiction in their writings, such as suspense and crime itself. Thomas de Quincey, in his essay "On Murder, Considered as One of the Fine Arts" (1817), stated that, in order for crime to be accepted as an aesthetic component, various sociological conditions had to be fulfilled, and that did not happen until the nineteenth century.

The creation of the genre, summarized above, is very interesting from the point of view of polysystemic analysis. Previous models are recycled in order to create a new model, and this new model is, at least initially, at the heart of the system, as it receives the approval of the "Institution."

Clearly, many canonical writers have used the crime novel as a testing ground, in search of resources which would lead later to canonical works. As Colmeiro remarks:

> A panoramic picture of the state of the police novel within the framework of literature in general must also include the "highbrow" use of police formulas on the part of established authors in the literary

canon. In a very symptomatic way, writers in all languages and widely acknowledged as prestigious have turned consciously to this genre from a great variety of perspectives. (Fernández Colmeiro 1994: 35)

Montalbán also talks about adapting the repertoire:

> There is a general paraliterary outlook based on creating a literature of supply, of the masses, which soon generates variants, mutants, which correspond generally to the literary, and moreover a relationship which channels elements that the police novel has discovered, technical and even literary and linguistic elements which are appropriated by literature in general: the characterisation of the literary voyeur, the investigator, the inquiry method, the type of crime which is introduced in relation to the traditional novel (organized social crime); "normal" literature embraces all of this and incorporates it into its attitude (...) for me, Chester Himes is as important a novelist as Richard Wright or any new negritude novelist, and Dashiell Hammett is as important as Hemingway or Faulkner. (Fernández Colmeiro 1988: 14).

Montalbán often situates Graham Greene and Leonardo Sciascia in this field. For this reason, and in addition to the aforementioned Eco, Sciascia, Greene, Puig, and others, several other canonized writers have written many works that can be considered crime novels. These include some Nobel prize-winners such as Dostoievsky, Faulkner, Somerset Maugham, Borges, García Márquez, Robbe-Grillet, Simenon, Highsmith, Dürrenmatt, Piglia and Modiano. And amongst Basque writers, Anjel Lertxundi, Bernardo Atxaga and Ramon Saizarbitoria. For Borges, it was a genre which deserved special attention, to such an extent that, together with Bioy Casares, he created and edited the "El séptimo círculo" series between 1945 and 1955 for the Emecé publishing house. During those years, around one hundred and twenty volumes were published in total. Borges himself also made his own contribution with the short stories "El jardín de los senderos que se bifurcan" (1941) and "La muerte y la brújula" (1944). Furthermore, ever since Alain Robbe-Grillet, a pioneer of the French *nouveau roman* movement, published his police-novel-like *Les Gommes* (1953), many writers of that generation have worked on the importance of the epistemological aspects of genre techniques in literary creation (Cillero 2000: 284).

On the other hand, some writers who place themselves within the genre have a clear awareness of what they are doing. They include Raymond Chandler and his essay *The Simple Art of Murder* (1950), in which he critiques mystery novels and those who write them and comes out in favor of the new model. Chandler is aware that he is working on the boundaries of a genre which is considered marginal, and admits that many dubious works are published. In that sense, he makes an effort to draw the boundaries between good and bad works in the genre.

Agatha Christie, too, one of the bestselling authors ever, was aware that she was a writer in the genre and tried to push herself to the limits, through some kind of experimentation. She did so through her narrators' words, for example. At a certain point, Christie decides to make the narrator himself the killer in *The Murder of Roger Ackroyd* (1926), which was later named the best crime novel of all time. Umberto Eco speaks ironically of this desire to experiment, observing the following:

> It seems that the Oulipo group constructed a matrix of all possible police story situations and found out that a book has still not been written in which the murderer is the reader. Moral: there exist obsessive ideas, but they are never personal; books talk amongst themselves, and any true police inquiry should prove that we are the guilty party. (Eco 1985: 83)

To cite another example, the French writer Pierre Lemaitre is also aware of the genre, but, at the same time, he demands that it be placed at the same level as canonical literature. One of his characters in *Irene* (2006) says the following:

> The detective novel was long considered a minor genre. More than a century passed before critics were prepared to mention it alongside "real" literature. Its relegation to the ranks of marginal writing owed much to what readers, authors and editors thought literature was supposed to be and therefore to normative cultural values, but it is widely believed that the genre was also dismissed because of its subject matter: crime. The popular fallacy—as old as the genre itself—seems to ignore the privileged position accorded to murder and detection in literary works by Dostoevsky and Faulkner, in medieval literature and in François Mauriac. In fiction, crime is as old as love. (Lemaitre 2015)

Therefore, by clearly writing genre works and disguising their genre in one way or another, many writers have taken crime and detective fiction to the next level. In that sense, we should question the absolute peripheral nature of the genre in the world literary system, and this position should be revised in light of the interest in publishing demonstrated by many central writers in the genre. All of this, of course, is in the hands of the abovementioned "Institution." This decides the central or peripheral areas of the polysystem, and hence the position of crime fiction is decided by the sociocultural code, "which tends to make this or that product literary in a general sense or as belonging to the crime genre in another more particular way" (Valles Calatrava 1991: 32).

Finally, apart from the general literary system, crime fiction can also be represented as a specific subsystem, as with other literatures in the genre. A study of this crime literary system would show that different repertoires have occupied a central place in the system throughout its short history. Even more, as in any other literary system, although models which occupy the central space at a specific time are useful, not all writers and works are in this central space. During the first two decades of the twentieth century, the Arthur Conan Doyle and Sherlock Holmes duo occupied the whole central space (it is not as clear from that point on whether Edgar Allan Poe's crime stories achieved the same standing, because this pioneer's work is often fraught with difficulty), and most of their followers and imitators had to make do with a peripheral position. Up to that point, one feature of the most important crime fiction was its format: they were short texts, thanks to Poe's short stories. All critics agree in saying that Arthur Conan Doyle was much better in Holmes' short stories than in his novels.

In the next twenty years, Christie, Van Dine and Sayers won the "Institution's" favor and, once again, many epigone followers were not so lucky. Whatever the case, the genre was incredibly successful, attracting an avid readership. Those readers, as P. D. James says, preferred novels:

> Although short stories continued to be written, gradually they gave way to the detective novel. One reason for this change was probably because the writers and their increasingly enthusiastic readers preferred a longer narrative, which gave opportunities for even more complicated plotting and more fully developed characters. (James 2009: 16-17)

The high demand led numerous authors to write crime novels. Many of these writers, like so many others who realize that the "Institution" "is condoning illegitimate literature, used nicknames to hide their true identities (and some behave the same way even today). This was likewise true in other non-canonical genres at the same time, yet it was a different story in the case of women writers. Shavit demonstrates this in the case of children's literature: "With women, however, the case was different. Having a subordinate position in society, women writers had nothing to lose. On the contrary, by writing they could only improve their status." (Shavit 1986: 39). In fact, there could be a kind of similarity between the English writers Agatha Christie and Enid Blyton. Both were born in the late nineteenth century, both wrote in non-canonical genres, both mastered the style of very long works, one of them a bestseller in her field, both lacked critical approval, but as regards social status, possessed fame and gratitude from readers. In *Talking About Detective Fiction* (2009), their compatriot P. D. James dedicates a whole chapter to the several women writers in the "golden age" of the genre, titled "Four Formidable Women": Agatha Christie, Dorothy L. Sayers, Margery Allingham, and Ngaio Marsh. These authors created women detectives, independent female characters, and they discussed their social problems (the situation of thousands of unmarried women because of the dearth of men in the aftermath of the World War I, or those who were obliged to choose between a career in education or marriage). From then until now, many other women have excelled in the crime genre, such as Patricia Highsmith, P. D. James herself, Maj Sjöwall, Sue Grafton, Donna Leon, Fred Vargas, and Camilla Läckberg. In the Basque Country, the main representative is Itxaro Borda.

The mystery repertoire gradually lost momentum because it was employing blueprints that were too clichéd. The variant we know today as noir fiction had already emerged by then, but it was on the periphery of the system, waiting for its chance to arrive. Dashiell Hammett was there, with his first short stories, until the early years of the Great Depression, when he published his novels and gained fame and approval. Mystery fiction did not, of course, disappear and it continued to be successful, although now from the periphery, and in certain cases converted into elements of some other systems (Poe, Doyle, and figures like that became reading material for young people's literature, as had happened with Dickens, Verne, and others). The "Institution's" tastes had changed, and had veered towards noir fiction. Then Raymond Chandler came out of hiding and in 1939 published his first novel, *The Big Sleep*. During the Cold War, spy literature predominated, and after May 68, the European police novel, by now not entirely noir nor completely mystery fiction, began to take center stage in the system. In very broad strokes, these were the ups and downs of the crime fiction system throughout history.

Introduction

The Structure and Elements of Crime Novels

All scholars of the genre agree in saying that the distinguishing feature that characterizes pure crime fiction is the back-to-front structure, in relation to its treatment of time. This is exactly what distinguishes crime fiction from adventure stories, which respect chronological order. At the start of crime novels, it is customary for a dead body to appear. From then on, two discourses are interspersed: that of the detective's chronological investigation and, as a result, the reconstruction of the crime, in a back-to-front way (Todorov 1971: 57), in general by means of a narration presented *in media res*. Bennett proposes a third element, as well as making a distinction: the reader's investigation. The investigation carried out by the reader, through reading the story, does not fully match the discourse of the investigation therein, which is coded and focused on genre requirements in order to maintain curiosity. As the narrator's discourse is more defined than that of the detective's story, it directs readers to conduct their own parallel investigation. To put it in Martín Cerezo's terms (2006: 113), the reader, by means of reading, is immersed in three structures: the trail of the detective, the trail left by the criminal for the detective and the trail of the reader in pursuit of the detective. This triple structure, in his opinion, is the reason for the success of the crime novel.

Linked to the organization of the discourse, there are two main ways to maintain the aforementioned curiosity: dividing up the information and delaying the information. The latter is carried out mostly through analepsis, but also through describing many places and characters, offering false clues and through the poetics of the text too. As noted in the previous quote by Todorov (1971: 60), interest in a story's past arouses curiosity; interest in the future, however, creates suspense.

Linked closely to the structure, there is the sequence of events. With a few small changes, the classic Introduction-Problem-Conclusion structure may change in the case of crime fiction, and with an equal number of small variants in each of the two main pillars that make it up (Valles Calatrava 1991: 64-69). In the case of the mystery novel, the basic structure of events would be the following: beginning order—wrongdoing-search for the guilty party—finding the guilty party—return to the beginning order, in which the "search for the guilty party" and "finding the guilty party" are carried out through rational investigation. In the case of the realist detective novel or the noir novel, however, it is: beginning—disorder—crimes-search—finding the offender—return to some kind of order, in which there is no order as such, rational procedures disappear, and in their place a dynamic search process appears.

After discussing structure and the treatment of time and the events associated with it, let us look at the qualities of the other elements in crime narrative (Fernández Colmeiro 1994; Martín Cerezo 2006). As for the narrator, it may be a character within the story or a narrator located outside the narrative. Generally speaking, the homodiegetic narrator is more common in realist novels in which the detectives themselves are often the narrators. Sometimes, mystery novels also make use of this variety, although the internal narrator is not a detective, but the detective's assistant. It is a question of credibility and identification: it would be very difficult for readers to identify with a very ambitious clever detective narrator in mystery fiction, yet easier with stories about a supposedly loser detective in realist novels. In terms of position of the narration, it may be simultaneous or after the fact. In the former, the reader gets the sensation of speed and, in the latter, the narration is more measured and often presented in the form of a chronicle. Besides all this, all narrators employ the previously mentioned dosage when it comes to giving information.

Regarding time, although we have discussed its treatment already, one can add that the notion of time in a story can be located anywhere. There are plenty of crime narratives that are set in the past; in the future too, because science fiction has often made use of a crime plot. That said, the contemporary stories of each writer are the most common.

With regard to space, as a rule, one main division may be made. The mystery novel prefers closed locations: rooms, isolated houses, campuses, small towns, islands, and the like. The realist detective novel, on the contrary, favors open urban locations: the detective in such novels moves around more, even though this space is also, in narrative terms, closed. Several observers have said that the noir novel must have at root a democratic bourgeois society (or, put another way, that it would be impossible in a dictatorial regime, regardless of its extremes). In practice, this is not the case, although detective narratives set in societies with capitalist and ultraliberal economies are more credible. The genre has managed to make headway in numerous European countries, but it has had a problem with the aforementioned credibility, for example, in South America.

Turning to the area of characters, from a structuralist point of view the main actants are protagonists and antagonists. Secondary-level characters, however, are the main characters' assistants, witnesses, and suspects. The typical protagonist is an investigator of some sort (private detective, police officer, judge, journalist ...). Nevertheless, the opposite is also true, and the criminal is sometimes the protagonist, either as the real criminal (seeking to maintain the disorder) or as an alleged criminal who wants to solve some injustice. Whether protagonist or antagonist, the investigator is, in Rodríguez Pequeño's words (1994: 30), the only essential character in a police novel.

Midway between the protagonist and antagonist is the victim and sometimes the crime itself as well. The victim is a character, but not an actant. They are in some way a metaphor for the transgression committed by the criminal, someone who instigates a yearning. What the police calls the cause or motive, in fact. In W.H. Auden's opinion:

> The victim has to try to satisfy two contradictory requirements. He has to involve everyone in suspicion, which requires that he be a bad character; and he has to make everyone feel guilty, which requires that he be a good character (. . .) The more general the temptation to murder he arouses, the better; e.g., the desire for freedom is a better motive than money alone or sex alone. On the whole, the best victim is the negative Father or Mother Image. (Auden 1974: 174)

Conversely, several other elements are actants, but not characters. Crime is the driving force behind action, and it gives the genre its nature. As stated, it is the fulfilment of the criminal's transgression, but also what the reader would like to do too. The investigator and the wrongdoer appear in the same way in opposition to one another, whether legally through justice or whether through ideological-moral values.

There is also another important component, readers themselves, and we will dedicate the next section to them.

The Reception of the Genre and the Conditions in the Reading Pact

As several literary theorists have contended, the meaning or interpretation of each work is decided on the basis of a pact between text and reader; a reading, at the end of the day. Thus, as Wolfgang Iser (1987) says, texts create those kinds of "gaps," and a reader must fill them in through their imagination; not just any reader, though, but an "implied reader," one that must interpret the potentiality of the text. Umberto Eco (1981) proposes something similar, and he refers to that kind of reader demanded by the features that each text possesses implicitly as a "model reader."

In the case of the crime novel reading pact, it generally channels a specific type of reading that is associated with rigorous genre coding. The text demands the active participation of the reader, ultimately revealing which of the clues it leaves here and there is correct (but not in too hurried a manner). Several authors have defined crime-intrigue as a labyrinth, and the reader is actively involved in interpreting the signs along this twisting path. The reader, for their part, demands respect for the rules of the game on the part of the text, a respect that is easily summarized in three features: having a rational solution to a criminal intrigue; being simple, consistent, and complete; and being created together with a mystery, as an explanation of the whole structure (Martín Cerezo 2006: 75).

Although superficially, the theme of speed has been explained. In part, because of the aforementioned pact, there is a tendency to read novels like these very quickly. The newspaper *El País* introduced a digital barometer to measure some dimensions of these kinds of topics:

> The subscription reading app 24Symbols has provided us with unpublished data about its users in Spain. Through this, we know that 19% of general fiction books are abandoned halfway through; that percentage falls to 14.2% in romance and 13.1% in noir fiction. If we look at those who have not reached even a fourth of the work, they are 9.5% of those who read general fiction, as opposed to 6.2% of those of romance and 6.9% of those of noir fiction (readers of these genres are not only faster—as we know from other sources—but they tend to finish the reading). (Millán 2018).

As Fernández Colmeiro says, that feature is a consequence of the structure itself of this kind of fiction:

> The intrigue of the story possesses at root a paradox: the longer it takes to conclude the hermeneutic code (question-answer, mystery-solution), the faster the impatience of the reader grows, thereby accelerating the rhythm of the reading in order to get to the end. The reader is obliged to slow down the reading in order to be able to weigh up the data presented (clues, evidence, interrogations) without losing the "crucial sign," and at the same time they are propelled to carry on ahead in order to satisfy their need for an answer. (Fernández Colmeiro 1994: 80–81).

In this sense, the efforts of writers trying to develop some kind of literary quality within the genre may not be rewarded, as the poetic texture will soon go unnoticed by the reader who is quickly seeking to untie the knot. One such writer is Umberto Eco, who is at the same time a theoretician and creator of fiction. He made use of the crime novel structure to write *Il nome della rosa* (*The Name of the Rose*) and, along the way, to reflect on the task of the reader. He speaks about types of readers thus in the essay *Postille al nome della rosa* (*Postscript to The Name of the Rose*, 1985):

> What model reader did I want as I was writing? An accomplice, to be sure, one who would play my game. I wanted to be completely medieval and live in the Middle Ages as if that were my own period (and vice versa). But at the same time, with all my might, I wanted to create a type of reader who, once the initiation was past, would become by prey—or, rather, the prey of the text—and would think he wanted nothing but what the text was offering him. A text is meant to be an experience of transformation for its reader. You believe you want sex and a criminal plot where the guilty party is discovered at the end, and all with plenty of action (…) All right, then, I will give you Latin, practically no women, lots of theology, gallons of blood in Grand Guignol style, to make you say, 'But all this is false; I refuse to accept it!' And at this point you will have to be mine, and feel the thrill of God's infinite omnipotence, which makes the world's order vain. And then, if you are good, you will realize how I lured you into this trap, because I was really telling you about it at every step, I was carefully warning you that I was dragging you to your damnation; but the fine things about pacts with the devil is that when you sign them you are well aware of their conditions. Otherwise, why would you be recompensed with hell?
>
> And since I wanted you to feel as pleasurable the one thing that frightens us—namely, the metaphysical shudder—I had only to choose (from among the model plots) the most metaphysical and philosophical: the detective novel. (Eco 1985: 56–57).

Colmeiro discusses this kind of reader when he speaks about the second reading option:

> For the average reader, whose interest in the crime story resides in the intrigue it generates, a second reading makes no sense (if

they have not forgotten the details of the story). Once the intrigue has disappeared, only the narrative mechanisms remain exposed. Clearly, the more sophisticated reader may find in later readings, at least in the best novels in the genre, other elements of interest independent of the intrigue factor (such as characterisation, description, style and composition). (Fernández Colmeiro 1994: 81, note 36).

Although many experts take at least one part of the genre to be realist, most concur in saying that crime novels, like other forms of fiction but even more so, demand a "willing suspension of disbelief" from the reader. In other words, they want them to interrupt their knowledge of reality for a moment and be willing to participate in the game proposed by the text: "The participation and presence of the reader in police literature is fundamental, possibly more visible than in any other genre, since its role is precisely that of filling in the 'empty boxes' which trigger the investigation" (Rodríguez Pequeño 1994: 29).

All of this reveals that crime fiction has a dual readership. In other words, it is aimed at two different kinds of readerships. On the one hand, there is a readership that likes "highbrow" literature: "The resilience of detective fiction, and particularly the fact that so many distinguished and powerful people are apparently under its spell, has puzzled both its admirers and its detractors and spawned a number of notable critical studies" (James 2009: 51). On the other, there are those that use it as a means of escape from their everyday problems: "there can be no doubt that the detective story produces a reassuring relief from the tensions and responsibilities of daily life; it is particularly popular in times of unrest, anxiety and uncertainty" (James 2009: 53).

Linked to the former, paratexts are very important in the reading pact: knowing that what the reader has to hand is a crime novel before they start reading it. Even though the most significant writers in the genre themselves have proclaimed it to be "highbrow literature," right from the start, publishers have marked the genre with identifiable paratexts. As will be seen in the next section, literature which seeks to go beyond mere police anecdotes, on the contrary, does not employ any special kind of paratext. This, however, can confuse the reader and lead them to read in a different key.

Finally, another topic that is constantly being discussed is the power of crime fiction to reflect (and critique) society. According to the most widely held opinion, mystery fiction, as a transmitter of Victorian values, reflected society through a conservative gaze, the crimes were clarified by pure logic and everything returned to normal. The realist variant, which took the name of noir fiction, however, creates a critical picture of a society dominated by real powers, denounces the lack of real social justice and, therein, criminals emerge constantly from every corner. Specifically, as Colmeiro remarks in his essay: "The distinctive criterion of these subgenres is based on the particular problematic articulated by its respective narrative formulas around two basic complementary elements in the ethical and aesthetic order" (Fernández Colmeiro 1994: 57). In his opinion, the game prevails in the classic detective novel, without ever neglecting the ethical aspect; in police fiction, however, the importance of ethics and aesthetics is reversed: "Here the criminal subject matter is maintained as an aesthetic game (suspense, mystery, ingenuity) but its importance is now displaced or reduced with respect to the ethical component" (61). Other observers, however, do not agree with this distinction. For example, Fernando Savater, ever the contrarian, does not believe that the noir novel detective is any more realist than the classic investigator of the mystery novel, nor any better morally: "One of the literary superstitions I most deplore (...) is that the so-called 'noir novel' implies a simultaneously literary and political-ethical advance on the classic detective fiction in the English style" (Savater 1983: 109). Martín Cerezo agrees with this perspective, contending that the noir variant, in which the good people are almost always humble and the bad ones powerful, is quite demagogic (2006: 108). Others underscore the individuality and ambiguousness of detectives in noir fiction, and their inability to truly change a rotten society or lack of interest in doing so. These two currents, as will be seen, would emerge among critics in the Basque Country too. Synthesizing the matter, it appears that the characteristics of the "realist" detective are not compatible with the Marxist transformative point of view, for example, and that the social critique which takes place in the novels in this series is closer to despair (hence so many open endings) or, at best, to a critique of irony.

Studies and Critiques on Crime Fiction Written in Basque

Few studies have been written about crime fiction in Basque. Examining the matter chronologically, the first important work was "Nobela beltza eta polizi nobela klasikoa" (Hard-boiled Fiction and Classic Crime Fiction) by Mikel Hernandez Abaitua in the Basque journal *Jakin* (1982). This article explains the origins and features of the genre, and right from the very beginning it defines the noir police novel as a subgenre. Classic detective novels are considered "intellectual" while the noir novel is "realist and authentic." Thereafter, Hernandez Abaitua differentiates periods within noir fiction and the most prominent authors and works, especially following the authors Chandler (1950) and Coma (1980). To conclude, in a section titled "Euskal nobela poliziakoa" (Basque Crime Fiction), he criticizes the simplicity of Basque authors in the genre, their lack of quality and their shift to the classic model:

> Our crime fiction fits completely into the intellectual model. As a whole, it is a crime fiction style which presents itself as a game of chess. And what is worse, our works do not even remotely reach the English level of intellectual style. Bad on both accounts, then. (Hernandez Abaitua 1982: 62).

One could say that Hernandez Abaitua's work was a declaration in favor of the noir variant of crime fiction. Hernandez Abaitua was a very active critic in the 1980s, above all in the Basque magazines *Argia*, *Susa*, and others. Specifically, *Susa* dedicated a monograph volume to police fiction in 1992. Thereafter, *Susa* published critiques and opinions about the genre. Amongst these, one deserves mentioning: Antton Azkargorta's short article "Philip Marlowek begikeinua egin zidanean... edo porrotaren lilura" (When Philip Marlow Winked at Me... or the Fascination of Failure) in volume 19 of *Susa* (1986). After reviewing the socioeconomic conditions that influenced the emergence of the "noir novel," Azkargorta critiques the revisionist perspective of the genre, the individualism of the typical detectives and the pessimism or, as he says, the "loser's aesthetic." In his opinion, the resignation, cynicism, indifference, lack of hope, and so on transmitted by the genre are of no help in effecting profound social change: "The presence of the law, the essence of the law, are always present, and the true heterogeneity, revolt and the destruction of the system, are left out" (Azkargorta 1986: 93).

These kinds of sociological interpretations of literature, rooted in Marxism, were quite widespread in the 1980s and, at a time when both committed literature and literary experimentation were very fashionable, such readings reflected a small but demanding readership that at one time considered police novels and similar literary products to be conservative. Despite such critiques, the aforementioned noir novel has constantly had a strong tendency toward social criticism. So much so that Manuel Vázquez Montalbán, a famous noir novelist and left-wing activist at the time, could not bear those, specifically, from the other extreme who criticized crime fiction:

> It was him [the scholar Vallés Calatrava], then a young recent university graduate who was studying the so-called Spanish police

novel, in a moment when just the statement drove me crazy, because it was being used by purist critics to denounce the conspiracy of a series of writers to return to the old ways of social realism under the guise of the police novel. (Valles Calatrava 1991: 7).

This is how Xabier Olarra, the translator of the work himself, interprets it, when he explains the hidden message behind the farcical image of the novel *1280 arima* (*Pop. 1280*), published in 1986, in his commentary for the journal *Literatur Gazeta* (Literary Gazette): "But behind it all has it not perhaps explained to us the essential nature of power, that is, severely denounced the violence used to maintain its situation, the blows and prayers used to maintain the blackmail and oppression and the essential necessity of using the coarsest cynicism?" (Olarra 1987).

In time, as noted above, the journal *Susa* published a monograph volume about the police novel in 1992. Among numerous original works on the topic, there are also short studies there, namely "Public Enemy Number One," authored by Andres Gostin, about the supposed decline of crime fiction; "Nestor Burma," a work about the detective of the same name in Léo Malet's comics, by Bego Montorio; "Larrüpean ebiltzen direnak" (What Under the Skin Is), on the *Navajo Tribal Police* series by the detective novel writer Tony Hillerman, by Itxaro Borda; and "Polizi nobela eta irakurlea" (Crime Fiction and Its Reader), on the distance that the reader should supposedly maintain, authored by Xabier Olarra. Furthermore, Iñigo Aranbarri interviews Emilio Lopez Adan or "Beltza" at length about the relationship between the political situation and police novels, in which it can be concluded that he acknowledges the capacity of the genre to convey social issues to a wide readership. Otherwise, one can also access several texts written in the ironic-satirical tone that was common in the journal *Susa*.

The next study cited here is titled *Atzerriko eta Euskal Herriko Polizia Eleberria* (The Foreign and Basque Police Novel, 2000) by Gotzon Garate, a writer who had published a copious number of crime novels. As he confesses in the preface, this Jesuit professor at the University of Deusto had long intended to write a book about the Basque police novel. In order to do so, he made use of the summer visits he made almost every year to New York to finally write an essay based on his experience as a writer, as well as books in Fordham University library in the Bronx.

Garate's work was published in textbook form, and it includes three main sections: "The Foreign Police Novel," "The Basque Police Novel" and "Summaries of the Best-Known Foreign Police Novels." After speaking at length about the success of the genre, in the first section he traces the history of police novels by citing the main writers and works, and thereafter he differentiates three kinds of police novel: the aforementioned "mystery novel," "the noir novel," and "spy novels." To conclude the first section, Garate discusses the literary values of the genre and offers information about works that have been made into films.

In the second section, the topic turns to authors from the Basque Country. He refers to the period from its inception to the 1970s; aside from himself: he cites Loidi, Izeta, Lartzabal, Peillen, and Gereño. The later names include Kintana, Zabaleta, Lertxundi, Txillardegi, and Velez de Mendizabal, although he mentions more Basque writers in the bibliography at the end of the section. In the last section, following a chronological criterion, he offers the contexts surrounding, summaries of and critical opinions about forty-six foreign novels, published between 1818 and 1971.

The same year Gotzon Garate's work was published, in Reno, Nevada, Javi Cillero presented his doctoral thesis *The Moving Target: A History of Basque Detective and Crime Fiction* (2000). Cillero taught at the University of Nevada for several years and earned his doctorate with the abovementioned work, under the supervision of Linda White.

Cillero's aim, evidently, was to write a history of detective and crime fiction in Basque. For this purpose, he first tries to clarify the origins, structure, and boundaries of the genre. Furthermore, the connections between the genre and canonical literature are also examined and, at the same time, the multiple ways in which the genre has developed in several national literatures.

The initial questions of the study are: what kind of work can be included within the boundaries of the detective and crime genre without distorting their elements? What elements of detective and crime fiction appear in the context of Basque literature under study here? How do these works relate to both canonical Basque literature and to detective and crime fiction and literature?

A large part of Cillero's work is devoted to recounting the history of detective and crime fiction in Basque, in four sections: the historical context and late emergence of gender, the post–Spanish Civil War years (up to the 1956 generation), from the Euskaltzaindia (Academy of the Basque Language) congress in Arantzatzu to the 1970s, the institutionalization process in the 1980s, and, lastly, the results of the last decade of the millennium. In each of these sections, there is a description of the Basque literary system, an account of the most important literary works and, finally, an examination of writers and works connected to the detective and crime genres.

As the author confesses, the choice of detective and crime works in Basque is neither narrow nor exhaustive. Indeed, as Cillero comments at the end of the methodology section, he first took into account all of the works related to a crime, whether they describe the causes, consequences or circumstances of a crime; secondly, he added several works in Basque clearly based on using suspense to maintain the reader's attention, even though it is debatable whether they are connected to the crime theme; lastly, he pointed out several other works which offer a hermeneutic or self-reflexive interpretation proposed by post-structuralist critics, to see what kind of link they generally have with detective and crime fiction.

Mari Jose Olaziregi published a chapter on the genre in both *Historia de la literatura vasca* (History of Basque Literature), edited by Patri Urkizu ("Novela negra y policíaca" (Hard-boiled Fiction and Crime Fiction), 2000: 561–565) and her own *Euskal eleberriaren historia* (History of Basque Novel) ("Polizi eleberriak (espioi eleberriak, misteriozkoak eta eleberri beltzak)") Crime Fictions (Spy Novels, Mystery Novels and Hard-boiled), (2002: 161–178). In the former, the final author she cites is Migel Angel Mintegi. In the latter, a longer version of the earlier article, after offering a general perspective, she examines the works of several authors: Gotzon Garate, Itxaro Borda, Hasier Etxeberria, Aingeru Epaltza, and Harkaitz Cano.

The last work contemplated in this section is a short book, *Beltzaren koloreak* (The Colours of Noir), published by Jon Alonso in 2016. As if he were seeking to take the customary subjectivity of an essay to the extreme, the author says that it is a personal approach in a kind of introduction: "Personal approaches, from an academic perspective on criticism, are of little value. Because they are necessarily partial and self-interested. Reductionist" (Alonso 2016: 10). A master of suspense techniques, Alonso warns the reader of a progress or prolapse in the aforementioned introduction: "I know that my opinions, sometimes, can also be surprising or provocative. I did not want to renounce that burden" (Alonso 2106: 11).

This work is divided into five chapters: "Origins" brings the most prominent authors in noir fiction to the topic, from the golden age of the genre to the 1970s, beginning with Hammett and ending with Highsmith, in short impressionist texts, linked to a motif and equipped with examples: the particularity of detectives, the connection to justice and politics, social criticism . . .

In the second chapter, "The 70s in Europe," Alonso discusses the issue of translation or transmutation. In other words, how a genre which had almost run out of steam managed to carry on in Europe, where the conditions were completely different. Here, he brings in the French writer Manchette, the German Arjouni, the Spaniard Montalbán and the Italian Sciascia: each one's ethical and aesthetic propositions, selections, and narrative problems.

The title of the third chapter is "The Age of Social Democratic Police." Here Alonso compares novels that portray reality with reality itself, in order to call into question some of the writers chosen. The police officers in contemporary novels and events are too close to reality, it would seem, and that leads him to a mechanistic comparison, to question the work of some authors, not just on account of what they have written but also based on what they have said in interviews too. He says this clearly at the end of the section: "The point is not what one is, much less what one should be, but that the reader has the right to know who the writer is" (Alonso 2016: 94).

The penultimate chapter is titled "From Noir to Green, from Noir to Noir" and it discusses the tempering apparently experienced by noir fiction in recent years. In Alonso's opinion, the police novel today has shifted far away from social criticism and has been used to whitewash some police officials and promote tourism. He cites the authors Donna Leon, Fred Vargas, Dolores Redondo, and Lorenzo Silva; among those who continue to make social criticism, he mentions Jean-Claude Izzo and Massimo Carlotto.

To conclude the essay, "A Sermon as Epilogue" is a kind of summary making it clear that all of the above have been ideological readings and, in this respect, the author sees the decline of the genre as time progresses:

> *The sigh of the oppressed, born of the vocation to be the heart of the heartless world,* has become another place of utterance for those who constantly speak from all loudspeakers, not infrequently, in a rougher and more subtle way, as the hegemonic message cannot leave uncolonised areas. (Alonso 2016: 113).

In order to conclude this section, we did not want to move on without mentioning that there is an annual cycle of talks and activities on the genre in the Basque Country. The initiative is called "The Noir Month, Basque Crime Novel Week in January." It has been held in Baztan since 2015, organized by a reading group there, together with promoters from Baztan and in collaboration with other institutions, and with the help of funding from the regional and provincial institutions, among others. There are several activities within the annual week, such as trips, talks, roundtables, book launches, film and music presentations, poetry recitals, exhibitions... Over the years many Basque writers have taken part in the talks and roundtables. In particular, Jon Alonso's aforementioned *Beltzaren koloreak* (The Colours of Noir) was the result of a talk at the 2015 edition of the cycle. At the same time, they have also fostered reissues of several works (*Dirua galgarri* [Ruinous Money], *Zaldi beltzak zeruan* [Black Horses in the Sky]...), and in 2018 the (H)ilbeltza Grant was established in a collaboration between the Baztan Town Council and the Txalaparta publishing house. This provides annual funding in turns for an original work and a translation in the genre. Some of those who have received the grant are Mielanjel Elustondo, Josu Barambones, Miren Gorrotxategi, and Koldo Biguri.

The History of Basque-Language Crime Fiction: A Summary

For this summary of Basque-language crime fiction, we have turned mainly to the works of Cillero (2000) and Garate (2000). As can be deduced from Cillero's initial questions, it is often difficult to find works that fit fully into the genre, especially from the 1980s onward. Generally speaking, the works he takes into consideration have something to do with a crime or violence. That said, as he confesses in the conclusion to his study, the genre has developed in a particular way within the Basque literary system. In relation to themes, the main subject matter is linked to power and its injustices, writings that favor downtrodden human groups. Even when it comes to portraying victims and culprits, he says that one notes a politicized approach. In any event, it seems that violence is quite a taboo. In fact, as Cillero says, crime fiction in Basque avoids showing extreme violence. In its place, he suggests, because political violence has occupied most of the symbolic space in the Basque Country, any other kind of violence is trivial. With respect to form, moreover, looking at the entire history of the genre, humor and satire have prevailed over realist models.

All historians agree in recognising that *Amabost egun Urgain'en* (1955; in English, *Fifteen Days in Urgain*, 2014), by Jose Antonio Loidi (1916–1999) from Gipuzkoa, was the first Basque-language crime novel. Loidi's work was one endeavor, in a very small novelistic tradition, in a literature that was late in developing and had no crime fiction whatsoever. Although it deals with an alleged crime in a rural setting, Loidi's work has a modern touch, in terms of both topic and technique. Moreover, the detective Martin Garaidi, based on the mystery fiction model, is completely believable, insofar as he is a representative of the middle-class merchants, lawyers, doctors, and small businessmen of the time, as Cillero contends.[1] In the 1980s, the Erein publishing house recovered Loidi's work in its "Auskalo" (Who Knows!) collection for children and young adults.

The next Basque writer to continue the tradition started by Loidi was Mariano Izeta (1915–2001). *Dirua galgarri* (Ruinous Money) (1962) by this writer from Elizondo was the second contribution to the genre. Izeta's novel, published in the Auspoa Liburutegia collection, is set in Paris and the main characters are Basques from the Northern Basque Country; that is how he managed to write a Basque-language police novel with a credible plot and dialogues. The crime in the novel is a robbery, and what the police officer cannot clarify is discovered by chance: it is revealed that the thief is the nephew of the owner of the factory in which the robbery took place.

The following Basque contributors to the genre were the Parisians Jon Mirande and Txomin Peillen. The fact that these two Basque-language writers were educated in French brought novelty to postwar Basque literature, in the sense of their use of European and American moulds.

The contribution of Jon Mirande (1928–1972) took the form of five short stories: "Ametsa" (The Dream, 1952), "Zazpi gizeraile" (Seven Murderers, 1954), "Maitarien ardoa" (The Lovers' Wine, 1956), "Eresi kantari" (Funeral March Singer, 1960), and "Gauaz parke batean" (In a Park at Night, 1963), published in the Basque journals *Egan* and *Euzko Gogoa*. These short stories are about several crimes, without any police investigations. They are influenced by Poe, Kafka, and Saki (Mirande translated several works by the three writers into Basque), their features are ironic humor, pessimism, and aestheticism, and they locate Mirande among the best Basque writers in the genre.

Txomin Peillen (1932–2022) wrote two crime novels: *Gauaz ibiltzen dana...* (Creature of the Night..., 1967) and *Gatu beltza* (The Black Cat, 1973). The former is the first noir novel in Basque, with a tough, tired, and contradictory detective by the name of Pettiri Sabuki. This same detective is the protagonist of *Gatu beltza*, although in this case suspense and even fear prevail. Peillen, like Mirande, used the themes and techniques of European and American writers in his novels, such as first-person narrators, complex structures, and open-ended conclusions, previously untried in Basque literature.

The last author in the post-war generation mentioned by Cillero is Jose Basterretxea or "Oskillaso" (1911–1996). In Cillero's words, Basterretxea's *Akatsbako gizonaren heriotza* (The Death of an Unblemished Man), which was serialized in 1967 in the journal *Egan*, is a humorous parody of romance novels and classic mystery fiction. What is more, it was the first Basque-language detective novel to employ a female protagonist. Basterretxea uses intertextualities and metaphysical resources to construct the parody. However, naturally, parody does not work if the reader is not familiar with what is being parodied. Because of this, Cillero notes, only readers who knew about these genres through reading in other languages would understand Basterretxea's playful storyline.

A few years later, now in the 1970s, the literary landscape had changed considerably. The standardization of the Basque language was taking place, as a result of the end of the dictatorship there was a little more openness and the creation of a movement to help adults learn and be literate in Basque began to take shape. If we add to that the development of the *ikastola* (Basque-language school) movement, it is clear that there was the beginning of growth in demand for Basque-language reading matter, even though the publishing infrastructure was very weak (Lur, Kriselu, Gordailu, Etor, Jakin, Gero, Hordago...). In this environment, two authors who would be especially important in the field of crime fiction began publishing: Xabier Gereño and Gotzon Garate. For both, writing such novels was a means rather than an end, both in terms of publicizing social themes and as regards to developing the language by means of attractive reading matter. In any event, they had to face not only the difficulties encountered in other systems of bringing the genre home, but also the obstacles that Basque literature had at the time. The principal difficulty was the issue of a lack of credibility. Themes such as corruption and crime situations in the huge cities of the United States and on a grand scale as well as the kinds of detectives depicted were hardly credible in the Basque Country and there was a need to adapt those elements to the Basque context. However, the biggest hurdle (as in other genres) was that of language, namely, how to construct credible underworld characters in Basque.

Xabier Gereño (1924–2011) was a very productive writer and worked in many genres, including short stories, biography, theatrical works, and novels. Among the latter, one must highlight his police, crime, and spy novels. Gereño's first work, within this genre, was *Hiltzaile baten bila* (On the Trail of a Murderer, 1975). With this publication, he introduced for the first time the detective Jurgi Arregi, who would appear again in several other works: *Jurgi kapitaina Bretainian* (Captain Jurgi in Brittany, 1978), *Espioitza* (Espionage, 1979), *Gudari bat* (A Soldier, 1977),[2] *Iruineako asasinatzea* (A Murder in Pamplona, 1978), *Osaba Gabrielen asasinatzea* (The Murder of Uncle Gabriel, 1978), *Xantaia kontesari* (Blackmailing the Countess, 1978), *Mitxino katua pozoiez hila* (The Death of Mitxino the Cat by Poisoning, 1979), and *Jurgi kapitaina Hong-Kong-en* (Captain Jurgi in Hong Kong, 1982). Jurgi appeared for the final time in the last of these and, additionally, Gereño began his transition to adventure fiction, abandoning the detective genre forever.

Gotzon Garate (1934–2008) also worked in many genres: short stories, essays, chronicles and novels, most of the latter being police novels, divided into two spheres by Cillero. Initially, his first three novels, following the path of mystery fiction, were set in a rural environment and focused on detective Jon Bidart: *Esku leuna* (The Soft Hand, 1978), *Goizuetako ezkongabeak* (The Unmarried Couple from Goizueta, 1979), and *Elizondoko eskutitzak* (Letters from Elizondo, 1979). Although they are simply structured (crime/questions and the search for clues/the detective's explanation), it is striking that in all three self-awareness of the genre appears in one way or another, through intertextual and metaliterary resources. With the two novels in the next sphere, Garate slips into the realm of noir fiction and uses the first-person narratives and tough detectives typical of this kind of novel: Haitz "Rocky" Zumeta in *Izurri berria* (The New Plague, 1984) and detective Jon Garai in *Alaba* (The Daughter, 1984). Likewise, intertextual traces, which are very prominent without becoming parodic, often appear in these two novels.

By the 1980s, the cultural conditions were very different. After Franco's death and by means of the statute of autonomy, specifically Basque cultural tools were developed, at least for part of the population. These included Basque-language public education, Euskal Irrati Telebista (the Basque public radio and television service), Basque-language newspapers, publishing grants, literary prizes, and writers' and translators' associations. All of this was a huge stimulus for Basque literature and, regarding crime narratives, it established the foundation for its growth, by means of translating into Basque a very distinctive genre.

Indeed, the first translations in this genre first appeared in the 1980s (López Gaseni, 2019). For example, James M. Cain's *Postariak beti deitzen du bi aldiz* (*The Postman Always Rings Twice*) was published in 1985, as well as Jim Thompson's *1280 arima* (*Pop. 1280*), both translated into Basque by Xabier Olarra. These were followed in 1987 by *Ligeia. Izu ipuinak* (Ligeia: Horror Stories), several poems by Poe translated by M. A. Unanua. Then in 1989 came Dashiell Hammett's *Gizon argala* (*The Thin Man*), translated by Koro Navarro. The first translation of Agatha Christie also appeared during that decade: *Monsieur Poiroten ikerpenak* (Poirot Investigates), translated by Xabier Galarreta, in 1989. They were attractive texts for Basque readers at the time and, simultaneously, did not present any great structural difficulties. In 1989, however, Xabier Olarra founded the Igela publishing house, which began its publications with the Noir series. Its first volume was

Zaldiak akatzen ditugu ba... (*They Shoot Horses, Don't They?*) by Horace McCoy, and in the years which followed the works of many authors were published: Bill S. Ballinger, James M. Cain, Jim Thompson, Chester Himes, Raymond Chandler, Dashiell Hammett, Patricia Highsmith, Ross Macdonald, and so on. That same year, the same publisher also started the Mystery series, whose first volume was *Zirriborro eskarlata* (*A Study in Scarlet*) by Arthur Conan Doyle. The same author was responsible for numbers 5 and 6 in the series: *Sherlock Holmesen abenturak I* and *Sherlock Holmesen abenturak II* (*The Adventures of Sherlock Holmes*, in two volumes). A further ten volumes by Agatha Christie were published in this series, including *Roger Ackroyden hilketa* (*The Murder of Roger Ackroyd*, 2004), *Orient Expresseko hilketa* (*Murder on the Orient Express*, 2004), and *Eta ez zen alerik geratu* (*And Then There Were None*, 2014). The Txertoa publishing house, meanwhile, published *Monsieur Poiroten ikerpenak* (Poirot Investigates, 1989) and *Hamar beltx* (*And Then There Were None*, 1990).

In the violent period that Spain, and especially the Basque Country, was experiencing at that time (ETA terrorism, state terrorism, corruption, and denunciation...), crime fiction could have been a means of offering a literary perspective on the situation. In a well-known interview which Vázquez Montalbán gave during that time, Fernández Colmeiro asked him about the subject, why the theme of terrorism was not addressed so much in Spanish police novels, and this was the writer's response:

> I think that it's because it has still not been digested sufficiently; in the mind of the Spanish writer the police and the repressive apparatus are still too guilty; it is very difficult to resolve to write something feeling sympathy for the repressive apparatus; you would have to choose, to approve that 'this one is good, and the other bad' and that still provokes a reaction. (Vazquez Montalbán, after Fernández Colmeiro 1988: 22).

Although with some nuances, Cillero offers similar reasons for this. As he remarks, Basque writers rejected the model of the detective/investigator who seeks and punishes the perpetrator of crime, and preferred to adapt crime-suspense models to their interests in order to portray "Basque activists" in a more positive way. This is what Txillardegi does in his novel *Exkixu* (1987), just as previously Saizarbitoria had done in his experimental narration *100 metro* (1976; in English, *100 Meters*, 1985) and Xabier Amuriza in his novel *Hil ala bizi* (Dead or Alive, 1973). Otherwise, although still used for social criticism, the writers' models of the previous decade and that element of defending the language disappeared. From the technical perspective, there was a tendency to bring film techniques into play, especially through the influence of American behaviorism. In line with this latter tendency, and repeating what was said in the section on the position of the genre in the polysystem, Mari Jose Olaziregi states the following:

> In any event, in our opinion, this is a matter that has rarely been mentioned in relation to the Basque novel: the benefits and novelties that the detective novel genre brought to the storytelling techniques of our narrators. Even through undertaking a simple superficial analysis, we would immediately note the important presence of typologies within the police novel in many of the novels published between the 1980s and today. (Olaziregi 2002: 161)

Two novels which could be located within the genre and written by Anjel Lertxundi (1948–) were published in the 1980s: *Hamaseigarrenean, aidanez* (It Happened the Sixteenth Time, 1983) and *Tobacco Days* (1986). In the former, in order to interweave a crime story into a rural setting, Lertxundi moves away from the usual molds and, via several narrators, skilfully builds the suspense, in order to eventually untangle the knot. As Jon Kortazar remarks:

> When describing the semantic level, we could say that it reinterprets the myth of the outsider. A journalist, a marginalized hero, will shed light on the truth about the crime that took place a few years ago. In this sense, it resembles a noir police novel (...). However, the text seeks to go further and two other issues have also been addressed as regards that direction: the situation of women in a closed community and the liberating power of the word, indirectly seeking to express what intellectuals should do in contemporary society. (Kortazar 2000: 156–157).

Therefore, it is organized as a chronicle novel with a strict structure. Therein, as opposed to the chronicler's objective point of view, the subjectivity of the dead man's wife Martzelina becomes the most important component.

Tobacco Days, however, is based on a film screenplay about smuggling at sea. In this case, the narrative follows and complies with the norms of the noir novel, by means of an objective fragmented narrative. Lertxundi explains a corrupt economic system through numerous references and structures typical in the cinema: arguments, card games, boxers, mythical drinks...

This book examines another work written by Lertxundi two decades later, in 2008: *Zoaz infernura, laztana* (Go to Hell, Darling). The novel looks into the problem of gender violence by using several resources of the crime genre, delving deeply into the ontology of the victim and the offender. In this work, whose very title, like *Hamaseigarrenean, aidanez*, locates it within the noir genre, the author seeks to contrast an objective point of view with the subjective story of the protagonist Rosa, here through a therapist.

Xabier Kintana (1946–) wrote only one crime work: *Ta Marbuta: Jerusalemen gertatua* (Tā marbūṭa: What Happened in Jerusalem, 1984). Here, too, we come across several perspectives in one narrative: Martin Bengoa's everyday life, a third-person voice that reports the police investigation, the criminal's internal monologue, and the dialogue of a Jerusalem tourist guide. As a backdrop to the web of the crime and the investigation, it reflects admiration for Israelis, most especially due to their efforts to recover their language. Perhaps because of this Judeophilia, and because the criminals in the novel are Palestinians, Kintana's work did not receive a very good critical reception.

Amongst many other works, Mario Onaindia (1948–2003) published several books with a touch of noir. The first of these was *Gau ipuinak* (Night Tales, 1983), a collection of stories dedicated to Kafka in a kind of rewriting of the Czech's themes. His next work, too, was a novel in the style of Kafka's *The Trial*: *Olagarroa* (Octopus, 1987). The protagonist is someone who is in prison for theft and tries to escape. However, the criminal dimension is an excuse (he did not want it to be part of the Basque Noir Fiction series) for publishing an existential reflection on the lack of individual freedom. Onaindia's third work in the crime genre was *Gela debekatua* (The Forbidden Room, 1988), a suffocating suspense novel about a woman in a locked house on the coast, recalling Hitchcock's films and, in Cillero's opinion, his best work in the genre.

Pako Aristi (1963–) is the author of two crime novels: *Kcappo. Tempo di tremolo* (1985) and *Irene, Tempo di adagio* (1989), both located in a rural setting in the 1930s. As Olaziregi observes, these novels and the third in the trilogy, *Krisalida, Tempo di tempo* (1990), "were clearly influenced by the noir novel (especially that of Chandler) and so-called American dirty realism, and have been considered one of the best examples in the Basque context of noir neo-ruralism" (Olaziregi 2002: 136). Aldekoa (2004), too, situates the novels within realism, and detached from *costumbrismo* and experimentalism. The events described by Aristi are very harsh, along the lines of Camilo José Cela's *tremendismo*, with large doses of sex and violence from time to time.

The works of the Jesuit Basque teacher Imanol Zaldua (1924-1996) are thesis novels that extoll the Basque character. Amongst these, two works are part of the police genre. *Herrimina* (Homesickness, 1985) is a mystery and suspense thriller and the first novel in a trilogy led by a journalist, Beñat Soraitz. *Urola ibaian* (In the River Urola, 1985), meanwhile, is a classic murder mystery, along the procedural lines of Conan Doyle and Christie.

Cillero locates one work by Txillardegi (1929–2012) in the crime fiction model: *Exkixu* (1987). Although this was the last step in the author's existentialist fiction, crime fiction elements are appropriated to move forward in the story of the activist Antton's trajectory. In Olaziregi's words, with this novel Txillardegi "slipped into the poetics which resemble orthodox critical realism" (Olaziregi 2002: 80).

Iñaki Zabaleta (1952–) published *110. Street-eko geltokia* (110th Street Station) in 1988, in the "Basque noir fiction" series by the Elkar publishing house. Set in New York, it tells the story of a young Basque man, Joseba. The main character, both a criminal and a victim, operates in an endless big city wasteland, perhaps in search of love, in an impossible search. When it comes to style, the novel uses a cinematic narrative, interspersed with a variety of shots and lively dialogues. Aldekoa includes the novel within the most successful works among high school and *euskaltegi* (a Basque-language learning center for adults) students, in the tradition of Gotzon Garate's oeuvre (2004: 204). Chronologically, the first one examined in this book is a crime novel.

The first novel by Hasier Etxeberria (1957–2017), *Mugetan* (On the Borders, 1989), is structured as a thriller by means of a few elements: two men who live on each side of the border and the woman they both love. Behind this outline, the action is political, pointing to the divisive and even lethal nature of the border, and the struggle to eliminate it altogether. Etxeberria's novel is told in a simple form, through short passages, in a journalistic style. Ten years later, he published another novel in the same style, *Arrainak ura baino* (More than Fish Water, 1999). It concerns a romantic story and the topic of political violence. The protagonist Simon Azkue carries out a violent attack on a public building in order to validate himself in the eyes of the woman he loves.

In the 1980s, moreover, crime fiction-like short story collections were published. Worth mentioning are: Mikel Antza's (1961–) *Odolaren usaina* (The Smell of Blood, 1987), which in Cillero's opinion brought a fresh perspective to Basque crime fiction on account of its more critical treatment of violence than previous authors, because of the elegant literary techniques it uses, for the intertextuality created by its documenting of stories, and due to the author's own personal biography; Andoni Egaña's (1961–) *Sokratikoek ere badute ama* (The Socratics Also Have a Mother, 1989), made up of three stories, which Cillero considers distinctive mystery fiction that in some way opened the door to police procedural fiction although the atmosphere of the time was not favorable to such work; and in one way or another, Koldo Izagirre (1953–) also entered the field of crime fiction through his collection of short stories, *Mendekuak* (Revenges, 1987).

To conclude with the 1980s, one must mention several works published in the field of children's and young adult literature: Anjel Lertxundi published *Portzelanazko irudiak* (Porcelain Images, 1981), under the penname Xabier Aldai, for the "Auskalo" series by the Erein publishing house, in the tradition of a group of young investigators; and the same author published six books in the "Madame Kontxexi-Uribe, Brigada & Detektibe" (Madam Kontxexi-Uribe, Brigadier and Detective), between 1986 and 1990; Xabier Mendiguren Elizegi also published *Tangoak ez du amaierarik* (The Tango Never Ends, 1988), a young person's mystery novel, for the first time with a female investigator. Children's and young adult literature in the genre is also explored in this book.

During the next decade, in the 1990s, the experimentalism of the previous decade was abandoned in general and there was a return to more traditional forms of storytelling. That said, this was carried out with a postmodern touch. There was another return during this decade: from rural to urban settings. A third especially important feature of the time was the striking development of translation. The "world literature" project was a cornerstone of this latter turn, and thereafter, some years later, as Anjel Lertxundi explains in his essay *Itzuliz usu begiak* (Turning Usually the Gaze, 2019), the dialogue between creative works and translations was more productive than ever. As for subject matter, moreover, the so-called Basque conflict was the most often repeated context, and there was a noticeable tendency in general to give visibility to marginalized characters and environments.

In terms of more closed crime fiction, as Cillero points out, at a time when collections of police and noir novels were disappearing in the surrounding countries and the characteristics of the genre began to appear in line with general literary trends, the creation of Igela in the Basque Country, a publishing house dedicated entirely to the genre, was significant.

Following the timeline in the specialist studies cited above, the first author during this decade was Joxean Agirre, via two works: *Gizon bat bilutsik pasiloan barrena* (A Naked Man in the Corridor, 1991) and *Elgeta* (1996). In the former, Agirre brings several police genre resources into play, in order to delve into a search for the meaning of the protagonist's life. Together with those resources, several others from canonical literature are explored, such as intertextuality with writers in whom he is interested. The second novel, *Elgeta*, adheres much more closely to the conventions of the genre.

Edorta Jimenez (1953–) published *Speed gauak* (Speed Nights) in 1991. The protagonist of the novel is an antihero who tries to prevent the conspiracy of some powerful figures in two days between reality and hallucination. The location of the work is Bilbao, a large city, and supposedly the best place to develop a crime plot. Retolaza and Egaña (2016: 55) locate this work within the trend of so-called dirty realism.

Laura Mintegi (1955–) is the author of a work which can be situated within the field of the genre: *Legez kanpo* (Out of the Law, 1991). Behind the main plot, a police novel is being written by a character that occasionally appears in dialogue with the main thread.

Xabier Montoia (1955–) published *Non dago Stalin?* (Where Is Stalin?) in 1991. The plot begins with the disappearance of a young man nicknamed Stalin. Through almost cinematic short chapters, he maintains the suspense of events, including the search for a lost document related to the "dirty war" at that time.

As the author of spy novels, Josemari Velez de Mendizabal (1949–) published three novels with a Basque spy protagonist, Koxme Zubia: *Yehuda* (1992), *Moskuko gereziak* (Cherries from Moscow, 1996), and *Samurai berria* (The New Samurai, 1999). Zubia is involved in international affairs, which are more elaborated than Gereño's writings. The aim was similar: to provide Basque readers with simple entertaining reading material, seasoned with features familiar to them from Spanish-language readings and genre films.

In 1993, Bernardo Atxaga (1951–) published *Gizona bere bakardadean* (*The Lone Man*) (1996). This is a great example of reaching the center of the literary system by manipulating some peripheral repertoires. Xabier Etxaniz (2007) observes that Atxaga's children's and young adult literature has been a field of experimentation for some of his canonical works. In the case of this novel under discussion here, Aldekoa says: "Realism is his thing, nonetheless, he handles deftly literary elements and resources from diverse literary traditions (noir fiction, children's literature...) but it contributes effectively to composing a good suspense novel" (2004: 262). That way, the result was not the typical police novel, but something more complex instead. Aldekoa and Cillero (2000: 304) have mentioned the novel's resemblance to a tragic play. All in all, the dosages of suspense, the political foundations of the plot, the use of symbols, the narrating voices, and the stifling atmosphere caused by the location have a lot to do with this tragedy.

The writer from Lapurdi Itxaro Borda (1959–) merits a special place in this overview on Basque crime and police fiction, and below we will examine her work in detail. She published three novels in the genre in the 1990s: *Bakean ützi arte* (Until They Leave Us in Peace, 1994), *Bizi nizano munduan* (Until I'm Alive, 1996) and *Amorezko pena baño* (More than Heartbreak, 1996). With the turn of the century, however, three more followed: *Jalgi hadi plazara* (Go Forth into Public, 2004), *Boga boga* (Row, Row!, 2012) and *Ultimes déchets* (The Final Waste, 2015). In all six, the protagonist is the atypical detective Amaia Ezpeldoi. Specifically, by means of the genre and protagonist chosen, Borda sees the possibility of giving visibility to socially excluded people, as she states in the aforementioned article in the journal *Susa* when discussing the monograph about police literature (Borda, 1992).

Itxaro Borda's first two novels are set in Zuberoa, in a rural environment, and they concern matters in this context in the local dialect. The third contribution, however, takes place in the Erribera region of Navarre. With the fourth, the detective Ezpeldoi moves to Bilbao. The fifth is set in Baiona (Bayonne). Cillero, following Sally Munt, classifies these novels by Borda as part of the satirical field of feminist crime fiction. In such cases, the protagonist questions the importance of herself, and Ezpeldoi's self-irony and humor distance the works from the typical strict seriousness of the genre (Cillero 2000: 320).

The next author in this chronological overview is Jon Alonso (1958–) and his novel *Katebegi galdua* (The Missing Link, 1996). The starting point of the story is the theft of an old book that could change the history of Basque literature and that of Navarre. The investigation of the crime and the measure of suspense are skillfully carried out, between the changes of pace and the intertextualities in the narrative, and behind all that the thesis of Alonso's work is developed: culture itself, specifically the rewriting of the history of literature, as an important tool for constructing collective identity and therefore for the struggle for power. In the same vein as the above work, in the novel-essay *Camembert helburu* (Mission Camembert, 1998) Alonso reflects on the function of art by making use of an investigation into a forgery of a painting by Toulouse-Lautrec. This adds elements of mystery and intrigue to the book, not only providing a pleasant read, but also allowing it to be placed in the realm of crime literature.

Now well into the new century, Alonso published *Zintzoen saldoan* (In the Group of the Righteous, 2012), which is explored in more detail in this book.

The same year that Alonso's novel was published, so was Miguel Angel Mintegi's (1949–) *Esker mila, Marlowe* (Many Thanks, Marlowe, 1996). As the title itself suggests, this is a tribute to the noir fiction of yesteryear. Mintegi sought to apply the noir outline to the Basque Country, while also adding nostalgia to his customary wittily ironic tone. If one had to choose, the secondary character, the detective's girlfriend, is more interesting than the detective himself. The death of the detective's brother, which forms the core of the investigation, is clarified in a classic closing encounter, more in line with Christie than Chandler.

Among many other works, Harkaitz Cano (1975–) published two novels with several features of the crime genre: *Beluna Jazz* (1996) and *Pasaia blues* (1998), both of which are interconnected not only through music, but also in terms of structure. The former begins with a murder. By means of a narrative on multiple levels, Cano presents the novel as a game to be completed, with a skilfully guided rhythm and a dreamlike atmosphere. Although the settings for that first novel are the United States and the Netherlands, in the second work Cano shifts the action to the Basque Country, and specifically to Pasaia. Here, too, there is a murder which the *ertzaintza* (the Basque police force) tries to clear up. As in his previous work, this takes place within the structure of a kind of puzzle, a music guide, and on this occasion by means of more realistic resources. Although the latter more fully matches the police genre than the former, it consciously refuses to do so, once again making use of the resources of the genre to undertake a more complex and profound work.

In order to end this overview of the 1990s, one must mention Aingeru Epaltza (1960–). In his fourth novel, *Rock 'n' Roll* (2000), Epaltza makes use of explicitly noir genre features to create a work about his generation: murder, suspense, lewdness, first-person narration, surreal comparisons, marginalized characters... All of this interspersed with intertextual quotes from rock music, film, and noir fiction itself. In a previously published novel, too, *Ur uherrak* (Muddy Waters, 1993), Epaltza brings marginalized figures into play: a black girl and an old *bertsolari* (a Basque oral poetic improviser). Hybridization between two worlds carried out brilliantly through the hybridization of melodies and genres. Indeed, as Olaziregi contends, "In the structuring of the work one can perceive narrative strategies that are close to the noir novel" (2002: 169). In one of this book's chapters, these two novels by Aingeru Epaltza, as well as his *Sasiak ere begiak baditik* (Even Brush Has Eyes, 1986), are examined.

Joxemari Iturralde (1951–) also wrote a book at the close of the twentieth century: *Euliak ez dira argazkietan azaltzen* (Flies Don't Appear in Photos, 2000). This time, Iturralde uses crime fiction to reflect on the transcendence of life. Julio Rekexo, a normal Bilbao detective, carries out minor investigations. It seems, though, that he is overcome by the scale of the world because it moves by the power of forces that he cannot control. Even the occasional romance is scarce consolation for the weary little guy. A few years later, Iturralde also published in the field of children's literature with *Sute handi bat ene bihotzean* (A Big Fire in My Heart) (1994). This is an adventure and investigation story about the protagonist Risky's group of young people, with whom readers were already familiar.

At the close of the twentieth century, regarding the position of the genre in the literary system, Cillero believes that due to the quality and reception of some works, it was losing something of its distinctive nature and was in some ways being incorporated into canonical literature. He is referring, of course, to a specific section of crime fiction. Indeed, he underscores the weakness of the genre, noting how difficult it is for authors who want to specialize in crime and police fiction. By means of data he states that, since Xabier Gereño's time (until that point), no author had used the same protagonist in more than three novels (Cillero 2000: 337–38).

Twenty years after the turn of the new century, in contrast, we believe that the clearly accurate diagnosis above needs qualifying to some extent. In fact, over the years, some "specialist" writers in the genre have appeared in the Basque Country, in a similar way to the figures that appeared in other European countries in previous decades (in the 1960s, the Sjöwall and Walhöö tandem in Sweden and P. D. James in the United Kingdom; in the 1970s, Vázquez Montalbán in Spain and Manchette in France; in the 1980s, Juan Madrid in Spain; and in the 1990s, Camilleri in Italy, Márkaris in Greece and Mankell in Sweden).

Within this current, the first name that should be mentioned is Jon Arretxe (1963–). After working in some other genres, such as travel literature and realist humor (Billelabeitia, n.d.), he ended up becoming a bestselling author. Likewise, through humor, he published two parodies of noir fiction: *Manila konexioa* (The Manila Connection, 2003) and *Kleopatra* (Cleopatra, 2005). Becoming a little more focused, he then began concentrating on crime fiction in general through the works *Morto vivace* (2007), *Fatum* (2008), and *Xahmaran* (2009). His next step was the book series centered on Detective Toure: *19 kamera* (19 cameras, 2012), *612 euro* (612 euros, 2013), *Hutsaren itzalak* (The Shadows of Emptiness,

2014), *Estolda jolasak* (Sewer Games, 2015), *Sator lokatzak* (Mole Mud, 2016), *Ez erran deus* (Don't Say Anything at All, 2019) and *Mesfidatu hitzez* (Mistrust through Words, 2019). As he is the chief exponent of a new tendency, a chapter in this book is dedicated to Arretxe too.

Alberto Ladron Arana (1967–), another productive writer in crime fiction, should also be placed within this same current. He started with some spy-based intrigue novels, *Xake mate* (Checkmate, 2002), *Eguzki beltzaren sekretua* (The Secret of the Black Sun, 2004), and *Arotzaren eskuak* (The Carpenter's Hands, 2006). From there, he passed on to the noir novel, with three more works: *Ahaztuen mendekua* (The Revenge of the Forgotten, 2009), *Zer barkaturik ez* (Nothing to Forgive, 2011), and *Piztiaren begiak* (The Eyes of the Beast, 2012). Thereafter, he published several works whose protagonist is Leire Asian, a woman officer in the Navarre regional police force: *Harrian mezua* (The Message in Stone, 2014), *Gezurren basoa* (The Forest of Lies, 2016), *Jainkoen zigorra* (God's Punishment, 2017), and *Film zaharren kluba* (The Old Film Club, 2018).

The third writer in this same current was Iñaki Irasizabal (1969–). In the field of noir fiction, he published *Mendaroko txokolatea* (Chocolate from Mendaro, 2005), *Igelak benetan hiltzen dira* (Frogs Really Die, 2011), *Bizkartzainaren lehentasunak* (The Bodyguard's Priorities, 2013), *Odolaren deia* (A Call to Blood, 2014), *Aita gurea* (Our Father, 2015) and *Gauzak ez ziren sekula berdinak izango* (Things Would Never be the Same Again, 2016). In addition, he also developed political thrillers in *Politika zikina* (Dirty Politics, 2017) and *Aramotz* (2018); and he has a book in memory of the Spanish Civil War: *Gu bezalako heroiak* (Heroes Like Us, 2009).

Besides the authors already mentioned, Aritz Gorrotxategik (1975-) published two novels in the field of crime literature: *Kafkaren labankada* (Kafka's Knife Wound) (2001) and *Kearen truke* (In Exchange for Smoke) (2005). The former, published by the Kutxa foundation after winning the Irun Huria prize, is based on the relationship between the literary professor Joao Boaventura and his former friend Marzel. This takes place in the context of a dark plot woven out of love and jealousy that unfolds in Lisbon. Joao, however, is not the only protagonist. In fact, the intertextuality t runs through the text is often predominant. *Kearen truke*, on the other hand, begins with an investigation into the case of a man apparently killed for losing a text by the seventeenth-century Basque writer Axular. This crime novel recalls, among others, Jon Alonso's *Katebegi galdua* (The Missing Link) in that it is about a mysterious death and the search for a lost book.

Several other authors and works which can be located to some extent within the genre during the years we are discussing must be cited. Joxemari Urteaga (1961–) published *Ordaina zor nizun* (I Owed You Compensation, 2001), about a photographer who receives mysterious letters. A few years later, moreover, the stories set in in this work were published separately in a collection for young readers and titled *Hilpuinak* (Deadly Short Stories, 2008), the subtitle of the original novel. Txema Garcia-Viana (1963–) published the noir novel *Sei lore* (Six Flowers, 2001), set in the same Bilbao in which, later, Arretxere's Toure would operate. Garbiñe Ubeda (1967–) brought out *Hobe isilik* (Best Keep Quiet, 2013) about memory; and Miren Gorrotxategi (1981–) published the interesting crime novel *33 ezkil* (33 Bells, 2016), with a nod, at the beginning at least, to Loidi's pioneering novel.

This tendency toward specialization in the first two decades of the century has led the genre to search for the periphery again within the Basque literary system, that is, generally speaking toward the typical crime and police novel coordinates. As proof of this, one only need turn to the paratexts used in works like these. The cover designs and the back cover summaries are aimed at readers who like this type of literature and provide a complete characterization of the genre. Specifically, on account of the importance of paratexts, an original work that explores the front covers of Basque police novels is also included in this collection.

One exception to this general tendency that has marked literary production during these years, and which is also addressed in a specific chapter in this book, is Ramon Saizarbitoria's *Lili eta biok* (Lili and Me, 2015). Once again, here we find gender hybridization, through some of the author's very own particular *topos*: a writer within a written text, the Spanish Civil War, memory, guilt, sentimental relations... There are also crimes, allegedly at least, and we consider this enough of a connection to incorporate this work by the great storyteller here. We are also able to include one of his latest works, dating from the new century, which is located at the center of the system and based on the play between genres.

Police Novels Written in Spanish

The relationships between systems that intersect with one other in a polysystem are complex. The work of Basque authors in Spanish is part of the Spanish-language literary system, and specifically the Spanish-language literary system of Spain. The same could be said, with the necessary adjustments, about those who write in French. According to the origins of the authors and the subject matter of some of their works, however, they are also part of the Basque literary system, at least according to some critics. This insertion is often difficult: sociologically, writers in Basque and those in Spanish/French in the Basque Country have lived in two separate worlds. Those who write in the hegemonic languages have generally looked toward the metropolises, while almost always ignoring those who write in Basque (very few of them have been able to get along in Basque, since the death of Pio Baroja, and, therefore, the interactions and influences assumed for any system have, if any, been unidirectional).

In the case of authors included in this collection of studies, however, observing the affinity is simpler. The native of Bilbao writer Ramiro Pinilla (1923–2014) was very committed to the Basque Country. He wrote about it constantly and it would appear that he worked in a dialectical way with Txomin Agirre on the basis of Basque themes, until creating his trilogy and main work *Verdes valles, colinas rojas* (Green Valleys, Red Hills, 2004-2005). His contribution to crime fiction came late, and he used the genre to express the moral and literary concerns repeatedly expressed in his work from a different perspective: *Solo un muerto más* (Only One More Death, 2009), *Cadáveres en la playa* (Corpses on the Beach, 2014), and *El cementerio vacío* (The Empty Cemetery, 2014).

The case of Dolores Redondo (1969–), from Donostia, is different, because she is a writer devoted entirely to the literary genre. Her most famous works are those that make up the Baztan trilogy: *El guardián invisible* (*The Invisible Guardian*, 2016), *Legado en los huesos* (*The Legacy of the Bones*, 2018) and *Ofrenda a la tormenta* (*Offering to the Storm*, 2018). The protagonist of all three is Amaia Salazar, a Navarrese police inspector, and she investigates crimes that take place in the Baztan Valley. Specifically, this character's formative years are recounted in the latest novel published by the author to date, *La cara norte del corazón* (*The North Face of the Heart*, 2019). This apart, the novel set in Galicia, *Todo esto te daré* (*All This I Will Give to You*, 2018), also includes the investigation of a crime. All of these works by Redondo have been translated into Basque.

Aside from those cited, many other authors have worked in crime fiction at some point or other. For example, Raul Guerra Garrido (1935–2022) has published three novels in the genre: *La costumbre de morir* (The Custom of Dying, 1981), *Escrito en un dólar* (Written on a Dollar, 1983), and *Tantos inocentes* (So Many innocents, 1996). Fernando Savater (1947–) debuted as a novelist with a political and police work: *Caronte aguarda* (Charon Awaits, 1981). Luisa Etxenike (1957–) is the author of a distinctive detective novel, *El detective de sonidos* (The Detective of Sounds, 2011). Eva García Sáenz de Urturi (1972–)

published the "Trilogía de la Ciudad Blanca" (White City Trilogy), crime novels set in Vitoria-Gasteiz: *El silencio de la ciudad blanca* (The Silence of the White City, 2016), *Los ritos del agua* (The Rites of Water, 2017), and *Los señores del tiempo* (The Lords of Time, 2018), whose protagonist is a police inspector nicknamed Kraken. The Donostia writer Ibon Martín (1976–) has published a police series about the investigator Leire Altuna: *El faro del silencio* (The Lighthouse of Silence, 2014), *La fábrica de las sombras* (The Dream Factory, 2015), *El último Akelarre* (The Last Witches' Coven, 2016), and *La jaula de sal* (The Salt Cage, 2017). Finally, the writer from Vitoria-Gasteiz, Álvaro Arbina (1990–) combines the historical and crime genres in the two works he has published to date: *La mujer del reloj* (The Clock Women, 2016) and *La sinfonía del tiempo* (The Symphony of Time, 2018).

References

Aldekoa, Iñaki (2004): *Historia de la literatura vasca*. Erein: San Sebastian.
Alonso, Jon (2016): *Beltzaren koloreak*. Susa: San Sebastian.
Auden, Wystan H. (1974): *La mano del teñidor y otros ensayos*. Barral: Barcelona.
Azkargorta, Antton (1986): "Philip Marlowek begikeinua egin zidanean ... edo porrotaren lilura." *Susa* 19, 91–93.
Barba, David (Ed.) (2005): *Primer Encuentro Europeo de Novela Negra. Homenaje a Manuel Vázquez Montalbán*. Planeta: Barcelona.
Billelabeitia, Miren (d.g.): "Arretxe, Jon," *Euskal Literaturaren Hiztegia*, UPV/EHU, http://www.ehu.eus/ehg/literatura/idazleak/?p=145
Borda, Itxaro (1992): "Larrüpean ebilten direnak," *Susa*, 29, https://andima.armiarma.eus/susa/susa2611.htm
Buschmann, Albrecht (2002): Introduction. Dossier La novela negra. *Iberoamericana*, II, 7, 93-96.
Cawelti, John (1976): *Adventure, Mystery and Romance: Formula Stories as Art and Popular Culture*. Chicago University Press: Chicago.
Chandler, Raymond (1988) [1950]: *The Simple Art of Murder*. Random House: London.
Cillero Goiriastuena, Javi (2000): *The Moving Target: A History of Basque Detective and Crime Fiction*. University of Nevada: Reno (NV).
Coma, Javier (1980): *La novela negra*. El viejo topo/Ediciones 2001: Barcelona.
De Quincey, Thomas (2004) [1827]: *Del asesinato considerado como una de las Bellas Artes y otras obras selectas*. Valdemar: Madrid.
Eco, Umberto (1981): *Lector in fabula*. Lumen: Barcelona.
——— (1985): *Apostillas a El nombre de la rosa*. Lumen: Barcelona.
Etxaniz, Xabier (2007): *Bela kabelatik Ternuara. Atxagaren haur eta gazte literatura*. Pamiela: Pamplona.
Even-Zohar, Itamar (1990): "Polysystem Studies," *Poetics Today*, 11, 1, 1–94.
Fernández Colmeiro, José (1988): "Desde el balneario," *Quimera*, 73, 12–23.

——— (1994): *La novela policiaca española: teoría e historia crítica*. Anthropos: Barcelona.
Garate, Gotzon (2000): *Atzerriko eta Euskal Herriko Polizia Eleberria*. Elkarlanean: San Sebastian.
Hernandez Abaitua, Mikel (1982): "Nobela beltza eta polizi nobela klasikoa," *Jakin*, 25, 51–67.
Hoppenstand, Gary (1987): *In Search of the Paper Tiger: A Sociological Perspective of Myth, Formula and the Mystery Genre in the Entertainment Print Mass Medium*. Bowling Green State University Popular Press. Bowling Green: Ohio.
Iser, Wolfgang (1987): *El acto de leer*. Taurus: Madrid.
James, Phyllis Dorothy (2009): *Talking About Detective Fiction*. Alfred A. Knopf: New York.
Kortazar, Jon (2000): *Euskal literatura XX. mendean*. Prames: Zaragoza.
Lemaitre, Pierre (2015) [2006]: *Irene*. Alfaguara: Madrid.
Lertxundi, Anjel (2019): *Itzuliz usu begiak*. Alberdania: Irun.
López Gaseni, Jose Manuel (2019): "Literatura estadounidense traducida al euskera," in Kortazar, Jon, ed. (2019): *Bridge / Zubia. Imágenes de la relación cultural entre el País Vasco y Estados Unidos*. Iberoamericana: Madrid. 229–243.
Losada Soler, Elena, and Paszkiewicz, Katarzyna (Eds.) (2015): *Tras la pista. Narrativa criminal escrita por mujeres*. Icaria: Barcelona.
Lotman, Juri (1977): "The Dinamic Model of Semiotics Systems," *Semiotica*, 21, 193–210.
Martín Cerezo, Iván (2006): *Poética del relato policiaco*. University of Murcia: Murcia.
Martz, Linda, and Higgie, Anita (Eds.) (2007): *Questions of Identity in Detective Fiction*. Cambridge Scholars Publishing: Newcastle.
Millán, José Antonio (2018): "Cuando un libro se nos cae." *El País*, retrieved from: https://elpais.com/cultura/2018/08/15/babelia/1534351691_997591.html.
Mullen, Anne, and O'beirne, Emer, (Eds.) (2000): *Crime Scenes. Detective Narratives in European Culture since 1945*. Rodopi: Amsterdam.
Olarra, Xabier (1987): "Jim Thompson '1280 arima' (beltzak barne)," *Literatur Gazeta*, 5. https://andima.armiarma.eus/gaze/gaze0507.htm.
Olaziregi, Mari Jose (2002): *Euskal eleberriren historia*. Labayru / Amorebieta-Etxanoko Udala: Bilbao.
Olaziregui, Mari Jose (2000): "Un siglo de novela en euskera," in Urquizu, Patricio (Ed.) (2000): *Historia de la literatura vasca*. UNED: Madrid. 504–588.
Resina, Joan Ramón (1997): *El cadáver en la cocina. La novela criminal en la cultura del desencanto*. Anthropos: Barcelona.
Retolaza, Iratxe, and Egaña, Ibon (2016): "The Contemporary Basque Novel," in Kortazar, Jon (Ed.): *Contemporary Basque Literature*. Center for Basque Studies: Reno (NV). 11-68.
Rodríguez Pequeño, Francisco Javier (1994): *Cómo leer a Umberto Eco: El nombre de la rosa*. Júcar: Madrid.
Sánchez Soler, Mariano (Ed.) (2009): *Actas de Mayo Negro. 13 miradas al género criminal*. Club Universitario: Alicante.
Sánchez Zapatero, Javier, and Martín Escribà, Àlex (Eds.) (2012): *El género negro. El fin de la frontera*. Andavira: Santiago of Compostela.
——— (Coord.) (2016): Monográfico: El género negro en el siglo XXI: Nuevas perspectivas en la literatura, el cine, la televisión y el cómic hispanos, *Pasavento*, IV, 1, 8–155.
Savater, Fernando (1983): *Sobre vivir*. Ariel: Barcelona.
Shavit, Zohar (1986): *Poetics of Children's Literature*. The University of Georgia Press: Athens (GA).

Todorov, Tzvetan (1971): *Poétique de la prose*. Éditions de Seuil: Paris.
Toury, Gideon (1980): *In Search of a Theory of Translation*. The Porter Institute for Poetics and Semiotics: Tel Aviv.
Urquizu, Patricio (Dir.) (2000): *Historia de la literatura vasca*. UNED: Madrid.
Valera, Luis (2009): "La novela negra actual en Europa," in Sánchez Soler, Mariano (Ed.). (2009): *Actas de Mayo Negro. 13 miradas al género criminal*. Club Universitario: Alicante. 185–214.
Valles Calatrava, Jose R. (1991): *La novela criminal española*. University of Granada: Granada.
Vázquez De Parga, Salvador (1993): *La novela policiaca en España*. Ronsel: Barcelona.

Notes

1 Cillero interviewed Loidi before he died and, in his essay, he provides a wealth of interesting information about the genesis of Amabost egun Urgain'en.
2 As Cillero says, *Espioitza* and *Gudari bat*, published by the Kriselu publishing house, did not appear in chronological order.

Chapter 1

110. *street-eko geltokia* (110th Street Station)(1986): A Basque's Harsh Exile or Homesickness in the City

Jon Martin Etxebeste

Introduction

Iñaki Zabaleta Urkiola published the novel *110. street-eko geltokia* (110th Street Station) in 1986. He wrote this noir novel two years earlier in New York, where the story is set. The Susa publishing house released it first (three editions) and from 1988 on it has been sold by the Elkar publishing house. In 2003, having gone through twenty-five editions, a special edition was published by Elkar. Therein, Zabaleta added an afterword.

It is one of the bestselling books in Basque literature, on a par with J. M. Irigoien's *Babilonia* (Babylon) (1989) and Pako Aristi's *Kcappo. Tempo di tremolo* (1985) (Olaziregi 2000). Up to 2019, it had sold 73,000 copies and between 2004 and 2006 it was the most downloaded Basque-language book in the Basque government library; the only Basque-language work in the top ten most downloaded books.

Zabaleta tells a story about loneliness, homesickness, and fear in this text, which is as much a screenplay as it is a book. It is the story of a refugee who lives in New York. Joseba is a young man who cannot return to the Basque Country because of the problems he has had with the Spanish police. He works in a café, preparing breakfasts; and that way he adapts to the loneliness and poverty

110. street-eko geltokia (110th Street Station)

of the big city. Simultaneously, the story recounts the life of Angie. She works for an advertising firm and will meet the protagonist through a campaign she is designing. A relationship will begin to develop between them. Meanwhile, Catherine (the boss of the café in which Joseba works) will use blackmail to get her worker involved in drug trafficking. After carrying out two deals, however, the protagonist will refuse to continue doing this work and the boss will order a hitman to kill him. Joseba will bleed to death at the 110th Street subway station; and, with his death, his nascent relationship with Angie also comes to an end.

Iñaki Zabaleta

Zabaleta was born in Leitza in 1952 and since 1989 has taught in the Journalism Department at the University of the Basque Country. He studied for a vocational industrial degree in automatism at Mondragon University (1971) and within two years of completing the degree he was working as a blueprint designer. In the 1980s, he studied journalism at the University of Navarre. The author lived in New York City at the time of writing the novel. Besides writing this work, he completed both a masters and a doctorate during his stay. His work was a finalist in the 1984 Resurrección Maria Azkue competition. He has been a journalist for the EITB (Basque public radio and television service) group and CNN, and contributed to numerous media.

He began contributing to the *Oh, Euskadi* journal in 1978 and won prizes in several literary competitions, including the Xalbador short story competition (1978 and 1980). In 1979 he brought out his first collection of poems, *Bertsoaren ezpata* (The Sword of Verse). He published his second, *Eskuaren fereka* (The Stroke of the Hand) in 1982. In 1988, another short story was released, titled *Carolyn Meyer, dantzaria* (The Dancer, Carolyn Meyer), after it had won the Ignacio Aldekoa contest. He published his most recent story in 2017: "Frantsesaren troka" ("Frenchman's Cliff"), in the book *38 idazle nafar* (38 Navarrese Writers), issued by the Pamiela publishing house.

The Noir Novel, Blood Shed Late

The book *110. street-eko geltokia* could be considered a noir novel. Zabaleta's novels do not begin with a death, as is customary. It is not therefore a classic detective novel. Nor does it fit in chronologically with those nineteenth-century works. There is no body, but the reader can surmise that they are reading that kind of novel and the lack of a hero only heightens the suspense. The canonical structure of these books goes typically like this: the book begins with a death and an investigator comes across clues as to how it happened, until the mystery is cleared up at the end. In this genre, death is central to the novel:

> We can define as a crime novel only that production in which the offence is not treated as an episode or a motive, but as the basic theme, out of which are derived or to which are connected, to some degree, all the human actions, dramas and conflicts. (Herrera 2008: 59)

The noir novel is usually told in four voices: that of the protagonist, the murderer, the victim, and the judge. In this case, the protagonist and the victim are one and the same. The death, that of the protagonist, comes at the end of the novel. Despite being a predictable act, the executioner and the method are both unknown.

Jorge Luis Borges said that any discussion of police stories implied citing Edgar Allan Poe, as he had invented the genre (1996: 189). Poe created the figure of the investigator Dupin and thereafter many authors would use an astute detective character (Hércules Poirot, Sherlock Holmes ...). Those writers follow the direction of the classic detective novel.

In the 1920s in the United States, authors embarked on the path of what was termed hardboiled storytelling. Terminologically, in regard to expressions like hardboiled, detective novel, noir fiction, and so on, there is debate about exactly where the boundaries of each are. The noir novel has predominated in the Basque case, but it may be confusing because in the United States the noir concept has also been used to refer to literature written by black authors (Hart 1987: 13).

Noir fiction quickly spread in English-speaking countries, followed shortly by countries like France. In Hart's opinion, (1987: 17), Pedro Alarcón's *El clavo* (The Nail) (1853) may be considered the first work in this genre (in other words, twelve years after *The Murders in the Rue Morgue*). The first noir novel in the Basque Country was *Amabost egun Urgain'en* (*Fifteen Days in Urgain*) by Jose Antonio Loidi, published in 1955.

In the context of the period between the 1920s and 1940s, noir fiction took on another tone. During the interwar period, when the mafia was very much in the news, detectives were no longer almost superhuman. The investigator's weaknesses were more visible and Zabaleta's work is much closer to this point of view.

As Todorov explains, the mystery novel is the sum of two stories, the story of a death (how it happens) and the story of an investigation (how what happened becomes known): as it is an investigation, there are long sections devoted to reflection. In 1945, Marcel Duhamel would baptise the genre *serie noir* as the two parts merging with the death story taking on more significance. However, the most important dimension is how that death is narrated. This new tendency would focus on power relations, violence, and capitalism. Zabaleta's novel, specifically, centers on that misfortune.

With respect to noir fiction in Spain, individual and separate works would be published. Up to the death of Franco, hardly any novels were published in this genre, and translations predominated; yet during what is termed the Transition publications multiplied: for example, Eduardo Mendoza's *La verdad sobre el caso Savolta* (*The Truth About the Savolta Case*) (1975). That same decade also saw the release of M. V. Montalbán's *Tatuaje* (*Tattoo*), the same Mendoza's *El misterio de la cripta embrujada* (*The Mystery of the Enchanted Crypt*) and Muñoz Molina's *Belternebros*. They had all the features of noir fiction; they were set in cities and were critiques of society.

Chronos, Eros, and Thanatos

The story of *110. street-eko geltokia* has three main plots, and depending on the subjectivity of the reader and the time in which they are reading, one of them may be more important than the others: First is the friction between Joseba's past and present. Second is the extortion of Joseba by his boss. Third is the love story between Joseba and Angie:

> One source of suspense is the story of Joseba's deal with Catherine, as well as his efforts to get out of that business. The other source of suspense is created by Angie's passionate searching for Joseba's underground messages, and the difficulties of meeting Joseba in a vast urban environment (Cillero 2005: 240).

Therefore, Zabaleta's noir novel is also a romance novel according to one of the plots.

In the universe created by Zabaleta, one can note a gentle touch of violence. The protagonist is surrounded by violence; time, space, and actions can be differentiated. He lives in a poor neighborhood, surrounded by violence; but his nonviolent nature steers him clear of that trouble. Moreover, there is violence pursuing him from his homeland and his past, that of the Spanish police; and the space situates him apart from that. The third kind of force is that exercised by Joseba's boss, and this violent attitude leads the protagonist to accept sexual abuse and immerse himself in the world of crime. Of the three types of violence, it is the second one that most frightens him, but it is the third one which really assaults him time and time again.

"Come on in, Gregory"

Joseba Telleria is the protagonist of the novel and he is introduced on the first page. He is a young twenty-seven-year-old man, born in Ezkurra, who has studied philosophy and is politically active. He has "That ruddy skinned beautiful face," says Angie when she meets him, transporting his rural origins to the metropolitan world. Joseba is a good-hearted quiet person. He lives in room 417 of a Harlem hotel and is working in a café during the time of the story. Although his story is optimistic, he represents a loser. Joseba is an antihero and the characters born in New York disconcert him, in the end reminding him that he is a foreigner in the city.

Joseba's best friend in New York is Gregory, a black alcoholic World War II veteran. He plays the role of a local living in wretchedness. He embodies the dignity of poverty.

Catherine is the novel's antagonist. She is presented later than the other characters. She is a high-class powerful woman. She feels attracted to Joseba and seeks to use and test her power over him, both in the business and in sexual pursuit of him. She owns a café in Manhattan and employs Joseba. She knows about Joseba's weaknesses and is ready to use extortion to achieve her goals. She personifies capitalism. As can be typical in this genre, the woman plays an unsettling role (Corbatta 1994: 169–170) and she may be the source of the conflict; her presence imposes difficulties in the search for harmony.

It is customary for sex to be very important in noir fiction novels and this topic appears connected to Catherine. Collateral damage of Joseba's loneliness is his sexual hunger, yet it would seem that the protagonist is in search of affection more than sex. He is under the control of sexual desire, and when Catherine forces herself on him there is a clash between the disgust he feels rationally and his bodily instinct. It is a very atypical passage in Basque literature and, bearing in mind the time at which it was written, of great value. It perhaps echoes the film *The Graduate* to some extent. There is a passage devoted to Joseba's sexual thoughts, but it is likely the author would have included it as a means of reinforcing Catherine's sexual assault on him.

Examining the passage in more detail, the scene can be understood as a switch of typical sex and gender roles. Catherine personifies capitalism and, with that, male values; and the nuances associated with femininity are obvious in Joseba. From that point of view, we would find a reversal of the traditional roles between the sexes in the rape, although the genders would remain the same therein. In short, sex is limited to power in this scene and it seems that this is what excites Catherine the most. Moreover, it serves to highlight Joseba's subordination and also to strengthen the character's rural Catholic particularities.

Joe is the murderer. He has barely any protagonism in the story. He is a drug dealer and is having some problems in carrying out a related job. He is a lower-level extension of Catherine.

Angie aims to be a high-class person, working in an advertising agency. She is the opposite of Joseba in that she leads an easy life, does not live in a foreign country, and her needs are not at the base of Maslow's pyramid, but at the top. Angie had a love affair with Kelly a few years ago and has not been able to get it out of her head since.

Tom is a strange person. Despite his limited appearances, he is one of the most psychologically complex characters. One assumes he is in love with Angie, but at the same time he pushes her toward Joseba or Kelly. Tom is an essential character that functions as a means of encouraging Angie to make decisions she would not otherwise make and as an interlocutor in order to provide the reader with information by means of conversations.

The characters appear in binary fashion: Joseba-Gregory, Angie-Tom and Catherine-Joe; as complements and extensions of one another. With the exception of Catherine, they are all good hearted and they have a firm ethical grounding. With the exception of Joseba, they are all locals and enjoy significant freedom.

As regards their psychology, the characters are quite unstable, and at first glance they are not very profound. It is an effect, in my opinion, consciously sought by the author: it is a cinematic presentation, in which readers must immediately position themselves either for or against them. Zabaleta does not reveal several aspects of their personalities and readers must fill in the gaps. Depending on the actions of the reader, then, more complex or simpler characters will be derived.

With the exception of the rape scene, when it comes to power relations, the relationship between the superficial indifferent woman and the brave responsible man prevails as the main plot, which resembles a stereotyped gender perspective.

The conversations between Gregory and Joseba are a pretext to discuss the Basque Country. The author uses this to sketch its true nature: Gregory says that they are "wonderful people" based on meeting a Basque, Marie from Baiona, in Paris. Gregory fell in love with her but one day she did not show up anymore and he deduced that she had fallen in love with another Basque, romantic ties between people from different cultures being very difficult. He predicts this at the beginning of the novel and he foresees the problems Angie and Joseba will have to face in their relationship. Cillero says that the conversations are held in Basque (2005: 239):

> Gregory is a World War II veteran who spends his last days in the hotel telling his stories for a drink in a nearby bar. Gregory's story is told from his own point of view, which introduces a new voice in the novel, a dialogical procedure used skillfully by Zabaleta. The illusion created by the author that Gregory speaks Basque is necessary to maintain the verisimilitude of the story. Moreover, in this case it was absolutely necessary that Gregory expressed himself in Basque for most of the readers would not have understood English, and Spanish was out of the question. Since it was not the case of creating a Spanish guardia civil character, but an American war veteran, the procedure was essential to the readability of the novel. One interesting way of introducing the character and making him believable is the relationship that Gregory had with a Basque prostitute in Paris. In this way, the reader gets immediately interested by the story and easily accepts Gregory's Basque as another narrative convention.

Jean Genet

Zabaleta admired the writer Jean Genet: his corrosive nature, dark side and the way he criticized the public. He came across the book *Funeral Rites* while he was studying English in San Francisco and from which he rescued the quotation in the book. He uses that as a bridge between Joseba and Angie, by means of a self-invented advertising medium. This passage is the protagonist's and Kelly's inclination, and Angie continues to look forward to reuniting with Kelly. This is the text: "Suddenly I'm not alone, because the night is blue, the trees are bare, the streets have learnt to speak and a girl, as alone as me, has been by my side." They also mention the unwritten last sentence in the conversation, "I sodomise the world." Otaegi (2008) says that "Genet's quote is a cry of solitude and despair":

> Angie at times brings back the memory of a lost friend. For Joseba, it means not being able to love his surroundings and the inability to love anyone in that area. Angie, though, is Joseba's counterpoint and is better adapted to this strange environment. She will show Joseba that he is wrong, that friends and affection are possible there too.

The praise of darkness and ugliness in Genet's work is in line with the idea of the city that Zabaleta wants to portray and contrasts with the sincerity of Angie's character.

The Story

The novel is written in the third person and in the past. It tells two parallel chronological stories: that of Joseba and that of Angie, in turns. This only underscores class differences. The story is very cinematic; the passages recall a film screenplay and the descriptions bear a striking resemblance to film images. Naturally, there is a film about the book's surroundings, titled *Menos que cero* (Less than Zero), yet set in Bilbao rather than in New York.

The narrative alternates between the story of Joseba and Angie, revealing class differences between the two. Lourdes Otaegi (2008) talks about its storytelling technique:

> His [Zabaleta's] television studies, on the other hand, provided him with technical skills. He wrote screenplays and learnt how to say everything he wanted to all the time through the camera's eye. In this novel, too, he worked out a structure through the help of images, but always as if to narrate the rhythm of a film. In creating the structure of the book, then, he first sought out some central themes, transformed them into foundations and established a structure on them, moving along chronologically or logically and linearly.

Zabaleta plunges the reader into a dark universe by means of his descriptions. In this case, he is favored by readers' preconceptions. Such violent areas in a big city like that are believable for the reader. However, I find that the dialogue between the characters hardly has the same credibility. Basque speakers have rarely heard police, detectives, and so on speak in standard Basque and it can be anomalous to read a war veteran like Gregory or a femme fatale like Catherine speaking in Basque. The shortage of dubbed films in the Basque Country may clearly have something to do with this.

Nevertheless, Zabaleta uses his ability to write screenplays to his advantage and employs a highly oral form of standardized speech which is natural and believable. He uses the kind of language spoken in and around Leitza to convey character's dialogues and his inclusion of several words in English is a valuable ingredient in the stories. If there is one weakness, it could be in not finding any language differences between the classes. The advertising executives speak in a very refined way ("I can assist you in that Thai guesthouse," 130) and that may be expected. Yet Gregory, a humble man from Harlem, speaks in the same way as Joseba ("hey, Joseba, that Catherine is a beautiful woman," 135) too. The use of the familiar *hika* form in Basque or some words in English would give the dialogue more credibility. Although one must bear in mind that we are talking about 1983, about a time when there were far fewer television series models.

As Otaegi (2008) demonstrates, the teachings of Gandiaga, his former literature professor, were a big influence. Zabaleta's main achievement is his narrative style. In an interview with Mikel Asurmendi published in the journal *Argia* (June 19, 2015), the author states that: "In the 1980s when I wrote it, I sought to imbue it with audio-visual features, believing that humanity's future and the way people adjusted their perception would come from audio-visual language, even though I was using a written register."The descriptions are also worth highlighting, for the impressionist techniques used and their striking poetic eloquence.

The author himself explained this in a previous interview in *Argia*:

> In some way, if as Horace believes, the core of poetry lies in such brevity and such condensation, I wanted to incorporate this attempt to summarize into the prose of this novel, writing in prose, but looking for words with a concept or heart: express in a few words what you have to say, but let those few words tell the truth or describe what you want. (...) It helped me try out a new method when it came to making descriptions: (...) I'm not saying I managed to do so, but that was my intention as regards the style: to express that feeling and that density without babbling on. (...) The golden rule has always been "express it concisely and forcefully" and in order to do that you also need that word contrast. I pay a lot of attention to that. (*Argia*, Oct. 27, 1985, 37)

Narrative Times

When it comes to structure, Zabaleta divides his narrative into nine chapters. He constructs a linear forward-looking narrative, but he also uses past facts. Gregory is one of the characters that recalls his reflections from the past (World War II) and Joseba's past itself is also described.

The author published the work in 1983, but the story is set a few years previously, in the late 1970s, because the protagonist is waiting for the dictatorship to end in order to return home.

110. street-eko geltokia (110th Street Station)

Altogether, the decision to narrate the story in the past is unusual. There would be no reason not to tell the story in the present. Indeed, the effect created by the narrator is basically that of what has been read in the present. Readers, Joseba, and Angie all find out information at the same time. Unlike the protagonists, though, the advantage for the readers is that they see the story of the two characters at the same time.

In the stabbing scene, the reader is aware of the person who is lurking. Consequently, readers feel a sense of suspense when the protagonist is stabbed unexpectedly. At a moment as important as the murder, they come down on his side and, again emphasizing the innocence of the character, readers moved by compassion for him are tempted to warn the protagonist. In the last chapter, without the protagonist, the narrator jumps from character to character. He narrates the closing lines from Gregory's perspective, as if he were the personification of the poverty-stricken face of New York.

The main motive for the author to choose the past is the end of a cycle. Written in 1983, the author expected that the political fugitive cycle would come to a close. This was an era that ended with an amnesty for political prisoners, and he wanted to capture that political phenomenon in a literary way.

On the other hand, when the new 2003 edition was published, the author blended reality and fiction. He traveled to New York and searched for Joseba's grave in the Holy Trinity cemetery in Brooklyn. There he came across two anonymous graves, one with a cross made out of tubes and the other made of wood; and he included that photo in the updated edition. One should in passing mention that the photographs in the book were taken by Zabaleta. The front cover image is also his and it was colorized by Joxemi Zumalabe. For the author, they express the friendship and respect between the two. Through that visit, the photographs and the story, he wanted to pay tribute to the fugitives. He wrote the book a few years earlier believing they would be the last fugitives, but that phase lasted longer than he expected. As Javier Rojo (2003) pointed out in a critique, this final paragraph is especially important:

> I reflected as I was on the subway from Brooklyn. Thirty years after Joseba's death, in the new century, there are still Basque fugitives, often new ones, and some of them could die abroad, as they do die. They can at least be given a gravestone with their names and surnames, the date and their birthplace, a real one made of stone that has a carved *lauburu* [a Basque symbol]. (Zabaleta 2003: 194)

Manhattan versus Harlem

Zabaleta describes the protagonist's odyssey. Joseba is a young Ulysses, fate robs him of his safe environment, and he has no other purpose than to return to his village. To do so, however, he must survive. Fernando Pessoa defined a life's unwanted journey as an experiment (2010: 169).

The setting for this story is the most metropolitan of all cities, New York. This is a space in which crime, threat, and murder are commonplace. From the beginning, the author cultivates images of this space on purpose: "He walked along 42nd Street wearily, a large raincoat draped over his body and an English-style cap on his head. He was somewhat hunched, hands in pockets and muffled up to his nose." The descriptions of the setting and character are prototypical of a noir novel and consequently the reader is completely immersed.

The noir novel can be set in the Basque Country, of course. Yet the stories that most people have seen or read take place in big cities. Moreover, if it were to be set in the Basque Country, mention of the police could be uncomfortable for readers. There is no intention to avoid political connotations, however, because the character is politically active and it fuels the fear he has of the police.

Authors chose to set most of the noir fiction in the 1980s outside the Basque Country: Xabier Kintana's *Ta Marbuta* (Tā marbūṭa: What Happened in Jerusalem) takes place in Israel and Mikel Antza's *Odolaren usaina* (The Smell of Blood) in different countries. Gotzon Garate's *New York, New York* and Harkaitz Cano's *Piano gainean gosaltzen* (Having Breakfast on the Piano) are set in the same location. In the latter, the writer from Lasarte includes a more positive portrayal of the city. There is no shortage of death in the book, but being in a different genre and more contemporary has an influence on the portrayal of the city. Zabaleta, Garate, and Cano put words to the feelings influenced by living there. In Garate's work, contemporary criminal actions are often understood in the terms of past offenders. Zabaleta's characters are constructed with greater Manichaeism.

A Map

The New York subway is important in the narrative. This is obvious because of the title taken from a station and because Grand Central Station makes an immediate appearance when one starts reading, on the first page.

The story takes place to the east of Central Park in a high numbered street. At that time, an invisible line between 92nd and 96th Streets distinguished different social classes. In this regard, Zabaleta's narrative is very realist.

110. street-eko geltokia (110th Street Station)

Zabaleta locates the hotel at 112th and Lexington Streets. It takes nine minutes for the protagonist to walk to the 110th Street subway station. He locates his residence in the Harlem neighborhood, in a dangerous area. In the opening pages, Zabaleta makes an effort to explain the danger by listing the necessary precautions and advice ("always keep one hand in your pocket"). Nor is the protagonist's home safe. "The room's two locks." He closes it securely once he gets inside and nor does he ever open the door to just anyone. Beyond the door, though, his room is a respite and his bed and coffee are a source of comfort.

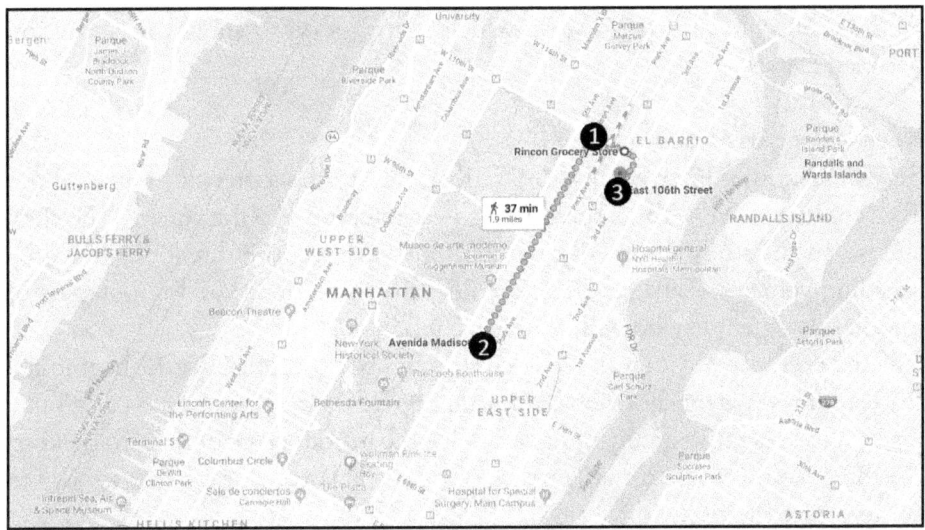

Image 1. The Protagonists' Home and Joseba's Café.

Angie lives on 106th Street in a much safer middle-class area. The café in which Catherine and Joseba work is situated in a safe area, too, close to Madison Avenue. These three settings are easily reached by a short journey on the green line.

The longest rides the protagonist takes are those out to Atlantic City in search of drugs. Joseba is ordered to pick them up in a casino and he takes them to Joe's store. He takes the bus out there. Zabaleta uses these trips for teleportation: Joseba receives word of what is happening in Ezkurra through his dreams and they tell him about his relatives (parents, sister, and two brothers). He also uses the journey to show what his life would have been like had he not gone to Iruñea (Pamplona) and escaped. Corbatta (1994) says that the dreams are used to give prophetic messages, yet in this case these dreams are more linked to wishes, that is, he dreams of a life he could have lived if things had gone another way.

The drugs are handed over in the South Bronx, in Joe's Grocery Store on Jackson Avenue. Zabaleta uses the reader's prior knowledge about the metropolis, in using areas like the Bronx or Harlem; but the zones (not specific areas) are real and the novel is completely geographically realist. The basis of the novel is the friction between classes and for that reason space is key. Perhaps that is why the subway was chosen too, because in fact, within the space of a few stops on an entire subway journey, there is a big change in class. It is reminiscent of Andrew Niccol's film *In Time*, in which space serves to show the separation between classes.

When Violence Is a Consequence

Several storylines intersect in the narrative. The story is a pretext to speak about class conflict in New York. There are endless references to the voices of Harlem sirens. Locals study resignedly, without any surprise, the directions taken by speeding vehicles. Zabaleta tries to reflect the indifference and remoteness of middle-class people who will experience upheaval.

The presence of violence is evident throughout the novel. At the beginning, the fear of theft is most obvious, a constant terror which threatens to carve out a place in the narrative at any moment. With the introduction of drug trafficking, the threat could come from the police. Yet Zabaleta does not use that tension to compromise the protagonist's task.

Throughout history, the siren of violence has been represented by light and sound and its direction emphasized. According to the recipient, they are received habitually in poor areas and by those of the upper class through newspapers. However, if speaking directly about violence, it is a story of the lower orders for this genre. The death of the protagonist himself is also quite clear and goes almost unnoticed; and here, too, losing one's life in solitude is almost more violent than by the stabbing itself.

Ultimately, one of the central themes of this novel is that of loneliness surrounded by people. Time and again, the description of people's inner feelings matches the weather.

On the other hand, there is a moral judgment that states that class differences are economic, but not so moral. In other words, there is good and bad in both; but lower-class people have no escape; they cannot avoid their fate. Catherine does not hesitate when it comes to using her privileged status: she blackmails Joseba, traps him because he has no papers. Further reading suggests that the origin of the violence is based on the well-being of the upper classes. To put it another way, the real violence is social injustice.

Nevertheless, in contrast, the first sentence in the novel states. "There is a saying in East Harlem: Anyone who lives in the ghetto really knows how to survive." It is a sentence published in the *New York Daily News* on October 21, 1983. This note can be taken as a warning of what is coming and Joseba, as he is from Ezkurra, does not know how to survive. He is too innocent. He has apparently adapted well to that violent environment, which seems to have concealed his goodness, but one small slip up is enough to die. That can happen to outsiders at any moment. The story of the protagonist in the Basque Country is not discussed in detail, but one can presume from the protagonist's psychology that his political activism did not go all the way, that he did not commit any blood crime (assassination), but rather that he got mixed up in political matters that were likewise all too much for him. However, at that time many young people were forced to flee from the police for trivial reasons.

On Homesickness

The climax of the story is the protagonist's death. As Joseba is getting stabbed, he mentions the word "mother," which confirms the meaning of the whole novel. In this regression, mother is his homeland, language, people, and protection.

The protagonist's homesickness pervades this work. He makes it clear where his place is. Above all, he mentions his yearning to speak Basque: at Joseba's moment of climax, he confirms his intention to go to the Basque Country because he was "longing to speak Basque" (136). What he does not write is important in Zabaleta's work and an example of this is the transition from homeland to living elsewhere. Moreover, this reveals the close relationship between Basque and much South American fiction:

> With respect to that generation (of the 1970s), in an interview with Eileen Dietz in 1976, Peri Rossi recalls: "I suspect that the sme thing happened to them (Galeano, Benedetti . . .) as to the country: their literature has been crushed by boots and obligatory silence. That's why I imagine that the best literature of my generation would be oral, transmitted from parents to children /. . . /. Maybe the best poems are written on prison walls or on drains" (Zabaleta 1884: 86-87).

Zabaleta's work is of immense sociological value because it portrays an image of the city at that time.

> The noir novel in the democratic period, that genre, demanding in its new context that it be removed from the most traditional realist praxis, but without abandoning it, was transformed into a liveable space for those that still considered it necessary to undertake critical social literature, often from a left-wing point of view, for which the most appropriate vehicle continued to be realism. In other words, the noir novel was transformed into a strategic cultural space to criticise the status quo (Balibrea 2002: 116).

Stereotypes of the Basque Country are strengthened: through Gregory, Zabaleta reinforces the idea that people from there are obedient, honest and sexually indifferent. He also reveals something about Basques, based on the worker he met in a Paris brothel.

Homesickness Abroad

Living abroad is a recurring theme in Basque literature, especially on the part of Joseba Sarrionandia. "The Basque language is our only free territory" said Sarrionandia, and Corbatta (1994: 169–170) also describes the mother tongue as a way to keep in touch with reality. The writer's language is their homeland and what they get out of writing creates complicity with a community capable of understanding that by means of history and humor. The protagonist arrives in a foreign city and that reality rubs off on his personality. It is a way of describing the city by appropriating reality and understanding that. Ultimately, the protagonist is engaged in a utopian search for a harmony that could only exist in his birthplace.

Jorgelina Corbatta terms that kind of exile transcultural integration:

> Facing up to the new, the creator assumes a double condition; that of the distanced witness and that of the protagonist; they seek to integrate, without losing what differentiates them whilst at the same time being nourished by what is different. That overcoming of borders imposed by the existence of races, national limits, ideologies, religions, languages, customs -if achieved- confers on the writer great universalisation. It facilitates, moreover, the establishment of a greater understanding which enriches both the exile and the community in which they are introduced (Corbatta 1994: 168).

110. street-eko geltokia (110th Street Station)

There are contemporaneous works by many writers that decided to leave their countries as a result of the dictatorships in Argentina and Uruguay. Many of those works have addressed homesickness and repression. Those that deserve a special mention are: *La nave de los locos* (1984; in English, *The Ship of Fools: A Novel*, 2000) by Cristina Peri Rossi and *Novela negra con argentinos* (1990; in English, *Black Novel (with Argentines)*, 1992) by Luisa Valenzuela.

In the abovementioned novel, one comes across these expressions describing New York: "full of detritus and vomit," "urinary city" (24), "an absolutely visceral city, the capital of filth" (19), and "ruthless city" (26). We can compare this to similar descriptions in Zabaleta's novel too. As such, it is a site of those displaced from their homeland, not a desired change of place. There is a pessimistic view of the present site that is at the same time a tribute to birthplace.

Basque literature resembles more developments in South America than that of English-language literature in Cillero's opinion:

> From the difficult postwar years to the flourishing end of the millennium, Basque detective and crime fiction has overcome many obstacles to find a place for itself within contemporary Basque narrative. The relatively late modernization of Basque literature was compounded by the constraints imposed on the genre by the sociopolitical composition of the traditional Basque Country—the lack of an autonomous police force, the lack of a literature that dealt with crime, and the lack of a strong judiciary system akin to the ones instituted in Western Europe in the nineteenth century. As a result of all this, Basque detective and crime fiction experienced an evolution similar to Latin American detective fiction, which was in turn impeded in its development by social and cultural problems. (Cillero 2000: 299)

Zabaleta's choice is worthy of mention. At a time when the Basque Country was experiencing violent periods, he goes to a big city and tells a story set there. The context of the late 1970s crisis, in which there was a high unemployment rate and drug trafficking was supported politically, would be great to give credibility to any novel. If it had to be a big city, Bilbao, the post-industrial city studied by Joseba Zulaika, would have been a logical choice, for example: "exposed to a tertiary service economy, but which in the process of reinventing itself it must deal with a growing army of unemployed, and with the social costs of this de-structuring: violence and youth declassing, civic insecurity, the massive influx of drugs" (Balibrea 2002: 115). Considering local violence could have been an option, yet at the same time it would have been very compromising for the writer; and readers would not have been able to enjoy the vulnerable distance that such a novel demands if it had happened there. A local setting would inevitably have involved choosing a side.

The Basque Country has been used as a setting for noir fiction. For example, in the novel *Demasiado para Galvez* (Too Much for Galvez) by Jorge Martinez Reverte (1948–), published in 1981. This novel tells the story of Sara Goicoechea, which involves a kidnapping by ETA:

> His inept charm serves better to point out the inconsistencies surrounding the struggles of Euskadi to be undestood and to undestand itself, than it served to point out the errors in the capitalistic sistem in *Demasiado para Galvez*. The villains of the first novel were wealthy capitalists who degenerated into stock bad guys by the end. By contrast, the author treats his etarras [members of the ETA terrorist organization] (all varieties of them) with more respect. He gives them background and motivation so that their ... (Hart 1987: 136)

Nevertheless, such works should be considered exceptions. Whilst Francoism persisted, the police novel was not fashionable. This was because Francoism delayed the economic development of Spain and because the fear of censorship also prevented writers from picking up their pens in a genre so involved in realism (Balibrea 2002:114). Clearly, the tendency to move away from especially painful and close issues prevails not only among Basque writers but in other nations too. The struggle for national freedom and Francoism were not addressed directly until the early 1980s (Balibrea 2002: 111):

> The strategic and ideological forgetting of these continuities in its day and until right now, justified by the need to bring the democratic project to fruition (...) was the hard core of what would later come to be called historical oversight, a characteristic which defined fully the transition period and the years of consolidating democracy during the successive governments of the Spanish Socialist Workers' Party (1982–1996).

One of Zabaleta's biggest achievements is describing Joseba's fear. He is consumed by a misery that afflicts him to his death, and homesickness, and yet he admits to a greater fear of returning home. Nor does Cillero (2005: 242) overlook this:

> Instead of using a direct approach to Spanish Basque politics of the time, Zabaleta skillfully proposes a metonymical approach to the conflict, making the Spanish police (political system) responsible for Joseba's exile and ultimately for his death.

In that regard, Zabaleta's work is one of the best depictions of the influence of torture in the Basque Country. This intention to leave a record of what is told and not told by official history through literature is in line with contemporaneous South American trends:

> For writers of the continent that came to configure their narratives as points at which one can surmise the real distance which exists between realities proposed by official history and the realities experienced by the subjects that constructe them (Salinas 2007: 7)

Zabalata has achieved what few other writers have: finding a widespread audience for a serious novel about the alienation of capitalism and fugitives. Ellipses, to some extent, were key to this broad appeal. Readers can fill in the gaps in facts that remain empty in the book and draw profound conclusions from the reading or use it as pure entertainment. It is, without doubt, a work of Basque literature in the 1980s which merits study.

References

Asurmendi, Mikel (2015): "Literaturak ez du balio eskluientea izan behar." *Argia*, Jun. 19.
Balibrea, Mari Paz (2002): "La novela negra en la transición española como fenómeno cultural: Una interpretación." *Iberoamericana* (2001–), 2 (7), 111–118.
Borges, Jorge Luis (1996): *Obras Completas*, vol. 4. Emecé: Buenos Aires.
Cillero, Javi (2005): *The Moving Target: A History of Basque Detective and Crime Fiction* (Doctoral dissertation). Director: Linda White. Unpublished.
Corbatta, Jorgelina (1994): "Metáforas del exilio e intertextualidad en *La nave de los locos* de Cristina Peri Rossi y *Novela negra con argentinos* de Luisa Valenzuela." *Revista Hispánica Moderna*, 47(1), 167-183. http://www.jstor.org/stable/30203382
Genet, Jean, and Dichy, Albert (1953): *Pompes funèbres*. Gallimard: Paris.
Hart, Patricia (1987): *The Spanish Sleuth: The Detective in Spanish Fiction*. Associated University Press. From the first chapter (Detective Fiction, Roman Noir, Novela Negra. What's in a Name?).
Herrera, Juan José G. (2008): "El canon de la novela negra y policíaca." *Tejuelo: Didáctica de la Lengua y la Literatura. Educación*, (1), 58–74.

Olaziregi, Mari Jose (2000): "The Basque Literary System at the Gateway to the New Millenium." *ASJU* XXXIV. 413–422.
Otaegi, Lourdes (2008): "110 Street-eko geltokia. Iñaki Zabaleta," in *Euskal Literaturaren Hiztegia*. EHU-Institute for Basque: Bilbao.
Pessoa, Fernando (2010): *El libro del desasosiego* (vol. 101). Ediciones Baile del sol: Tenerife.
Rojo, Javier (2003): "110. street-eko geltokia." *El Correo*, May 10. https://kritikak.armiarma.eus/?p=902
Salinas, A. (2007): "Novela negra y memoria en Latinoamérica." *Poligramas 27*, 1–13.
Zabaleta, Iñaki (1985): "Iñaki Zabaleta Urkiola. *110 Street-eko geltoki*a." *Argia*, Oct. 20, 4.
——— (1984): *110. Street-eko geltokia*. Susa: San Sebastian.
——— (2003): *110. Street-eko geltokia*. Elkar: San Sebastian.

Chapter 2

Aingeru Epaltza's Three Intrigue Novels: *Sasiak ere begiak baditik* (Even Brush Has Eyes, 1986), *Ur uherrak* (Muddy Waters, 1993), and *Rock'n'Roll* (2000)

Asier Barandiaran

Aingeru Epaltza (Iruñea, 1960–) has written a copious number of novels (Egaña 2008) and will soon (in 2024) celebrate his fortieth anniversary as a writer. Several of his works fall squarely within the field of the intrigue novel or the police novel, with his distinctive way of developing suspense and "noir" fiction. In this chapter we have selected three novels by the Iruñea (Pamplona) author with the aim of examining his police style. In this study, we want to pay special attention to the notion of place in the fiction chosen by the author, in order to be in some way more aware of how places help him to fulfil and reveal his narrative intentions.

Sasiak ere begiak baditik (Even Brush Has Eyes) (1986)

Aingeru Epaltza's novel is set during the time of the First Carlist War, taking place between 1830 and 1842. We know that in that war, the Carlists were strong in the Basque Country, that they had followers and some kind of organization and wanted to besiege certain cities, especially Bilbao and Iruñea. The novel begins on the road to Iruñea, because there were several battles between Carlists and Liberals in towns and areas around the city (although always on the way to the capital of Navarre).

Having said that, one might think that this is a historical novel. In fact, and this is our opening hypothesis, we would argue that this is an intrigue and "police" novel. Indeed, several historical events are taken into account, but all the characters are fictional and the story is full of intrigue and "searching." The term "searching" in this case brings us closer to the "police" type of concept.[1] Although there are no police officers, there are many searches and clarifications of puzzles in this novel. Besides these, the action, which intensifies through the core of the book, is swift. That is why we can situate it within the tough or hardboiled[2] subgenre.

Basque literature has not often set its stories in the Carlist Wars. Aingeru Epaltza's work is, then, according to our data, the first to do so. Several more would come later, including Bernardo Atxaga's *Sara izeneko gizona* (A Man Called Sara) (1996), set in the First Carlist War, which in certain ways "borrows" elements from Epaltza's novel: suspense, intrigue, adventure, the cruelty of war, a touch of picaresque. Amongst Navarrese who write in Spanish, Pablo Antoñana (Viana, 1927–Iruñea, 2009), for example, dealt with the subject of "Carlist" stories in his narrative fiction, in the novels like *No estamos solos* (We're Not Alone) (1962) and *Relato cruento* (Bloody Story) (1977) (Martín Nogales 1989:190). Of course, among Carlist writers, in Spanish, there have been those that maintain a "romantic" approach (López Antón 2000:15–20) when discussing the Carlist Wars. Aingeru Epaltza, one should underscore from the start, does not reflect any romanticism at that time: on the contrary, there is cruelty, cynicism, and treachery in the novel (rather than any nostalgia for the era), sprinkled with a touch of mischievousness. Yet that is the narrative environment in which the writer from Iruñea functions more comfortably, as can be seen in his later novels.

The story is set mainly in Navarre, and although most of the action takes place in Iruñea, other rural areas are also used as locations. Aingeru Epaltza's decision was significant and, at the time, bold: he transports us to the First Carlist War (1833–1840) and therein, in Basque, develops a story which has something of intrigue and police novels, all in the author's first novel. The attempt was not exactly a failure; in fact, because he had been awarded a grant for new authors by the Iruñea City Council in 1985 to develop the story, a year later, in 1986, the Elkar publishing house released it. Moreover, in this novel, as Ibon Egaña states, one will see three characteristics of Aingeru Epaltza's literature:

On the one hand, recreating well-known histories and narrating the collective history of a specific era by means of principal characters; on the other, taking the margins, sidelines or periphery to the center, and reformulating Basqueness from the somewhat peripheral perspective of Navarreseness; third, showing that Navarreseness by using standardized Basque which tends towards the Navarrese dialect. (Egaña 2008a)

The protagonist and fictional intradiegetic narrator is Pedro Mari Arrieta. Indeed, as a resource that he has repeated at other times, Epaltza focuses on the strategy of "lost manuscripts" at the beginning of the story. In other words, Epaltza, under the pseudonym "Etxebertz," states that at the beginning of the story ("Some instructions for the reader"), he found the manuscripts of a man named Pedro Mari Arrieta and that what will be read thereafter is his narrative, his children the narrators, because they want to relate his life and ups and downs.

Suspense, Mysteries, and Picaresque

In these initial "instructions," however, the first mystery of the story appears: who is this Baztan writer that tells the story of the first Carlist War in Basque? Because of the manuscript resource,[3] "Etxebertz" apologizes, saying that he has not managed to find out any information about the text; and that it would have been a solitary "island" in the history of Basque literature, something that did not apparently have anything to do with the pro-Basque (Euskaro) movement which was founded in the late nineteenth century. We will proceed through the novel, in dosages, becoming an expert in Arrieta's vicissitudes.

Alongside this mystery, the reader's curiosity will be maintained by what Pedro Mari Arrieta has to say and why he left his descendants some manuscripts. Thus, in what follows we will delve into this in order to aquaint ourselves with Pedro Mari Arrieta's adventures and misfortunes.

When the Baztan native Pedro Mari Arrieta, a farmer and *mugalari* (expert in crossing the border clandestinely) working as a smuggler, joins the Carlist side to take part in the First Carlist War, it has a touch of adventure. Having left Baztan, they set out to "take" liberal Iruñea, but as soon as they arrive, through a series of mix-ups, they will first be mistaken for well-known Liberals by the Carlists and, then, by the Liberals themselves.

Suspense

Aingeru Epaltza knows how to ration out samples of suspense very effectively. In this, his very first novel, he puts what we may term the technique of "suspense dosage" into practice. Once he manages to escape from the Liberals, the character Arrieta (dressed in another person's clothes) manages to find another Carlist troop location. When he is getting near there on his donkey Panpoxa, a Carlist shouts "halt" at him unexpectedly. In the quote, we will observe that it gives the reader time to explain the suspense or mystery:

> And I was going along when suddenly I heard "stop!" behind me. I'm not lying, right there and then I was on the verge of falling to the ground from the violent blow in my heart. I raised my quivering hands and thought "they've caught me at last!.." Imagine my surprise, then, when he ordered me calmly to turn round, instead of seeing the blue uniform of the liberals I was looking at our beloved white beret. What joy!
>
> —Amongst my own again!—I think I cried out, lowering my arms and going up to the serious-looking soldier aiming at me with the intention of embracing him.
>
> —Stop right there if you don't want any holes in your head! —and the fusilier threatened him. (Epaltza 1986: 31)

The protagonist Pedro Mari Arrieta risks his life on several occasions and, in those situations, the game of suspense consists of narrating how he will avoid death. For example, in chapter 3, "On the Gallows," following an escape, a Carlist troop comes across him and decide to hang him as a Liberal spy. The moments up to the hanging are described in detail, with the protagonist himself as narrator: that gives him an opportunity to explain his feelings of fear and his thoughts in general, and this leads to prolonging that moment, delaying the mystery and information on how to get out of it.

The "muddle" from which he must free himself is the following: what will happen from now on in relation to those (Liberals) that believe him to be Lieutenant Torres and whether they will "find out" or not. This leads the main character to a bewildering situation, living in Iruñea as a lieutenant: at first, happily, but gradually becoming more serious, for fear of being "discovered":

> It was great, yes, definitely, being Lieutenant Torres!

> Imagine. As soon as I arrived in the city of Iruñea they put me up in a charming loft with a single bed, including a fireplace too. As if that were not enough, for the first time since I went to off to war, they began serving me plentiful breakfasts, lunches and dinners. In my head I was still wondering if I was dreaming and that's when they brought me a tailor to measure me for uniforms "appropriate" to my level. (Epaltza 1986: 41)

Furthermore, until those puzzles and mix-ups are cleared up, the main character will experience several dark and ethically "obscure" situations and that leads us to the conclusion that this novel has something of a "noir novel" to it. The noir novel can be considered part of the police genre. This is where the epithet "black" or noir comes from:

> The epithet "noir" is due on the one hand to the dark atmospheres they reflected, but especially to those stories which were published first in the journal *Black Mask* [...] (BNE 2019)

During his walks in Iruñea, the protagonist Arrieta enters an inn called the Golden Clog, in which there is a Basque leader who they call *Ahetza*.[4] *Ahetza* (Luis Juanena) realizes that the supposed Lieutenant Torres is a Basque speaker, and informs him, flatteringly, that he may have the "service" of a prostitute there. That prostitute, though, is from the same village in which he spent his childhood. She is Graziana, known by the nickname Maria Eugenia in her "profession." Therefore, Arrieta moves in dark circles during this urban sojourn, in Iruñea. Simultaneously, however, there is a break with the romantic perspective of Basqueness during the Carlist era: although *Ahetza* is Basque, his only principle is business and making as much money as possible (living in what was at one time the capital of the Kingdom of Navarre). Likewise, Graziana, who left her farm to go to the city, is a woman whose only goal is to make money in a murky way. Arrieta, on the contrary, because he entered into that environment inadvertently, will be able to get out of the mixed-up situation one way or another. Yet how he gets out of that is what brings part of the intrigue[5] to the story.

As the novel progresses, so the tension increases, when the character of Alfontso appears. Alfontso is aware that Pedro Mari Arrieta is looking for a bag of gold coins and because he believes that he has already found it, at a moment he is trying to escape from Iruñea, he confronts Pedro Mari Arrieta, threatening him with a pistol. Then the pace, tension and intrigue of the story increase in an exponential way until the end of the novel.

Picaresque

Besides intrigue, as this section's epigraph states, we observe several picaresque dimensions in this novel, even though it does not exactly comply with the goals of picaresque novels. Above all, the character of Pedro Mari Arrieta appears quite picaresque on more than one occasion. In fact, this man from Baztan displays several "traditional" picaresque features:

> He is an inexperienced big hearted young man, to whom the surrounding reality shakes him in a bad way and makes him become lost in scepticism and tricks. Systematically, life lays down traps for him from which he barely knows how to free himself, and he ends up giving himself in without any remedy or regret to the means which forces him to defend himself and cheat. Yet he is not a professional delinquent, but has plenty of sense and liveliness and lacks ambition. (Zamora 2002)

In that vein, in a clash with Liberals, he is the only one to come out alive (luckily) from a small troop of Carlists and he flees the pursuing Liberals by managing to climb down from a rocky mountain precipice and get to the bottom of the mountain. Down there, he will come across a "mysterious" jenny donkey, loaded with a pile of clothes (Liberal clothes, it appears) and a striking quantity of money in some baskets (as he will find out later).

As noted above, the Liberals will take the protagonist Pedro Mari Arrieta for Lieutenant Torres and because of that, he will have lodging in Iruñea (until he heals from his wounds), with a lieutenant's prebend. Initially, the protagonist accepts this in an almost humorous way, misunderstanding the benefits involved, without thinking any further, cheering with a touch of euphoria (without being very aware of the danger of the situation):

> "You're surrounded by these 'blacks'" I thought, but I didn't run out of a long list of surprises. Didn't they just give me a servant and order him to obey my every command quickly as quickly as an expert? (Epaltza 1986: 41)

As he is playing the "role" of Lieutenant Torres, Pedro Mari Arrieta has an unexpected "helper" who does not speak Spanish and who will reveal to Torres the "news" of his Basque side. A psychologist or an apparent doctor will examine Torres's "amnesia" in Spanish, and the protagonist explains the consequences without any sense of humor or irony:

> when I was taken prisoner, I suffered mistreatment and, especially, being on the point of dying on the gallows, I laughed inside, because the consequence was losing my language and embracing that of my captors. What a puzzling thing to say! It would have been better if he had said I was crazy.
>
> However, he also knew how to calm the hearts of those gentlemen, for my illness, me not speaking Spanish at length, is said to be short lived. "The treatment I prescribed him"—added that wise thicket—is already achieving positive results." Absolutely! That was it, yes. How on earth did I not learn more Spanish in that twenty-day spell when everyone around me knew nothing else? (Epaltza 1986: 44).

When he was in Iruñea, the mix-ups he freed himself from and positive surprises did not end there. The liberals would also give him a medal and a great deal of money too, and the protagonist speaks about all this with imprudent euphoria:

> Therefore, lips scented, while the whole Iruñea garrison was standing firm, the general—Damn! Why does his name not come to me?—pinned a shiny medal on my chest when there was a noticeable "improvement" in my state. "For the merits and work undertaken in defence of our Queen Isabel." Gosh!
>
> Still, the bag full of coins I was given for the same reason was more agreeable: two hundred silver coins! Father would not, to be sure, have made more than what the queen gave me in five years of working his fields. Then, to mention everything, think of the consequences of loosening your trousers. It's like the world turned on its head! (Epaltza 1986: 44)

The picaresque has of course been created historically (and literarily) in poor social circumstances, and therein several characters try, by means of ruses and tricks, to climb the social ladder or improve their living situation. In this story, as in many picaresque stories, as well as the protagonist, there are two "poor" Basques who have gone to Iruñea from a small village to improve their lives: Luis Juanena, "*ahetza*," the owner of the Golden Clog inn and Graziana, the prostitute who works there.[6] Both help to give the story a picaresque touch. They have a bitter, argumentative relationship with the protagonist because each one's (material) interests do not often coincide, although they do not reject taking advantage of Arrieta's improved economic situation.

The case of Graziana is significant and in creating this character, as well as showing that he is knowledgeable about literary history, Aingeru Epaltza has added a lively option, blending an intrigue novel with a picaresque one. That way, he joins the dynamism of the literary system and, thanks to that contribution, he takes a step toward the center of the literary system.

Graziana is a woman who is out of place, a Basque speaker, the daughter of a well-known family (the hope of the house), from the same village as the protagonist, in her youth desired by the young men of the village (including the protagonist himself), church going, and from a family that appreciates reputation:

> For the time being, the categorisation of the rogue as a public woman in picaresque texts serves to accompany indirectly the treatises, reports and sermons in their construction as a woman out of place. (Zafra 2009: 4)

She is out of place and it is a huge surprise for the protagonist, leaving him disturbed and shaken because he did not expect to come across Graziana in that "profession." There is a misogynous position as regards this female character, because she is the only woman and a prostitute. Of course, all of that is a mirror of the mentality of the time. In fact, being a prostitute is linked somehow to the picaresque nature and that transforms the character into an outsider, leaving her in a position of being criticized socially:

> In particular, it is the female picaresque's separation of the *pícara* from 'decent' society that underscores its male-authored critique of women's sexual freedom. (Cruz 1999: 144)

The range of picaresque characters is not just made up of the abovementioned three figures. In one moment during the story, the "real" Lieutenant Torres himself will show up before the protagonist, demanding the two thousand "lost" gold coins along with the jenny donkey. The Liberal Lieutenant Torres confesses to him that he only embraced the Liberals' ideology for pecuniary reasons, and in truth, instead of Torres, he was Fermin Goñi (he also carried out an exchange of identity) and was born in the village of Asterain.[7]

> —Yes, Arrieta my friend, you're still very young and you don't understand things like this. I, on the other hand, spent fifteen fruitless years going from one place to another in search of work

because of the revolution. I know, "progress," the constitution and similar silly slogans... [...]

This is what I said to myself: "Well, Fermin, you'll show up in Iruñea like a hero, fully playing this dirty role when you arrive, but also with all the coins from your Carlist countrymen well sown into your pockets." I wanted no more than to fulfil all of this. (Epaltza 1986: 71–72)

Places in Sasiak

It seems that a nineteenth-century intrigue story calls for a capital city and for Aingeru Epaltza, Iruñea is, whether he wants it or not, his point of reference and focal point. In fact, in Basque nationalist discourse, Iruñea has always been a special place and a constant reference for Basque speakers in Navarre. In the late nineteenth century, the city of Iruñea would hold some fascination as a territorial model for Navarrese Basque speakers and hence the protagonist narrator's reflections about Iruñea: "In his sermons, Don Kaxildo told us that everything he saw was like Jerusalem or Babylon" (Epaltza 1986: 46). It is also often equated with Babylon, from a traditionalist point of view, because Iruñea was attracting the menaces of "novelty" (liberalism and so on):

Before us, many people from the Olloibar Valley were arriving and a few locals, too far off to be able to see the walls of Iruñea, owned by non-belivers and "blacks." (Epaltza 1986: 17)

Indeed, most of the Navarrese soldiers on the Carlist side were from rural and farming backgrounds. Those from Baztan, additionally, were involved in smuggling. But enlisting in the Carlist ranks was more rewarding than this lifetsyle:

Before joining the army of our king Carlos, at that time when we were involved every day in guiding the cows from the sheds to the fields and the fields to the sheds, and the odd night now and again in smuggling, all I knew was what my oldest brother Bernardo told us when he showed up at home now and again: "Zumalakarregi! That's our general, and he's from Gipuzkoa too! He's really stuck it to the Liberals now!, "We're going to take Bilbao. It is said that Zumalakarregi remarked that Bilbao will fall like an apple tree and be in our hands." (Epaltza 1986: 16)

Babylonia was mentioned above and the tendency to equate Iruñea with biblical toponyms would surface again some years later in the texts of the writer from Iruñea. Aingeru Epaltza himself would once more turn to the "leitmotif" of Jerusalem in his novel *Gure Jerusalem galdua* (Our Lost Jerusalem) (Barandiaran Amarika 2015), the third and last in a trilogy about the Conquest of Navarre. A few years previously in that trilogy he uses that image of Iruñea in the mouths of those loyal to the Kingdom of Navarre. Indeed, it could also be said that there is intrigue and adventure in this trilogy, even though the protagonists of the adventure are some troublesome antiheroes, following the tendency that began in the novel *Sasiak ere begiak baditik* (Even Brush Has Eyes).

Ur uherrak (1993)

Since Aingeru Epaltza published this novel in 1993, he has moved in murky waters; indeed, in this small "closed" village in a Basque-speaking area of Navarre the relationships between characters would become increasingly "darker" with the first bloody consequence of what would later be the Basque "conflict."[8] For example, he says this about some of those involved in the "Basque conflict" in that village:

> Most of those in the Old Convent were from the City or even beyond, and it is said that those lodged there wanted to learn to speak the same way as in the Village. As heard in Joxefelixenea, however, they were dangerous because they were making bombs and killing people. (Epaltza 1993: 19)

In part, the "conflict" arrives in that Basque-speaking village from the city (in the case of Navarre, although the novel does not say so, the main city is Iruñea). It does not emerge naturally in the village. Talk of the conflict takes place in the dark atmosphere of those young pro-Basque bar clients. Right there, in those "bar" environments, some old people in the village mistrust the decisions the new village corporation wants to make; in other words, about the new secretary and doctor, always underscoring the fact that this new policy comes from outside this Basque-speaking village in Navarre:

> they'll bring in someone from Gipuzkoa, for sure, a terrorist from Gipuzkoa, who'll make a lot of bombs in the Village ... BOMBS!! (Epaltza 1993: 22)

Yet that "black" or "dark" situation begins with several characters. One of them, one of the protagonists, is a young black woman called Billie, the daughter of a man who left the village to go to the United States—Juanito's daughter—who ended up an orphan after her mother's death and for that reason came to the Basque Country, to her father's village. Another character is Jazinto, a *bertsolari* (popular improviser of verses in Basque) of the old school who is disillusioned with many things.[9] However, Billie also occasionally performs *bertsos* in the rock group she leads, offering a performance with an "exotic" (postmodern) touch. They are two "losers," in that village, who feel marginalized or lonely living among the other villagers:

> The theme of this book is loneliness. The writer introduces characters who, although they live together, do not understand one another. Each their own, intrinsic and particular life; a volcano has erupted inside each of them at some point in their lives, or an earthquake occurred that left a lasting mark on them. Each of them has tasted defeat in their bones, which has led them to look inwards, distancing them from the rest. Because a lack of communication stems not from not talking to each other, but from not being able to understand one another. (Juaristi 1993)

In this closed village, there are other kinds of losers: violent aggressors. A character named Xantux, a local councillor (for the "opposition" to the dominant left-wing Basque nationalist party, which in Basque-speaking Navarrese towns often means being in the UPN party), will suddenly without any prior warning show up dead in the story, shot in the head by some unknown person. His wife Maria Eujenia shows up in front of the councillor Martin Jabier wanting to embrace her husband (Xantux) and crying out loud.

> —Xantux, "Marisonekoa"... a councillor... He was apparently shot in the head. (Epaltza 1993: 85)

The narrator will not tell us at all why the assassination was carried out. The thread of suspense starts like that: readers, especially Basque readers, may suspect that it was a politically motivated violent act, but the narrator prefers to approach that "ugly" incident by means of different characters, slowly, giving information in doses, asking the reader's curiosity to wait.

One of the main plots in the story, as noted above, is the assassination of the councillor Xantux. One of the people who will investigate this is Lieutenant Medina, a civil guard who was posted to this Basque-speaking village against his wishes, and who will try and fight the political violence spreading to the area with another form of violence. Yet Lieutenant Medina is also a dark character, someone with "dirty" ethics. In fact, the novel attempts to show this dirty reality time and time again.[10] In the case of this character, above all, he is portrayed beating up suspects unethically:

> The cold water of the sink brought a little peace to Medina's hands. They were completely battered, especially his knuckles, in the living flesh. He hadn't handed out a beating like that in a long time. First to those of the Old Convent, in a harsh post-lunch period, and then those detained in the bars, from the afternoon right up to midnight, thwack-thwack relentlessly except for the matter of dinner. (Epaltza 1993: 118)

Lieutenant Medina's job is routine, cynical, without any heroism, although now and again he will reveal some arrogance. His goals are not very ethical, but nor is he very capable of achieving these aims. He will appear again at the end of the novel, seeking to carry out a bad act, maintaining the suspense.

Halfway through the novel more or less, as Xantux's killer is Juanito "Kulunka," Billie's father, he goes to prison. Yet either by leaving or escaping, he will return to the village secretly with the intention of carrying out another bad act. Making use of the "experience" he has from the Vietnam War, and still with the opportunity to use some weapons from here and there, the suspense will be activated at the end of the novel again, through the carrying out of several bloody events. The reader, perhaps lulled into a false sense of security by that dirty realism, will, in this way, be woken up at the end of the reading.

Places in Ur uherrak

This novel presents the atmosphere of a Basque-speaking village in Navarre. Not a very big village, perhaps intensifying the asphyxiating aspect: "*herri txiki, infernu handi*" (small village, great hell). These Basque-speaking villages in Navarre (always as places) already dispense wordless information, from their history and customs, and from what the architects of the villages transmit, from the meanings of the names and natures of each of the houses in the villages. Although the village in *Ur uherrak* was completely Basque-speaking during the Spanish Civil War, many locals were in favor of the Requetés and in the atmosphere of the novel there are still some people who look with distrust at the "new" political environment of the town, which is completely different from the history of their lives:

—Look, it hasn't escaped you that a Requeté can never change. Too much, then, for you. You likely have a covered pile of red berets from thirty-six in some corner of your home

The *bertsolari* pulled a face.

—What a thing to say! You of all people . . .! You don't think you sang "Oriamendi" less often than I did. Weren't you, then, going to take Iruñea with me that July? (Epaltza 1993: 47)

The titles of each chapter in the novel indicate narrative places, but most often refer to this rural area:

I. Ugaldeko bluesa (The Ugalde Blues)

II. Kartzelako bluesa (The Prison Blues)

III. Ziudadeko bluesa (The City Blues)

IV. Mendi gaineko bluesa (The Mountain Top Blues)

V. Akabaileko bluesa (The Concluding Blues).

It is clear that setting the main location for the story in a rural village in Navarre brings with it another consequence: being strange and misunderstood by city dwellers. The focus of the narrative also switches endlessly from one character to another, with secondary level stories appearing time and time again, even though it seems that they coincide with the "main" one at the end of the story. Thus, secondary level "places" appear, and in the case of Navarre, this takes place in the Navarrese Basque-speaking zone,[11] the author also wanting to rescue those secondary level places from their dirtiness. This, moreover, muddies or darkens the logic of the story because the thinking of people from small villages shares some knowledge that the city folk do not know. This is how the journalist Xabier (a Basque speaker from Iruñea), the omniscient narrator, depicts someone's thoughts as he went to that small village:

> I got in the car, started it up and set off for the Village, glancing at the open landscape. The same as ever: mist, ruined farmhouses and livestock, nothing else. I don't even need to change gear in that shitty area. Whoever crosses the pass that leads there feels as strange as a lone explorer entering a dangerous jungle, only missing a pith helmet. Everything here, things, animals, human beings,

feels like it's eight thousand kilometres away, unreachable, incomprehensible. (Epaltza 1993: 95)

Those that live in the village are also aware that the "City folk," that is, the people from Iruñea, could care less (to use the cleanest expression) ... about them:

—One must think ... You'll see... They'll also have something to tell us from up there,

—From up there? The city folk? That lot couldn't care less about us or last year's winds! (Epaltza 1993: 111)

They have very Basque-speaking customs in the village, even though among the Basque speakers it is said (at the end of the twentieth century) that the discourse of left-wing Basque nationalism has "problems" in "attracting" the local older people. Among those Basque customs it is stated time and time again which house each person is from (Ikatzeta, Petrineko, Etxandi, Aurkasia, Errero, Bordazar, Dorreto ...). Another one is giving people nicknames (Paxtor, Xantox, Kulunka, Beltxista, Miru Zaharra, Arraska ...).

Everything to this point corresponds to every chapter in the novel, except one. Chapter 3 is titled "The City Blues" due to the fact that part of the story is set in the "City" (in Iruñea, clearly, although the name of that place never appears at all), because once Billie's group become successful they are there and the old *bertsolari* Jazinto has gone there to live, because in the music group's concerts he gives his "ethnic touch." The bars, precarious flats of the group members, the Old Quarter of the city, the dark recording studios ... are always "outsider" places.

Rock'n'Roll (2000)

In the novel *Rock'n'Roll*, the protagonist Eduardo is also submerged in a dark moment in his life. At the beginning of the novel we meet a man who is separated from his wife, depressive, and who has turned to alcohol, for whom life is ironic, and who is disillusioned. Eduardo himself, the narrator, does not deny his alcoholism:

I will not deny this if it's obvious. I owe it to myself to drink a lot on account of the many bad things that have happened to me in my life: totalling this car, scaring that girl away, making her boss fall out with her, making my relationship with Kristina worse ...

beginning in more detail, my case could be used as a model for the Health Departments involved in campaigns aimed at protecting the population from the dangers of alcohol. I would truly be convinced to say on the TV screen, completely shamefully, making mistakes in my terrible English, in other words, that drinking is the gun I have to flee from the sudden kicks that life gives me, and all the normal things that come with such problems. I'm human, at the end of the day. (Epaltza 2000: 114)

This reputation gives him the appearance of an antihero or loser, peppered with cynicism, of course. Moreover, since he separated, he has lived with his brother Josu and the "success" Josu has with young women contrasts with his own failures in love and that also increasingly diminishes his self-esteem. The protagonist's friends, Charly, Ttipi, and Ximurra like both alcohol and drugs: lines of cocaine, joints, and so on:

Charly was next to me, mixing chopped up dried leaves with red tobacco on the palm of his left hand. His second bottle of vodka in my hands was warming me up; the first, lying among my things, was empty. Ttipi showed me again how one had to take a drink, directly now, without spilling any on your shirt. (Epaltza 2000: 22)

But mysteries which have something to do with a crime typical of a police novel must emerge. In this case, a dead body shows up in a river (the Arga River in all likelihood) next to the city.[12] When the first "corpse" appears, then (an old woman drowned or found in the river), another young person will appear for the first time in the story: Manuel Sarasa Gonzalez, nicknamed "Spikey hair," "Hedgehog," or "Roly-poly Manolo." The protagonist will be surprised to find out (because he has not seen him since they were young) that he has become a police officer (an inspector, to be precise), and he has gone there to begin an investigation into the death:

—Wow, Tomas! If that's not Roly-poly from my youth: a fucking policeman, Tomas, a fucking police chief! (Epaltza 2000: 46)

Things like this can happen in a capital city like Iruñea, because that is what the sociology of the place is like. It is the sociology of a generation that were adolescents in the 1970s, specifically, and Aingeru Epaltza is capable of showing "social surprises" like that, even though he does frame all that in irony. What is more, this character's cynical "role" aids the noir police dimension of the story, because he is a truly disillusioned[13] (and disappointed) character, to a postmodern extent.

The protagonist is a journalist, but he is not passionate about his job, and even less so when the story takes place, in mid-summer, at a time when the news in cities like Iruñea is very boring:

> Three minutes later I would be outside and they, on the other hand, would continue to reward the sunny August Friday devil, heaven knows up to how much, in the exciting news that usually occurs in the summer: the number of visitors to the municipal swimming pool, the world hoe throwing championship in I-don't-know-where, or a really interesting poll on the most popular ice cream flavour. (Epaltza 2000: 48)

One should underscore the fact that, in the last two novels by Aingeru Epaltza under study here (*Ur uherrak* and *Rock'n'Roll*), the two journalist characters have a dark nature and both fulfill, at one time or another, the "detective" role or task, seeking to clarify a mystery[14] (a murder, for example) or undertaking a search.

He is seeking to clarify a mystery, yet he starts from an unstable and not very enthusiastic personal situation, separated from his wife, when his passion for the young women around him is aroused, thoughts emerge that he clearly recognizes, on the way to becoming an arrogant sexual predator (although he does not have the energy to fulfil his "lascivious fantasies").[15]

One of the other elements that makes the story darker is the possibility of black magic or Satanism being a factor at some point (in the story); indeed, when the body of the seventy-six-year-old dead woman, Milagros Celestina Soria Aramendia, was retrieved from the river, one of her fingers was missing, and this could have indicated that the death may have been linked to the occult.

Yet the old woman Milagros Celestina will not be the only person to die. The abovementioned friend Ttipi[16] will also show up dead and that will be an unresolved mystery in the story. The protagonist (Eduardo) will also have to cover the story for his newspaper. In his search for information about the murder, however, Roly-poly (Manolo Sarasa) will have to turn to the friends from his youth, because he is an inspector in the city (Iruñea) police station.

The story will slowly unravel (too slowly, perhaps, with digressions that lead to a delay in the narrative, reflecting the lethargic summer atmosphere of the city) toward the core of the mystery. Key to that will be the protagonist's decision at a specific moment to follow his wife and her lover, Ximurra, when they go out one night. They have gone to a "suspicious" grill restaurant outside the city to have dinner and later they head out to an industrial estate owned by Ximurra's company. Over several pages, the narrative is filled with ellipses and a focus on intrigues and there, precisely, the narrative fully takes on the appearance of a police novel. In order to intensify the intrigue, Aingeru Epaltza knows very well how to add some cliff-hangers in the fictitious narrator Eduardo's narrative, at the end of chapters.

Places in Rock'n'Roll

Despite not being named, Aingeru Epaltza has once again chosen Iruñea—the city—as the setting, and in doing so he has chosen a classic trend that corresponds to noir fiction.[17] Yet this is "contemporary" Iruñea, Iruñea during a sweltering summer, decadent, boring, half asleep. Iruñea is typically bustling throughout the San Fermin festivities, becoming the Basque festival capital and the wild activity which starts on July 6 is very famous among old-world European festivities. Some of Ernest Hemingway's novels managed to reveal this special Iruñea.[18] But later, Iruñea is plunged into a state of "depression," once again becoming (in spite of being the capital of a former Kingdom) the boring capital of an ordinary province. How does Aingeru Epaltza try to reflect this atmosphere in his novel? Above all, with everything the journalist Eduardo has to look for interesting (and out-of-the-ordinary) news in the summer.

As Maider Aristi states, there is a resemblance in this approach to other well-known novels:

> The city of Epaltza's novel exudes the same literary character as the secondary villages or out-of-season landscapes in Ignacio Martínez de Pisón's novel *Carreteras secundarias* [Secondary Roads]. And the journey of a journalist trying to unravel the noir tale of the novel reminds us of Antonio Tabucchi's novels *Sostiene Pereira* [In English, *Pereira Maintains*] and *La testa perduta di Damasceno Monteiro* [In English, *The Missing Head of Damasceno Monteiro*]. We can situate this work in the same vein as the aforemtioned three excellent novels [...] (Aristi 2001).

Nevertheless, the urban dimension of the story does not overlook the fact that Navarre has another side, in other words, its rural part. He points out that rural areas are inevitable places of escape for urban journalists like himself, and especially at this time when he is separated from his wife, he is compelled to do so. Indeed, he goes there with his son Unai to visit grandma on some weekends (those weekends when it is his turn to be with his son). The inclusion of this place seems only to indicate his lack of attachment to the rural area and his urban nature:

> Inevitably, because he was unforgiving, I spent the first eighteen years of my life in his birthplace. [...] I saw only wild young mountain men amongst the young lads of the village; [...] As for the girls there, it's been so long since I escaped—embarrassment? Good sense?—that I can't remember, but in that regard they weren't too different from those I knew in my usual surroundings. As for the rest, little else: a horrible smell of shit in the streets, the endless attacks of flies at night, and the irritability and discomfort that our mother's family cultivated from generation to generation in the household. (Epaltza 2000: 58)

It is strange that this feeling toward the Basque rural area is the same as that of the journalist Xabier in the novel *Ur uherrak*, as noted above. He has an "image" because the character has come back and in that return we do not find any attachment to the Basque-speaking areas that one supposedly attributes to a Basque cultural "activist," thereby breaking a kind of cohesive icon (and transforming the character into even more of an outsider).

In addition, as well as his workplace (both the office and the streets, both being the "workplaces" of journalists), the Lisbon Bar stands out in the city of Iruñea as a setting for events and dialogue. It is the dark witness of the ethylic existence of the protagonist and his friends, possessing a symbolic name to some extent (an echo of the melancholic capital of Portugal) and the confessional of the misery he experiences with his friends or the ironic court of his friends' "complaints":

> —Well, Eduardo, don't insult me, for I remember it well. At the start of each summer, fresh tender meat, newly brought from the faculty flocks, under the care of the dirty wolf Edu (Epaltza 2000: 110)

Iruñea, when it comes to places, is (at least) one dichotomy: the dichotomy between the Old Quarter and the Expansion District. The Old Quarter, besides being the supposed "original" site, is also home to a certain kind of youth (now the home of Josu, the protagonist's brother): thus, those people seeking more humble accommodation, who do not have a very "prosperous" profession or occupation (often artists and bohemians), live there. The Expansion District, however, is an urban zone mostly constructed during the Franco period, for people with financially comfortable professions, who were once in favor of the regime and "order." The protagonist went to school there, a monks' school, as he lived in that neighborhood. The rebellious era of their adolescence also started there. Eduardo the protagonist says the following about his friend Xamur's aunt's house from that time:

> Thanks to the good hospitality of the old woman, between the ages of 17 and 20, we turned Aunt Milagros' house into a real operating center. It wasn't just any old place: 200 metres squared, right in the middle of the Expansion District. There, between walls plastered with ugly flowery wallpaper, we began our Saturday nights out. Sometimes we didn't even go out, until the time came for someone to go home. (Epaltza 2000: 132)

Of course, just as the story takes place, the Expansion District is in decline; the residences, although still large, have gone out of fashion, because of the smell of mothballs, their appearance and the "outdated" connotation of the people who live there. Furthermore, the protagonist is aware that the Expansion District residents are bourgeois, even if during the transition period he took part now and again in political clashes.

Conclusions

In these three works by Aingeru Epaltza, it is difficult to distinguish which are noir and which are police novels. That said, when we say "police" novels, it is clear that whoever plays the "detective" role is hardly ever a police officer (even though some police officers do make an appearance, above all in the novels *Ur uherrak* and *Rock'n'Roll*, in the case of Lieutenant Medina and Commissioner Roly-poly, respectively).

Above all, in the novel we enter the "noir" realm via dirty realism, and especially through the main characters, those who seek the "truth" because they are "disillusioned" and, so to speak, postmodern. There seems to be an idea behind the story: truth comes after disappointment, because ideologies prevent us from seeing the cruelty of reality.

The "truth" of reality is best reflected in the narrative of the intradiegetic protagonist who is on the decline. This is what Aingeru Epaltza has done with two of the three novels: with *Sasiak* and *Rock'n'Roll*. It seems that he achieves this decadence with a picaresque point of view, as long as criminal or illegal events appear in a cynical kind of way.

The aforementioned narrator's picaresque (and counter-heroic) atmosphere is no obstacle to complex moments of intrigue at the end of the novels. In all three, there are narrative spaces in which he increases the doses of information which clear up some of the mysteries about the criminal events narrated and the perpetrators in those narratives, in line with the cynical and ironic nature of the narrator. Aingeru Epaltza's truly strong and consistent narrative ability is clearly evident in these kinds of novels.

References
Andrade, Pilar (2010): "Novela policíaca y cine policíaco: una aproximación." *Ángulo Recto. Revista de estudios sobre la ciudad como espacio plural* 2, no. 1: http://www.ucm.es/info/angulo/volumen/Volumen02-1/varia02.htm.
Aristi, Maider (2001): "Asfaltoaren zaporea," in *Gara*, Feb. 3: https://kritikak.armiarma.eus/?p=157.
Barandiaran Amarika, Asier (2015): "Aingeru Epaltza y la forja de la navarridad en sus novelas históricas," in Esparza, Iratxe, and López Gaseni, José Manuel (eds.): *La identidad en la literatura vasca contemporánea*. Peter Lang, Berna, 141–164.
Biblioteca Nacional de España (BNE): *Novela policíaca: guía de recursos bibliográficos*. Ministry of Education, Culture and Sport. Retrieved Jul. 15, 2019 from http://www.bne.es/es/Micrositios/Guias/novela_policiaca/index.html
Cerqueiro, Diana (2010): "Sobre la novela policiaca." *Angulo Recto, Revista de estudios sobre la ciudad como espacio plural, 2*, no. 1: http://www.ucm.es/info/angulo/volumen/Volumen02-1/varia01.htm.
Colmeiro, José F. (1994): *La novela policiaca española. Teoría e historia crítica*. Anthropos: Barcelona.
Cruz, Anne J. (1999): *Discourses of Poverty: Social Reform and the Picaresque Novel in Early Modern Spain*. University of Toronto Press: Toronto.
Egaña, Ibon (2008): "Epaltza, Aingeru (Iruñea, 1960)," in *Euskal Literaturaren Hiztegia (ELH)*. Retrieved July 2, 2019 from http://www.ehu.eus/ehg/literatura/idazleak/?p=350.
Epaltza, Aingeru (1985): *Sasiak ere begiak baditik*. Elkar: San Sebastian.
———. (1993): *Ur uherrak*. Pamiela: Pamplona.
———. (2000): *Rock'n'Roll*. Elkarlanean: San Sebastian.
Fierro, Juan Manuel, and Nitrihual, Luis (2010): "Cinismo y parodia de América en la novela *Daimon* de Abe Posse. Una aproximación a la filosofía de Peter Sloterdijk." *Letras*, 52, no. 81. Caracas. Retrieved April, 2010 from http://ve.scielo.org/scielo.php?script=sci_arttext&pid=S0459-12832010000100001.
Juaristi, Felipe (1993): "Bakardadearen ibaian," in *El Diario Vasco*, Jul. 31: https://kritikak.armiarma.eus/?p=2194.

López Antón, José Javier (2000): *Escritores carlistas en la cultura vasca*. Pamiela: Pamplona.
Mackler, Tasha (1991): *Murder. . . by Category. A Subject Guide to Mystery Fiction*. The Scarecrow Press. London.
Martín Nogales, Jose Luis (1989): *Cincuenta años de novela española (1936–1986). Escritores Navarros*. Promociones y Publicaciones Universitarias: Barcelona.
Martínez Aragón, Antonio (2015): *Espacio del realismo sucio*. University of Granada: Granada.
Mendizabal, Mikel (1987): "Sasiak begiak ere baditik," in *Argia*, Jan. 11: https://kritikak.armiarma.eus/?p=3085.
Santos, Francisco (2002): "La primera guerra carlista en Navarra (1833–1939)," in *Euskonews & Media* 189.zbk (Nov. 22–29): http://www.euskonews.eus/0189zbk/gaia18903es.html
Zamora, Alonso (2002): *Qué es la novela picaresca,* in Biblioteca virtual Miguel de Cervantes: http://www.cervantesvirtual.com/obra-visor/qu-es-la-novela-picaresca-0/html/ff70f412-82b1-11df-acc7-002185ce6064_3.html#I_0_.
Zafra, Enriqueta (2009): *Prostituidas por el texto. Discurso prostibulario en la picaresca femenina*. Purdue University Press: West Lafayette (IN).

Notes

1 The word "detective" has also been used for this kind of novel, and detectives must "search" in their quest for information. This is the common ground between "detective novels" and this novel by Aingeru Epaltza: "This genre, of basically English-language origin, is given in English the generic term *detective story* or *detective novel* (according to its narrative extent) or, in a more comprehensive sense, *detective fiction* (which includes the two previous ones), all of which make explicit reference to the importance of the central role of the private or *amateur* investigator" (Colmeiro 1994:53–54).

2 "The second subgenre [. . .] is given the name in English, in the absence of a specialized epithet, the adjectives *tough* or *hardboiled* which are used normally to designate an incisive style, tough characters and narrative of frenetic violent action, not necessarily of a 'police' kind" (Colmeiro 1994:56).

3 This has been used in intrigue novels and here Epaltza has adapted the hypothetical resource very well to our culture: "Manuscripts and rare books figure prominently on the pages of the mystery story. Rare books disappear, old manuscripts surface, and priceless collections go on the auction block—all to the delight of the reader and to de detriment of the victim" (Mackler 1991: 248).

4 The demonym for someone from the Aezkoa Valley, although nowadays Euskaltzaindia (the Academy of the Basque Language) corrects it to the form *aetza*.

5 Because of the intrigue, Lieutenant Torres, at least in the logic of this story, is a former liberal spy, which exacerbates the novel's intrigue; in fact, the appearance of the "real" Torres will shed light on how successful his work was: "As long as we have international conflicts, we'll have spy stories and mysteries with intrigue. But some of these tales involve various branches of our own soil, and leave the average citizen aghast" (Mackler 1991: 198).

6 In literature, too, there are "livelihoods" which have gone hand in hand: prostitute and pimp, linked by certain interests: "Long referred as the world's 'oldest profession', prostitution is, in fact, only the second oldest: pimping ranks as the first. Be that as it may, prostitution is the

situation in which any number of murders are committed, in fact as well as fiction" (Mackler 1991: 315).
7   Nowadays known as Muru-Astrain, within the municipality of Zizur (in the Iruñerria region), until the nineteenth century it was said to have had a very numerous Basque-speaking population.
8   In Aingeru Epaltza's words, the very mention of "our sad story" very often provokes a sense of shame amongst us, even those of us who do not feel influenced by the "conflict."
9   "The *bertsolari* Jazinto in the novel *Ur uherrak* does not speak the same way as many contemporary *bertsolaris*, not even close. *Ur uherrak* is a novel by Aingeru Epaltza, and as the writer admits, he is trying to achieve distance in the narrative [...]" (Barandiaran Amarika 2011: 24).
10   Dirty reality, not always because it uses minimalist language, no. He resorts to Baroque language, resorting to ironic descriptions in the narrator's speech. Yet in dialogues, yes, short, coarse responses full of ellipses... are plentiful: "[...] abstraction, economy of language, use of the elipsis, precision and descriptive sobriety" (Martínez Aragón 2015: xii).
11   "That is perhaps the most interesting thing about this literature and this architecture, the second history, the profound history, the rescuing of all that which appeared lost, but that with intelligence can be recovered without thinking about an aesthetic or dogmatic result [...]" (Martínez Aragón 2015: 140).
12   We are thus faced with a so-called "mystery novel," because a death is typically the door to enter into a police novel, which was already being developed in the late nineteenth and early twentieth centuries (Andrade 2010).
13   "In this sense, the modern subject, the western subject, is transformed into a modern cynic lacking any hope. Modern cynicism lives alongiside the discomposure appearing before its very eyes, but it continues to function as if it did not exist" (Fierro and Nitrihual 2010).
14   "[...] we could define it as the set of mysterious and confusing events of a criminal kind which make up a difficulty for the investigator's reasoning and which are ultimately ordered and explained by means of logical procedures." (Cerqueiro 2010).
15   Here is an example of the attitude of the protagonist Eduardo himself towards female interns: "It happened four years previously. It only lasted a couple of weeks. After making a lot of fuss in all the newspaper offices to the point of being ludicrous, it was hard for me to get a second contract for her. Two dizzying weeks. Two whirlwind weeks. Two weeks of lies. Two weeks of grief. Then, she dumped me:
—Did you think I went to bed with you for your pretty face, or what?—idiot." (Epaltza 2000: 111).
16   In chapter 6, the protagonist has had a long and broad conversation with Ttipi, or Anjel Urtxipia; in fact, since he was a young man Ttipi always liked gossip about people. Forty years later, he has an office in the expansion district and works in confidential information and consultancy in a successful business. Eduardo will turn to him regarding the old dead woman: to see if there is an "occult" group or a cult behind it, and so on. In the middle of chapter 7, though, we are shocked to learn of Ttipi's murder, marking another twist in the story.
17   "The urban nature of the scenery was already a normal pattern in the classic detective novel, which only in a few cases located its stories in the country. But the importance of the city is more significant in the noir story, which due to its realist dimension transforms many

of these works into authentic portraits of different city environments, places and types" (Cerqueiro 2010).
18 Above all, the novel *The Sun Also Rises* (1926) reveals the San Fermin atmosphere to the English-speaking world. Other novels by Ernest Hemingway also depict the festive atmosphere of Iruñea. For more information, see: https://www.sanfermin.com/en/party-guide/hemingway-and-sanfermin/.

Chapter 3

Bernardo Atxaga's *Gizona bere bakardadean* (The Lone Man) (1993)

Xabier Etxaniz Erle

In December 1993, *Gizona bere bakardadean* (Pamiela; in English, *The Lone Man*, Harvill, 1996) was published, following the first novel written by Atxaga, the award-winning *Obabakoak* (with *Behi euskaldun baten memoriak*, Memories of a Basque Cow, 1991, Pamiela, published in between). During those years there was immense pressure on Atxaga; it was the first time that a Basque writer had achieved that kind of success, both within and outside the Basque Country, and all readers, critics, and experts were waiting to see what Atxaga would do after *Obabakoak*. When Atxaga wrote *Behi euskaldun baten memoriak*, he received harsh criticism, perhaps because readers expected *Obabakoak II* ("We all fall into the temptation of comparing it to Bernardo Atxaga's other works, but I think this book does not have a lot in common with those, maybe only in terms of technique" in Felipe Juaristi's words, 1992; or "The history of Basque literature will not say that this book is the most memorable book in Atxaga's work, one would hardly think so," J. L. Zabala, 1992), or for whatever reason. In Anjel Zelaieta's words, "It has just been written that Atxaga's novel *Behi euskaldun baten memoriak* will not be great, or, in other words, that this will not reach the level of other creations by the Asteasu native" (Zelaieta 1992).

Leaving the rural environment and fantasy literature aside, he made the leap into realism, at first with *Behi euskaldun baten memoriak* and then by means of the novel *Gizona bere bakardadean* (*The Lone Man*) (Pamiela 1993).

That change was also made under the aforementioned pressure, and in Juan Luis Zabala's words, "social pressure time and time again asked him to do that without forgetting or selling out his very own literary identity" (Zabala 1994), and even more, "the writer has carried out his work faithfully, contrasting a strong and elegant bridge between what was asked of him and what he wanted to do, maintaining the spirit of Obaba whilst distancing himself from Obaba" (Zabala 1994). To be sure, although Zabala said that, he also observed the following about the latter novel: "It is true, yes, and it was known beforehand too, that, to the extent that he has distanced himself from Obaba needing to respond to the aforementioned pressure, to the extent that he has had to achieve a new way of creating literature, a new cycle, Atxaga's writing style and literature has lost something of its distinctiveness and its tenderness" (Zabala 1994); whatever the case, none of this would stop him from winning the Critics' Prize that year.

This novel, moreover, marks a watershed moment, not just in regard to style, but also regarding the very perspective of literature. As Figueroa (1988) says, literary works in diglossic situations display multiple features (the influence of philology, communicative and not so literary texts, the importance of folklore, the lack of constructive trajectories . . .); in the face of all that, *The Lone Man* introduced modernity by these means; the work was published in Basque and immediately translated into other languages (three months later into Spanish) and then in several countries (Catalonia, Czech Republic, Denmark, Germany, France, Greece, Hungary, Israel, Italy, Netherlands, Portugal, Slovenia, Turkey, Britain. . .). A few years after the novel was published Atxaga said the following about the translation of his works and the creative process:

> Now I have decided which way I will go with the novel. I will write it in Basque at first, then, imposing the necessary discipline and by force of will, I will translate it into Spanish and, finally, I will rewrite the Basque version taking into account the variations that emerge from the Spanish translation. (Zabala 1996: 30).

This was after Atxaga's first award-winning novel *Obabakoak* and he was criticized for writing a work aimed at "foreign" more than "local" readers. It was clear from the beginning that the book was going to be published in Spanish (something that was not typical at the time in Basque letters) and this led to the criticism. But just as there were such criticisms, there have been those who have praised Atxaga's contribution at the time:

Basque, thanks to Atxaga, has been made *literary*, in other words, it has been transformed into a literary language before the world. All of this gives confidence to the Basque reader, it normalises reading works in Basque, it takes the reading of works created in Basque out of the confined circles of cultural activism. (Apalategi 2001: 48).

Now, with the passage of time, and some decades later, with another perspective, readers and critics can look with fresh eyes at how the novel *The Lone Man* changed Atxaga's narrative fiction. Furthermore, by changing styles, they can see how Atxaga, although he depicted realism and the customs and actuality of contemporary society, maintained a fine thread from *Obabakoak* through to his latest novel *Etxeak eta hilobiak* (Houses and Graves, 2019). Indeed, Obaba has always been present, in one way or another in the writer from Asteasu's works, and besides the village, its voices, as a place for reflection, or a desire to make our identity known are always evident.

When *The Lone Man* is discussed it is described as an action novel, "in the first sense of fear" in Itxaro Borda's words (1994), a tale of suspense, mainstream fiction, and in Ur Apalategi's words (2020), "that it is Atxaga's first realist work (the first work set historically), that through social pressure Bernardo Atxaga dares to speak about the 'Basque problem' for the first time, that although he has used the mechanisms of a thriller masterfully, he has achieved a profound reflection on the end of ideology." Felipe Juaristi, too, says that "Absolutely everything is connected, like fitting the pieces of jigsaw puzzle together (that is exactly the police novel tradition)," yet later clarifies: "I do not mean that this work of Atxaga's is a police novel, because the main characters are not police officers, although there is police intrigue, in good doses and which grabs the reader's attention" (Juaristi, 1994). In other words, whilst both Apalategi and Juaristi say that Atxaga's book uses the mechanisms of a thriller or police novel mechanisms, no one else has considered this novel a police novel. Amongst many other features of *The Lone Man* there is also, as Andreu Martin said, a playful suggestion (Martin 1989: 29); this is a novel full of mystery and inquisitiveness from the very beginning, a work about the future of ETA members who are in hiding that captures the reader; in short, it is about the organization, about the armed conflict, about human needs, about love . . . It is true that it does not follow the typical outline of a police novel (Martín Cerezo 2006), a murder, suspects, an investigation, the end. Yet in this novel, Atxaga's narrative space or focus is, specifically, on those who have committed "evil" or suffered the force of the police. From that perspective, this novel is also original because the protagonist is not, as in typical police novels and as is customary, an investigator, someone in search of the criminal, but someone in hiding from the police. This perspective has something to do with the Basque conflict, because in the Basque Country people (readers, we should say, in this case) have been closer to people fleeing than to the police.

From the beginning of the novel, the reader gets to know Carlos, the main character. He is the omniscient protagonist narrator of this novel. We will learn about his past, his experience in the organization and in prison, how he kidnapped and killed a businessman... and also about the present, when, together with his colleagues, he owns a hotel near Barcelona and that two ETA members are in hiding in the basement of the hotel bakery. Moreover, the players in the Polish national football team, who are taking part in the World Cup, are in the hotel and being watched over by policemen and security guards.

Carlos is a solitary man who has only left the hotel a dozen times in ten years. He is a baker and because of his work, he likes being alone; the bakery is "his" spot and his hotel partners never show up there. He goes for walks with his dogs Belle and Greta, with whom he does have a close relationship. Carlos, though, is hiding two young people in a corner of the bakery: Jon and Jone, and when the novel begins, on June 28, 1982, the two young people have been in hiding for two weeks. He takes the young people food in the evening and in a chat with the girl he finds out that a child from the hotel has seen them:

> The conditions I set haven't been respected... Unfortunately, you're abolsutely right... What's worse, someone saw us... It happened the day before yesterday. Around eleven o'clock at night. Jon and I walked to the spring down below and while we were cooling off there, a little boy of about five shone a flashlight at us. I almost shot him, really I did. I came that close (Atxaga 1996: 20)

The child, Pascal, is the five-year-old son of another owner of the hotel and it will be hard to hide the fact that the child has seen someone with a gun. Carlos, in addition to the pressure he is under, realizes the need to get the ETA members out of there, even more so since the press publish an advertisement every day with photos of Jon and Jone, offering three million pesetas to anyone who may be able to give the police some information.

To further complicate the situation, a young man who has been assigned to take the young people back to the Basque Country, the fishmonger Mikel, tells Carlos (and also the two hidden people) that they have to stay for another week, that the trip is apparently too dangerous. In the meantime, Carlos discovers that the guards around the hotel are special, that they are monitoring all the comings and goings in the hotel, and, what is more, that some people impersonating journalists are policemen and that they are suspicious.

The reader, then, can tell that the pressure is building on Carlos. Moreover, there are external as well as internal factors in that growing pressure. Some of those are mentioned, as is the suspicion that someone has informed on him (how else would one understand the police attitude and the control around the hotel?), yet the internal factors correspond to Carlos's past, his activist experience, his relationship with his hotel colleagues, his hiding of the fact that he is sheltering two young people, his internal past voices: the advice Sabino his teacher gave to him; the comments of his brother Kropotky, who is in a psychiatric ward, and the words of the critical internal voice, the "Rat"; all of these voices increase Carlos's uneasiness and his loneliness. They constrict his life, environment, and situation to the point of suffocation. The tension, in that closed environment, has to do with the past as well as the net that the police form around Carlos; not just around him, but Carlos himself knows that their goal is to capture him, even though the police do not realize that. In Ur Apalategi's words, "Carlos (. . .) is the paradigm of an existential predicament that appears in Atxaga's work for the first time. In other words, a torn character who cannot choose between two competing spaces" (2007: 120).

In such a situation, the former activist's past, revealed in events that happen time and time again in flashback form throughout the novel, does not help. The actions he carried out, his prison experiences (also reflected indirectly in the texts of Rosa Luxemburg), his behavior with his brother, the deaths of his friends and, one should say, above all, the killing of the businessman are a heavy burden on Carlos' everyday life. The reader becomes more aware of that burden, namely the events in the protagonist's life, as the novel progresses. What will happen with the hidden activists? Will Stefano or Fatlips catch up with them? And Carlos, what will Carlos do? His life becomes more and more complicated for the reader, as the more they get to know him, the more difficult it becomes to guess Carlos's true character and behavior.

Carlos is very private, likes to do things his own way and sometimes he even does things in a way that others do not understand. When he explains the escape to Jone, the girl gets worried because Carlos has written the plans down on paper: "Is it safe to have things written down?" (Atxaga 1996: 163), and the answer Carlos gives also explains his personality:

—While I was an active member of the organization, which I was for quite a long while, I always had bits of paper on me. At one point, my alias was 'Confetti'. I never had any problems. I have a very idiosyncratic method of taking notes (...)

—I can't understand a thing.

—Nor can anyone else. (Atxaga 1996: 164)

In the end, Carlos himself will take charge of finding a solution to the situation of the fugitives. It is clear that no one else can help him, that he alone will have to manage if he does not want to risk the future of his friends and the future of everyone at the hotel. Fear, specifically the fear that they will be caught, is ever present, yet in Carlos's view, there is still time to resolve the situation:

—They (the police) don't know anything definite, but they know enough. If they've got this far, they must know quite a lot, and if they do, it's because someone has betrayed us. The little boy probably said something. (...)

—There's no point getting all worked up. That may have been what happened, or it may be that the police have looked in their files and realized that nearly everyone in this hotel is an ex-militant. (Atxaga 1996: 165)

The novel incorporates the events in a five-day period. As noted earlier, the narrative begins on June 28 (by that time, the hidden activists have been in the bakery basement for two weeks) and extends over the next four days. Initially, the writer shows the situation, where and who they are, what they are like, the characters' past ... but on the second day Carlos notes the close police presence (an unexpected encounter with Fatlips on the way to the petrol station; verifying that policemen are masquerading as journalists; Stefano wanting to record him at work ...), and that speeds up the rhythm of the events. It is true that the novel is 349 pages long in Basque (325 in English) and much more than a thriller (the capitalist and communist system appear on a par with each other in reality—Poland at that time was a communist country—in hotel get-togethers, conversations and stays; there are also accounts of social relations; relationships between men and women, for example, women "who serve only to incite desire or sex" in the words of Itxaro Borda (1984); but then the Basque conflict, the armed struggle, reflections on past dreams and feelings of despair are explained in the novel, among many other matters). The reader, of course, knows that this novel admits multiple interpretations, but as we get closer to the police dimension, the author accelerates the events as the tension increases, giving a more intense rhythm to the events of the final days. In the words of Ur Apalategi (2020):

> In the second part, though, together with the appearance of the police that go to the hotel, the accelerating rhythm establishes the thread of a true suspense novel. Putting into practice the well-known techniques of suspense fiction, the author takes the story of Carlos back in time—how much time he has left to organize and bring about the ETA activists' escape—and that novelesque novelty coincides with the process of compressing space, creating real angst (in the sense expressed above) in the reader.

Atxaga, like Patricia Highsmith, uses the character's lies, despair, and feelings of guilt to reveal the unease he is enduring. Carlos is increasingly alone, sensing more and more pressure, but the polyphonic voices within him also influence this feeling of despair and loneliness. Sabino's advice draws Carlos back again and again, to another time, to another struggle, to the friends and events of that time; the Rat, meanwhile, constantly criticizes Carlos' actions, calls into question the baker's behavior, and he must be constantly attendant to such doubts. This is, precisely, one of the values of this novel, maintaining that intrigue (will they catch them or not, will they escape free or be caught as a result of Carlos's conduct) from start to finish. The intrigue of or interest in the novel is not, unlike in other police novels, knowing who committed the murder or attack, no, in this case we know from the beginning what has been done and by whom, and through the book the reader's curiosity lies somewhere else, wondering whether the police will catch the two young people in hiding or not.

As mentioned above, that relationship between Carlos and the police, whether they will catch them, whether they will find out where the two ETA members are hiding, will increasingly weigh on Carlos' mind. "The police obviously had some definite information" (Atxaga 1996: 157), thinks Carlos at one stage, and that reflection has something to do with Fatlips' fixation with Carlos:

> Why is he watching me closely? he asked Sabino, as he set off again. The policeman's behavior couldn't be explained away as a matter of temperament or as a purely personal problem. He was clearly more suspicious and aggressive than other policemen, but

even so, his zeal still seemed to him excessive. He knew that Carlos was Jon and Jone's contact, that it was him, not Guiomar, Ugarte or anyone else. (Atxaga 1996: 193).

But as the hours go by, Carlos also notices the burden of others on him:

> The police hadn't just turned up there spontaneously, they had done so after receiving a phone call from someone and it had to be someone living in the hotel. He was the man Stefano was looking for; Stefano knew that he, Carlos, was the contact for Jon and Jone, and he was watching and waiting for the one false move that would show him the way to their hiding place (...) Fatlips and the other policemen would know too. How else could he explain the shot fired at him in La Banyera? (Atxaga 1996: 232).

The guards provoke him, they want to unnerve him so that he makes a mistake and thereby show them where the two young people are hiding. Therefore, guards will appear when he is least expecting it, they will stop him at checks even though they know him, they will treat him badly at a checkpoint when he is going back to the hotel with Maria Teresa... the thing is that they all know something, but they do not know the most important thing, where Carlos is hiding the two young people. That said, Carlos is increasingly being pushed into the realm of fear, he is increasingly worried and that fear will lead him into a dead-end.

As is customary in noir novels, Atxaga uses the plot of the novel as a pretext to discuss other matters; there is a noticeable discussion about what is termed the "Basque conflict," Carlos talks about the past and its distance from the present, he decides to hide the two young people but does not agree with their ideas, does not share the goals of the current organization ("I find your present struggle absolutely absurd," 33). Carlos gave up the goals of the struggle and believing in the methods used long ago, and that is mirrored in his reflections and conversations with Guiomar. At the outset, by means of a warning, in a letter from his brother it is stated that:

> A few days ago I saw a pamphlet bearing a photo of the day of your trial. You're all standing there with your fists raised and—according to the caption—singing the song of the Basque soldier: "*Eusko gudariak gara Euskadi askatzeko, gerturik daukagu odola bere alde emateko* ... We are Basque soldiers fighting for the freedom of our country and ready to spill blood for it." Well, the day will come

when that song will hold no charm for you whatsoever. (Atxaga 1996: 236).

Then, reading what he wrote at the time:

> Carlos tossed the piece of paper violently into the air and that greeting: How are you, Basque soldier?" and all the other words written in red biro landed on the floor by the door. He found it impossible to read the letter. It came from another planet, from another century, as did the pamphlet he had written eleven years before. (Atxaga 1996: 238)

Yet Guiomar's is the clearest comment of all. After the former combatants, who know each each so well, get together, when Carlos tells him that he has been hiding Jon and Jone: "in recent years you've done nothing but tell me how you don't believe in anything any more and how our struggle was all in vain" (Atxaga 1996: 304).

Social relations are also a constant throughout the book: among the hotel workers, amongst former members and activists, on matters between men and women, and also those relating to human wishes. Regarding this latter point, Danuta Wykak, the interpreter for the Polish national football team, has an important role in the novel. Danuta lives in a communist country and really likes beauty items; some earrings, a necklace, those humble details that she cannot have, those bourgeois whims, will be decisive in the development of the novel. Yet that wish of Danuta's starts to be explained as revolutionary, because the desire for treats is explained in Rosa Luxemburg's texts:

> "I can't stop dreaming—I've become terribly vain, I think!—of having a pretty new suit decorated with braid," Rosetta wrote in another letter, this time from Cracow. "Here, I've been shown the tomb of Kociuszko, the tombs of the Polish kings (. . .) but all I can think of is: I'd love to have some braid here and here and here." (Atxaga 1996: 196)

The account, however, comes from a television report that is showing at the beginning of the novel. On the Basque coast, forty thousand years ago, people apparently went to great lengths to collect some shellfish, with which to make necklaces, "all to satisfy a whim, a trifling desire, that of self-adornment" (Atxaga 1996: 204) in Carlos's words. Specifically, the lone man tells the interpreter from a Communist country the following: "in my view, that episode is a clear demonstration of something: the importance of the unimportant"; and then, "Caprice is really important (...) When we were in Cuba, (...) All the people who were frustrated in the satisfaction of their caprices despised socialism." (Atxaga 1996: 205-206).

Kropotky also addressed the importance of those needs in a letter to Carlos when he was in prison:

> "Most of the revolutions of the past don't merit the name (...) In my view, revolution doesn't take place on the level of primary need, but on a higher level, once those primary needs have been satisfied. It's only then that people might start wanting a different world, except that most people don't, because they're quite happy with the old world and because they've assimilated bourgeois values" (Atxaga 1996: 207–208).

There is a climax in this conversation between Carlos and Danuta, a question that will completely change the future of the characters: "How far would you go to satisfy a caprice, Danuta? (...) What would you do for some good earrings? I mean what would you do to get some real emeralds" (Atxaga 1996: 208).

> Danuta's answer is that she is poor and "it always affects me when people remind me of it" (Atxaga 1996: 209). "There are terrible shortages in Poland, and I'm a very proud person" (Atxaga 1996: 209).

Atxaga gradually fits together a jigsaw puzzle throughout the novel or, as Guillermo Cabrera Infante describes it (cited in Martin Cerezok 2006: 45), a game of chess. The hidden young people, Carlos' decision-making and solitude, Danuta's desire for caprices, Pascal's innocence, the guard's rancour, unfortunate fate ("Nemesis doesn't strike the guiltiest person, or even the most dangerous, it always strikes the weakest" in R. Luxemburg's words, 1996: 249). He leaves us several clues throughout the novel so as to guess what can be foreseen, such as the quote from the Polish poet Cyprian Kusto:

> "But life, as those who are capable of looking back know only too well, has no firm base, and we live like someone swimming alone at sea. We should always be on the alert, we should never allow ourselves to rest, not for a moment. One day, a large wave carries us towards one place" (Atxaga 1996: 71)

Danuta's pleasure in jewelry, and Maria Teresa's comment to Carlos at a dinner: "I have a rest in Danuta's room, and do you know why? Because she usually has lots of fashion magazines" (Atxaga 1996: 267); the presence of an informant in the hotel, and the increasingly violent behavior of the police, the news about the fires on the TV news, the hut Guiomar built for Pascal...

All these pieces fit together, slowly at first, then faster and faster in the concluding storm, as Nemesis said, until the weakest is knocked out.

As Ur Apalategi (2007: 124) mentions in relation to this novel, Atxaga launches "the realist tendency which, later, would come to dominate Basque literature." It is true that *The Lone Man* was very important in the work carried out to open up that predominance, and more than that. In the *Times Literary Supplement*, Horspool states the following about this novel: it "is apparently linear, but it is what has happened before the beginning of Carlos's plan, and what will happen after it, that enrich the plot, raising the novel above the level of a conventional thriller." In other words, seemingly Atxaga has constructed a psychological novel or thriller, but within that structure he narrates a simple life story and, among other themes, he also includes a reflection on a generation that was involved in an armed struggle. When he was young, Carlos joined the organization and therein the messages, slogans and orders he received marked him for years. They date from other eras, as do the references to revolutionaries that appear in the novel (Kropotkin, R. Luxemburg...). At the same time, gone are the days of militancy, imprisonment, armed action, and the last robbery to buy the hotel. Sabino, his brother Kroptky, the events of the struggle, and so on are all gone... now, however, it is a time framed by the people in the hotel near Barcelona, the hidden ETA members, the Polish national football team and the police guarding the hotel. Atxaga builds the structure of the novel between past and present; the initially slow rhythm (above all, through leaps into the past and internal voices) speeds up with each passing day. That way, after several suffocating moments in the rhythm of the first four days, we reach the last decisive and dynamic day. The mystery is clarified and, thus, in the end, the intrigue concludes. For the reader, however, because of the previously read dialogues, reflections, and passages, *The Lone Man* is a mystery novel, but much more than that too.

References

Apalategi, Ur (2001): "Errealismoaren eraberritzea eta kokapena 90eko hamarkadako euskal literaturan" in K. Uribe (Pub.) *Azken aldiko euskal narratiba*. UEU. Bilbao. 41–56.

———. (2007): "Gizona bere bakardadean" (1993), in J. Kortazar (Dir.) & I. Retolaza (Pub.) *Egungo euskal eleberriaren historia*. UPV/EHU: Bilbao. 117–127.

———. (2020): "*Gizona Bere Bakardadean* (1993). Bernardo Atxaga," in *Auñamendi Entziklopedia*. http://aunamendi.eusko-ikaskuntza.eus/es/gizona-bere-bakardadean-1993-bernardo-atxaga/ar-154487/.
Atxaga, Bernardo (1993): *Gizona bere bakardadean*. Pamiela: Pamplona.
———. (1996): *The Lone Man*. Harville & Secker: London.
Borda, Itxaro (1994): "Hotel Atxaga," in *Argia*, 06/19/1994, https://kritikak.armiarma.eus/?p=3386.
Figueroa, Antón (1988): *Digloxia e Texto*. Galaxia: Vigo.
Juaristi, Felipe (1992): "Ingenuitatearen omenez," in *Euskaldunon Egunkaria*, 02/01, https://kritikak.armiarma.eus/?p=2450.
———. (1994): "Pertsonaiak beren bakardadean," in *El Diario Vasco*, 01/08, https://kritikak.armiarma.eus/?p=2210.
Martin, Andreu (1989): "La novela policiaca/negra como hecho lúdico." In J. Paredes Nuñez (Ed.) *La novela policiaca española*. University of Granada: Granada.
Martin Cerezo, Iván (2006): *Poética del relato policiaco*. University of Murcia: Murcia.
Zabala, Juan Luis (1992): "Tamaina ttikiko desertua, oasiz inguratua," in *Argia*, Jan. 26, https://kritikak.armiarma.eus/?p=3349.
———. (1994): "Obaba barru-barruan," in *Euskaldunon Egunkaria*, Jan. 23, https://kritikak.armiarma.eus/?p=2516.
———. (1996): "Hemendik 25 urtera izango ditu euskal literaturak arazo benetan latzak," in *Euskaldunon Egunkaria*, Dec. 4, 30–31.
Zelaieta, Anjel (1992): "Behin baten anabasisa," in *Euskaldunon Egunkaria*, Feb. 22, https://kritikak.armiarma.eus/?p=2452.

Chapter 4

Itxaro Borda's Detective Cycle: The World of Amaia Ezpeldoi

Ur Apalategi

Amaia Ezpeldoi is, without doubt, the most enduring and far-reaching character in Basque fiction. One might say that, since 1994, the character has been the epicenter of a calculated literary universe that has been enriched and partially modified from novel to novel, a fictional spokesperson, in large part, for the completely idiosyncratic worldview of her creator. There is no intention here to fit in with the orthodoxy of the genre, nor any aim of resembling the classics of the genre. On the contrary, over the years Borda would bring the genre more into line with her own distinctive identity as a writer, creating a unique as well as hybrid literary object.

An Ambitious Literary Project
At the time when the first novel constructed around Amaia Ezpeldoi—*Bakean ützi arte* (Until They Leave Us In Peace)—was published, in a 1994 interview for the journal *Argia*,[1] Itxaro Borda states clearly that she seeks to write one work made up of five novels (therefore a pentalogy, although eventually a sixth volume would also be added to the scheduled series). Borda presents a written cycle about territoriality, which would seek to reveal the space/peripheral structure of a language and social system. In fact, after traversing Zuberoa, Amikuze (Lower Navarre), Bilbo and Araba, Amaia Ezpeldoi would never reach Donostia, as Borda declared in the interview. Instead of reaching the Basque-speaking heart

of the Basque Country (Donostia), Amaia would continue in Baiona and once again in Lower Navarre in the last two novels in the cycle.

These are (to date?) the novels that make up the corpus of the hexalogy,[2] listed in chronological order of publication of the novels and specifying the geographical locations of the plots that take place therein:

Bakean ützi arte (Until They Leave Us in Peace), Susa, 1994 (set in Zuberoa).

Bizi nizano munduan (Until I'm Alive), Susa, 1996 (set in Lower Navarre).

Amorezko pena baño (More than Heartbreak), Susa, 1996 (set in the Erribera region of Upper Navarre).

Jalgi hadi plazara (Go Forth into Public), Susa, 2007 (set in Bilbo and Gasteiz).

Boga boga (Row, Row!), Susa, 2012 (set in Baiona).

Ultimes déchets (The Final Waste), Maiatz, 2015 (set in Baiona and Lower Navarre).

It seems reasonable to consider that Amaia Ezpeldoi's tendency to move from one periphery to another has something to do with the way writer Itxaro Borda sees herself in the Basque literary system (and more generally among the population of the Basque Country). The ambition to escape her personal periphery and assault the center has always been present in Borda's career.[3] Itxaro Borda decided to make the leap into the center of the system by releasing her first novel with the Susa publishing house (the controversial *Basilika* (Basilica) in 1984, which is mainly a text that is critical of the prominent cultural figures of the Northern Basque Country). With that move she placed herself at the center of the system, thereby managing to avoid the circuit of expected notions and risk of censorship associated with the Northern Basque literary subsystem. She would go and live in Paris for ten years, having achieved a job in the public sector as a postal worker. This temporary economic exile served her very well when it came to avoiding the exclusion she could have suffered in the cultural world of the Northern Basque Country. Indeed, she began to develop the Amaia Ezpeldoi cycle precisely upon her return from Paris. These detective novels, then, are directly related to Itxaro Borda's return, and, as will be seen, can in some way be interpreted as an expression of the contrasting feelings stemming from that return: on the one hand, as a positive effort to reestablish herself in local society (that is, Zuberoa, the Northern Basque Country, and the Basque Country as a whole) by publishing and celebrating local dialects and references; on the other, as a deep and bitter humanistic reflection on identity and the difficulty of taking root anywhere. The melancholic lament of a wandering writer who feels doomed to be an outsider anywhere and always.

Itxaro Borda wants to embrace the entire Basque territory and the Basque language, by focusing on the paradoxical ways that dimensions of the tradition of Basque modernity appear both backward and progressive. Her reclamation of Basque dialects, for example, can be interpreted as a backward and nostalgic ploy, from the perspective of the cultural system that is linked to standard Basque modernity. Itxaro Borda does not deny this wistful dimension of her work. She understands her literary task as an act of leaving a linguistic and ethnographic record of what is going to disappear, which gives a testimonial value to this series of books.

Yet, as noted, paradoxically, the literary reclamation of linguistic (ultra) localisms and Basque dialects can also be understood as a postmodern turn because Itxaro Borda does not confine herself to writing about a dying language, with tears in her eyes. On the contrary, she seeks to turn these peripheral, ultra-local, and wounded dialects into a weapon in order to shake up the stable structure of power relations between speech and cultural references within the Basque cultural system. In her opinion, she juxtaposes a polynomial alternative based on diversity with the domination of a Basque language and culture in the center that is incapable of embracing the totality and nuances of the Basque reality. Borda advocates a hybridity between old and new, as well as between center and periphery, following the same postmodern current as Atxaga in *Obabakoak*, in order to overcome the damaging effects of the monolithic modern model and its power.

Borda's behavior, however, is not the same when it comes to the use of Basque language from one novel to another. Thus, as the hexalogy progresses, Itxaro Borda does not, in the strict sense, maintain the same territorial disposition she did at the beginning, and in the final books many characters seem to contaminated by Amaia's dialect. However, generally speaking and especially in the dialogues, each character speaks in the dialect of their birthplace and we come across a Romanesque group of great dialectal diversity, in which the only

Basque dialect that is missing is the standard central form of speech, fulfilling her promise at the outset.

We should add, in the interest of accuracy, that Amaia's Navarrese-Lapurdian Basque is not at all pure but instead a blend of all the kinds of Basque in existence (she mixes words from all the Basque dialects, often in the same sentence, as well as all kinds of different historical varieties and registers of Basque, because her prose is littered with literary references). In a provocative way, one could say that Borda's is the true *unified* Basque and not the standardized, poor Basque of the center that she implicitly criticises. It is hard to deny that she is the Basque writer who uses the most global, diverse, and lexically rich Basque. Borda's Basque model is such a mouthful that it becomes a linguistic utopia in its richness.

For all these reasons, one could not contend that this is a conservative or nostalgic linguistic tendency. On the contrary, Borda's complex linguistic choices present the reader with a postmodern aim. Borda declares that it is time to give up the narrow concept of standard Basque around which Basque modernity has revolved. Her utopian as well as heterogenuous cultural-linguistic proposal thus takes on the form of a postcolonial uprising against the imperialist tendencies of the language and culture at the very center of the Basque Country.

The subject of colonialism is mentioned on more than one occasion throughout the cycle, whether on the part of Spain or France across the centuries, or the more recent internal colonization among Basques (the latter mostly in the final books in the series, and it is insinuated especially in BB[4] (Row, Row!). In BUA (Until They Leave Us in Peace), Borda conceives or mentions the concept of "*Herenerria*" (The third land), comparing the Basque periphery of Zuberoa to the Far West of the United States, considering it necessary to conquer the territory of the last Indians (the need of capitalism to conquer, in this case).

We may say, likewise, that these novels also have a prominent didactic dimension. Borda appears to be writing for the politico-historical education of the Basque people.

Traversing and embracing the whole of Basque geography (with the exception of Gizpuzkoa and the diaspora), it seems that the average Basque reader would like to expand the knowledge they may have of their country, its local customs, and history. Furthermore, the Amaia Ezpeldoi cycle is used to rescue parts of the unofficial history of the Basque Country. It recounts history linked to different Basque regions and places, as the plot develops, acknowledging its aim to illustrate the reader's Basque historical culture.

The Borda Definition of a Police Novel

Borda locates her cycle within the subgenre of the police novel, because she fully assumes the code and rules of that subgenre.

In this series of novels constructed around Amaia Ezpeldoi, the same sequential outline is always repeated, with a few generic details or nuances. First, we witness Amaia's solitary melancholic everyday life. Then someone contacts Amaia because they have heard that she is a detective and because they would like to clear up a mystery (a disappearance, in most cases). In the next stage, Amaia gets to work, with her scarce resources (because she is an amateur detective). As the investigation proceeds, Amaia has an affair (or several, sometimes simultaneously) and she befriends this lover and other people who help her with the investigation, becoming an investigative group. The investigation brings with it too the discovery of an unexpected mystery (a political, economic, environmental, or social scandal). Lastly, in most cases two mysteries combine (solving the first mystery involves resolving the second, and vice versa) and Amaia's affair ends with the investigation, in a very sweet or more bitter way. Amaia returns to her solitary existence. As noted, there are exceptions and one or the other of these sequences may be different from one novel to another, but this is the general outline.

That outline leads us to the classic detective novel. The originality of Borda's work does not lie in her effort to revamp the outline. In fact, she makes no effort in this regard. It can be said that we are dealing with conventional police novels because the conventions and frameworks of this type of novel are fully respected. These conventions and frameworks, however, are employed in a detached way and Amaia Ezpeldoi is not a realistic character (as a detective, of course) and nor are the investigations she carries out very believable but the author does not seem to care too much about that. On the other hand, the intrigues are just an excuse to develop the story and the surroundings. For that reason, it could be argued that we are sometimes dealing with police novels that verge on pastiche.

Thus, Borda reclaims a simple—what Aresti might have termed "cheap"—literature, in order to confront the overly serious literature at the center of the Basque literary system (Atxaga's political allegories or Saizarbitoria's realism, for example). She deems the police novel, because it is understood as secondary level literature with its own codes, an appropriate medium through which to begin rejecting the domination of the center from the periphery.

On the other hand, her description of and reflection on Basque society, as well as, of course, everything that she depicts about the complex identity of the main character, is completely realistic, profound, and convincing. It can be surmised that the author attaches real importance to this aspect.

The question, then, would be the following: why has Itxaro Borda chosen the police novel genre, if she does not take the genre too seriously? The fact is that the police novel has been used for a long time, all over the world, to make sharp and critical radiographs of the public. It is probably the most popular and best-selling way to carry out social criticism, because it is easy to read, and because it is based on some well-known conventions. That is possibly what encouraged Borda to make her choice. On the other hand, brought to the peripheral context of Basque letters, this subgenre has still not yet been overdeveloped or too frequently employed and the Amaia Ezpeldoi cycle has also had an air of originality, since it appeared in the mid-1990s.

We should specify, however, that Borda has not developed just any kind of police novel, but, rather, the social critique branch of the genre. The left-wing police novel, in other words. Once again, Borda's identification with this genre has something to do with her outsider self-perception. As is logical, the guilty parties or criminals will always be people from the dominant classes. In UD (The Final Waste), to give one example, the murderer is a businessman, a sixty-year-old corrupt businessman—involved in tax evasion—and sexual predator by the name of Bernitz Mendiol. As stated above, though, ordinary crimes and social crimes (which cause unemployment among the local population or harm farmers' lands) go hand in hand in the novels, as the intrigue serves to link the two.

If the outline of Borda's social critique police novel writing is undervalued and sometimes indifferently crafted, it cannot be denied, however, that the specific contemporary Basque reality—the experience of associations and institutions, that of social movements, of *ikastolas* or Basque-language schools, and many other things—is represented throughout the cycle like nowhere else. The following could, once again, be highlighted: although it may appear surprising, there is a piece of Basque(-language) social reality in Itxaro Borda's texts that does not appear in contemporary Basque literature. There is no place for those aforementioned elements in the texts of the two main realist authors today. In Atxaga's texts, for example, contemporary popular or institutional reality is never mentioned (there is no mention of the Basque Government or *ikastolas* in Atxaga's texts). In contrast, Saizarbitoria's novels only reference "an aristocratic" part of that reality, such as *gudaris* (Basque soldiers) and ETA members, or intellectuals and the Basque urban bourgeoisie. In her police novels, Itxaro

Borda mentions the most everyday prosaic Basque reality that never reaches an epic level. It is Basque life devoid of glamour; a true literary alternative in opposition to the central culture and references.

Borda's novels also have a second major distinctive quality, namely her detective's rural personality (that is how Amaia Ezpeldoi describes herself). Some of the most prominent authors in the rural branch of detective fiction, which seems to derive from the nature writing established in the United States by Henry D. Thoreau, are Daniel Woodrell, Craig Johnson, James Crumley, and Tony Hillerman. The narrator Amaia Ezpeldoi refers directly to the latter—and especially his Navajo detective Jim Chee, a tribal police officer—in BNM (Until I'm Alive), acknowledging her literary debt. Amaia Ezpeldoi would, too, in her own way, be a member of the nascent Basque tribal police.

Moreover, as in the work of the pioneering Thoreau, these authors (including Borda) also constantly blend and intersperse their observation and autobiographical considerations of nature, maintaining a genuine lyricism. It is worth stating that many of the crimes mentioned in the novels that make up the cycle are environmental.

Applied to the Basque context, of course, any literary representation of rurality cannot avoid the intertextuality of our long fertile romantic tradition. Borda is well aware of its echo, as we will confirm in the next section.

The Police Novel and Popular Literary Forms

Besides being police novels, the works involving the main character Amaia Ezpeldoi are also many other things; they are made up of other heterogeneous components, and the presence of some of these other components is so great that it can be concluded that we are dealing with hybrid works. However, all of those other components share a common point, namely their simple popular nature. Borda's literature is written on the basis of regular folk for regular people and out of love for normal society. One senses, especially in the initial books in the cycle, that her goal is a loving depiction of the local Basque people and way of life. Significant, in this respect, is her use of certain forms of narrative, such as speaking directly to the reader from time to time, as in some of Dickens's novels, or more generally in the Romanesque pamphlet tradition. "Popular" writing is, often, easy. Thus, Borda is not afraid to use clichés or stereotypical metaphors, because it prioritizes an immediate communication with a wide readership. In the same way, Borda employs a simple language register, without concerning herself too much with the pedigree of her prose.

As for the use of popular literary forms, though, her main conduit is the use of popular music. The music—but above all the songs—in the novels in the cycle becomes the soundtrack of Amaia Ezpeldoi's adventures, because the character-narrator constantly mentions the music she is listening to or the lyrics of the songs on her lips as a comment on what she is experiencing. Moreover, it is notable that the titles of three of the novels in the hexalogy are taken from Basque songs (*Bakean ützi arte*, *Jalgi hadi plazara*, and *Boga boga*).

Itxaro Borda pays tribute to the popular Basque literary tradition, imbuing her narrative fiction with the cultural value of songs by means of intertextuality. She believes that songs are important because they are able to reflect and express people's emotions. At the same time, she declares that she would like her novels to be consumed in a regular way, as if they were songs. Or as if they were a television show (a soap opera). In that regard, Amaia Ezpeldoi's tribute to the Basque soap opera *Goenkale* (High Street) in UD (The Final Waste) is significant. Borda wants to see herself as a modern-day bard, even though she produces police novels rather than songs. Blending allusions to popular songs and Basque rock music, she constructs a bridge between two eras and styles and proclaims that they constitute one culture, art created by and for the people.

Nevertheless, Borda demonstrates her familiarity with high culture by including numerous learned or cultured references (to thinkers like Hanna Arendt and artists like Louise Bourgeois) in the words of her main characters and using an educated language register when the narrative calls for it (mostly with an ironic touch, as when speaking, for example, about the Lower Navarrese Basque bourgeoisie in Until I'm Alive), but in doing so she shows no intention of placing herself above the average reader. It is not a tool about which to boast. On the contrary, she seeks to demonstrate that anyone can access such culture, to assert that high culture is not the preserve of the privileged classes. She also wants to show that a high culture or register is not the only way to communicate reality. Therefore, one of the most important features of Borda's writing is her carnivalesque blend of high and popular registers and references, in the Bakhtinian sense of language.[5]

There is something physical, dirty, in the way Borda describes things, and in her characters' experiences, in line with the dirty realism movement. At the same time, purity and sublimity are a constant presence, in Amaia Ezpeldoi's innate melancholy, or in the lyrical gaze she offers on nature as well as regular people.

One also notes traces of beat literature in Borda's work, as Amaia Ezpeldoi's comings and goings embody the Kerouacian topos in the emulsion between the dirty and the sublime or an intransitive journey without any money. One could also mention the constant presence of music linked to beat literature, as noted above.

If one had to give other quick partial definitions of this idiosyncratic and complex literary hybridization, one might say that these police novels are, among other things, a remarkable mixture of popular satire in the Northern Basque tradition and the punk spirit, or a mixture of (almost) romantic ethnography and gonzo reporting.

On the other hand, one could say that these novels are closely linked to certain different forms which are found in the popular literary tradition of the Northern Basque Country, as the author herself explains in a 2007 interview.[6] Borda embraces the marginalized rowdy tradition of *charivari* (some types of popular drama) such as the *toberak* or *galarotsak*, *maskaradak* (masquerades), and *bertsolaritza* (oral poetic improvization), in order to denounce the shameless injustices within the social structure.

In that sense, the Amaia Ezpeldoi cycle has a lot in common with the neo-ruralist novels and short stories developed by Borda's generation in the 1980s. Yet at the same time Borda distances herself from the main demystifying anti-romantic goal of neo-ruralism: in fact, she does not write in order to critique the romantic rural view of the Basque Country; she addresses the present, without filtering the allegory of the past.

The Construction of a Character

One of the main features of these six novels is that the narrator-character is at their epicenter. This character's experiences are central to the action and storyline, and her hypertrophic narrative voice has complete protagonism, with an expressive function predominating in her discourse. Two things define Amaia Ezpeldoi: her function (as a detective) and her personality (her self).

In terms of function, here is how she defines herself in the inaugural novel of the cycle: "On the silver plaque next to the door, full of pride, I read my name: AMAIA EZPELDOI—PRIVATE INVESTIGATOR FOR LIVESTOCK AND PEOPLE—MAULE" (chapter 2).

Note the humorous touch of self-definition and the tendency of the character to laugh at herself. It is clear from the outset that the police novel genre will be approached from an ironic postmodern distance. It is also noteworthy how the character's egalitarian left-wing ideology, albeit in a caricatured way, envisages from the outset this way of putting people and animals on the same level.

One of Borda's strategies to give her character a minimum of literary credibility (next in line alongside pure social or real credibility) is to summon up the mythology of noir fiction and the police novel. Throughout the hexalogy, there are countless references to other well-known detectives, or to famous characters in thrillers and noir fiction.

Amaia Ezpeldoi's sources are diverse in this respect and mostly devoid of cultural hierarchies. The character-narrator refers to literary, film, and television detectives as her colleagues or sources of inspiration.

Amaia Ezpeldoi generally identifies with anyone of a noir or detective nature, being a consumer and fan of this kind of character and the mythology associated with a detective.

There is a major temptation for any reader who knows something of the writer's life experiences and traits to interpret Amaia Ezpeldoi as a fictional analogy of Itxaro Borda. Let us first list the most noteworthy similarities: they are both lesbian women from the Northern Basque Country who have lived in Paris for several years and a physical resemblance could also be mentioned, as can be deduced from the passages in which Ezpeldoi describes herself. Both hold humble public positions (Borda is a postal worker while Ezpeldoi initially works for a gas and power company in France and later becomes a refuse collector for the Baiona city council). Outside her official job, Borda has also been an amateur but passionate rural writer and likewise Ezpeldoi has been a private investigator. What is more, they are the same age, give or take a year or two. The private investigator is thirty-three in the first volume in the cycle, published in 1994, when Borda was thirty-five (having been born in 1959).

There is another similarity between Borda and Ezpeldoi in relation to their manner of speech. They both experience linguistic seclusion, to the point of feeling marginalized from or outside the center of the Basque population or cultural system, as this passage in JHP (Go Forth into Public) demonstrates: "I was the wrong soul. A chameleonic soul who thought *mertzi biziki* ("Thank you" in dialectal Basque) and uttered *mila esker* (Thank you very much). I could multiply the examples. Sometimes I would go to the village cemetery and break down in tears and mourning with linguistic loneliness" (In the first chapter, "Introitus" (Introduction)).

Indeed, one could define Amaia (and this is one of the main dimensions of her personality) as a misfit, as an ogre (physically, sexually, geographically, socially, linguistically, and so forth), someone who does not fit her social context at all. She has an unusual physique, is a lesbian, a tomboy, and a proletarian (on the boundaries of the *lumpenproletariat* in several events) who speaks in a Basque dialect that is disappearing. Her deeply melancholic nature, her misanthropy and dose of self-hatred stems from all that. The character's self-contempt or self-hatred is often evident through the hexalogy. Thus, on page 49 of UD (The Final Waste), she states: "I am also travelling waste."[7] She feels a fleeting love for, identification with, garbage. She identifies with all the marginalized and stigmatized and finds only a kind of peace alongside them. There is a moment in UD (The Final Waste) when she goes to Bidaxune to take refuge in the Jewish cemetery there. Every so often Amaia becomes a misanthrope: "If Nolwen hadn't been too busy, I would have recognised my inner truth: I was looking for closeness, a desert and silence" (BB [Row, Row!], chapter 16).

That reference to a desert directs us logically to the poetry of Pierre Topet Etxahun. In the poem "Desertuko ihizik" (Wilds of the Desert 1833), Etxahun portrays himself as a victim of men, explaining that he, too, was condemned to wander hidden like the desert beasts. Ezpeldoi is sentimental and moving when she mentions openly her loneliness and desire for love. Simultaneously, she is *malevolent* and provocative (as the itinerant troubadour from Barkoxe would have been: weeping and teasing). The character's impudence/insolence is constant and she is not only aware of that but proclaims it.

To some extent, Itxaro Borda could be interpreted as a female Etxahun, because like him she has led a marginalized existence and, because of that, she responds to the cruelty of society through her literary provocation and talent, thereby paradoxically finding a way to integration. The cantankerous romantic poet and the sharpshooting novelist become siblings through a connection that overcomes centuries, in a provocative role, as it is curiously anagrammatically possible to combine the two: Itxaro Borda = Bardo Txiroa (a play of words, an anagram of her name meaning "the poor bard" in Basque).

Although she is vindictive, Amaia Ezpeldoi is not portrayed by her creator Itxaro Borda as monochrome. In numerous passages she demonstrates that she is a character of great sensitivity. In UD (The Final Waste), for example, while she is watching a TV detective show with her partner Nolwen, the macabre events of the television images make her start to vomit. In the same way, Amaia Ezpeldoi shows that she is very aware socially, and ultimately very human.

The character's sensitivity is also evident in her narrative style. Amaia Ezpeldoi is lyrical and sensual in her narrative forms (like her author). Her originality is that she describes rural and urban landscapes in the same expressive way.

If we were to summarize Amaia Ezpeldoi's philosophy, we would define it in terms of hedonistic pessimism. In line with that hedonism, there are numerous references to and descriptions of sexual relations in the novels, as a welcome cheerful counterpoint to a desperate and pessimistic worldview in general. Furthermore, the frequent sexual scenes are narrated in a sensual and/or imaginative way, combining content and form.

Even though the world around her may be falling apart, the character never loses her sense of humor. She likes to laugh at herself, as much as anyone else.

In the end, Amaia Ezpeldoi is a character defined by her culture, in the widest sense of the term culture, namely that which also embraces ideology. In line with the cultural and political references that appear in the first three books in the hexalogy, it can be easily concluded that Borda's implicit reader is a book-loving member of the Basque nationalist left. A sign of Amaia Ezpeldoi's clear politico-cultural identity is the use of the pronoun "we." She comments on the current Basque (cultural as well as literary) reality constantly and her prose is written for those who experience the Basque-speaking world very closely; it is prose for initiates, because its author Borda appears to believe in a left-wing Basque nationalist readership community.

What Is the Real Crime of These Police Novels?

Borda suggests that the real crimes against our society are not those that are discussed at length in the media, but other more silent crimes, linked to the idea of oppression, which media noise about these common crimes drowns out. In these politically charged novels, an anti-elite discourse prevails, systematically, leading the way to an inherent (subversive or conservative?) ideological ambiguity on the part of the detective genre, which inadvertently blends a hint of a leftist perspective with that of populism.

Yet one must acknowledge that this tendency is more pronounced in the first three novels in the cycle and that things are blurred and confused, from an ideological point of view, in the second part of the cycle, in which Ezpeldoi's character moves away from the ideas and the mental universe of the Basque nationalist left.

However, it seems to us that, if the hexalogy is taken as a whole, there is another crime that emerges in a more silent way that is at the heart of Borda's literary work, to the point of being the key to her whole literary oeuvre. The Dostoevskian dialectic—the feeling of guilt and the complex work of cleansing that guilt—about that more silent and more indeterminate crime is a component that gives cohesion and narrative tension to the adventures of Amaia Ezpeldoi. What, then, is that crime? The crime is an atypical crime that Amaia Ezpeldoi attributes to herself, under the pressure of the public eye, of course.

Amaia Ezpeldoi is a freak, as suggested in the previous section: physically, sexually, geographically, socially, and linguistically. She feels guilty about her monstrous nature; the superego embedded in her psyche by society is merciless toward her and constantly reminds her that she does not fit within the confines of the normal. The adventures she experiences and the investigations she carries out serve to fight her sense of guilt, above all else. The reason for the cyclothymic nature of the character, therefore, lies in this intimate struggle. Thus, we will see her make use of and develop different strategies throughout the cycle against that feeling of guilt. It is a huge, endless, and tiring struggle against the feeling of guilt, for it is truly a powerful enemy, and for that reason, from time to time we see Amaia Ezpeldoi worn out by her audacity and drowned in melancholy, having turned into a trembling kid and almost acknowledging the curse of her supposed abnormality. This desperate fatalism is, in all likelihood, the reason for choosing the surname Ezpeldoi—we should recall that, as an old song goes, in the fifteenth century at a place called Ezpeldoi in Zuberoa, the Beaumonts killed the Agramont knight Bereterretxe by tying him to a tree and probably torturing him, and the people of Ezpeldoi did nothing to help the martyr. Therefore, the Ezpeldoi patronym is a name imbued with a tragic connotation, and one used by Borda to underscore the victim-like quality of her character (as well as to denounce the impunity of crimes and the indifference of crime witnesses).

Amaia Ezpeldoi is a psychologically tortured character who is repeatedly judged by the public in the court of normalcy, as if her feeling of guilt were like carrying the stone of Sisyphus up a mountain, only for it to roll back down again and again. Her crime, that for which the court of normalcy judges her repeatedly, is being outside the norm (in other words, because she is a woman, a lesbian, proletarian, and her connection to the culture and language of the Northern Basque Country). Language is, of course, one of the areas in which the question of normalcy becomes most intense. Amaia Ezpeldoi denounces the exclusion she suffers from the center of the Basque world.

In that regard, it is noteworthy that the paradigm of that normality changed as the six novels in the cycle were published. At the outset, the imaginary court of normalcy—that which controls the castle of her mind—was the most common imperialist-capitalist French or Spanish world, yet as the cycle reached its conclusion the court of normalcy turned into something closer, because it was, precisely, the supposedly progressive left-wing Basque nationalist world. Nevertheless, although the ideological nature of the court changed, the basis and meaning of the struggle were the same, that is, a struggle against the dictatorship of normalcy, which Borda-Ezpeldoi conveys with great consistency from beginning to end.

Borda alleviates the pressure of her non-normalcy by demonstrating the grubbiness of the normal Basque world. Now we understand much better why she has chosen the police novel genre. The genre helps to shine a light on the hidden or camouflaged grubbiness of society, and there is no more appropriate objective for any writer than that. But let us not be deceived; the real criminal in these novels is neither the businessman nor the petty local tyrant, nor capitalist society either, but the very idea of normalcy. The dictatorship of normalcy may come from anywhere (and thanks to that, Ezpeldoi's denunciation is useful and potentially extendable to a universal level), even the periphery of the periphery. We are always someone's normalizers or someone's peripherals.

She seeks protection from this intolerance of inequality, as best she can, via fatalism. She would like to be normal, to break free of the condition of being indigenous, although it seems impossible; it seems like a curse.

The Aesthetics of Coming Out

What constitutes individual human identity? And, in passing, that of a group. That is the question at the heart of the novels. The answer Borda gives is complex. As much as identity itself. Amaia Ezpeldoi is an unsettled character, both as regards certain dimensions of her nature and her ideology, to the extent of destabilizing the reader. That, in truth, makes reading the hexalogy interesting. The real narrative suspense does not lie in the solving of the crime, but in the seismograph of the main character's identity. Indeed, we are dealing with the chronicle of a changing world—between 1994 and 2012—and, what is more, we discover this changing world through a changing gaze, because the narrator herself is also changing, both deeply and unexpectedly. Amaia Ezpeldoi comes out of various closets throughout the hexalogy, or this large closet, which is gradually opening, has many drawers. The shape of the series or cycle made up of many novels derives, it seems, from an internal need on the part of the author in this case, from the need to show little by little the integrity and truth of her character to the Basque readership, in a huge exercise in redemption. In this way, the defendant in the court of normalcy becomes, via these police novels, the judge and refuse collector of (overly) normal Basque society.

In Amaia Ezpeldoi's transformation from the beginning to the end of the hexalogy, we note that the items that make up her identity include some that are stable and others that have been altered or completely reversed.

The following items, those in the novels BÜA (Until They Leave Us in Peace) and BNM (Until I'm Alive), make up her identity at the outset:

A - Womanhood

B - Heterosexuality

C - Basqueness

D - Basque nationalism

E - Northern Basqueness

F - Rurality

G - Proletarianism

When we get to the end of the hexalogy we note that some of those items have changed, because the character is much more audacious in embracing her differences, or because her worldview has experienced an evolution. The following items have remained stable: womanhood, Basqueness, Northern Basqueness, and the proletarian identity. Those that have changed, however, are the following: rurality (she goes to cities), sexual orientation (the character has fully embraced her lesbianism), and political orientation (she seems to have abandoned her Basque nationalist nature).

Let us examine the first change.
The character herself summarizes her new situation or feelings of identity in a profuse sentence which encapsulates her most accurate self-definition on page 27 of UD (The Final Waste): she is "an out lesbian, embraced from now on, a Basque, without being a Basque nationalist."

However, we should add another change to these major transformations—that which has something to do with a change in her political orientation. In fact, alongside her author, Amaia Ezpeldoi proclaims her French culture—together with her Basqueness—at the conclusion of the hexalogy, the most obvious proof of which is the publication form of the last novel in the cycle. The novel *Ultimes déchets*, unlike the previous five (which were published in the

Southern Basque Country by the Susa publishing house and just in Basque), was published by the Maiatz publishing house in Baiona in 2012, in a bilingual edition. It only has a French-language title, with no equivalent in Basque. The method of publishing the novel (verso page in Basque and recto in French, so that both versions can be read side-by-side) parallels Amaia Ezpeldoi's French cultural coming out.

Nonetheless, Amaia Ezpeldoi is still Basque and, ultimately, a Basque nationalist as well, however much she may deny that. In other words, we can conclude that, when she is in the company of Basque nationalists, Amaia Ezpeldoi does not feel like a Basque nationalist, yet on the other hand, she continues to feel like a Basque nationalist when around those who do not understand (or do not want to understand) Basques, in her own idiosyncratic way. Despite being exasperated or annoyed with Basque nationalists, Amaia Ezpeldoi is still in love with the Basque Country (if only for the landscape).

The Two Sides of the Hexalogy
The novels can be divided between those of the 1990s (the first three) and those from 2000 onwards (the last three). As highlighted in the previous section, what separates the two periods is, essentially, the lack of an acknowledgment of lesbianism and the subsequent acknowledgment and all the identity changes that seem to bounce off from that—the urban turn, recognition of French culture, and a cooling attitude toward Basque nationalism. The use of the police novel mechanism does not change at all throughout the hexalogy (the mystery plot is stable and repetitive).

Yet at the same time, one can also note another kind of evolution by reading the six novels one after the other. This evolution has something to do with Amaia Ezpeldoi's self-confidence and level of self-esteem, with her overall existential state of mind. BUA (Until They Leave Us in Peace) is quite melancholic, like BNM (Until I'm Alive), because Ezpeldoi does not feel comfortable among people, but instead different and marginalized, and yearns to be integrated in Basque society. On the contrary, a sunnier, more positive period emerges in the third novel, which continues through to BB (Row, Row!). We view Amaia Ezpeldoi as more confident and increasingly proud of her identity in the three mid-cycle novels (that is, in APB [More than Heartbreak], JHP [Go Forth into Public], and BB [Row, Row!]). In the final novel, though, in the bilingual UD (The Final Waste), we once again come across the early mournful Amaia, imbued with major self-loathing or self-hatred.

Looking at this from the perspective of literature, in the 1990s novels—and especially in the first two—we are dealing with placid police novels without much narrative tension, as befits the stereotype of rurality. There are no striking or bloody acts in the early novels. If we look at the ideological dimension, the novels of the initial phase evince naïve optimism, and they are also heavily ironic with respect to socially and culturally reprehensible elites.

Turning now to the three post-2000 novels, the change is conspicuous. First of all, on the literary level. The use of conventions and stereotypes in noir fiction or police novels also changes—unlike the plot and narrative mechanisms—in this second phase, with the increased use of polar mainstream codes. Here, Borda reveals a willingness to refresh the storylines, with the aim of adapting to the new tastes of and desire to seduce the Basque-language readership. Basque narrative fiction had also improved and many writers had begun to produce and succeed in secondary level genres. As such, there are more murders from JHP (Go Forth into Public) onward, the urban setting predominates, police officers and forensic investigators appear in the plots, and as Borda's writing more closely approximates the hardboiled style, Amaia uses guns. The evolution of the character, and the novels, is perhaps connected to Itxaro Borda's changed status, because between those two dimensions of the cycle she won the Euskadi Prize (given to her for the novel *%100 basque* [100% Basque]), imbuing the writer, and by association her fictional alter ego, with some authority.

Ideologically, too, the change is salient. In the three works of the second period, the author does not avoid using the pronoun "we," but when it is used, it does not refer to the same thing or human being: there is mention of a lesbian group of friends (in other words, a much more reduced collective, quantitatively speaking, than that of the Basque nationalist left) or queer community (that is, a broad body which makes a different kind of social distinction). The nature of the implicit reader changes, then, once we enter into the second part of the hexalogy, in that it is no longer a young activist in the Basque nationalist left but, rather, a transnational/transcultural utopian in the queer community. At the start of the hexalogy, there is one character—tormented by loneliness—and compared to that person, the minority but dynamic Basque world appears rich and appealing. In the second phase, however, the Basque world seems solitary and broken, and Amaia in contrast becomes the center of a group of friends.

In the well-known essay *Gender Trouble* (1990), which Itxaro Borda would have read, Judith Butler defends the subversive value of specific parody, from an activist point of view. It could be said that Borda uses the character Ezpeldoi—in the second phase of the cycle—to make a lesbian parody of gender, overacting homosexual identity, showing it exuberantly. On the contrary, one could argue, and herein Itxaro Borda is completely original and pioneering, that in the first three novels of the hexalogy, she tries to legitimize Northern Basqueness by applying the same strategy so that it can have its place at the center of the Basque cultural system, with the same level of dignity and respect for other Basque identities. In other words, she exaggerates the stigmatized features of Northern Basqueness—its Basque dialect, of course, but not just that—in a parodic way, turning the display into a performative provocation. By means of parodic theatricalization, what was once humiliating becomes a source of pride.

References

Apalategi, Ur. "Iparraldeko azken aldiko literatura euskal literatur sistemaren argitan (eta vice versa). Zenbait hipotesi." *Lapurdum* X, Centre de recherche sur la langue et textes basques IKER (CNRS), 2005, 1–19.

Atutxa, Ibai. *Tatxatuaren azpiko nazioaz*. Utriusque Vasconiae, 2010.

Borda, Itxaro. "Autojustifikazio erreza." *Hegats* 4, EIE, June 1991, 229–238. (Text of a talk given in some November 1990 meetings in Donostian).

———. *Bakean ützi arte* (Until They Leave Us in Peace), Susa, 1994.

———. *Bizi nizano munduan* (Until I'm Alive), Susa, 1996.

———. *Amorezko pena baño* (More than Heartbreak), Susa, 1996.

———. *Jalgi hadi plazara* (Go Forth into Public), Susa, 2007.

———. *Boga boga* (Row, Row!), Susa, 2012.

———. *Ultimes déchets* (The Final Waste), Maiatz, 2015.

Butler, Judith. *Gender Trouble*. French edition: *Trouble dans le genre*, Paris, La Découverte, 2006).

Egaña, Ibon, coord. *Desira desordenatuak*. Utriusque Vasconiae, 2010.

Evan-Zohar, Itamar. "Polysystem studies." *Poetics Today*, vol.11, no.1 (1990). Monographic issue.

Gabilondo, Joseba. *Before Babel*. Barbaroak, 2016.

———. "Erbeste amatiarretik utopia pertsonalera: emakumezko idazleen politika kulturala." *Nazioaren hondarrak* (1998), 243–252.

———. "Itxaro Borda: migrantzia melankolikoa eta ni lesbiar nazional baten idazketa." *Nazioaren hondarrak* (2000), 253–277.

Interviews

"Euskal lurraldetasunaz bost eleerritako lehen urratsa da." Argia, May 29, 1994, 56–57.

"Barnekaldeko herrietan bizia bada, komunikabideetan agertu ez arren." Argia, Apr. 14, 1996, 22–26.

"Iragana mitifikatzea gure jaidura nagusietarik bat da." Argia, Jul. 29, 2012.

"Euskal munduak euskaraz guti irakurtzen du." Berria, Dec. 30, 2015.

Notes

1. "Euskal lurraldetasunaz bost eleberritako lehen urratsa da," in *Argia*, May 29, 1994, 56–57.
2. From now on, each time a passage from one of these novels is cited, the initials of the book title will be used in order to expedite the reading. Thus, respectively, *Bakean ützi arte* (Until They Leave Us in Peace) will become BUA, *Bizi nizano munduan* BNM (Until I'm Alive), *Amorezko pena baño* APB (More than Heartbreak), *Jalgi hadi plazara* JHP (Go Forth into Public), *Boga boga* BB and *Ultimes déchets* UD.
3. Ur Apalategi, "Iparraldeko azken aldiko literatura euskal literatur sistemaren argitan (eta vice versa). Zenbait hipotesi," in *Lapurdum* X, Baiona, IKER, 2005, 1–19.
4. The novel *Boga boga*, for example, denounces ETA for at one time fascinating, intimidating and symbolically raping Northern Basque society. Among other things, Borda denounces the existence of a network of local Basque brides, termed the "soldiers' fiancées," for male ETA members who took shelter in the Northern Basque Country in the 1980s.
5. See the works of Mikhail Bakhtin, especially those on François Rabelais and the Middle Ages as well as the popular culture of the Renaissance.
6. "I don't want to pontificate, I don't want to talk about our situation as an expert or a great writer. I think I'm closely tied into the Northern Basque tradition, because a lot of tragic themes have been mentioned ironically or jokingly. What's more, due to the difficult situation, we need to move forward in a positive way so that we can overcome the sadness" (*Argia*, 04/05/2007).
7. In the French-language version of the work that Borda adapted herself, she is even harsher, cruder: "*je suis un tas de merde ambulant*" ("I'm a walking pile of shit").

Chapter 5

Constructing Harkaitz Cano's Literary Universe: The Influence of the United States

Aiora Sampedro Alegria

The Police Novel

It is well-known that the roots of this literary subgenre are normally traced back to Edgar Allan Poe's Detective Dupin trilogy and Arthur Conan Doyle's romantic writings and that a few decades later, around the mid-twentieth century, it reached its zenith with the essays of Agatha Christie and Dorothy Sayers. All of those works in English would intrinsically involve a detective who would lead an investigation into a crime. For that reason, generally speaking, the investigator would solve a puzzle by means of clues left by the criminal and reasoning. At the same time, in their denoument, all of the works coincide in that, through the work of the investigator, the balance at the beginning of the story would be restored.

Together with the emergence of the police novel, the creation of the anti-police novel is also often mentioned; as is understood, it was created as a distortion of the former. In fact, as the name implies, critics would consider texts constructed in contrast to the typical structure of the original genre as anti-police texts. As we will attempt to explain below, Harkaitz Cano's novels *Beluna jazz* (hereafter BJ) and *Pasaia blues* (PB) will be of use when it comes to trying to describe the similarities and differences in those categories. Moreover, the connection of the two novels with the United States and its art will be essential to do so.

Harkaitz Cano's Places

Born in Lasarte, Harkaitz Cano (Lasarte-Oria, 1975) moved to Donostia when he was young and has lived there ever since.

He studied law but is a writer and translator. He does not just work in literature, but also as a scriptwriter for television and radio, as well as collaborating with several newspapers. Cano began publishing his work when he was very young: he published his first written work, a collection of poems titled *Kea behelainopean bezala* (Like Smoke in Low Mist, 1994), when he was nineteen and, at the same time, in 1993, it was reported in the journal *Susa* that he was a member of the Lubaki Banda literary group. From that moment on he set out to be a writer.

Following his first publication, he brought out some works made up of several genres; for example, *Pauloven txakurrak* (Pavlov's Dogs, published originally in 1994) and *Radiobiografiak* (Radiobiographies, 1995). Following these, he released his first novel: *Beluna jazz* (1996). Later, Cano also published another four novels: *Pasaia blues* in 1999; *Belarraren ahoa* in 2004 (in English, *Blade of Light*, 2010), winner of the Euskadi Prize; *Twist: izaki intermitenteak* in 2012 (in English, *Twist*, 2018), winner of the Euskadi Prize and the Spanish Critics' Prize; and *Fakirraren ahotsa* (The Fakir's Voice) in 2018. He also published more poetry: *Norbait dabil sute eskaileran* (Someone on the Fire Escape) (2001), *Dardaren interpretazioa* (The Interpretation of Tremors, 2003) and *Malgu da gaua* (The Night is Flexible) (2014). Besides poetry books and novels, two books which are considered the highpoint of his storytelling are worth mentioning: *Telefono kaiolatua* (The Caged Telephone, 1997) and *Neguko zirkua* (The Winter Circus, 2005), as well as *Bizkarrean tatuaturiko mapak* (The Maps Tattooed on the Back, 1998), *Hipotesiak gordinkeriaz* (On the Vulgarity of Hypotheses, 2007), and *Beti oporretan* (Always on Holiday, 2015).

Otherwise, he has also worked on less developed genres: the graphic novel *Piztia otzanak* (The Tamed Beasts, 2008), the chronicle *Piano gainean gosaltzen* (Having Breakfast on the Piano, 2000) and the essays *Zinea eta literatura. Begiaren ajeak* (Film and Literature: The Eyes' Defect, 2008), and *Txalorik ez, arren* (No Applause, Though, 2014). In the meantime, he also tried his hand at children's and young adult literature: *Sorgin moderno bat / A Modern Witch*

(2002), *Itsasoa etxe barruan* (The Sea inside the House, 2003), *Omar dendaria* (Omar the Shopkeeper, 2005), *Lesterren logika* (Lester's Logic, 2006).

Finally, it is noteworthy that the projects carried out in collaboration with various plastic artists, musicians, and dancers are an indicator of his tendency to mix different disciplines. His books can be read in Dutch, Galician, Greek, English, Spanish, Russian, German, and Italian.

In his early poetic works, Cano followed avant-garde literature. We can see that *Radiobiografiak*, a collection prepared for the radio show "Goizean Behin" (Once a Morning), repeated a tendency toward fantasy, perhaps in honor of the magic realism of the earlier generation of Basque short story authors; in which the rupture of time planes, the appearance of fantasy elements, and so on, were striking. Even in his first published book of poems, *Kea behelainopean bezala* (Like Smoke in Low Mist), the writer appeared to be the heir to the generation of Basque literature in the 1980s, borrowing references and literary trends: Rimbaud, Artaud, and so forth.

In the works that would follow, a change of style could be perceived. Thus, we can see interspersed in *Telefono kaiolatua* (The Caged Telephone) some features of the American literary style: minimalism, depressing environments, marginalized characters, and the like.

Having acknowledged all of this, we would like to examine BJ (1996) and the subsequent PB (1999), above all, together with *Piano gainean gosaltzen* (Having Breakfast on the Piano, 2000) from his time in New York, *Norbait dabil sute eskaileran* (Someone on the Fire Escape, 2001), and even *Belarraren ahoa* (*Blade of Light*, 2004), which will be situated in the beginnings of the aforementioned transition.

Compared to the previous works, spaces would take on a special significance in BJ (1996). This was because it was the first time in the writer's career that an entire work would be set in one specific place and, in order to do so, he would use a real space: the United States. We could say the same about what can be considered a continuation of the former, namely about PB (1999), although now changing subject matter and style, because the setting also changes to the Basque Country.

BJ would be the first novel in Harkaitz Cano's literary career that was set in the United States and, as a result, also the first appearance of a police novel in the United States. It was published in 1996 and two years later, in 1998, he spent a year in New York City. Even though the whole story is not set in the United States, many characters and passages are located, among other places

(Paris, Rotterdam . . .), in New York. The novel recounts the mental breakdown of Bob Ieregui, an American trumpeter of Basque origin, beginning with the first signs of madness and telling his story through to his ending up in a psychiatric facility. BJ is considered to be a tribute to the main cultural contributions of the United States in the twentieth century: film and music, the surrealist touch in narrative fiction, film noir, and jazz music styles are combined to construct the narrative.

As noted, Harkaitz Cano's literature reveals a significant fascination with the United States and the influence of dirty realism that has bound his work to the United States can be seen even in his first books. In particular, discussions of his work (Esparza 2017) mention the influence of Raymond Carver, Charles Bukowski, and Paul Auster. In BJ, this presence would be decisive for the first time. As the title declares, this is a novel built on the rhythm of jazz music: each chapter is constructed around the verse of a jazz song and is structured by sewing together long sentences written to the rhythm of the slowest beats.

Cano himself has clarified on several occasions that the novel is constructed in the form of a jazz concert (see Egaña Etxeberria 2019): a constant foundation (Bob Ieregui's life), and variations on that (sub-plots, parallel narratives, the oneiric world . . .). As in jazz, narrative sections and motifs are repeated, always in a variation, a detail, a nuance added to the characterization of a figure or the thread of the story. In order to join the passages together, interspersing jazz lyrics is also a strategy used throughout the work; to the story that is told by playing a kind of game of mirrors. Once he gets to the music, it is worth noting that Cano chooses an American musical genre created in depressed areas of the large southwestern cities in which to set the novel. The nature of the story is characterized by playing a game of mirrors in the storyline with music. The abovementioned rhythm of the narrative is compared constantly to songs and the rhetorical resources inserted by the writer here and there bring the writing of the work closer to jazz music: chaotic confusions of images intended to slow down the tempo of the sentence repetitions and, when necessary, to achieve a faster speed.

In truth, Cano has pursued a fascination with film noir throughout his writing; in the essay *Zinea eta Literatura: begiaren ajeak* (Film and Literature: The Eyes' Defects), among other things, he admitted liking noir style filmmakers: pointing out Hitchcock, Billy Wilder, and Orson Welles. At the beginning of BJ too, Cano pays tribute to the images, conventions and myths created around police films and film noir (Aldekoa 2008: 417). Dark surroundings and appearances by marginalized human groups inevitably frame the opening pages. The dreamlike setting in which the events of this example take place is sometimes reminiscent of the sublime atmosphere of film noir (Aldekoa 2008: 11):

> Movement and stillness. The cosmos represented two things in this living room: an old record player constantly spinning a record on the one hand, and, on the other, this tiny lead owl that was on the floor next to the record player. As for the rest, this yellow-walled and narrow high ceilinged living room was almost empty. In the window, a Gothic cathedral, a pair of wet suede shoes and a diamond-shaped wire bridge were in view. The shoes had been placed in the window to dry out. The lifting bridge and the cathedral also looked for all the world like they had been hung out to dry, there in the window. A penetrating melody, like the smell of black bitumen, could be noted from almost any corner, making the gleam of the street cobblestones audible.
>
> And when it had just rained, the streets of that city smelled of rotten fish, perhaps because the wet parallel beams of the railway tracks seemed to have been made of broken wooden boxes from the fishmongers.

It is well-known that the noir genre was created in close connection to the socio-political atmosphere in the United States, in the aftermath of the World War I (1914–1918) and the Great Depression (1929–1939), and hence that crime, violence, political corruption, a lack of public safety, and so on are reflected in American film and literature.

In this variant of the English-language police novel created by the pen of Raymond Chandler and others, the narrator delves into the psychology of the characters in order to know and reflect on the motivation for the crime. That way, rather than shedding light on the crime in comparison to the detective novel, the goal is to understand the crime. For that reason, the boundary between good and evil is often blurred in these works, humanizing the criminal and bringing to light the darkest aspects of the detective.

The principal feature that distinguishes them from detective novels lies in the origin of evil. We know that the motive or reason for crimes is always some human weakness: anger, a yearning for power, jealousy, hatred, desire, lust, and so on. BJ has a significant connection to the noir genre in this way; in fact, the characters will come to resemble the representative criminals and perpetrators of crimes in those noir films, with the narrator delving into their psychology. For example, the character of Klara Miao, who fulfils all the criteria of the novel's femme fatale, is linked to a murder that will take place in the opening pages. Furthermore, the principal example of humanizing a marginalized figure is the trumpet player Bob Ieregui. As well as breaking the time planes, the narrator who delves into the characters' psychology reveals to the reader a kind of collage of completely different images that come together in the psychology of the characters. Thus, in light of everything examined, we consider it more accurate to place this work within the traditional noir fiction category.

From BJ to PB there is a noticeable stylistic and thematic shift. In order to do this, the author's active position and outside influence are significant; in other words, the demands of his readers: in 2006, through the Basque Summer University, Edu Zelaieta and Ibon Egaña, both teachers at the University of the Basque Country, published a collection of essays that addressed the links between the Basque conflict and Basque literature. Cano mentions works created about the topic of the conflict in the text he prepared for the collection and therein, he explains why he made the leap from his first to his second novel:

> [As regards texts prior to *Twist*] Readers approach the writer; writers can tell them to go to hell, of course—Get away from me, get lost!—but readers will tell him or her "you're the one getting lost." Write about us. Write now. Write here, they will tell him or her. (Cano 2006: 37)

Thus, the transition from a location to the other reflects a kind of relationship with the work that the writer feels encouraged to offer to her or his readers. In this text, Cano confesses that the texts the writer creates are in a constant dialogue with readers and to illustrate that, he goes into detail about his personal experience. That dimension will be a window onto his literary work, by recounting the personal relationships he has with proximate artists. That way, alongside the setting, the writing style also changes, because the noir of the previous work is not valid in the Basque Country and the result is a more classic detective novel.

Three years after publishing the earlier noir novel, PB was released. Yet looking at the origins of the characters, we may consider this a police novel, in which there is an exchange of hunters and the hunted, more than a noir novel. Set in the Basque coastal town from which the novel takes its name, this work, which more approximates a detective novel, narrates the surveillance activity between two ETA members and the Ertzaintza (Basque police force). In fact, unlike BJ, beyond aesthetic elements, the story is based on the dispute between detectives and criminals that are watching each other. The storyline is divided into two planes, one about ETA members living clandestinely in an empty flat and the other about the vicissitudes of the Basque police officer Cesar Telleria, who is observing them. Both planes are intertwined when the two protagonists on one side find out about an infiltrator; whose identity will not be known and which will lead to growing mistrust between the two. As the plot thickens, it is revealed that the person who may have been the infiltrator at the beginning is the wrongly suspected member, shifting the focus from the traitor onto another character. In this plot complication, the watchers will unwittingly turn into the watched and the watched become watchers in the story.

The passages begin diverging on two separate planes in the opening pages: after appearing initially, Cesar Telleria is following someone; then the second plane emerges, namely that of the town of Pasaia Antxo. There, dialogues occur between Olatz and Marta, two ETA members in hiding in a safe house; the empty flat plane views the protagonist Cesar Telleria in antagonistic terms; while the protagonist walks around freely all the time here and there (he is on a work trip on the trail of a character unknown to the reader), the cell is dormant, when the activists are in a limited space. As the storyline progresses, so the relationship between the main and secondary characters that will appear later is structured in a multi-directional network.

Another aspect of the fiction is based on the couples. They go from being a symbolically objective mirror to constituting a narrative game. The opposition between the police officer Cesar and the infiltrator Veronica is the basis of the opposition between the ETA members Marta and Olatz; in both cases, one of the characters assumes the identity of their partner. Such character evolutions are reminiscent, as the writer has noted on several occasions, of Ingmar Bergman's film *Persona*.

Telleria's transformation is linked to deliriums, to another dimension. As in BJ, here too the characters' relationship to the oneiric dimension is marked by uncertainty, leading ultimately to psychotic references. The text acknowledges a wide horizon of expectations on the part of the reader as a result, because more than one level of interpretation is facilitated.

The protagonist's deliriums affect the reader's uncertainty about the literary world. This is what the author brings about through several narrative strategies; the most significant of which may be the appearance of paradox: paradoxical events drive life as well as the goings on of the characters in the novel. Indeed, this is the case because the fine line between madness and mental clarity is called into question in mid-plot.

Meanwhile, the reversals of time and space increase doubts on the part of the reader about the events narrated. The writer deftly leads the reader into dead-end twists. The novel operates in the form of paths that follow multiple and parallel times. The narrator builds a horizon of possibilities in which the past and present real and possible events of the characters intersect, thus combining different spaces at the same time:

> In a few weeks, the building societies would send many letters and the honey would turn out to be more bitter for them. In the meantime, those in love would complain about the postal service in the coming days because they did not receive letters from each other, because the bits and pieces that reached the corresponding address were said to be very sticky and contagious, and several letters of complaint would appear in the newspapers asking whether postmen washed their hands. Perhaps it was only a hypothesis, [. . .]. And close the parenthesis, and light a cigarette. (2008: 44)

We can also situate predictions between prolepsis and analepsis. In PB, those first words beyond the street echo that surrounds the protagonist are transformed into a basic feature of the plot: "open up your hands sir, I'll *predict* your future" (2013: 11).

Returning to that the theme of the characters, in contending that they are mirror-characters, it symbolizes the fact that they are also readers to each other. One can therefore conclude that readers may also be characters in a novel. That is possible, because the mirror characters are the same in different dimensions and, therefore, they become each other's illusions.

> [Cesar] He was behaving like a schizophrenic. He was recalling the dark times of old and after thinking about it three or four times, he went into a pharmacy. He did not have a prescription, but it didn't matter, they pulled out the shelf and didn't give him any problems. Later, that was a strong drug. [. . .] He picked up the phone and called one of those prostitutes in the newspaper. He needed to fuck. [. . .].

> He thought he could make out something like a fight on the other side of the door. Two women were shouting. It wasn't a good sign.

> Schizophrenia again. When he opened the door, someone closed the door to the ground floor. But Telleria did not notice that. The thing is, in front of him, instead of the prostitute he had ordered, a woman called Veronica showed up, or that's what he thought, because it could also have been just the effect of the drug, even if a physiognomist like him found it quite easy to confuse drugs. Whether it was Veronica or not, that was the best fuck of his life.
>
> The next morning, when he woke up, the chaos in the room was more disgusting and unbearable than ever [...]. But had someone really been in his home? Wasn't it all just the feverish consequence of his sick disturbing imagination? (2013: 182)

In the chapter titled "Shot," the network unfolds, revealing the hunter to be the hunted and the hunted as the hunter. The observer is informed that, right from the beginning of the story, he has been the observed, because it is really Veronica who has decided that he is an ETA member and reveals that Cesar Telleria was masquerading as a police officer. Thus, the story becomes a tragedy. The observer police officer depicted as the observed is killed and the ETA members, masquerading as observers, escape. Likewise, after plotting the whole scheme, Veronica flees.

In this second novel, although the writer has stated that he is coming to the Basque Country, precisely in light of the preceding paragraphs, one must also mention the United States; specifically, Paul Auster and his *New York Trilogy*. Readers will find three stories in the *The New York Trilogy*, published between 1985 and 1986 in an anthology: *City of Glass* (1985), *Ghosts* (1986), and *The Locked Room* (1986).

In the first story, titled *City of Glass*, a writer slips into a complex web of madness following a phone call. The presence of some ghosts will catch the detective in the strangest case of his career.

Some of the keys to Auster's literary production—chance, the nature of will, and a special way of understanding suspense—appear in this collection of stories (Gómez Vallecillo 2011). Taking into account the narrative analysis we have just seen in *PB*, it seems inevitable to make a connection between the literary suggestions of Cano and those of Auster.

Conclusions

As we have seen, the presence of the United States makes a difference in Harkaitz Cano's writings and, whether to a greater or lesser extent, in the novels discussed here too.

At the same time, one cannot overlook the link between setting and artistic environment, because the police novel appears together with the United States in Cano's writings. Moreover, it is worth noting that the novel's setting conditions the subgenre of each work: one can understand the text set in New York as a kind of tribute to the artistic atmosphere of the United States and, as a result, it is closer to noir fiction. In PB, however, that atmosphere no longer works, and thus, it takes the shape of a detective novel that is closer to the Basque conflict.

In truth, the two works under discussion here could both be situated within the police novel genre, as noted, because their features are displayed by means of some shared strategies in both works; murders and police investigations that take place in the first chapter and that are not resolved until the last emphasize a police procedural air in both cases. In contrast, we also see anti-police novel features. Therein, the plot influences the protagonist (Holquist 1971) and, typically, three kinds of plots can be differentiated: the detective that becomes a victim, the detective who goes on to become a criminal and the detective who is forced to leave the question unanswered (Tani in Pardo García 2007: 251). We can locate Cano's works within this classification, especially in the third section. Both the case of BJ and the end of PB show the reader that the whole plot has been built around a crime that did not happen. In the first case, Bob Ieregui, who tries to solve the crime, sees that no crime ever took place. In the second, the police officer Cesar Telleria finds out that the criminal he is watching is watching him, so the detective becomes a victim and directly annuls the crime that Telleria is investigating. Moreover, an unexpected criminal appears: Veronica. Put another way, in traditional police novels (whether detective or noir), the writer normally creates a puzzle and offers it to the police character in the novel so that this character, following certain clues, can put the mosaic together. The detective's work is usually straightforward: catch the criminal; in which the perpetrator, through the clues offered and through the character's exceptional intelligence, is usually found out at the end of the novel. The reader typically follows the detective's same steps. That being the case, in light of the narrative strategies we have seen, we may consider the two works by Cano, in a closed sense, as anti-police rather than police novels; each in its own style, BJ as noir, PB as a detective novel.

Along the same lines, Fernando Lázaro Carreter (1990: 131) underscores the fact that the goal of a literary work is to construct a fictitious reality; that is, instead of reproducing a genuine world, it creates an intrinsically artistic world. If one acknowledges this, in these two works, the first chapters naturally connect to the last passages in the story. Thus, that reflection which the reader will see in the opening pages would be a summary of the writer's worldview. That means that Harkaitz Cano makes use of a chaotic reality to create an intrinsic world, based on random events and repetition. The construction of Cano's literary universe, in general, is carried out through connecting those two previous features. Events are linked to each other in a row of constant repetitions and with that, reality becomes an exaggeration for the character. It escapes the character's understanding and multiplies the horizon of possible choices. In most cases, therefore, the effect of coincidence disappears, and the characters fall into making a leaden effort to understand reality; endlessly trying to interpret what is happening all around them.

Additionally, these two works share another point: a tangled plot. Cano gives the reader the key to interpret his literary texts at the beginning of the novels: giving unreliability to what the narrator is telling from the beginning. The author has found another place in the book for the passage corresponding to the last part of the plot; it lies at this final point, the connection of these narratives; the mistrust of explaining any reality, in fact.

References

Works by Harkaitz Cano
Cano, Harkaitz (1996): Beluna jazz. [Updated edition in 2008] Susa: Zarautz.
Cano, Harkaitz (1999): Pasaia blues. [Updated edition in 2013] Susa: Zarautz.

Cited bibliography
Aldekoa, Iñaki (2008): *Euskal literaturaren historia*. San Sebastian: Erein.
Cano, Harkaitz. (2006): "Mina eta artifizioa," in Zelaieta, Edu & Egaña Etxeberria, Ibon. *Maldetan sagarrak*. UEU: Bilbao.
Egaña Etxeberria, Ibon (2019): "*Beluna jazz (1996)*. Harkaitz Cano." In *Auñamendi Entziklopedia* [online], Retrieved March 4, 2019 from http://aunamendi.eusko-ikaskuntza.eus/eu/beluna-jazz-1996-harkaitz-cano/ar-154513/.
Esparza Martin, Iratxe (2017): *Identitatearen eraldatzea XXI. Mendeko euskal narratiban: subjektu literario posmodernoa. Transformación de la identidad en la narrativa vasca del siglo XXI: el sujeto literario posmoderno*. UPV/EHU: Bilbao. (Doctoral dissertation).
Gómez Vallecillo, Ana Isabel (2011): *Paul Auster. El narrador en la oscuridad. Estudio narratológico de sus novelas 1982-1992. Motivos e imágenes*. Catholic University of Avila: Avila. (Doctoral dissertation).
Holquist, Michael (1971): "Whodunit and Other Questions: Metaphysical Detectives Stories in Post-War Fiction," in *New Literary History* (3).
Lázaro Carreter, Fernando (1990): *De poética y poéticas*. Cátedra: Madrid.
Pardo García, Pedro Javier (2007): "El relato antipolicial en la literatura y el cine: *Memento*,

de Christopher Nolan," in Alex Martín Escribà, and Javier Sánchez Zapatero (Coord.): *Informe confidencial: la figura del detective en el género negro*. Difácil: Valladolid.

Urkiza, Ana (2001): "Ihesean," in *Euskaldunon Egunkaria*. 06/09/2001. Retrieved March 23, 2019 from https://kritikak.armiarma.eus/?p=248.

Chapter 6

Taking the Genre to the Limit: On Jon Alonso's Novel *Zintzoen saldoan* (In the Group of the Righteous)

Javier Rojo Cobos

Jon Alonso's relationship with noir and police fiction is quite unusual. First, he is clearly very familiar with the keys to the genre and its whys and wherefores, as he has demonstrated visibly in the essay *Beltzaren koloreak* (The Colours of Noir) (Alonso 2016). Like some previous writers (beginning with Chandler—1995a and 1995b in the Spanish-language version I have used—who, together with Hammett (cf. Galán Herrera 2008), as well as creating fiction, also wrote some interesting notes about the genre), he has reflected on this literary genre. Indeed, the ideas which appear in his text in the form of an essay can be used as a compliment to the literature that the writer has created. Moreover, in his literary career, he has created writings that can be placed within the parameters of noir fiction. But here one must bear in mind that he has not limited himself to rewriting the clichéd components shown in such literature. He has gone further: insofar as he uses the genre, when he uses the keys and clichés that appear therein, he takes them to the limits, seeking to offer something else. The reader must be aware of that something else, because it is unequivocally important.

In this chapter, one of Jon Alonso's novels will be taken as an example, in order to see how the literary genre is adapted and transformsed in the writer's hands, how he plays with clichés, using, reinforcing, and destroying the reader's prejudices. The work which will be used as an example is titled *Zintzoen saldoan* (In the Group of the Righteous), published in 2012.

At first glance, the plot told in this book has all the ingredients to place it within the field of noir fiction. The story developed in the work can be described in summarized form thus:

Following a series of ups and downs in his life, the protagonist, Enekoitz Ramirez, steals from restaurants. That is his profession, so to speak. One night, after having dinner at the restaurant of the celebrated chef Kepa Pedrotegi, the chef shows up dead and suspicion falls on Enekoitz Ramirez. Seeking to prove his innocence, he begins his own investigation in order to find out who the real killer is. The investigation will be full of mistakes and complications and, as usual in this genre, next to him cannot be missing the presence of a woman, who seems to be a femme fatale, who helps him (Weinrichter 2005).

In the storyline, then, there are basic ingredients for the novel to be noir, because on the one hand there is a crime, in this case a murder, and on the other, the appearance of a special character that must carry out an investigation into this, as the genre demands. What is more, when the plot has as its background famous chefs, in some way it could bring to mind a film which premiered in 1978 that also imitated stories and used the pivots of comedy as they appeared in Agatha Christie's literature: *Who is Killing the Great Chefs of Europe?*

Among all of the ingredients that a noir novel must contain, an investigator who must solve the crime on the basis of different reasons is central, and that happens in Jon Alonso's novel too.

As noted, this character is called Enekoitz Ramirez, and besides fulfilling the role of investigator and protagonist, he also plays that of the narrator. In his discourse, often imitating the style of traditional novels, the first-person resource becomes an appropriate tool with which to give not only facts but also opinions on various topics, in such a way that it sometimes seems to function as an alter ego of the writer himself.

As presented in the story, the protagonist is not a professional investigator. Unlike in other Basque noir novels, the protagonist is reluctantly obliged to become the investigator by chance, if he is to prove his innocence. It has often been mentioned: in noir and police novels written in Basque, it is very rare to come across investigators that can be placed in the professional group, because these, with the exception of officials, are viewed with mistrust in our literature. When the noir genre is used in Basque novels, amateur sleuths are chosen, yet that does not mean that sometimes the professionals have better resources and skills at their disposal, because it is surprising how unintentionally, too, the amateur sleuths who are involved in such a complex investigation can carry it out without any technical preparation.

Turning to the nature of the protagonist, it is evident that the character that plays the investigator is a disillusioned romantic who wants to show that, at root, he is a cynic. He has a troubled past and although at one time he was willing to fight for romanticism or the like, with the passage of time he is only concerned with his own self-interest. Whatever the case, he retains traces of romanticism that are often reflected in personal ethics. These kinds of characters with problematic pasts can call to mind, for example, someone like Pepe Carvalho, the investigator created out of Vázquez Montalbán's imagination, whose past was almost bizarre (a communist and ex-CIA collaborator). Enekoitz Ramirez likewise has a mixed-up past, sometimes mysterious, insofar as he reveals that past in dribs and drabs, and in that past components that seem quite unlikely to come together, because after being a former ETA member and prisoner, he worked in the art market and ended up stealing from luxury restaurants.

One must also take into account the character's opinion. In traditional noir fiction, romanticism and cynical disillusionment combined in the character, following the canon. Just as Alonso, likewise, consciously uses components of the canon, here too, there are those kinds of features: one can almost say that he is a romantic turned cynic by reality, although he does make a special effort to hide the romantic component. Cynicism, on the other hand, gives him a kind of ethical supremacy, and, that being the case, whilst he plays the role of amateur sleuth, it seems like he wants to show that he is better than other people, ethically at least, as if he were the only one who understands how reality really works. Because he moves in a mysterious kind of world, and whilst no one else knows what hidden threads exist behind reality, he is capable of discovering this hidden reality. This ethical superiority sometimes leads to contempt for people who do not understand the world as he does.

To summarize the main thread of the story, it has been stated that the character is forced to investigate in order to show his innocence, but the matter is more perplexing: the characters who force him to investigate (those who represent power, those identified with the law and the police) know that he is innocent. Yet they use him to drive the investigation. And here the reader comes across the material incentive behind the events: if he has no experience in such investigations, why do they choose someone like him to find out who the murderer is? Ultimately, if what they find does not clarify what happened, why do they launch the investigation?

Of course: first of all, one must have an investigation if what is stated in the novel is to be carried out. Yet this incentive, not being part of the plot, must be placed in the discourse. If there is no investigation, then there is no novel titled *Zintzoen saldoan* (In the Group of the Righteous).

But as well as this discursive necessity, there are two other concepts that we need to consider, which are related to Aristotle's poetics: credibility and coherence.

Stories which usually unfold in noir fiction tend to be located within realistic parameters, but in order to understand the nature of realism, three pillars must be taken into account: in fact, what the writer offers, when influenced by a both a reference outside the discourse and the reader's expectation, creates credibility out of the interaction between them.

Andrea Camilleri's words in the notes at the end of his *La muerte de Amalia Sacerdote* (The Death of Amalia Sacerdote, 2013, 201–202; in Italian, *La rizzagliata*) can be of use in clarifying this matter, especially as regards two of those three pillars. Camilleri equates his text to a historical novel, with the difference that the plot is related to a contemporary story. As a historical novel, some components are taken from reality, while others are the result of the author's imagination. In this specific case, those taken from reality were the main events in a well-known crime in Italy. Everything else is the result of the writer's imagination. The following paragraph may be a little long, but it is very illustrative:

> What, then, are the elements of my invention? [...] everything else. [...] I have never set foot in a RAI editorial office, [...] and, therefore, I have never known how an editorial office worked from the inside. [...] Just as neither have I ever attended a meeting of the Regional Assembly. [...] I am totally removed from the banking world [...]. I have the same crass ignorance when it comes to the legal offices of the different prosecutors, investigating judges and the rest: I only know what the newspapers write about them. [...] Amongst all those who understand something of which I have just spoken, many will find obvious incongruences with regard to the reality. (Camilleri 2013, 202)

As the writer admits, he knows nothing about the inner workings of those institutions and enterprises. In the novel, this inner working is an indispensable component of the plot. Naturally, those who know something of the institutions mentioned will immediately find that there are several errors in the story told by the writer. What the writer has offered and the outside reference, then, do not coincide. But what happens with this if the third component (the reader) is inserted in between? To the extent that the reader does not know this outside reference, the story will seem totally credible to them, insofar as the writer has connected the components presented coherently. Indeed, from the point of view of these readers, credibility in such literature does not come from the connection between the subject matter and reality, but from the connection between the components explained by the writer, that is, the internal coherence. Specifically, this is the same thing that was said about credibility and truth in Aristotelean poetics. Thus, by way of a conclusion, it can be deduced that the appearance of the credibility generated by such literature stems in large part from the reader's ignorance: many readers find plots set in Los Angeles much more believable than those set in (for example) Gasteiz, in this case, the closer they are to the more well-known and the much stronger their knowledge of the reference, readers regard events that seem possible in Los Angeles as impossible in Gasteiz.

In that matter of credibility, the nature of the protagonist is also important, along the lines of what Alonso states too in *Beltzaren koloreak* (The Colours of Noir, 2016). In this essay, when explaining noir fiction models that can be read in Basque, he places the image of the investigator front and center and explains how a figure like that fits into European literature. In fact, this genre of novel, which is by nature and origin from another place and another time, demonstrates weaknesses in terms of believability, along the lines explained in the chapter Alonso titles "The Age of Social Democratic Police" (2016: 71–95). In European novels, the person who seeks to solve a crime is not now an investigator who mistrusts police forces, but a likeable character from within the police itself who seeks to solve the crime against all odds, and a person like that is not credible at all. Here, it approximates the classic Basque literary model. Delving deeper into the argument, Jon Alonso's perspective moves away from literature and focuses more on ideological approaches, in which the image of the pleasant democratic police is implausible to him. Credibility has its weaknesses, rooted in ideology, when a professional investigator (in regard to proximity, whose references are therefore well known) is used. As a consequence, if an amateur sleuth is preferred, while that implies a special reading pact in which understanding the novel in a realist way and the link with reality are in some way suspended, the material incentive for the events is somewhat lost.

By delving deeper into this idea, because the credibility weakness is related to ideology, one can see how sometimes the discourse of the novel seems to be an excuse to explain ideological approaches that have little to do with storyline.

Time and time again in Alonso's literature we come across works of a hybrid nature in which a narrative thread leads to speaking about something else. Arguably the best known of those works is *Camembert helburu* (Mission Camembert, 1998). In the preface to this text and in the publicity released by its publisher, the reader is advised that it is an essay disguised as a novel and that it was published as part of an essay series. Indeed, in one way this text has all the ingredients one imagines of a novel: characters and actions, the use of space and time, and a fictitious account. When it comes to a novel, there is also a story that could be taken for intrigue: some mysterious people contract an art thief to inquire into a painting that Toulouse-Lautrec is said to have painted. That thread of intrigue, however, seems very weak, yet since the book is about much more than this intrigue, such matters are not so important. This is because this text, which resembles a novel, allows him the opportunity to offer some reflections and information on Toulouse-Lautrec and art in general. This way, readers interiorize topics like this and, without the reader realizing it, the writer will insert them into a world about art, making this chapter as much about intrigue as a novel. The discourse of the novel has made the field of the essay more attractive, because this field is also a component of intrigue.

Art and the like are discussed in *Camembert helburu*, yet ideological matters are not so important. In *Zintzoen saldoan* (In the Group of the Righteous), using a similar approach regarding technique, intrigue is used as a pretext to speak about a lot of other things, aided by clichés, and here ideology does assume special importance.

There is a dual use of cliché in this text, because alongside the clichés of the literary genre we also come across those in Basque culture and elsewhere in the world, both portrayed as quite closely linked. In noir fiction, the typical idea is contrasting (surface) image and (internal) reality. Normally, behind the gleaming surface there is a rotten and degenerate interior. This approach often appears linked to the idea of wealth, because the wealthy always have another side. In Alonso's novel, the cliché of the genre is presented to the reader as an inclination in Basque culture and the world as a whole, when quite a negative perspective is presented, and almost inevitably ideology appears as another component of the discourse in the novel. In fact, all of the official aspects of the Basque world are stirred up without any qualms in the disillusioned words of the character, who is also the protagonist and narrator at the same time. Yet as he is ideologized (and as his point of view is not equidistant), non-officials are treated differently, because they remain outside his criticism. In this case, we can see that the noir novel can also be a political novel, in the same vein as Colmeiro noted (Colmeiro 2015).

Entering into the ideological process, among the clichés one sees, that which is front and center, above all because of its symbolic value, is gastronomy. In official circles in the Basque Country, extraordinary importance is given to gastronomy, looking outward as if this were the only or most basic thing that could be on offer for locals or visitors. Viewing it that way, gastronomy is a product of the central space of Basque culture, one that puts all others in the shade, because culture, in official circles, is mixed up with the publicity aimed at foreign tourists, becoming an example of superficiality and mere appearance that hides dark interests.

On the other hand, in making a critique, humor is also often used in the form of parody and sarcasm. There is no shortage of passages which seem like jokes and this use of humor can be cathartic or liberating, because what is today termed political correctness must put up with its endless stings. In that regard, there is no problem in making issues that have become almost taboo today a target for humor.

Although Enekoitz Ramirez is a thief, he is part of the "righteous" group and he is obliged to appear alongside the "righteous," but those righteous people, those that make up official society integrated into the system, are not at the end of the day as righteous as they seem, because they also have something to hide (skeletons in the closet, and in noir fiction that is literal) and they function according to their own self-interest.

One can say that this text is a noir novel, but only if one understands noir fiction in a loose way, as a broad flexible genre that can be used to express anything, in which the only essential element is the appearance of a crime, while the disillusioned romantic investigator makes an effort to explain this.

In this specific case, the noir plot is used to make a harsh critique of Basque culture and the official world.

References

Alonso, Jon (1998): *Camembert helburu*. Susa: Zarautz.
——— (2012): *Zintzoen saldoan*. Txalaparta: Pamplona.
——— (2016): *Beltzaren koloreak*. Susa: Zarautz.
Camilleri, Andrea (2013): *La muerte de Amalia Sacerdote*. RBA: Madrid.

Chandler, Raymond (1995): *Obras completas* (2 lib.). Debate: Madrid.

—— (1995a): "El simple arte de matar," in CHANDLER (1995): *Obras completas* (2nd book). 1097–1111.

—— (1995b): "Comentarios informales sobre la novela de misterio," in Chandler (1995): *Obras completas* (2nd book). 1121–1128.

Colmeiro, José (2015): "Novela policiaca, novela política," in *Lectora* 21: 15–29.

Galán Herrera, Juan José (2008): "El Canon de la novela negra y policiaca," in *Tejuelo* 1: 58–74.+

Palacios, Juan, and Weinrichter, Antonio (Pub.) (2005): *Gun Crazy. Serie negra se escribe con B.* T&B Editores: Madrid.

Weinrichter, Antonio (2005): "Kiss kiss bang bang: La femme noire," in Palacios and Weinrichter (2005) (Pub.): *Gun Crazy. Serie negra se escribe con B.* T&B Editores: Madrid. 321–331.

Notes

1 The film, in truth, is based on a novel: *Someone Is Killing the Great Chefs of Europe*, published by Nan and Ivan Lyons in 1976, yet as I do not know the novel, I cite the film.

Chapter 7

The Gaze of the Other: Jon Arretxe's Noir Fiction

Javier Rojo Cobos

Jon Arretxe is a very well-known writer among Basque readers. One can find many different kinds of works in his literary production and he demonstrates in all of them a close relationship with his readership, to the extent that his books are examples of a bestseller in Basque literature. This does not mean that, as regards literature, he does not pay attention to the writing he carries out. In his production, above all, one encounters funny stories focused on adults who do not want to leave their adolescence behind (recall the success achieved by *Ostegunak* (Thursdays) and the works that followed it) and texts which have something to do with noir fiction, and in all these cases he has met with a very positive reception on the part of readers.

Those last works mentioned above will be discussed here, and specifically the novels created around a character named Mahamoud Toure.

These novels involving Toure were published in a series by the Erein publishing house with the emblematic name "Tough Harvest" and, up to now, that is as these sentences are being written, the writer has released seven volumes based on this character. These are the titles and the years in which they were first published:

19 kamera (19 Cameras, 2012)

612 euro (612 Euros, 2013)

Hutsaren itzalak (The Shadows of Emptiness, 2014)

Estolda jolasak (Sewer Games, 2015)

Sator lokatzak (Mole Mud, 2016)

Ez erran deus (Don't Say Anything at All, 2018)

Mesfidatu hitzez (Mistrust through Words, 2019)

As can be seen, between 2012 and the present, a novel featuring Toure has been published almost every year. The novels that appear in this series naturally offer independent stories and each one has a closed storyline, because in each novel a story with an end is developed. But the writings published in the series appear to be bound together as in the form of a chain, for the beginning of each story starts with the end of the previously published novel, and the end of each marks the beginning of the next. If we turn to the series as a whole, then, the novels are presented as if they were boundary markers in a bigger story that is developing from one volume to the other, as the general direction of this larger story is undetermined. This often implies that it is essential to know information in the previous novels in order to understand the new story. As this information is essential, the writer uses techniques (introducing a summary and so on in the new story, for example) to recall the previous information in the new novels, extending the thread which runs through all of them.

This relationship between the novels has another consequence: a kind of evolution appears both in the nature of the main character and in the nature of the conflicts which are raised in the storylines.

At first glance, it seems like these stories suggest an often ironic rewriting of the components we see in classic noir fiction. In other words: based on classic models (in that classic model established by Dashiell Hammett or Raymond Chandler, for example, on the canon, see Galán Herrera 2008), an update appears in Arretxe's novels, which also begins with the main character's nature. As Óscar Urra says, "crime fiction is almost always based on clichés" (2013: 35), and knowing these topics and identifying the variations which take place in them is essential if the text is to be understood properly.

In noir fiction, there is often an investigator who fulfils the role of protagonist (for a general study of that character: Martín Cerezo 2005). The character functions according to personal ethics and in one way or another can be interpreted as equivalent to characters rooted in romanticism: they are loners, they do not have a very balanced personal life and their relationship with authority is insecure, because ultimately they carry out a function that is not fulfilled by the institutions in the power structure. They also believe in justice to some extent, although justice in this sense does not have a lot to do with the law, but rather with their personal ethics. Those kinds of components appear in the traditional investigator model.

When Arretxe takes these components and assigns the role of protagonist in the storyline to the Mahamoud Toure character, we are confronted with the classic model.

First of all, there are his origins. Mahamoud Toure is an illegal immigrant, from Burkina Faso specifically. As in the case of many such people, he left his homeland for wealthy Europe in search of a better life, leaving his family at home. In search of the supposedly easier life in Europe, he ends up in Bilbao, in the San Francisco neighborhood. In that district, and as a means of survival, he has begun to work as an investigator solving small problems. Yet being African, he still uses magic, even though he does not believe in it, because at the end of the day he behaves like a modern picaresque rogue. Indeed, one should not forget that, sometimes, picaresque components also show up in noir fiction (Urra 2013: 64).

Toure is a Muslim, but he does not grant much importance to the topic of religion, because he is quite lax in his beliefs. As for his personal life, as noted, he left his family behind in Africa, and while he is in Bilbao he does not mind if white women feel attracted to him, becoming lovers, and the odd one ends up being a colleague in some of his adventures. In that regard, Arretxe, aided by irony, time, and time again plays with the clichés built on white Europeans and black men from Africa.

The character's main goal is survival, and that means that he must make money somehow and somewhere. He is a character located at the margins of society, a loser at the end of the day. Therefore, he works as an investigator in small matters. He thus also gets into more and more complicated problems, because, as we will observe later, when Toure is working to make a little bit of money in investigation like that, he will inadvertently become entangled in increasingly complicated and serious problems. Faced with these problems, the character reveals his true nature.

As regards being a character who carries out minor investigations (clearing up minor thefts in the neighborhood, for example), Toure has a lot to do with picaresque cheating; when increasingly complicated and serious problems arise, though, such picaresque behavior will not be enough to get by and in this latter case he shows that he has some ethics. Within the boundaries of those ethics, he will not have any problems using violence and the like to defend not just himself but also his friends. In any event, even when things go against him, he tries to maintain his dignity (cf. Urra 2013: 25).

On the other hand, one must remember that, besides being the protagonist of the stories, in many of the chapters in these novels Toure also plays the role of narrator. This gives him an exceptional opportunity to give his opinions, especially about what happens around him through the filter of someone else's eyes. By means of this change of perspective, one may say that, from being condemned to being a character who is "other" (locals see him that way), he has turned into a subject who identifies himself as an "I" and that he inspects and analyses what he sees and what happens to him on the basis of that awareness of self, for example giving an opinion on Basques and especially people from Bilbao.

He is an investigator, and, as is customary in our literature, an amateur. One must contrast this with professional investigators, police officers, *ertzainas* (Basque police officers), and so forth. This contrast has two dimensions. On the one hand, institutions that can be included in the field of professional researchers are viewed, in Basque literature in general, as very suspicious on account of a fairly widespread prejudice against power, and as a consequence, it is hard to find a professional like that as the protagonist in any text. Yet on the other, bearing in mind the legal status of the characters in Arretxe's novels, it is unsurprising to consider professional investigators as the enemy. In fact, professional investigators must maintain order, and whilst they concentrate on doing that, they do not worry too much about everything that happens in the San Francisco neighborhood, as long as whatever happens takes place in the neighborhood and among foreigners.

In this situation, the noir novel can be the right tool for social critique. As Urra says:

> [...] the classic noir novel [...] aspires to fit the plot into a social, moral and human background, dense and violent, which leaves the contradictions of the system to be discovered in a somewhat critical way. (Urra 2013, 24)

This idea of social criticism that appears in the background of noir fiction has often been mentioned (for example, Corcuff 2014 and Cuadrado 2010). In Jon Arretxe's novels, too, there is no shortage of such critiques, as one can see in different fields: opinions about foreigners; the behavior of those who represent power; social control; law and justice; gentrification, and so on. Themes like this appear directly or indirectly in Arretxe's novels and are raised in the form of an important frame around a specific anecdote, because they can also affect Toure's adventures.

In classic noir fiction, there is a typical general idea behind the development of many storylines: specifically, the corruption that hides behind wealth. In Arretxe's novels, too, although sometimes he does not take into account the marginal nature of his characters so obviously, he leaves the odd clue. In the classic novels, a superficial image and an internal nature came face-to-face in topics like money, with wealth always hiding something underneath, which is unlikely to go away. In Arretxe's novels, the protagonists are characters who live on the margins. This is both physically, in the sense that they live in a neighborhood that is increasingly farther away from the city center, and also symbolically, because "respectable" Bilbao society does not want to know anything about what happens in that neighborhood. Thus, to the extent that they are on the fringes of society, their relationship to wealth is indirect. Yet even so, at least in some small way, we see the approach repeated and one can see that the offences are disguised as a layer of normality. Nevertheless, one should emphasize this idea, bearing in mind the nature of the characters, namely that wealth, real wealth is remote to them.

If we turn to the nature of the characters in these novels, among the social issues mentioned, perhaps the most important of these is the behavior of foreigners. Besides being the protagonist, Mahamoud Toure also plays the role of narrator in many chapters. He makes the most of this to explain in his own eyes how he sees Bilbao and the behavior of its people, by means of an approach that could at the outset be termed estrangement. It also means that in the initial novels in this series, Toure examines the behavior of the local people as if he knew nothing about them, and in this change of perspective he plays with the habits of readers. The reader is normally accustomed to sharing the subject's point of view, because it is presented as the autochthonous "I" in Basque literature. In Toure's eyes, though, locals are turned into the object, and by examining what seems like typical behavior from afar, it is seen as strange. As a consequence of this role reversal, parody is frequently created. The Basques (us) that Toure sees are foreigners (we are foreigners). They are quite strange in his eyes, in regard to the unusual customs they (we) have. Inevitably, humor emerges out of this change of perspective, dark humor but humor nonetheless. This humor, moreover, will increase as the protagonist plays the rogue.

As Basques are transformed into the object, one notices the racist conduct that goes almost unnoticed by the locals. Generally speaking, the locals mistrust the foreigners, and that takes place on two levels. Those who live in San Francisco have seen how their neighborhood has changed in recent years on account of the influx of foreigners. Although they live in the neighborhood itself, one cannot say that they have been integrated, because each sticks to their own areas. They live alongside one another, yet without mixing together. Additionally, in the neighborhood, residents organize themselves into groups according to background and, with the gentrification process taking place, some hidden powers have a special interest in the deterioration of the neighborhood, in order to be able to speculate.

Racist attitudes outside the neighborhood are exacerbated, as people of African origin are more isolated in white Bilbao (as they say in novels), without the support of any group, operating in an environment other than their own.

We see that social criticism of clichés highlighted when explaining the situations that are set out about social control and power. We should remember the nature of the narrator who appears in these novels, because this has something directly to do with what is meant. There are also chapters with the narrator-character Toure. Told in the first person, fulfilling the role of subject in those chapters, he gives his opinion on what he sees around him. But in addition to those chapters, there are other chapters which have a heterodiegetic narrator. The narrator in charge of these chapters in the novel seems to have a mysterious voice, and it introduces the presence of a hidden power. The hidden power, resembling that of a Big Brother by means of a camera, sees and controls everything that happens in the neighborhood, as if it were an omniscient and omnipotent being, and it moves other characters from its watchtower according to its wishes, as if they were puppets. The mysterious being that seems like God is a police officer, a cunning and deceitful character who wants to control everything seemingly according to the guarantee of law but who disobeys the law in line with his own self-interest.

Toure is subjected to an incomprehensible power in the face of this situation, which drives him to become muddled up in increasingly serious problems. Moving from his situation to his nature on this point, this is clearly a metaphor for the human condition.

In any event, the power which seems absolute also has its own problems, because there are other hands at work behind it (it is a powerful police officer who thinks he is God, but in the end he is a human being), and when no benefit can be derived from it, those more poweful hands abandon it without any problem.

At the very beginning, the storylines in these novels headed by Toure are set in Bilbao, and looking from that perspective, the city is very present. As noted above, Bilbao is a city divided into two parts, the San Francisco neighborhood (which is also called Little Africa) and white Bilbao. The city is the protagonist, and those who live there appear full of contrasts and peculiarities from Toure's gaze, to the extent that the clichés of Bilbao's inhabitants are highlighted. But as the character's trajectory develops and evolves, those clichés are reflected directly in the location of the plots and the general nature of the storylines.

This relationship may be summarized thus: while the storyline is set in Bilbao, components that may be connected to humor appear in relation to locals being viewed with irony. Insofar as the character, though, appears to get embroiled in increasingly complicated events, those components which could be connected to humor diminish in importance. In their place, more and more violent events appear in the plot. In this violence-irony balance, as the stories slip into violence, so the spaces are extended too.

In *Estolda jolasak* (Sewer Games, the fourth in the series, published in 2015), the character had gone to Africa in search of vengeance. Yet leaving Bilbao in such a way at that time was unusual, and he returns. In the last two novels, however, this distancing becomes the norm.

In *Ez erran deus* (Don't Say Anything at All, 2018), the character leaves the streets of Bilbao and settles in a small town in western Navarre. In an attempt to escape problems that have led to increasingly serious difficulties, Toure ends up working for a shepherd in a small town in Navarre. It would seem that his situation has calmed down to some extent. He can escape from a place. Yet evading fate is impossible, and in this novel, the same outline that appeared in previous works is repeated, because here, too, without wanting to, he gets involved in another investigation. Because it is a rural town, the investigation is also dependant on this rural nature and, in this case, he has to investigate the murder of a donkey, even though it all gets more and more muddled and problematic. As if the small town were a mirror of what remains in the city, here too we see the contrast between the idyllic surface image and the underlying decay, as there are tensions that everyone in the village knows about but which rarely emerge. When these tensions are highlighted, they do so with a ferocious explosion, in a fully violent way. In this volume, one can still come across a small trace of humor, but any smile that may emerge is wiped off one's face. In the stories set in the streets of Bilbao, we always note the presence of a character who controls everything by means of cameras. There are no cameras in the small town, but it is almost impossible to keep a secret in silence. This is because, at the end of the day, the character comes across the same control in the town as in the city. Clearly, in this novel a counter-image to the city is presented, when the small town that was the realm of idealization in the Basques' traditional imagery is demystified, as is an aggressive place like the city.

Those changes appear to have started to mark a trend and in what is to date the latest novel in the series (*Mesfidatu hitzez*, Mistrust through Words, published in 2019) they have increased. Seeking to escape the problem that was introduced in the previous novel, in this latest work, Toure changes location and shows up in Paris. As well as changing places, it seems that his situation has also improved and instead of being on the brink of starvation, thanks to robberies, he is much more comfortable financially. When he was in Bilbao, it seemed that an uncontrollable fate was moving the character's life. As if to show that it is impossible to escape from that, he will once again become immersed in a complicated investigation. In this case, the investigation is more serious, because it has to do with a missing person and while he tries to solve the matter, he will cross paths with the Chinese mafia. This novel clearly demonstrates the dark side of the city, the underbelly of gleaming Paris (recalling a cliché) and the aggressive city of those whose aim is to survive. In this city, too, the novel reveals the presence of a dark power that pulls the strings as if the characters were puppets, the comings and goings of police officers who are calmly involved in corruption, prostitution, scheming, and the parallel hidden world that tourists do not see. The attitude of the narration also changes, because ironic humor has almost disappeared here, and the storyline is wholly focused on a noir plot, with a predominance of violence in the events.

Throughout this chapter, it has been shown how some themes are repeated in this group of novels presented as a series: the behavior of those whose only goal is survival, the presence of power, the reverse and dark side of cities (and small towns), and so on. Those themes appear through the eyes of a normally invisible "other" and this change of perspective is seen as an unusual exchange, especially in the novels set in Bilbao: in the exchange of subject and object, "we" and "others" change place, so as a result, features that are difficult to objectify "for us" stand out. Using the clichéd features that appear in noir fiction storylines, Arretxe places a kind of mirror before our eyes and this mirror reflects our flaws.

It is true that, as mentioned at the beginning, he writes bestsellers, and as is inherent in such literature, popular appeal may have been the main purpose of these texts. Yet Arretxe does something else: through that role change he also carries out social criticism, and it seems to me that this is the fundamental value in his literature.

References
Arretxe, Jon (2012): *19 kamera*. Erein: San Sebastian.
———. (2013): *612 euro*. Erein: San Sebastian.
———. (2014): *Hutsaren itzalak*. Erein: San Sebastian.
———. (2015): *Estolda jolasak*. Erein: San Sebastian.
———. (2016): *Sator lokatzak*. Erein: San Sebastian.
———. (2018): *Ez erran deus*. Erein: San Sebastian.
———. (2019): *Mesfidatu hitzez*. Erein: San Sebastian.
Corcuff, Phillipe (2014): "Novela policial, filosofía y sociología crítica: referencias problemáticas," in *Cultura y representaciones sociales*, 8th annual journal. 16, 30–51.
Cuadrado, Agustin (2010): "La novela negra como vehículo de crítica social," in *Letras hispanas: revista de literatura y cultura* 7-1, 199–217.
Galán Herrera, Juan José (2008): "El Canon de la novela negra y policiaca," in *Tejuelo* 1: 58–74.
Martín Cerezo, Iván (2005): "La evolución del detective en el género policíaco," in *Tonos. Revista electrónica de estudios filológicos* 10: 362–384.
Urra, Óscar (2013): *Cómo escribir una novela negra*. Ed. Fragua: Madrid.

Chapter 8

Ramon Saizarbitoria's *Lili eta biok* (Lili and Me, 2015): The Spanish Civil War and the Investigative Novel

Miren Billelabeitia and *Jon Kortazar*

Objectives

This chapter has two objectives. First, it seeks to present an explanation of a methodology with which to study investigative novels about the Spanish Civil War. Then, it also aims to introduce here and study the investigative novel *Lili eta biok* (Lili and Me), published in 2015 by Ramon Saizarbitoria. It is a study, therefore, of methodology and practice.

José Martínez Rubio, a researcher at the University of Castellon, has published two works on the themes of Spanish Civil War studies and explorations of questions about what happened therein. In 2012, he published a long article titled "Investigación de la memoria. El olvido como crimen" (Investigation of Memory: Forgetting as Crime). Three years later, in 2015, his ideas appeared in a book titled *Las formas de la verdad. Investigación, docuficción y memoria en la novela hispánica* (The Forms of Truth: Investigation, Docufiction and Memory in the Hispanic Novel).

His main thesis is the following: novels whose focus is to enquire into and investigate the Civil War do not follow the typical directions in police novels.

Specifically, as the main reason, the main objective of such enquiries and investigations is not to identify who the killer is, precisely because it is often the case that there is no murder.

In *Lili eta biok*, a murder is believed to have taken place, but in the last chapter it is revealed that it did not in fact happen. However, a rape was committed and this indeed was the real crime. To some extent, *Soldados de Salamina* (in English, *Soldiers of Salamis*) and *Lili eta biok* are similar. Yet in Ramon Saizarbitoria's novel, the main reason for investigating the murder is to reveal the truth, emphasizing the value of truth and the importance of having to tell the truth for future generations.

Our objectives will be to determine adaptations of investigative novels about violence in the Civil War and to explain the discussion of truth that appears in *Lili eta biok*.

Methodological Explanation

Although we have summarized the main thesis in a general way, let us slowly examine Martínez Rubio's work. He constructed an argument and a summary of the hypothesis in the article. Therein, he proposed a term for the investigative novel genre, specifically to name those that examine the Civil War. In his opinion, and he gives data for this, the number of novels which employ this technique—specifically, he studied a painful act which took place in the Civil War, liberating it from the state of oblivion into which it had fallen—is expanding, and in his view, it reached a peak in 2010.

In his opinion, three influences created that trend: on the one hand, the success of noir fiction; on the other, the fondness for nonfiction and the link that historical accounts reveal with readers; and third, the impact of the novel *Soldados de Salamina* in 2001 on the triumph of memory. To put it in his words:

> This interest in the investigation-of-memory novel is based in my opinion on three fundamental pillars: the boom in the noir novel at the end of the century; the growing regard for non-fiction narrative and for some specific events and the publication in 2001 of *Soldados de Salamina* as a forerunner of the so-called memory novel. (Martínez Rubio 2012: 71)

In Martínez Rubio's opinion, this investigative novel, constructed around an act or a situation in the Civil War, has not followed the main outline of the noir novel. On the contrary, it has transformed it, creating a new narrative framework. Comparing Manuel Vázquez Montalbán's (1939–2003) *Asesinato en el Comité Central* (in English, *Murder in the Central Committee*) and Javier Cercas's (1962–) *Soldados de Salamina*, his conclusion is clear: the investigative novel did not follow the narrative outline of noir fiction, specifically because there is no murder, no murderer, no victim, and because the investigator begins the investigation on his own account. It is evident that the investigative novel does not fulfill the main criteria of noir fiction. In a relatively long paragraph, the researcher outlines how it is different:

> In this case [in reference to *Soldados de Salamina*], the narrator (Javier Cercas) investigates a crime which was not committed (there was no murder), and then washes his hands of the matter after careful study of a victim that was never a victim (Sánchez-Mazas), and moreover he does so on his own account without the mediation of any client; that is, not only are the classic roles of criminal and victim subverted (we could ask ourselves perfectly logically whether Miralles is more victim than criminal, or if Sánchez-Mazas is more criminal than victim), but also that of client and of investigator (he is not a typical investigator that must reveal a truth, but rather he must construct that truth, that "essential secret" which explains the why of a heroic act like saving a life and the why of an unjust situation such as the forgetting of heroes), of crime and of truth (there is no death but there is forgetting, in the same way as there is no solution but there is memory, I am already getting ahead). (Martínez Rubio 2012: 75).

The objective of the investigative novel, then, was placed at a higher level: at the level of ethics and history (connecting truth and memory) and unlike in the case of noir fiction, which is at the level of entertainment and light reading. It is true that *Soldados de Salamina* was more important when it was published and that the narrative features presented are too closely linked to that novel. Anyone might ask: What happens if there is a murder in this investigative novel? Let us look at Jokin Muñoz's (1963–) *Antzararen bidea* (On the Trail of the Goose, 2007). It is merely a theoretical issue, but if the methodology is only linked to *Soldados de Salamina*, it also demonstrates its weak aspects. In Jokin Muñoz's novel (Serrano 2011, Kortazar 2018), Lisa, Igor's mother and a simple housewife, together with her friend Gigi, a bartender, examine a murder committed as a result of the repression that took place. The two investigators carry out the inquiry without any goal of financial gain. Their aim is something else, to get at the truth, to know what happened, and they will look into a death, a homicide.

But the investigative novel is more precise when it comes to providing narrative features, and in this aspect, too, it makes a direct distinction between investigative and noir novels.

1. In the noir novel the main objective is to clear up a death. In an investigative novel, however, the investigative process is predominant.
2. The beginning forms are different. By the time the noir novel starts, everything has happened, both the death and (although not always) the investigative process, and after it has happened, it is all recounted. In the investigative novel, though, the main aim is the investigator's account, and it is told while the process is taking place.
3. If death is the main space of the noir novel, forgetting, and the struggle against forgetting would be the main theme in the investigative novel. An effort to get at the truth drives the investigative novel. That is, above all, the direction it takes.
4. The nature of the offender would be the last feature: in noir fiction the offender has a special (physical) feature, a feature that has been made special and often marked by a scar, but it is not like that in the investigative novel: there, the offender has hidden the offense in the greyness of society (Martínez Rubio 2012: 76–80).
5. Yet there is a feature that has taken the investigative novel to another level. The investigation does not just take place in the field of fiction, for its task lies in its power to make what is private public. The private, what was hidden, becomes public and therefore its plea is ideological, political (Martínez Rubio 2012: 80).

If we apply these features to *Lili eta biok*, we see that most appear in Ramon Saizarbitoria's work. First, we see the journey Faustino goes on to find out what really happened in the war, the place in the novel occupied by the process, and the recounting, the writing, of that process. Getting to the truth is the main aim in the novel and, paradoxically, this murder that was considered to have happened did not really take place. To put it one way, at the outset Faustino goes off in search of a false objective. Yet going the wrong way, by means of paradox, will enable him to find out what is correct. In the case of the offender's image, the offender from the war, Julio Cesar, and the contemporary offender, Cesar, now appear integrated into society. It is clear that Ramon Saizarbitoria's aim is to create a political discourse aimed at young people.

Although everything we have seen to this point is very useful for our literary study, we should see what Martínez Rubio says in his second text and reflection. Specifically, we will do so by looking at the opinions he expresses in chapter 3 of his *Las formas de la verdad*. Although his main hypothesis (noir and investigative novels are two different literary genres) has been confirmed, he offers other interesting resources when it comes to defining the investigative novel. There is a noticeable difference between the article and the book. In the latter, the reflection is much broader and deeper, which space precludes going into here. Likewise, we cannot examine the greater connections that he makes either with other kinds of narrative (with the reception contract, with the ambiguity of the story) or also with other storytelling techniques (with the endings of novels, for example). We could say that while the distinct ideas in the article do not change, they are enriched and described more precisely.

Although he discusses the usefulness of the aforementioned distinction, Martínez Rubio also offers five analytical methods which appear in investigative novels:

1. The memory process. In novels set in such environments, the voice that speaks in the first person recounts something that happened a long time ago and alternates between present and past. The voice recalls a forgotten or lost initiative that will clarify and make sense in the context of the current issue. Because Martínez Rubio's study takes Hispanic novels into account, he gives many different kinds of examples. In order to show the memory process, in his opinion Roberto Bolaño's (1953–2003) *Nocturno de Chile* (2000; in English, *By Night in Chile*, 2003) would be a fine example. Or Rafael Chirbes's (1949–2015) *La buena letra* (Good Handwriting, 1991). In our case, Ramon Saizarbitoria's (1944–) *Bihotz bi. Gerrako kronikak* (Two Hearts: War Chronicles, 1996) is an example of the technique.
2. Construction. In this case, as well as memory, the protagonist would need some other help to achieve totality, whether photographs, or a document or the like which will help to recover memory. Construction typically uses memory and forgetting to make up a game between the two with the aim of achieving a totality of the event.
3. Appearance. The investigator does not want to undertake an enquiry, yet suddenly and unexpectedly they become aware of something and it pushes them to explain that. We should understand this as if it were the appearance of something new rather than the investigator going looking for something, but it comes to them through other sources, a witness from the time, or

via other characters. The most striking example of this tendency is Jokin Muñoz's (1963–) *Antzararen bidea* (On the Trail of the Goose, 2007). In *Lili eta biok*, Lili tells Faustino the story her grandfather told her about a doomed love story in the war. It is this that pushes him to explore and write about the history.

4. Exploration. This method of investigation finds its chief expression in contemporary life, and its main goal would be examining the here and now. There is, then, no leap and change between times. When it comes to giving examples that have used the method, Martínez Rubio takes television series into account. Programmes like *Callejeros* (Street Guides) and *Vascos por el mundo* (Basques around the World) are taken into account, because they reveal an exploration of this contemporary life.

5. Investigation. The investigator introduces all the others into this method, expressing their personality and importance, however.

He has mentioned four cultural resources, as a guide to the tendencies:

Contemporary life/The past

Ignorance/Knowledge.

Logical recovery/Methodological action

Passive/Active

In addition, examining the structure of the novels he has presented the following main outline:

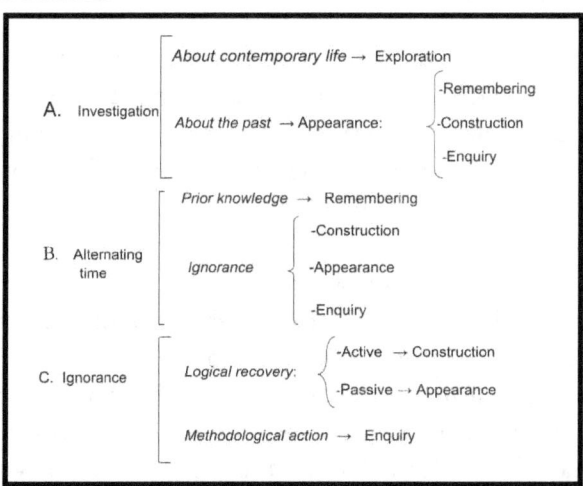

Martínez Rubio differentiates two methods in the field of investigation: that which moves forward, the progressive, in which we know the actions as they are recounted, yet we do not know what comes next; and that which looks backward, the regressive, in which the storytelling work of the text begins after everything has happened, and the narrator recounts the events that have taken place (Martínez Rubio 2015: 153–175). In the progressive, in which we know the actions as they are recounted, examples are Eduardo Mendoza's (1943) *La verdad sobre el caso Savolta* (*The Truth About the Savolta Case*, 1975) and Manuel Vázquez Montalbán's *Galíndez* (1991; in English, *Galíndez*, 1992).

On this point, Martínez Rubio carries out a theoretical development. In the first text on the subject (the 2012 article), he calls works like *Lili eta biok* "investigative novels." In the 2015 book, however, he uses the term "writer's investigation" for novels like this. It is just a matter of the concept, but although we will use it, we give priority to the older term: the investigative novel, because the expression "writer's investigation" is not so clear whether we are discussing Ramon Saizarbitoria or Faustino. When we have used the latter term, we clarify that the writer was Faustino, the character.

> Regressive investigation [...] is that typical of the writer's investigation. Therein, everything has already happened: the case investigated and the investigation itself, and therefore, the novel begins when the story, the discursive and ideological explanation of reality, starts factually. (Martínez Rubio 2015: 175–176)

He once again reveals the features of this literary genre. But here, he has time to emphasize the ideological and ethical aspect. The chief aim of this kind of novel is not examining and clearing up a murder, but rectifying historical forgetting through the truth and reflecting on the nature of History and breaking the greyness of the offender.

Lili eta biok: A Summary of the Storyline

Before entering into the analysis, it seems to us appropriate, especially for those who have not read the novel, to supply a summary of the storyline. At the same time, one must also bear in mind that it is a very distinctive story, full of coincidence, which is often close to the unbelievable and always close to the technique that Ramon Saizarbitoria has used in recent times. He wants to express the truth through fiction, and as we are reading fiction, it is based on chance and several inappropiate encounters. The thread is dense, yet several small currents appear along the way.

In this novel, Ramon Saizarbitoria presents the psychologist and former writer Faustino Iturbe. Faustino left his job as a psychologist after his treatment of a patient failed and the patient committed suicide. He is an ex-writer on account of the fact that it has been a long time since he has written anything and he is ensconced at home, because he spends his days without being able to contact anyone. In the first three chapters in the novel, three narrative threads are opened up which are linked closely to Faustino. Each thread develops one aspect of the narrative, but the links among all three appear time and time again, are related to Faustino's daily life and rekindle the competition to unravel the unresolved mystery mentioned in the story.

The first thread is that of Ana, Faustino's former work colleague and friend. Ana asks Faustino to do her a favor as a go-between, specifically to buy a book that her uncle owns at present, an issue of Larramendi's Trilingual Dictionary which Ana's Falangist grandfather rescued from a fire in the Civil War. Because her uncle is having some financial problems, he wants to sell the dictionary, but Ana wants to offer it to the Provincial Council in order to clear the name of her Falangist grandfather, Julio Cesar.

The second thread, that of Lili, is extended by Ana to Faustino, in introducing the teenage Lili, who apparently needs psychological help. Lili, knowing that Faustino is a writer, shows him a book of poems by Cernuda that her grandfather gave her, and tells the tale of the doomed love story of the Falangist soldier Juan Aramendia, who gave it to her grandfather. The tale immediately elicits Faustino's sympathy, because it describes a tragic love story during the Civil War, because he is attracted by the literary penchants of the Falangist, because the story has a secret, a dark ending that was never resolved, and, at the end of the day, because Lili's grandfather remembers the love between the Falangist Juan Aramendia and Rosarito, which was interrupted by Juan's disappearance and perhaps murder, with remorse and heartache. In order to alleviate the responsibility that her grandfather's situation creates for Lili, Faustino tells her about his grandfather's wartime experience, how he admired his image as a *gudari* (Basque soldier) when he was young, and how he got angry at his grandfather-hero when he was interviewing witnesses of the Civil War for a report, when someone informed him that his grandfather would go mad with fear when he heard the planes and bombs near the trenches. The stories told by

Lili and the gaps in Juan Aramendia's disappearance remind Faustino of unfinished business in his own life: the death of Maite several years earlier due to his erroneous psychological treatment and the fact he never dared to answer her father's phone calls. This memory reminds him of his cowardice, as he lives on his grandfather's inheritance. As a result, they go to the house in which Maite lived. Although he is prepared to explain this remorse that Lili puts in his mind to the teenager he has just met, this is the time to face up to his responsibility to the father who was calling him. This is how Faustino ends up going to the home of Maite's father, Juan Arrese. He welcomes him in and shows him Maite's room. There, Faustino sees an old photograph in which a young girl appears in front of a farmhouse that resembles Rosarito from the love story Lili has just told him. Juan Arrese tells Faustino that it is his mother and that the photo was taken before the war, that his mother had him at a very young age as the result of the love she had experienced in the war, that his father disappeared in the war and that his mother had to leave home and her village and go and live in the city. The similarities with the story Lili told him drive him to leave that house as soon as he can, go into a bar, and write down notes on everything he has just heard quickly on some paper napkins. That afternoon, without missing the opportunity, he starts writing again, going into the story and delving into the nature of the characters. With the help of a friend who works in the Municipal Archive, he then gets several pieces of information about Juan Aramendia.

Furthermore, Ana sets out to have Faustino make an appointment with her uncle Cesar to talk about her grandfather Julio Cesar's dictionary. While he is in Cesar's home, he sees a picture of a farmhouse that, he thinks, is the same one as that in the photograph in Juan Arrese's house. It is his wife's family's farm which Cesar is selling. Sensing Faustino's interest, Cesar offers to show it to him and takes him to the village of Otzeta. At the farm, he begins to imagine the first meeting between Juan Aramendia and Rosarito. While he is walking around the farm, he runs into an old man. When Cesar goes looking for him, he shocks the old man, who looks like he has seen a ghost. In Donostia once more, he continues to delve into Juan Aramendia's details, developing what he has begun writing, reaching some affirmations. He knows that Rosarito lived in Otzeta, and he is almost sure that the farm he saw was her home. When he tells Lili all this, she answers him that her grandfather has had a serious turn and is ill. A few days later, Faustino returns to Otzeta of his own accord. There, in a talk organized by a group working on historical memory, he learns that some builders have found a dog's skull with a bullet hole buried underground, that the discovery has stopped work and that excavations have begun to search for the bodies of those shot or missing during the war. While all this is going on, he receives a call from Lili; she is in Otzeta too and they go to see the surroundings where Juan Aramendia and Rosarito had their love affair, a nearby church and the priest's house. They know that Juan often went there to speak to the priest and consult his books. A man who comes out of the house next door tells them that the priest is his uncle and that during the war he went to Argentina, taking a lot of books with him to spare them from being destroyed. With the help of some relatives from Mutriku, the priest intended to leave with a Falangist who lived on a nearby farm, but apparently the Falangist did not turn up at the appointed time. Thereafter, Lili takes Faustino to her grandfather's house, and there he realizes that he is the very old man he saw the day he went with Cesar to Otzeta. After lunch, the three of them remember the story of Juan Aramendia and Rosarito and begin sharing the details. Lili's grandfather was a go-between for the two lovers because he knew Rosarito and because the Falangists lived in his house; Julio Cesar knew this and he intercepted a letter that Juan Aramendia had written to Rosarito with plans to elope, but instead of delivering the letter, he ordered Lili's grandfather, still a child at the time, to tell Rosarito another meeting time. He threatened that if he ever told anyone he would kill his entire family, and to show that he was telling the truth, he [Julio Cesar] shot his grandfather's dog in the head and threw it into a pit. Thereafter, her grandfather regretted having taken part in the deception perpetrated toward Rosarito and the misfortune it brought: her rape and Juan's disappearance. Lili's grandfather is convinced that Julio Cesar killed Juan Aramendia and buried the dog in the pit.

The third thread is structured around Lore. Faustino sees Lore swimming on Ondarreta beach in the first chapter. From that moment on, he tries to go every day to the beach to see Lore. He also sees her once at Ana's uncle's house when he goes to view the dictionary that he is selling, but he does not speak to her until bumping into her in the doorway of the hospital to which Lore's father has been admitted. The pretext for the encounter is the dog Faustino has by his side. Faustino found it at the hospital entrance when he went to find out if Juan Arrese had been admitted there. They strike up a conversation and while chatting, Lore invites Faustino to have coffee because she wants to get some clothes for her father from his house on the way. Thus, Faustino finds out that Lore is Juan Arrese's daughter, the sister of Maite who committed suicide (the half-sister, really), and Rosarito's granddaughter. Lore explains to him the tragic end of the love story between Juan Aramendia and Rosarito. Julio Cesar raped Rosarito. Thus, her father Juan Arrese is not Juan Aramendia's son, as everyone thought, but the result of Rosarito's rape. She clarifies to him the deception engineered by Julio Cesar with the aim of raping Rosarito, and also that when Rosarito found out that she was pregnant as a result of the rape, she left for the city and started life again officially as if Juan Aramendia were the father of her son. After spending some years in Panama and getting married there, recently arrived back in Donostia, Lore introduced her husband at a family dinner. There, Rosarito confessed to Lore that she had noted a resemblance between her husband and her rapist, Julio Cesar, but she did not reveal the secret to her son Juan Arrese. Cesar, Lore's husband, did know though about that and he uses the knowledge when his financial difficulties pile up to blackmail Lore, so he can get his hands on her father's and grandmother's possessions. After Lore's confession, Faustino knows that Rosarito did not want to run away with Juan Aramendia, but that she had always lived with that memory in her heart. Faustino tells Lore the connection of what Lili's grandfather did and the suspicion that Julio Cesar murdered Juan Aramendia. But Faustino still doubts whether that murder really happened. In the end, he returns the dog he found at the hospital entrance to its owner. And look who it was, Charo, Juan Aramendia's daughter. Charo clarifies that Juan Aramendia managed to escape, that he made it to Bilbao, and from there to England and then on to Argentina.

Igniting the Flames of the Novel: The Need to Remember

Remembering has been a useful way to receive the memory of relatives or anyone associated with the passage of history. That memory launches a trigger, a call, a letter, a report . . . In *Lili eta biok*, Lili's grandfather's illness is the trigger. Lili is very concerned and she tells Faustino about the tragic end to the love story her grandfather experienced closely during the Civil War era and the serious regret he felt about what he thought was a murder. In the novel, as the nameless grandfather tells Lili, in his opinion, Juan Aramendia's murderer was Julio Cesar Lasa, the man who shot her grandfather's dog dead and threatened his family with a similar fate without carrying out the threat. Sixty years later, the dog's skull was found and, his opinion, his suspicion that the murdered Juan Aramendia will emerge has revived the anxiety of the memory. How and why the dog was killed and who did it brings to the surface what has been hidden in the recesses of his mind for years. Regarding that discovery, it brings to light the grandfather's memory.

It is obvious when the old man's personality disorders began. It relates the problem to the initial activities of the historical memory recovery group (...) from the moment an anthropologist who showed up in the village began interviewing people who had lived through the war, apparently, with the aim of finding traces of the disappeared, and following the questioning, the gossip and rumours that had remained silent in household kitchens for seventy years began spreading and it made the grandfather feel uneasy (...) Many people were buried in sites in Gazteluzarra and several other places. (516)

The faint possibility that the body of Juan Aramendia, who he thinks, was murdered by Julio Cesar, may also appear terrifies him. He is also horrified by the responsibilities of years of silence and the consequences of this for the lovers Juan Aramendia and Rosarito. He has remained silent for many years, ignoring the sites of memory that have hidden legally the recollection of events regarding society as well as the village.

The distinctive feature of this novel is that it is not about unknown conditions or history, but about the consequences of forgetting or exclusion. This is why memory, through its restorative tendency, ties us to an ethic of writing because it values exposing hidden events, the value of showing and verifying the truth, the value of truth for future generations because what happened was not clarified at the time. For that reason, Lili's grandfather explains his memories and thoughts to the writer Faustino, his remorse and guilt, in order to alleviate the awful tempest that has remained in his head.

In reconstructing memory, the protagonist needs a foundation on which to construct the narrative, and to give meaning to the totality through the unknown section that needs to be investigated. In order to recover what has been forgotten, re-memorizing legitimizes the exercise of memory. Reconstruction is linked to memory, and at the same time to the unknown. In this novel, Juan Aramendia's escape and exile in Argentina remain unknown to the reader until the last chapter and, for Ramon Saizarbitoria, helped by much needed chance, it gives a new twist to the story. That lack of awareness on the part of Faustino and other characters offers another voice with which to tell Juan Aramendia's story, that of Rosario-Charo, the daughter Juan had in Argentina.

Among those single voices that are talking about knowing how to re-memorize, the reproduction corresponds to at least two characters who exchange information: to Faustino and to Lili's grandfather, or to Faustino and Lore, when it comes to revealing Rosarito's rape and its consequences, and, also, to Faustino and Charo as regards the escape and exile of Juan Aramendia.

The Faustino that Became a Writer: The Investigation of the Truth

In investigative novels, it is customary for a writer protagonist to have another job besides writing, and in *Lili eta biok* Faustino is a former psychologist. In novels like this, protagonists who carry out an investigation, whatever their profession, will all end up functioning as writers. This condition of becoming a writer character legitimizes metafictional resources. On this point, we follow José Martínez Rubio (2012, 2105).

As Manuel Alberca (2007) says, today the image of writers has lost that classic shadow that emphasized them as model intellectuals and they have become intellectuals more closely connected to their readers, thereby democratizing their image. The result of this is that the protagonist often takes the form of a sterile creator and a parasite, a strange misanthropic character portrayed with a weak personality.

That is exactly what Faustino shows us. At the beginning of the novel, Ramon Saizarbitoria presents him as concealed at home and hiding away from society; laying on the sofa, without any wish to meet anyone, eating junk food. He is consumed by a long illness. The death of his patient Maite, who committed suicide, pushed him to give up his job in a psychologist's office. He blames the psychological problems that have overwhelmed him by increasing his image of fragility on failing his former patient and on laziness that, he believes, he has inherited from his grandfather. The protagonist takes the shape of a character that is very common in the desacralizing evolution of the writer, playing on everyday simple characters, but in the end, it frees him up to do the work of writing the story told by Lili. Yet Lili also frees up Faustino; this time, Galatea unleashes a new twist on the Pygmalion myth. Faustino's memory is presented at the beginning of the novel as the loss or lack of a main dimension of personality or life, even though Ramon Saizarbitoria presents it at that moment as the traumatic and pathological result of something that is not very well known.

The writing work he took up when he left his job in the psychologists' office has also contributed to the loneliness he has chosen, but lately he has not been doing that either. The narrator continues to explain the origins of his trauma, and he seems to contradict himself when he considers what has happened to him as "the result of what other people did." This is because Faustino bases what he sees about himself on his grandfather's cowardice, his timid personality.

Sarobe explains why he is always calling, and the reason is that he wants to ask him permission to use some of the interviews in that unfinished documentary in another work he had been commissioned to do on Historical Memory (. . .) In truth, the matter doesn't worry him that much because he is convinced that Sarobe will not use that part, an interviewee with mouse teeth questioned his grandfather Faustino's courage. (14)

He does not know what else to say, and says that his grandfather was a coward, like Ledor (p. 271 or.).

When a character becomes a writer in an investigative novel, and when they lead the investigation, there can be four motives:

1) To create a report. Faustino set out to make a video report on the Civil War *gudaris* (Basque soldiers) but was suddenly cut off by an eyewitness because he mentioned the cowardice shown by his grandfather in the trenches:

Amongst the speakers, it had a *gudari* from Antzuola (. . .) There was apparently a man in his battalion that, as soon as heard the engine of an airplane, burst out crying and they had to go up to him so that he would not jump out of the trenches in the panic, running off into the exposed countryside. He was, it was said, a lad from Donostia by the name of Iturbe (. . .) He was Faustino by name and Iturbe by surname, the grandson of the battalion coward. (271–273)

2) To write a novel. After hearing Lili recount the tragic wartime love affair, and after seeing the prewar photo in Juan Arrese's house, in which Rosarito herself appears as a teenager, Faustino cannot keep up with the pace of his writing and hurriedly goes over the similarities surrounding the stories he heard on a bar napkin.

Overcoming his regret at using a sticky free publicity Keler pen, he begins writing on the paper napkin: "Juan Aramendia arrived in Otzeta in the autumn of 1936, two years after that photo in which Rosarito appears in front of the house was taken." Then, putting the paper note in his wallet, he swears to himself that, since it is proven that the characters mentioned by the girls in Ana's neighborhood and the father of the suicidal Maite are from the same story, he will endeavour to write that story. (129)

3) To do an essay.

4) To assemble a personal truth. By means of a period of sorrow in his investigation into the disappearance of Juan Aramendia, Faustino acknowledges his grandfather's fear in the trenches of the Civil War.

> It is good to hear the grandson of the *gudari* who wept in fear of enemy attacks, the cowardly Faustino Iturbe, speak with compassion and love about cowards. (275)

But Faustino the writer is capable of meeting those initial aims in order to transform his investigative work into a metaphor for the very writing of a novel. As he investigates, he writes his own literary work, and that writing leads to a change in his personality. In this novel, all of the characters who tell their story to Faustino believe that the text is also an announcement, because all of these characters acknowledge the higher aim of developing the novel about them and the need to do investigative work. That way, the novel fulfils two goals: telling a story and also describing how it is told. One novel is created within another novel.

When the writer appears as an investigator, investigative novels, using a metafictional level, explain the problems, efforts, failures, and achievements in the process of the writer character writing a novel. Within the same discourse, they link the concision of what has been created and its explanation, the recounting of history and all the information needed to do the novel, in search of the whole supposed truth. This complex work leads us to reflect on the effectiveness of fiction when clarifying reality, and faced with some other discourses that are typically termed true stories, literature tends to make discourse much more effective. *Lili eta biok* draws the reader into that plot, when the young Lili needs to be heard and her truth known.

> A writer's investigative novels narrate a detective process which gives an account, combines with fiction to some extent, of a factual or fictitious reality, historical or particular, from a strict position in the first person. This narrative process unfurls the entire ethics about a writer's intellectual labour (about their responsibility to narrate, about the right to disclose painful stories and about the necessity of doing so in an honest way and so as to get over a trauma at the heart of a community). And this writer, in turn, constructs the story of the collective from their own cognitive process, [...] they become the builder of an external reality, or at least their

gaze prefigures and configures the reality it expresses. (Martínez Rubio 2015: 267–268)

Although Faustino does not write in the first person, the novel is ultimately placed above the documentary, above testimony, above nonfiction and above biography. The "novel in progress" dominates the novel itself and that encourages the narrator to begin writing, not like those who present information but in the manner of those who make a discovery, forming the narrative over and over again through data. Thus, the literary text is a model between truth, reality, and the subject, the endless work of constructing the effect of reality. The end-of-the-century variant of "postmodern realism" theorized by Joan Oleza (1993) favors an aesthetic that delves deeply into the "representation" of memory and forsakes "mimesis," demonstrating imagination and construction (Martínez Rubio 2015: 261).

The Thesis Novel

Lili eta biok goes in two directions. Faustino begins investigating the tragic love story between Juan Aramendia and Rosarito and Juan's disappearance, and the investigation leads him to another extreme. Juan Aramendia was not murdered and there is no crime as such in that sense (as if it were a parody of the first Basque-language police novel, *Hamabost egun Urgainen*, in English *Fifteen Days in Urgain*) but the investigator comes across another crime, Rosarito's rape and its consequences.

Is a writing that reveals suffering and shame worth it? Does the truth perhaps liberate? Does it perhaps save us? *Lili eta biok* seeks to answer those questions.

We will present *Lili eta biok* as a novel that has a message or is a thesis novel. The work, as Ramon Saizarbitoria has explained on more than one occasion, is for an adolescent readership, or, if one prefers, it ranks among others—*Kandinskyren tradizioa* (Kandinsky's Tradition), *Miren eta erromantizismoa* (Miren and Romanticism)—written with young readers in mind. He has never revealed whether he wrote it with the aim of instructing, but he has not denied that either.

> The writer is not sure if it is worth disputing it. He does not think that there are any boundaries between young adult literature and literature *without going any further*. When you're young, you read in another way, and you get something else out of the same book. (184)

In line with some of the best historical novels, specific facts and events that were revealing of the violent atmosphere before and during the war are mentioned again and again when Faustino walks the streets of Donostia with Lili:

Ana and the little girl live near the crossroads of Kolon and Peña y Goñi. Being right there, right now reminds Faustino Iturbe that, on 10 September 1934, just before nine at night, Manuel Andrés Casaus, the Acción Republicana [Republican Action] leader, was shot dead by the head of the Falange, that he was shot dead in revenge for the killing of the Falangist head Manuel Carrión Damborenea (...) As he was heading home, at number 15 on Peña y Goñi, with a friend of his, as the latter declared, two shots were heard, the two friends turned around and Casaus apparently shouted "they've killed me" (57–58).

Number 32, Prim Street is at the junction of Moraza and the Catholic Monarchs, almost. (...) he says to the girl that almost certainly Juan Aramendia (...) often crossed that portico (...) because Aizpurua's study was the meeting place for Falangists in the city. In itself, that's where the local head of the Falange, Manuel Carrión Damborenea, was shot dead as he was going to a meeting with his fellow party members, two years before the war broke out, on 9 September 1934, on a Sunday, at around ten in the morning. He ran into him, and stopped for a chat, as one witness explained, who was waiting for eight or ten people, looking like workers, one wearing mechanics' overalls, and hearing three or four shots. (86)

Since then he's known that the well-known Basque scholar and bibliophile Julio Urkixo, and Carlist politician, lived on the top floor of that building (...) He had a library of more than fourteen thousand volumes (...) When the coup took place, Urkixo fled to the side of the Nationals; the cultural heritage and economic wealth that his library entailed disappeared completely, as a result of the action of an uncontrolled group, even though the militias sent by the then secretary of the Provincial Council, Jesus Maria Leizaola, and men of confidence could not stop it (...) Leizaola was also a member of the Defence Council, when Andres Irujo was the commissioner ... (95)

The priest Jose Ariztimuño, a Basque nationalist journalist and writer, better known by the nickname "Aitzol" (...) Aitzol founded the Basque Renaissance (...) in 1933, opened Freedom Avenue and he survived until 1936. The thing is that Aitzol put the architect

Aizpurua in charge of the building project and the work management, so, (...) they would speak, and sometimes, perhaps, right there in the studio at number 31 Prim Street too. When they executed Aizpurua on 6 September, Aitzol had taken refuge in the Benedictine Belloc Abbey, but he did not feel comfortable (...) in order to return to Bilbao he set sail on the Galerna ship, but the fascists intercepted it opposite Pasaia, on 15 October, a month or so after Aizpurua, took him to Ondarreta prison, and he was tortured cruelly. Two days later, on the 17th, those on the architect's side executed him. (96)

When he mentions the events that took place in several towns in Gipuzkoa:

Because he was Navarrese, he was in Lizarra in the afternoon of 18 July (...) In Beasain, when they entered on the 27th, he was right there, and for the first time, he witnessed the atrocities committed by his people, and they took the towns on the N1 road, Ordizia Tolosa, Aduna, Urnieta ... The last of these in the middle of a huge rainstorm, and under the violent bombing of the Republicans, on 6 September. (147).

He lived in Irun, because his father was employed on the railways (...) he confirms that after the cannons of the warships *España* and *Admiral Cervera* severely punished the city, the anarchists, in retreat, burnt almost everything, including his parents' house too. (174)

Terror in Beasain: a woman pretending to be her father, kneeling in front of the bloody corpse of a civilian thrown next to a canyon; leaving his rifle on the ground, his comrade removes the watch from his wrist ... (221–222)

That texture of data networks and serious events is a support, providing a base, but at the same time it could also be true to the development of the love story, even if it is fictionalized:

Whilst he was constantly talking about Juan Aramendia, how he dreamt about escaping to France, living in Paris (...) it was not possible, but, even so, he seemed to be happy (...) the relationship lasted barely three months, but the feelings it incited would last forever. (332)

These data have given credence to Rosarito's account of the rape:

> It was Julio Cesar who got Rosarito pregnant (...) Returning to Otzeta during the war, he says that a couple of young lovers used a boy from a nearby farm to send messages to each other. One day, the boy told Rosarito, he doesn't recall now at what time, at dusk, that he would be waiting at the place they normally saw each other. She appeared at the appointed time, but Julio Cesar was there. He apparently beat her before raping her. After the atrocity, he told her that if she didn't keep quiet about what had happened, everyone would find out that she was whore, and that he'd tell it to the world. (336)

The separation of the two lovers, Aramendia's escape and Rosarito's torment:

> That Juan Aramendia's motorbike was found abandoned; he was said to have escaped, and that he was also killed. (337)

> She says that Rosarito was raped around twilight, the poor woman almost sleepless, that she was awoken by some cries, and she recognised Juan Aramendia's voice outside, calling for her to come out. She says that grandmother doesn't remember anything coherently or sequentially; just a few odd images and phrases (...) Father recalled that outside she told him "well, she doesn't want to go," and that it was true that he didn't want to leave. She didn't want him to see her, because she felt dirty and she didn't want to see him either; she wanted to be alone, to die alone. (511)

In regard to the harsh conclusion:

> Mother banished her from the farm without any pity. (126)

Faustino writes a description of the grief throughout the novel in one c sentence, putting the words he is writing into Rosarito's mouth:

> You are hell. (553)

We will once again return here to the questions posed by this novel: Is a writing that reveals suffering and shame worth it? Does the truth perhaps liberate? Does it perhaps save us?

Faustino sets the story in a time steeped in cruelty and bloodshed, at a time when neighbors and friends had to be separated and hostile to one another in order to sustain the war:

> About Jose Manuel Aizpurua, though, he informs him that he was the architect who designed the Nautical Club. Being the head of Falangist propaganda was no impediment to being friends with Lorca and Buñuek (. . .) Aizpurua and Lorca saw each other one spring morning in 1936 at the Biarritz Hotel in Zaragoza Square. The two friends, the red poet and the blue artist, the summer of that same year, were killed within twenty days of each other, each shot by the other's friends. (79–80)

> Beasain was one of the first sites of an execution in Gipuzkoa, along the lines of what had already happened in Navarre, collectively, and to a great extent, indiscriminately. The most terrible thing in that industrial town in the Goierri region (. . .) was that in order to be able to flesh out the war, it was necessary to make enemies of those who were not enemies beforehand. (222–223)

In this yearning to clarify and expose the truth, Ramon Saizarbitoria makes Faustino the narrator. Faustino sees what needs to be examined in detail and the correct direction to take. In order to set his explanation of a wartime story in the perfect novel (text), there are three values that are given to the truth:

1) Young people need to know. In chapter 6, an old acquaintance who was a friend of Faustino's father who lost his brother during the Civil War and had to leave his home is very curious about the subject of Faustino's new novel, about the events he is researching. He attaches great importance to putting young people on the path of truth and clearly states so. "The young need to know" he tells Faustino:

   > –I wondered if you were writing something about the war or not.
   >
   > –Maybe. I'm thinking about it.
   >
   > –That's good. The young need to know. (175)

2) What do we do with the truth? Lore calls into question the value of truth. Is it worth telling the truth after being hidden for a long time? The situation cannot be resolved, the truth that was initially hidden and rejected without any bad faith has created the consequence of severe complications seventy years later.

> It was a tough blow for her to find out that her grandfather was not an attractive noble disillusioned Falangist, but Rosarito's rapist (...) she clearly saw that her husband looked like her. She couldn't understand why she didn't realise earlier that he was an unscrupulous individual, someone that lived off her, deceiving and humiliating her since the day they met. When Rosarito became a participant in the secret, she got the impression that it was not something new for the husband. "So we're uncle and niece" (...) that he would in no way allow her to abandon him, that the poor woman did not know what he was capable of, and in a sweet voice he began listing a long list of ways he had thought up to ruin her life. (...) Naturally, denouncing the truth to her father became his main weapon of blackmail. (338–340)

In chapter 10, that idea is once again specified:

> –Tell me what we do with the truth—the old swimmer
>
> (...) that she was sacrificed to protect father. "To protect him from the truth." (340–341)

says Lore to Faustino when she clarifies her grandmother's rape and its consequences to him. The answer, however, is four lines faster than the question as she recalls Grandma Rosarito's words:

> She always maintained that hiding truths was a mistake, because they get more and more hidden and because, in the end, they always end up surfacing at some point (...) She died without telling her son the truth. (340)

Sharing the truth with Faustino has given her the courage to acknowledge her father and leave her husband's blackmail groundless:

> They called her from the hospital, to tell her that her father had come out of the coma. (...)
>
> –However, I don't know if it will be for the best, in all honesty -she says, once again when they are face to face with another. (...)
>
> –I don't think think life will bring him anything good any more. Quite the contrary

For sure. (345)

—I'm no longer afraid of him. I regret letting him blackmail me; because I've been a coward.

The man infers that her father has died, and because of that she feels free of her husband's rape. When asked how she is, the answer is that she remains unchanged, but that she will have to face up to the truth if she is to get on with life. "And I will also have to face up to what I did at one time; I don't want to go on with life conditioned by his threats." (509)

In deciding to confess the truth, Lore frees herself from overpowering connections and conditions from long ago events which she herself had nothing to do with.

3) Truth is, then, presented as a liberator and a source of courage. In chapter 16, while Faustino, Lili and the grandfather are chatting, the grandfather recalls the importance of truth, the importance of telling the truth and the importance of not hiding it, as well as the grief and pain that hiding events would bring. "One should always tell the truth, and face up to brutality..." At the end of the day, he hides the deception and rape committed against Rosarito because the rapist Julio Cesar threatens to kill his relatives.

—If I had had the courage to tell the truth, Belabeltza would perhaps have carried out his threat, but it would have been no worse for the Iturrinos or the Jauregis, and Juan Aramendia and Rosarito would have been saved, possibly. One should always tell the truth, and face up to brutality, because you end up crushed all the same when you give in, and you only end up hating yourself. (478)

As the grandfather admits, hiding did not prevent the break-up of his family, or the break-up and torment of the relationship between Juan Aramendia and Rosarito, or the fall of the latter's family either:

The question was whether he was who gave her the message from Juan to meet at eight in Gazteluzarra, if he really gave it to her on his behalf. He said yes, and she insisted on him telling the truth, please, to see if it was not Belabeltza, and he kept lying again and again, because he knew that something very serious had happened because of his guilt (...) He thought of giving her a book of poetry

> as a gift from Juan, but Rosarito told her to keep it for himself and read it, which would no doubt be good. From that point on, he never saw it again.
>
> The Jauregis shut themselves up in the house, stopped working the land, lost their livestock. The men went down to the village at dusk to get drunk (...) His father also began drinking, because his mother stopped speaking to him. (476–477)

Hiding the truth resulted in his feeling guilty in the years that followed:

> He never ever admitted that Julio Cesar had taken the message for Rosarito off him, he only revealed to his father how he found out about Aramendia's disappearance when he saw him very early that day and he ordered him never to tell anyone.
>
> –The grandfather thinks that he was guilty of his death, because he didn't warn him that Julio Cesar had taken the envelope from him.
>
> –I don't think it was because of that. If he wanted to kill him, he would have managed to do so one way or another. (393)

At this moment, it was essential for Faustino to follow in Juan Aramendia's footsteps in order to clear up his disappearance—or murder in Lili's grandfather's opinion—and put an end to the remorse and regret. Along the way, the only thing to clarify the connection between past and present would be his text, which is also an excellent way of clearing up the connection between each and every one of them.

Chapter 15 of the novel underscores the responsibility of literature in this area:

> The one that has made a not very short reflection on literature and history; that literature perpetuates, he says in conclusion, even though it is intense for those who experienced it, a memory of events that history does not know how to remember. (455)

The chief message of this novel surrounds the value of stating the truth. Yet in order for the clarification of truth to alleviate internal grief and shame, although it is useful to put things in their rightful place, some of them, for Ana, for example, fall on her like a ton of bricks.

In the end, he decides to place his hand on Ana's shoulder to console her. "Come on, come on, don't be like that" he repeats and "forget about the war and about your grandfather's damn things too." He is honest when he tells her that he is too conditioned by the choice his grandfather made in the war, and that it's not her fault her grandfather was a Falangist either—nor, it came to him, that he also was a rapist and almost certainly a murderer (. . .) he thinks about revealing to her the secret of his Basque nationalist grandfather's cowardice, because he also regrets explaining his overly idealised image of him. He's not too bothered about confessing the truth, after telling Lili once about it. It also makes him feel better. "You're not to blame if it that was your grandfather"—truth be told, it doesn't seem to him like a big deal to say that he was just a Falangist—"and I'm not to blame if mine started crying in terror in the trench, as soon as an airplane would appear in the sky." (373)

Ana, on the contrary, finds it impossible to accept her grandfather's choice or the consequences of that and his violent attitude, becoming aware of behavior that is still no more than a suspicion:

–But yours was on the side of the Republic.

–I'm telling you that a lot of men had to grab hold of him, because of the panic attacks it gave him.

–Being a fascist and being a coward are not the same thing -says Ana. (374)

In this situation, Faustino clearly comes down on the side of culture. He reclaims culture as the main form of resolving the prejudices linked to history and our forebears and he places the responsibility of choosing to follow or face up to the course of history in our hands:

The thing is that culture gives us a way to choose our *ancestors*. That's our real responsibility: what we choose. (374)

Conclusion: The Real Crime Is Forgetting the Truth

Ramon Saizarbitoria leaves a clear message on the table through this novel. The real crime is forgetting what happened, at least in our study of this novel.

Faustino investigates two crimes. One did not happen, namely the murder of Juan Aramendia. He escaped without anyone realizing, and although Lili's grandfather thinks that Julio Cesar killed him, that was not the case. The second is the rape of Rosarito.

Both Lili's grandfather and Rosarito kept quiet about what happened; they did not tell the truth. A consequence of this is that Lili's grandfather lived his whole life in anguish and guilt. Rosarito's silence, however, has brought about much more serious social consequences. Lore, without realizing, has married the son of her grandmother's rapist, Cesar (her step-uncle), and what is more, has had to endure his blackmail. Cesar wants to take control of Rosarito's possessions and he will achieve that.

The winners always win. That is the main reward for covering up the truth.

References

Alberca, Manuel (2007): *El pacto ambiguo. De la novela autobiográfica a la autoficción*. Biblioteca Nueva: Madrid.

Kortazar, Jon (2018): "Memoria, violencia y utopía en *Antzararen Bidea* (2007) / *El camino de la oca* (2008) de Jokin Muñoz, una novela vasca sobre la Guerra Civil," in *Rassegna Iberistica*, 41, 109. 119–134.

Martínez Rubio, José (2012): "Investigaciones de la memoria. El olvido como crimen," in Hans Lauge Hansen and Juan Carlos Cruz Suárez (2012): *La memoria novelada. Hibridación de géneros y metaficción en la novela española sobre la guerra civil y el franquismo (2000-2010)*. Peter Lang: Frankfurt. 69–82.

——— (2015): *Las formas de la verdad. Investigación, documentación y memoria en la novela hispánica*. Anthropos: Barcelona.

Oleza, Juan (1993): "La disyuntiva estética de la postmodernidad y el realismo," in *Compás de letras*, 3. 113–126.

Serrano Mairezkurrena, Amaia (2011): "Por los senderos de la memoria: *El camino de la oca* de Jokin de Jokin Muñoz," in *Cuadernos de Alzate*, 45. 109–132.

Chapter 9

The Police Novel in Basque Children's and Young Adult Literature

Xabier Etxaniz Erle and *Karla Fernández de Gamboa Vázquez*

Beginnings

In discussing children's and, especially, young adult literature, the term "gained literature" has often been mentioned. In other words, this is literature not created expressly for children and young adults, but which has become part of that genre. Many of the classic 19th-century texts have come down to the present in the form of children's and young adult literature. Something similar happened with the first police novel written in Basque: *Hamabost egun Urgainen* (1955; in English, *Fifteen Days in Urgain*, 2014). This work, written by Jose Antonio Loidi Bizkarrondo, was presented for a literary competition organized by Euskaltzaindia (the Academy of the Basque Language) and received a special mention; the competition was not for children and young adults, but for adults, and that is how our first police novel came about. From 1990 onward, however, the Erein publishing house began publishing it as young adult literature, so that young people could read Loidi's work.

In the 1950s, Euskaltzaindia recognized the need to encourage book production in Basque. As Etxaide (1984: 10) noted: "'Euskaltzaindia' was the first in the post-war period to begin doing something in favor of Basque, (...) to begin collecting things from among Basque culture sympathisers and to encourage us to work." Among these initiatives, it established a literary competition and, as noted above, Loidi achieved a special mention for the novel he presented in 1955. There is a prologue in the book by A. Irigarai, in which he states: "He employs a lively and interesting theme (the police theme never before addressed in Basque-language books), written in a simple popular Basque. One does not need a dictionary to read this novel, and saying this about a book in Basque is no small thing." *Hamabost egun Urgainen* had two features, namely, its attractiveness in regard to the storyline (its ability to draw the reader in, as it was a police novel) and its simplicity as regards language. We should not be surprised, then, that as time went on, this novel gained a young readership. What is more, in the 1961 edition published in Catalan, J. Alberti said the following:

> *Fifteen Days in Urgain* is a work of a police nature, with a completely original storyline in the genre. An action-packed novel, all Basque critics have coincided in underscoring the interest that emerges from the first pages. The style is simple, direct and colloquial.

The starting point of the work itself expresses very well the pace and direction of the novel: Txomin, the Urgain gravedigger, must prepare the grave for the deceased rich man Eguermendi, and sees the body of Eguermendi's young wife, with a bullet hole in her head. Disturbed, he tells Mr. Herriburu's wife about the discovery, and she asks her friend, the private investigator Martin Garaidi, to solve the murder.

This is how the novel, divided into thirty short chapters, starts. It is constructed right from the very beginning to captivate the reader. Throughout the chapters, the private investigator Martin Garaidi examines events that took place several years earlier and begins to search for the murderer. In his prologue, although Irigarai mentioned the originality of the novel, he offers the names of several authors who were taken into account when it was written: Poe, Chekov, Alarcón, Verne, Simenon, and so on. We do not know to what extent these and others influenced Loidi, but at the beginning it clearly resembles Ruiz de Alarcón's work *Iltzea* (The Nail) (in both cases, the text begins with the discovery of a skull with a hole) and as for Simenon's influence,

> In order to make writing in Basque normal, he supposedly thought about translating a detective novel that he liked a lot, specifically a book by Simenon, but he realised that translating it could be a daunting task and decided to start writing a novel on his own, without giving up the police genre. (Otaegi, 2020)

Olaziregi, on the other hand, challenges Irigarai's words: "To tell the truth, Loidi's technique does not reach the level of that master of the genre, E. A.

Poe, because, to the weakness of the conversations one must add his meta-comments, which spoil the suspense and slow down the rhythm" (2002: 68). M. Hernandez Abaitua (1982a) echoes this when he admits to not valuing the book very much as a police novel.

Yet from his mid-twentieth-century perspective, this work was also a useful means by which to introduce themes in Basque that had been detached from our language, as E. Mas said in 1958 in the prologue to the Spanish-language version of the book:

> At first sight, a police novel in Basque appears incongruent. This ancient language seems appropriate to describe the simple life of fishermen and peasants with their rustic and primitive problems, apt perhaps for the lyrical expansions of simple people or for religious instruction, but incapable of expressing the mobility of modern life, with its continuous concerns, alarms and startles. Nothing further from the truth.

The ease with which one can read *Hamabost egun Urgainen* (*Fifteen Days in Urgain*) has been noted since its first edition. Indeed, besides employing a lively, natural, simple, and popular form of speech (as Mitxelena, Garete, and Sarasola have noted), it uses an ironic writing style with a humorous tone (Cillero). If we add to this a chapter structure that creates interest for the reader (giving a clue at the end of each chapter about what will happen in the next and, through titles at the beginning of each chapter, "Garaidi Worried," "Slippery Slope," "Larrola's Confession," creating expectations), it is understandable that the work draws in contemporary young people as well as adults, and, as we mentioned before, that it has also been published in Spanish, Catalan, and, more recently, in 2014, in English. This is because it was, and this recognition must be acknowledged, "the first book to be translated [from Basque] into another language (it was published in Catalan in 1961)" (Sarasua).

L. Otaegi (2020) says that *Hambost egun Urgainen* (*Fifteen Days in Urgain*) was the most read Basque-language police novel until 1977. Furthermore,

> Together with this, Txomin Peillen's *Gauaz ibiltzen dena* (Creature of the Night..., Zarautz, Kulixka 1967) and *Gatu Beltza* (The Black Cat, Bilbo, Gero, 1973) and Mariano Izeta's *Dirua galgarri* (Ruinous Money, Tolosa, Auspoa, 1962) are mentioned. The ones after 1977 are those of Xabier Gereño and Gotzon Garate, so this novel by Loidi filled a time in which there was a clear gap.

Due to their subject matter and the Basque used, the works mentioned here were (and are) not very appealing to young people. Yet during the era before Basque-language children's and young adult literature emerged, Xabier Gereño's contribution with works published in straightforward Basque is worth noting. The Bilbao writer made use of literature in order to promote the language, so the reader might study Basque. J. Sarrionandia (1977a) commented the following on that para-literary offer:

> If Basque-language literature is to survive, it will have to discriminate completely between literature and para-literature, and this distinction is not based on the criteria of quality but on objectives. Xabier Gereño's novels, and he also admits it, are para-literary (or would be if Basque-language literature was established) and he has a very legitimate approach and goal within this field.

Gereño wrote, above all, theatrical works, biographies, short novels, and police novels, and among those latter texts we find the following titles: *Hiltzaile baten bila* (On the Trail of a Murderer, Kriseilu, 1975), *Espioitza* (Espionage, Kriseilu 1977), *Iruineako asasinatzea* (The Murder in Pamplona, Kriseilu 1977), *Jurgi kapitaina Britainian* (Captain Jurgi in Brittany, Egilea editore, 1978), *Osaba Gabrielen asesinatzea* (The Murder of Uncle Gabriel, Egilea editore 1978), and *Xantaia kontesari* (Blackmailing the Countess, Egilea editore 1978). For those learning and those becoming literate in Basque, many of these books by Gereño would end up in the hands of young people.

Joseba Sarrionandia (1977b), made the following comment about Xabier Gereño in the weekly *Zeruko Argia* (Heaven's Light):

> Lately, Xabier Gereño has been writing police novels. In fact, the police genre is the most appropriate to embody such texts in a consistent narrative, because it has the advantage of a general structural connection and some form of suspense. It is said he likes Agatha Christie, Simenon and Conan Doyle, more than the American noir novel, as regards genre trends. Moreover, among Basque-language writers, Xabier Gereño is the only one that cultivates effortlessly the noir novel.

Yet after this time, together with releasing texts in the early 1980s for Basque children and young adults, Xabier Gereño began publishing his first police or mystery novels. In many ways, the reference point for these works was the "Famous Five" series by Enid Blyton. The protagonists are young people, girls and boys who seek to solve a mystery, whose curiosity and interest push them into adventures.

From the 1980s Onward

From the 1980s onward, many books were published and clearly, in addition to the nature of that young gang mentioned above, in those books there is no violence or death, there is no blood . . . or very little.

In 1981, Anjel Lertxundi, under the pen name Iñaki Aldai, brought out *Portzelanazko irudiak* (Porcelain Images, Erein, 1981), in which a girl and two boys, Idoia, Xabier, and Mikel, try to solve a mystery with their dog (as did Enid Blyton's girls and boys and their dog Timmy in the "Bostak" series in Basque published at the time). In this case, those three children from Donostia find a piece of paper in a porcelain image and that gives the location of some treasure. In order to get the treasure, however, they must find and put together three pieces of paper. On the way, they come up against some bad people and, in the end, in a happy ending of course, the young people take the treasure to Donostia.

In the mid-1980s, Joxemari Iturralde created the character of Risky. This boy, while on holiday in a village, has a group of friends and, together, they get up to all kinds of things, including looking for an innocent person in the book *Sute haundi bat ene bihotzean* (A Big Fire in My Heart, Pamiela, 1994). The girls and boys come to the aid of the man who is in no way guilty when he is arrested for starting a fire. Among the group, after having several adventures, the man's innocence will be proved and the origin of the fire clarified.

Xabier Mendiguren Elizegi, on the other hand, set *Tangoak ez du amaierarik* (The Tango Never Ends, Elkar, 1988) a long way from the Basque Country, in Buenos Aires, and the investigator is not a group but one young person. Seeing the lights of the spotlight as a clown faints, the protagonist investigates the world of circus people in an attempt to unravel the mystery of his dizziness. Starting from this premise, young Pantxo will come across circus behavior, the movement of some suspect packages and mysteries, as well as political repression.

Previously, we referred to the fact that the mystery genre is very appealing to young people, that it is a very appropriate subject with which to draw in the reader, for readers to take a shine to, and for that reason, the release in 1990 of the mystery book *Erinias taberna* (The Erinias Bar, Elkar, 1990), written by sixteen-year-old Amaia Ormaetxea, should not surprise us. It was a school project, which was turned into a police novel for young people with the help of her teacher and the publishing house.

In this case, the investigator is a police officer, Jennifer, whose first case is a death resulting from a fire. James Maccrae dies when his house is set on fire, leaving his children orphaned. The firefighters, however, conclude that the fire was started deliberately and from that point on, the investigator Jennifer has to deal with the difficulties and complex problems caused by inheritances, gambling debts, children's problems, and many other issues. Little by little, she resolves all the complexities of the police cases until clarifying the matter in the end.

At that time, there were not just prominent original mystery books but also translations. To cite three very different styles, we could mention the writer M. Neuschäfer-Carlón's *Gaizki ateratako argazkia* (A Badly Taken Photograph, Elkar, 1992), H. Jürgen Press's book *Eskubeltz taldearen abenturak* (in English, *The Adventures of the Black Hand Gang*, 1976; Elkar, 1984) and *Postariak beti deitzen du mila aldiz* (The Postman Always Calls a Thousand Times, Elkar, 1994) by the Catalan writers A. Martín and J. Ribera. The first of these is a work in the style of a group of friends, as we have commented on. A little girl is kidnapped and Uwe and her friends investigate the matter until they reach the enlightening clue: a badly taken photograph. *The Adventures of the Black Hand Gang*, in contrast, being a very simple book, stands out for the importance of its images in addition to the text, posing a mystery game (the reader must find the answer to the question in the text in the picture that fills the whole right-hand page). Martin and Ribera's novel, meanwhile, is a book for young people, in which a young man who wants to date a girl inadvertently also finds Silvia and himself involved in the midst of a whirlwind of robberies, kidnappings, and numerous activities. This unusual novel thus includes intrigue and mystery, together with humor.

In addition to all these, the aforementioned Bostak series, comprising sixteen volumes, was published in Basque between 1981 and 2000. Although not as well-known, the Giltza publishing house brought out nine books between 2009 and 2013 in its "Lau lagun eta erdi" (Four and a Half Friends) series. Therein, too, the protagonists are four children and a dog, but unlike in Enid Blyton's well-known series, the books, written by Joachim Friedrich and illustrated by Mikel Valverde, are situated in contemporary society.

Yet if there has been one important contribution to Basque children's and young adult literature for works created in the realm of the police novel, it is the Madame Kontxexi-Uribe Brigada & Detektibe (Madam Kontxexi-Uribe, Brigadier, and Detective) series in the late 1980s, written by Anjel Lertxundi and illustrated by Antton Olariaga.

Madame Kontxexi-Uribe

In June 1988, the first two books in the "Madame Kontxexi-Uribe, Brigada & Detektibe" (Madam Kontxexi-Uribe, Brigadier, and Detective) series were released and the last two to make up the six-book sequence were published a year and a half later (the remaining two books—*Harakin deskalabratuaren kasua* (The Case of the Injured Butcher) and *Bertsolari hitz totelaren kasua* (The Case of the Stuttering Basque Oral Poetic Improviser)—were also announced, but never published).

Lertxundi wanted to offer young people mystery books, but, above all, his approach was humorous and based on wordplay. This is evident from the beginning.

Kaxkajo bahituaren kasua (The Case of Kidnapped Kaxkajo, Erein, 1988) is the first book in the series, and therein it is explained how Madam Kontxexi Uribe started out as a detective. As the first book, it offers a presentation right from the very outset:

> Her generous enormous bottom had sunk the mattress and, afterwards, when she stood up, the mattress that had been devastated by Madam Kontxexi's weight eased up as if taking a deap breath, the straw mattress wrinkled, the bed beat up. (Lertxundi 1988a: 5)

Together with Madam Kontxexi, her son is also introduced: "He was there, sat happily at the table, her son Bixentiko, who had been working tirelessly for seven years with the aim of getting through the first term of his first year of medical school." (Lertxundi 1988a: 5–6).

Madam Kontxexi is a schoolteacher who is on the verge of retiring, but a telephone call will completely change the life of this calm, quiet, and serene woman. As Bixentiko says, "they gave the same number as our phone to the Ertzaintza [Basque police force], and every time there is a robbery, or when someone has an accident, either because of nerves or the victims get confused, they call our house" (Lertxundi 1988a: 9).

Because of the call, Madam Kontxexi gets an idea in her head: "Someone is calling here? Let's try and solve their problems. (. . .) The poor Ertzainas [Basque police officers] have so much work, apparently . . . Why don't we help them, then, as much as we can?" (Lertxundi 1988a: 12).

Of course, that decision has something to do, as Bixentiko says to his mother, with the fact that hidden underneath Madam Kontxexi's pillow there are books by Agatha Christie, Simenon, Patricia Highsmith and so on. Thus, by chance, because of a phone call, the schoolmistress becomes a detective in Anjel Lertxundi's books. In the book which opens the series, the starting point for the investigation is a dog's disappearance: "my dog ran away from home last night and hasn't turned up since (. . .) it's a special dog: it brings us the newspaper every day from the newsstand" (Lertxundi 1988a: 17).

Madam Kontxexi tells the dog's owners that she will find it, and thus, when she arrives at her school, she asks her pupils for help: "Have any of you seen a lost dog near the *ikastola* [Basque school]? A red Labrador retriever. . ." (Lertxundi 1988a: 29). After tweaking their interest, she throws down the gauntlet to them: "Kaxkajo's owner is very worried. Shall we help him to find his poor dog? Let's see, aren't you all part of the clever, daring and shrewd Kalimotxo team?" (Lertxundi 1988a: 29).

One pupil responds to the sense of compeititon she creates among her pupils, because he has news for Madam Kontxexi about a ship that has arrived from the Labrador Peninsula. Amidst the din, revelry, uproar, and fidgeting of the students, the head, Madam Maripetral, decides to open a case against Madame Kontxexi and expel her from school. . . naturally, she receives what should have been bad news happily, because that way, she will have time to unravel the mystery of the missing dog.

Madam Kontxexi clears up the mystery very quickly when she goes to the aforementioned ship, where she is taken prisoner. The schoolmistress frees herself from the ties around her hands and soon solves the mystery of the kidnapped dog. That, and the next day she goes back to her job calmly and proudly.

The books in this series do not have any special merit with regard to the genre of mystery or police books. As we can see, our protagonist goes straight to the ship and resolves the complexity of the mystery (after fighting the people there. . . of course), and in that regard, it seems like the writer is using her as an excuse to write the work and to achieve his real objective. In *Paris de la France-ko pateen kasuan* (On the Case of the Paris de la France Pâtés, 1988, Erein), the same conclusion is even more noticeable. This is because here, there are two cases in one hundred pages; the first, the murder of a parrot, and the second, that of the theft of some pâtés. In both cases, the mystery is solved very simply, and resolved through marriage. Anjel Lertxundi seeks to write works that have a fresh and humorous tone. He makes the reader laugh by playing with words, and in his descriptions and dialogues.

The very titles of the chapters reveal this. Here are some chapter titles in the books:

Jaiki beharra beti da triste,/ hori ez da inorentzat albiste (The need to get up is always sad, / that's not news to anyone, *Kaxkajo* ...)

Tori ezan espedientea, maitea,/ eta etxean pasa ezan aste betea (Take the file, darling, / and spend a whole week at home, *Kaxkajo* ...)

Odolkiak izaten du ordaina / eta seko haserretu da kapitaina (The black pudding pays off / and the captain is very angry, *Kaxkajo* ...)

El Corte Ingles-eko beherapenak / eta Demetrioen penak (Sales in El Corte Ingles / and the sorrows of Demetrius, *Paris de la France* ...)

Aperitibo eta bazkari, / ekin dio madamek lanari (Aperitif and lunch, / madam started work, *Paris de la France* ...)

Nahiz basoan otsoa topatu / Madame ez da Txanogorritxu (Although she meets a wolf in the woods / Madame is not Little Red Riding Hood *Eskiatzaile* ...)

Nola duen arrosak arantza, / hala Santi Mamiñek arrantza (As the rose has a thorn, / so Santi Mamiñe fishes, *Estalaktita* ...)

Yet the chapter titles, those which reveal the story within, give the narrative a direction and therein we can find all kinds of wordplay and humorous descriptions. To begin with, these are based on descriptions of the characters, as we have already seen with Madam Kontxexi and Bixentiko. But apart from personal descriptions, Lertxundi uses action, such as, for example, when discussing Madam Maripetral: "The Head's nostrils flared like a hunting dog chasing a hare, suspecting something, smelling it, spying on it ..." (Lertxundi 1988a: 36); or that of the incapable pupil Dexpaxio ["Slow"]:

Everyone in the class turned their heads towards Dexpaxio, who was sitting at the last table. Well, Dexpaxio wasn't Despaxio, but Jose Maria Iturrimendi Larrarte, but everyone called him Dexpaxio, because, well, he was slow, and because he reacted very late, and because he was never in a hurry to do anything and ... It's clear why everyone in the class called Jose Maria Iturrimendi Larrarte Dexpaxio, right? (Lertxundi 1988a: 38)

In Madam Kontxexi's philosophy, in her lifestyle, this touch of humor is also evident, and it is maintained throughout the book and sometimes appears prominently. For example, in the matter of eating. One feature of this woman (as well as her intelligence and her relatively fair treatment of people, among other things) is her love of eating. For that reason, the handle on Madam Kontxexi's fridge was on the lower part, "so that every time she wanted something to eat, she also had to do some exercise" (Lertxundi 1988a: 52), after exercising. . . "Girl, if you enjoy the pleasure of eating by doing a little bit of exercise, the kilos may stay the same, but at least I could say that I'm following the doctor's advice" (Lertxundi 1988a: 52).

As for the matter of eating, Madam Kontxexi's opposite is Bixentiko (indeed, we should say not just in the question of eating, but in everything else too). This is made very clear in a letter written by the mother to her son, in which the reader is able to see the irony and food similes used by the mother:

Bixentiko, my beloved cod in pil-pil:

I have to go out. Get your own lunch. For today, you'll have to manage with a boiled egg. Do you know how to do that? First, get a pan, fill it with water and heat it up. When it begins to boil, the water not the pan, you have to put the egg in. If you want it not so done, make your bed, because the time it takes you will be perfect for the egg. If you want it well done, however, vacuum the whole house and by that time the egg will be quite well done. So, well, next, take the egg out of the water, break the shell (careful, because it'll be very hot, don't burn yourself, like a poor fresh peach), put it in a glass, add a touch of salt, and then start eating it with some bread.

Enjoy, my beloved sweet little Chantilly.

Your mum Kontxexi." (Lertxundi 1988a: 53)

As well as humor, by playing with language, the author uses repetitions of similar terms to give more strength to the idea, emphasizing the aim of the speaker or narrator. "The Ertzain [Basque police officer] is always at the service of the people, that's the motto we were taught over and over again at the Academy. So, say, express, declare, mention everything that worries you, bothers you, makes you nervous" (Lertxundi 1988b, 20).

This wordplay tendency is also evident in other works by Lertxundi for children ("The simple way of storytelling is very successful and that simplicity is not a coincidence. In this way, this written prose is full of playfulness in relation to both language and subject matter too," as Mikel Hernandez Abaitua (1982b) states in a comment made for *Tristeak kontsolatzeko makina* -The Machine to Confort Sad People).

When writing a police novel (that was also the case in the work *Hamaseigarrenean aidanez* (It Happened the Sixteenth Time), Lertxundi must create a believable investigator and, in this credibility, he must bear in mind the society and situation of the Basque Country. As J. Kortazar said,

> each country frames its police novel according to its corresponding features. In the contemporary Basque Country, detectives from the USA are of no use, because they are not from here and, what is more, because it is very difficult to show the police sensitively here. For that reason, whether or not there is a detective, attention has not been paid to the police novel: the reason stems from choosing an investigator. (Kortazar, 1983)

That lack of sensitivity toward the police which Kortazar mentions changed, to some extent, with the implementation of the Ertzaintza [Basque police force], or that is what Madam Kontxexi thinks because she is sorry that those Ertzainas have so much work on their hands ... and in the face of that, Lertxundi creates a distinct and different investigator (as we were able to see above too). Lertxundi's investigator is not a police officer or a professional investigator, but an *ikastola* [Basque language school] teacher, and moreover a very fat and bold woman. This fatness is an aid throughout the books, as in Camilleri's Montalbano books, in which food enjoys an almost constant presence. It is used to the point of humor. The presence of humor, a feature in the works of the aforementioned Italian writer, would likewise be another similarity in the works about Montalbano and Madam Kontxexi. That said, while one is a police officer who investigates murders, the other is an *ikastola* schoolteacher who loves mysteries and solves much simpler matters.

There are various merits to the six books about Madam Kontxexi, including first the language used by the writer, which is comprehensible, simple and offered in a playful way; then there is the character of Madam Kontxexi herself, a spirited woman full of life and with a fine talent for irony; and lastly, their critique of society and culture today, yet still without losing their humor, which is ever-present. The mysteries, in the end, are just pretexts in these books to link everything that has gone before. This is because, as is customary in the noir novel, any investigation into a murder is a pretext for making a critical reflection on society, someone in particular or our social relations.

Recently, Irati Jimenez commented very succinctly on the value of these works by Lertxundi in the magazine *Elkar*:

> And today, here, I am going to applaud a kind of precious stone. I have just reread the six books in the Madam Kontxexi-Uribe, Brigadier and Detective series by Andu Lertxundi and Antton Olariaga and they seemed more mischievous and better than when I originally read them. When I was younger, *Sardina Ezpain Gorriaren Kasua* [The Case of the Red-lipped Sardine] made me laugh, but I only understood half of what I do now. Read it. Reread it. You will see that no other book has been written in Basque literature which so clearly reveals all our elitist-purist-absurd cultural characteristics. Tell me, really, if you have ever come across a better parody than Bixentiko going to Seville when his mother is kidnapped. Bixentiko is our very own Ignatius J. Reilly, a silly quixotic man who wants to be bohemian and bad, without any talent to create literature, someone who pronounces theories about literature, wasting time in the windmills of absurd Basque-language purity, like a foolish native Basque speaker, without realising that the adult learner of Basque next to him is far more intelligent. Immature, puny, monkish, a Basque speaker and dull, in the end we will warm to Bixentiko and maybe you will be moved to some extent when his mother gives the best advice that anyone who wants to be a writer has ever been given. What can be given to all the Bixentikos in our literary world and, especially, to each of us that deep down inside is tempted to dress Basque up in a cassock, is revealed to us through the intimacy of Bixentiko. "You like literature. That's fine. Make literature."

> Make a note: Madam Kontxexi-Uribe, Brigadier and Detective's *Sardina Ezpain Gorriaren kasua*. The most mischievous and moving analysis of Basque literature and Basque culture. Along the lines of *The Bonfire of the Vanities*, as anarchic as *No Word from Gurb*, a kind of avant la lettre Spanish Affair predating *Spanish Affair*, which manages to reach the terrific comic heights of a Tom Sharpe. Therein I have found the sharpest diagnosis that can be made of our culture and, alongside that, medicine to save us from all the nonsense and sickness. (Jimenez 2019: 7)

A Few Works at Century's End

At the end of the twentieth century, many mystery novels were published, some of them translations like Agustin Fernández Paz's *Lore erradioaktiboak* (Radioactive Flowers, Elkar, 1993), a mystery work about a radioactive spill in an Atlantic trench. Others, meanwhile, were created in Basque. Pako Aristi's *Din-dan-don... Kanpai lapurrak non?* (Ding-Dong...Where Are the Bell Thieves? Elkar, 1996) is a mystery set during the Second Carlist War and begins with a deal between the thief Baptiste Lizarraga and a jeweller in Baiona to get a 500-kilo silver weight. The thief will seek, in the middle of the war, to steal a bell in Beizama, where a one-ton bell has been made that, in order to get a good sound, is half silver and half bronze. It is full of adventure and mystery, but not a police novel at all. In contrast, *Hauts madarikatua* (The Cursed Powder, Elkar, 1996), published by Imanol Zaldua that same year, is. Therein, Detective Bidegain has to investigate a drug dealer who operates between Antwerp and Bilbao. It is a sprightly novel about drugs, with lots of action and a happy ending. It is somewhat moralizing, and one only need see the quote that appears at the end of the novel to realize this:

> The source of joy and tears is deep inside the heart, and the empty heart cannot be filled with anything external, let alone drugs.
>
> We make getting numb a foundation and everything established on top of that immediately crumbles to dust. (Zaldua, 1996: 125–126)

We can also find mystery and a police investigation in *Margolana* (The Painting, Alfaguara/Zubia, 1999), written by Igor Elortza. Elortza sets the novel in the near future (it takes place in 2002) and it is about a valuable painting which goes missing in a school; the narrator is a pupil in the school who investigates the disappearance. In fact, from the start it is obvious that this is a mystery or detective book (a quote by Agatha Christie opens the work) and Elortza uses numerous elements—the international police, a suspect caretaker, the behavior of young pupils, et cetera, to attract the reader. In the words of Manu Lopez Gaseni:

> This has all the ingredients to capture young readers; set in a high school, a fondness for comic books, the use of new technologies, young people's parties, first loves and bad adults. (Lopez Gaseni, 2000: 53)

Panic Attacks

In 2003, among books for young people, the Elkar publishing house released noir fiction and police novels within its "Panic Attacks" (Izu-taupadak) series. In the beginning, they were translations of police novels, including Robert Swindells' *Kale gorrian* (*Stone Cold*, Elkar, 2005), Sinclair Smith's *Inork ikusi ezin duena* (*Second Sight*, Elkar, 2006) and Andreu Martín's *Wendyk hegan ikasi zuen gaua* (*The Night Wendy Learnt to Fly*, Elkar, 2009). Initially, together with Jaume Ribera, several of Andreu Martín's works were published in Basque in the Falnaga series. In this case, he appears as the sole author of the novel and it concerns what happens to the young woman Wendy over the course of a night. A long time ago, a witch told Wendy that she would die on her twenty-third birthday. Today, that day has come, and the police officer Wendy (she is a *mosso d'esquadra*, a member of the Catalan police force) gets involved in numerous tangles during this unforgettable night.

Among works created in Basque, however, there is one author who stands out for his work in recent years, Jokin de Pedro.

This writer from Bilbao had already brought out children's books and mystery or horror fiction (*Izu-izua*, Terrifying Horror, for example), when he published the first Inspector Gorospe book in 2008: *Irurac bat* (The Three Are One, Elkar, 2008). Previously, too, as in the case of the short stories in *Izu-izua* (Terrifying Horror), if there were noticeable references to films in de Pedro's work, so now we see an attempted murder that we have seen so many times before. Gari wants to kill his wife and, so as not to fall under suspicion, he contracts a professional killer. The events, however, do not turn out as Gari thinks they will, and instead of killing Lidia, his wife, a friend of his is dead. From the police suspicions, Lidia, in the end, clearly sees that her husband is guilty.

Five years later, de Pedro published *Etsai gordea* (The Hidden Enemy, Elkar, 2013). In this case, a well-known television presenter receives threats and nearly all the chapters cover a period between April 15 and May 3, 2010. Toward the end, a couple of chapters take place a couple of months later. In that regard, it is a very dynamic novel. Mr. Arriola is threatened and sees his world turned upside down, and thus Inspector Gorospe begins to investigate the presenter's lifestyle and past.

De Pedro maintains a touch of tension throughout the novel, which at times rises dramatically, and that way he manages to intensify the threat (from letters to bombs) while also increasing the reader's interest. Indeed, as in his latest novel *Elurpean* (In the Snow, Elkar, 2016), he uses intrigue, a lot of action, dynamic events, a stubborn inspector, and so forth to enourage the reader to find out how everything unravels at the end.

Another police work has been published in this Panic Attacks series by Elkar, J. Urteaga's *Hilpuinak* (Short Death Stories, 2008), which includes six stories: "Txerriak txerritegira" (Pigs to the Pigsty), "Susmorik ez" (No Suspicion), "Perfumea potto ttikian" (Perfume in the Small Bottle), "Basoko zarata mutuak" (Mute Forest Noises), "Laster amaituko diagu" (We'll Finish It Soon), and "Ipuin bat dugu bizitza" (Life is a Short Story); each short story is about a murder and as the last story concludes: "Life is a short story; / we write on blank pages, / until the ink runs out" (Urteaga, 2008: 163).

In Recent Years

In recent years, in order to conclude the panorama, we must cite a work published in 2017 by the Erein publishing house: *Iraganik gabe* (Without Any Past, Erein, 2017), written by Felipe Juaristi. This intrigue novel starts in a very cinematographic way. The protagonist wakes up, without any strength, with his arm tied to a pipe. He flees and, on the way, his colleagues and the police seek to capture him. The fugitive finds shelter in a house, in which a grandfather and a young girl live, and he will develop a very special relationship with the latter, with Venezia.

As usual in noir fiction, the novel reveals the aim to show different realities apart from actions, interpersonal relationships, the society in which we live, and, above all, a demonstration of one's fears, feelings, and contradictions:

> The grandfather knew that it was just a question of time, that they would catch up with him, the police or the Zumarraga friends. At the same time, he knew that he could do very little about it. He was tempted to pick up the phone and call the Ertzaintza [Basque police force], because he thought it best to leave Nicolas in the Ertzaintza's hands than those of the others. In the end, he didn't dare. The man hiding at home was Venezia's friend; she had never had any friends. That stopped him. He also asked himself what might happen if the Zumarraga friends arrived before the Ertzaintza. He didn't get to the end of the question (Juaristi, 2017: 85).

As one can see, Felipe Juaristi, using agile writing, reflects the grandfather's thoughts, fears, and worries attractively, encouraging the reader to continue reading. This is often one of the most striking features of police novels, as they seek to capture readers and keep them engrossed until the last knot in the plot is untied.

In 2020, meanwhile, Juan Kruz Igerabide published *Arrastoa* (Traces, Alai, 2020). Set during the 1936 war, the person narrating the events is a Civil Guard detective. There has been a murder in Lekunberri and in July 1936, when the atmosphere is very tense, this detective decides to investigate the murder without revealing his identity. A pro-Republic schoolmaster has been arrested (the victim was a fervent Carlist), but the investigator does not believe the schoolmaster Donato is the murderer.

The starting point of the novel gives a clue in order to demonstrate that this is a police novel; as does the text which appears on the back cover of the book, but, although there is an investigation into the murder, one would say that this is a *costumbrista* novel. In the eight chapters, the first must be understood as an introduction, the next five about the life of the local police officer and baker Justino, and the writer only uses the last two to clarify the murder.

It is an enjoyable novel because of the hard-hitting narratives (the corruption and hatred of politicians, revenge, political assassinations, etc.) but, as noted above, as the narrator is a detective, and that detective's job is to shed light on a murder, it is clear that the protagonist of the novel does not have anything to do with the murder. This time, then, the police novel may be a pretext to attract readers to the novel.

With the coming of the twentieth century, police novels came to occupy the center of the literary system in adult literature and at the international literary level. There have also been attempts in Basque, and there are, as in the case of Alberto Ladron Arana, many writers who have appeared therein; but even more than in adult literature, it could be said that the main contribution has been made in children's and young adult literature. This is because, in order to attract readers, a direct dynamic language is used, because it is a suitable field for humor and exaggeration and, why not, because it also creates a space for critique.

Basque childrens' and young adult literature has experienced good and bad times in regard to police novels, and now, although too many works are published, there is a very interesting set of quality readings with which to create fans, as well as to stimulate the imagination and the reflection of readers.

References

Aristi, Pako (1996): *Din-dan-don. . . Kanpai lapurrak non?* Elkar: San Sebastian.

Cillero, Javi (2000): *The Moving Target. A History of Basque Detective and Crime Fiction*. Doctoral

dissertation. Reno. Unpublished.
De Pedro, Jokin (2008): *Izu-izua*. Elkar: San Sebastian.
———. (2008): *Irurac bat*. Elkar: San Sebastian.
———. (2013): *Etsai gordea*. Elkar: San Sebastian.
———. (2016): *Elurpean*. Elkar: San Sebastian.
Elortza, Igor (1999): *Margolana*. Alfaguara/Zubia: Bilbao.
Fernández Paz, Agustín (1993): *Lore erradioaktiboak*. Elkar: San Sebastian.
Garate, Gotzon (2000): *Euskal Herriko Polizia Eleberria*. Elkar: San Sebastian.
Gereño, Xabier (1975): *Hiltzaile baten bila*. Kriseilu: San Sebastian.
———. (1975): *Espioitza*. Kriseilu: San Sebastian.
———. (1977): *Iruiñeako asasinatzea*. Kriseilu: San Sebastian.
———. (1978): *Jurgi kapitaina Britainian*. Egilea publisher: Bilbao.
———. (1978): *Osaba Gabrielen asesinatzea*. Egilea publisher: Bilbao.
———. (1978): *Xantaia kontesari*. Egilea publisher: Bilbao.
Hernandez Abaitua, Mikel (1982a): "Nobela beltza eta polizi nobela klasikoa," in *Jakin*, 25: 51–67.
———. (1982b): "Tristeak kontsolatzeko liburua," in *Susa*, 1982-01. Available at https://kritikak.armiarma.eus/?p=3998.
Igerabide, Juan Kruz (2020): *Arrastoa*. Alai: San Sebastian.
Iturralde, Joxemari (1994): *Sute haundi bat ene bihotzean*. Pamiela: Pamplona.
Jimenez, Irati (2019) "Gora genero txikiak, Gora Bixentiko!," in *Elkar* 55, 7. Available at https://postdata.elkar.eus/wp-content/uploads/2019/03/Aldizkaria-55.pdf.
Juaristi, Felipe (2017): *Iraganik gabe*. Erein: San Sebastian.
Jürgen Press, Hans (1984): *Eskubeltz taldearen abenturak*. Elkar: San Sebastian.
Kortazar, Jon (1983): "*Hamaseigarrenean aidanez*: iragarritako sari baten kronika," in *Jakin*, 1983-09. Available at https://kritikak.armiarma.eus/?p=3870.
Lertxundi, Anjel (1981): *Portzelanazko irudiak*. Erein: San Sebastian.
———. (1988a): *Kaxkajo bahituaren kasua*. Erein: San Sebastian.
———. (1988b): *Paris de la France-ko pateen kasua*. Erein: San Sebastian.
———. (1988): *Eskiatzaile herrenaren kasua*. Erein: San Sebastian.
———. (1989): *Estalaktika rockeroaren kasua*. Erein: San Sebastian.
———. (1989): *Alarguntsa sikodelikoaren kasua*. Erein: San Sebastian.
———. (1989): *Sardina ezpain gorriaren kasua*. Erein: San Sebastian.
Loidi, Jose Antonio (1990): *Hamabost egun Urgainen*. Erein: San Sebastian.
Lopez Gaseni, Manu (2000): "Margolana," in *Behinola* 3: 53.
Martin, Andreu (2009): *Wendyk hegan ikasi zuen gaua*. Elkar: San Sebastian.
Martín, Andreu, and Ribera, Jaume (1994): *Postariak beti deitzen du mila aldiz*. Elkar: San Sebastian.
Mendiguren Elizegi, Xabier (1988): *Tangoak ez du amaierarik*. Elkar: San Sebastian.
Mitxelena, Luis (1955): "Amabost egun Urgainen," in *Egan*. Available at https://kritikak.armiarma.eus/?p=6671.
Neuscháfer-Carlón, Mercedes (1992): *Gaizki ateratako argazkia*. Elkar: San Sebastian.
Olaziregi, Mari Jose (2002): *Euskal eleberriaren historia*. Labayru. Amorebieta-Etxanoko Udala: Bilbao.

Ormaetxea, Amaia (1990): *Erinias taberna*. Elkar: San Sebastian.
Otaegi Imaz, Lourdes (2020): "*Hamabost egun Urgainen (1955)*. Jose Antonio Loidi Bizkarrondo," in *Auñamendi Entziklopedia* [online], 2020. Retrieved from http://aunamendi.euskoikaskuntza.eus/eu/hamabost-egun-urgainen-1955-jose-antonio-loidi-bizkarrondo/ar-154309/.
Sarasola, Ibon (1976): *Historia social de la literatura vasca*. Akal: Madrid.
Sarasua, Asier (2011): "Amabost egun Urgain'en," in *Eibartik*, Feb. 28. Available at https://kritikak.armiarma.eus/?p=5366.
Sarrionandia, Joseba (1977a): "Gudari bat," in *Zeruko Argia*, Dec. 18. Available at https://kritikak.armiarma.eus/?p=2911.
——— (1977b): "Paraliteratura militantea," in *Zeruko Argia*, Dec. 10. Available at https://kritikak.armiarma.eus/?p=2919.
Smith, Sinclair (2006): *Inork ikusi ezin duena*. Elkar: San Sebastian.
Swindells, Robert (2005): *Kale gorrian*. Elkar: San Sebastian.
Urteaga, Joseba (2008): *Hilpuinak*. Elkar: San Sebastian.
Zaldua, Imanol (1996): *Hauts madarikatua*. Elkar: San Sebastian.

Chapter 10

Ramiro Pinilla's Police Novels: Contesting the Lack of Memory

Santiago Pérez Isasi

Ramiro Pinilla's (1923–2014) narrative work has received, in recent years, moderate if not scant attention from academic criticism, in spite of the recognition that it deserves, following the publication, above all, of his monumental trilogy *Verdes valles, colinas rojas* (Green Valleys, Red Hills, 2004–2005). The volume coordinated by Mercedes Acillona López, *Ramiro Pinilla: el mundo entero se llama Arrigunaga* (Ramiro Pinilla: The Whole World Is Called Arrigunaga, 2015), is for the moment the only work dedicated in monograph form to the author from Getxo, to which one should add the individual works published by Javier Feijoo Morote in recent years (2018a, 2020, among others) and the analysis in *Aquella edad inolvidable* (That Unforgettable Age), Ramiro Pinilla's latest novel (with the exception of the police series studied in this chapter), edited by Jon Kortazar (2019).

Feijoo Morote is responsible, likewise, for several works which have addressed Ramiro Pinilla's police novels (2016, 2017, 2018b), following the pioneering work of Bautista Naranjo (2011), which highlighted accurately the Cervantine nature of Ramiro Pinilla's police narrative, and following the chapter by Jorge Chen Sham (2015) in the aforementioned collective work coordinated by Mercedes Acillona. These three novels, *Solo un muerto más* (Only One More Death, 2009), *Cadáveres en la playa* (Corpses on the Beach, 2014a), and *El cementerio vacío* (The Empty Cemetery, 2014b), as such a late harvest in Pinilla's narrative, offer a parodic approach to the police genre. They include the detective/bookseller Samuel Esparta/Sancho Bordaberri, who investigates various crimes committed before and after the Spanish Civil War.

In this work, however, I propose to undertake a different analysis from the approaches of the previously mentioned authors, which are focused, for the most part, on the relationship between Ramiro Pinilla's works and the police genre itself, with the rest of the author's work or with the already cited quixotic model. Thus, in what follows, I will suggest a review of the three novels mentioned in order to analyse how one of the central themes and preoccupations in much of Pinilla's work is manifested therein: the construction of memory, whether through assembling a narrative about the past, or the conservation of and return to what are termed "sites of memory," according to the concept proposed by Pièrre Nora.

The Construction of Memory and the "Battle for the Story"
Narrating against Forgetting

As Feijoo Morote explains, the police work of Sancho Bordaberri/Samuel Esparta does not have the basic goal of discovering the criminal in order to restore order (social, economic, or political); nor even necessarily the punishment (moral or penal) of the offender. Instead, it seeks to recover the truth and memory relating to events in the past: "Samuel Esparta's struggle is [. . .] against forgetting" (Feijoo Morote 2016: 25–26). In this way, Pinilla's police narrative is integrated into the whole of his work, in which the theme of recovery of a memory faithful to the past occupies a fundamental place: not just in *La higuera* (The Fig Tree), a novel that revolves precisely around trauma, memory, and reparation (Beti 2007, Ibarrola-Armendariz 2015), but also, for example, in the trilogy *Verdes valles, colinas rojas* (Green Valleys, Red Hills). In the latter, many of the conversations between Asier Altube and the schoolteacher Don Manuel are, precisely, about the most appropriate way of recovering, recording, and remembering the past. Thus, Ramiro Pinilla's work in general, and his three police novels in particular, could be located within the context of the (broad) current of historical memory narrative, even if with a few particularities, as we will point out later:

> Pinilla is part of the group termed 'critical memory': they pose a narrow correlation between the past and its present legacy, assuming the consequences of a conflict which condemned to the past many of its protagonists, but with the firm intention to restore its memory. (Muñoz López 2009, cited by Feijoo Morote 2016: 25)

The chronological, social, and political contextualization of the crimes is without doubt essential to understand this need to recover the past. In *Solo un muerto más* (Only One More Death), in 1945 Samuel Esparta investigates a crime that happened in 1935; in *Cadáveres en la playa* (Corpses on the Beach), the investigation takes place in 1972, while the crime was committed in 1935. Only in *El cementerio vacío* (The Empty Cemetery) is the action contemporaneous to the crime, so that, in this case, forgetting, or, if one prefers, a blindness that must be corrected, does not have so much to do with the passage of time, as it does with ideological prejudice, as we will examine later.

The idea of recovering the truth about the past, of bringing to light what is close to being definitively buried by forgetting, is a constant presence right from Detective Samuel Esparta's first case. At the same moment in which he renounces his failed career as a writer of police novels and decides to give life to Detective Samuel Esparta, Sancho Bordaberri is aware that his work consists of recovering a chapter buried in forgetting due to historical and political circumstances:

> The crime was committed in 1935, and I suppose that if he wasn't found guilty, it was because it was not a political crime. Later, Franco would have said: "Those Basques won't miss one of their own after having lost so many." The police, the municipal police and the judges did very little, four questions and a nice goodbye. So that today, in 1945, we still have the murderer out there. Why has everyone, including me, forgotten about this matter for so many years? The thing is, Franco was right, it was a time with too many deaths, those of the imminent war and those of the repression, which had still not ceased. (Pinilla 2009: 8)

This search for a past truth about something that everyone has forgotten or would prefer to forget becomes the categorical imperative that drives the detective's action: respect for the truth is identified with the very concept of justice or integrity, "gentlemanly" values adopted from hardboiled models, and, in the final analysis, from Don Quijote himself. Giving voice to those who have lost theirs seems to be an obligation or mission of universal dimensions and a huge moral and philosophical burden: "It is unjust to close the mouths of those who ask, simply, to tell a story. The world would be better if every living being—including the dinosaurs and the Neanderthals—had had the opportunity to tell their history" (Pinilla 2014a: 16).

It is significant that this recovery is carried out in the form of narrative, as "telling a story;" in other words, it may be perceived with clarity that remembering is narrating, that without narrative there is no memory. "I could care less who has killed and who not, I only seek a consistent development of the facts... and, why not? To do justice?" (Pinilla 2014a: 43). This "consistent development of the facts," an almost literal definition of the narrative plot since Aristotle, leads to the almost invisible pairing between detective investigation and the composition of the novel by Sancho Bordaberri, *Solo un muerto más* (Only One More Death) [which, in a new quixotic game, will appear referred to and commented on in *El cementerio vacío* (The Empty Cemetery)].

One must ask oneself, for that reason, if it can be considered that Samuel Esparta is successful in his search for the truth, justice, and memory. On the one hand, the initial crime (the death of the twin Eladio) is solved in the final pages of the novel, and therefore one may believe that there exists a certain mending and recovery of the past; the very publication of the novel (in an intradiegetic sense) would seem to guarantee that the events narrated cannot now be concealed once again by forgetting. Even so, the epilogue to *Solo un muerto más* (Only One More Death) offers a somewhat more pessimistic vision, since a new crime (that of the other twin, Leonardo) suffers once more a similar process of forgetting ("It was just one more death: civil protocols were stifled by the minor characters of the Regime and the same 'old nothing has happened here' was implemented" Pinilla 2009: 184), which allows for asking questions about the relationship among narrative, memory, and power; or between the diverse types of memory and forgetting: individual and collective, or also institutional(ized) and what is posed as alternative.

Narrating Against Power
In effect, it is not a question of just constructing a narrative that rescues the voice of the forgotten and which may construct an individual and collective memory of the past. It is also, and in a very obvious way in the three novels, one of constructing an alternative memory to that imposed from authority, from the dominant or hegemonic discourses. Naturally, within the historical context in which the action of the novels is situated, the power to construct the discourse was held by Francoism and, at least in the immediate postwar period, the Falange as his propaganda and indoctrination body. This is a mission shared by Samuel Esparta, the detective, and Sancho Bordaberri, the bookseller. The latter manifests, for example, his intention to "counteract children's publications like

Flechas y Pelayos (a children's magazine of Francoist ideology, published from 1938 to 1949) and other Francoist jingoisms" (Pinilla 2014a: 6), and in another passage he states the following:

> There was some Mathematics from 1937 eulogised with the 2nd Triumphal Year; some Natural-Physical Sciences from 1938 and a History of Spanish Literature from the same year, both with the 3rd Triumphal Year; a School Encyclopaedia had left the printers without such excess, and if it made it into bookshops it was due to the fact that the oversight was remedied with a hastily hand-stamped "2nd Triumphal Year"; the Church fulfilled education covering all the materials and publishing them, purified, by companies titled, for example, Anti-sectarian Publications of Burgos, the Caudillo's headquarters city. On the eve of every October, the bookshop was filled with these outpourings, which soon passed and we would return to other fictions, those of the rest of the year. (Pinilla 2009: 40)

This classification as "fictions" for discourses originating in the Francoist regime could lead one to pose a broader question: that of whether all discourses originating in institutional authority (historical, educational, political, etc.) can be equally considered as fictions, or if this is only applicable to those that originate in authoritarian or ultranationalist regimes. This is not a topic developed by Pinilla, at least explicitly, in these novels, even though, as we will see a little later, that of Francoism is not the only hegemonic discourse contested therein.

Furthermore, this opposition between official Francoist discourse and constructed memory (or in the process of construction) through Sancho Bordaberri / Samuel Esparta is personified, at the intradiegetic level, by the confrontation of the detective with the Falangist Luciano Aguirre, who aspires to be a poet, in *Solo un muerto más* (Only One More Death); and with the Political-Social Commissioner Cayo Fernández, in *Cadáveres en la playa* (Corpses on the Beach). In both cases, there is an attempt to construct two parallel narratives, one stemming from within institutional authority and endorsed by it, and another, that fictionalized by Sancho Bordaberri, alternative to the former and which aspires to be more compliant with truth and justice:

—[. . .] We have two versions of the same case; you could make a novel out of either of them.

–Only one would be real. (Pinilla 2009: 177)

In the case of *Solo un muerto más* (Only One More Death), the conflict between both versions extends up to the dénouement of the investigation, in which two possible explanations about Eladio's death confront one another both on the intellectual and the physical plane:

> –You die and I'll carry on with the novel. I'll write that the other investigator missed the shot, took aim incorrectly, and I have Etxe, the real murderer. More pages, more density. What's more, inserting a body doesn't do a noir novel any harm. [...]
>
> –You'd be lying. You'd be inventing. And are you not afraid of imagining? You'd be contaminating the whole story.
>
> –Remember, bookseller, that, what's more, I'm a poet. I'd resolve the incident through a single borderless poem.
>
> I lift the heavy chains as far as the length of my arms.
>
> –That's the real ending of the novel, damn it! (Pinilla 2009: 180)

In *El cementerio vacío* (The Empty Cemetery), for its part, the Political-Social Commissioner seeks to write an aseptic, neutral, and objective report on the crime of Anari. However, as happened with Luciano Aguirre in *Solo un muerto más* (Only One More Death), Cayo Fernández also interferes in Samuel Esparta's investigation, provoking the fatal dénouement of the plot and managing, given his position, to make the official discourse of the Regime frame him as the central hero in solving the case (Pinilla 2014a: 186). It is thus demonstrated, perhaps, that the official discourse cannot be neutral or remove itself from its position of power, since it conditions not just the representation of the facts, but the facts themselves. Only the future publication of the novel written by Sancho Bordaberri would be able, once more, to arrive at "imposing the truth," constructing an alternative memory to the official one.

In this novel, though, the Francoist discourse (already worn out and with signs of exhaustion) is not that which most clearly confronts the process of reconstructing the crime; this place corresponds, in this case, to the hegemonic discourse (at least in the Getxo of Ramiro Pinilla's universe) of Basque nationalism. One should recall that this representation (and parodic deconstruction) of nationalist discourse was also one of the central elements in *Verdes valles, colinas rojas* (Pérez Isasi 2015a); in *El cementerio vacío*, the death of a young Basque woman by (allegedly) an immigrant *maketo* [a historically derogatory term for non-Basque immigrants][1] provokes the externalization of xenophobic discourse and dominant stereotypes in the nationalist discourse of the era. The opposition between Basques and the external "other" (recall the character of Ella in *Verdes valles, colinas rojas*) is manifested again in history, resembling *Romeo and Juliet* or *Bodas de Sangre* (*Blood Wedding*), the forbidden relationship between Anari and Pedro. In this specific case, however, it is only a one-off manifestation of a (supposed) timeless war between Basques and the outside world, "the other": "In our land, in the past they were Cagots and now they are *maketos*, although their differences are substantial, beginning with those of time. [. . .] Cagots or *maketos*, always "the other" (Pinilla 2014a: 13).

Hence, the identification of the *maketo* Pedro González as the murderer of Anari is not based so much, nor solely, on the available evidence, but on prejudices projected onto him as someone outside an idealized community, which is peaceful and incapable of carrying out acts of violence.

Although in a less relevant way, a similar approach appeared already in *Solo un muerto más*, in a brief scene in which Sancho Bordaberri chats with the schoolteacher Don Manuel, a spokesman, both here and in *Verdes valles, colinas rojas*, of the Basque nationalist worldview. For Don Manuel, the mere hypothesis that Eladio's murderer may be a Basque is unacceptable:

> –Do you know where I'm going with this? . . . Someone from amongst us killed him! Who? Another Basque, allegedly. And here's the danger: it couldn't have been another Basque . . ., even if in Getxo the immense majority of us are. But there are also those from elsewhere, non-Basques. And it had to have been one of them. Because, Sancho, we Basques don't kill, and even less that way.

> It's an issue from which I'm somewhat removed, but the expression of the man I have before me is almost desolate. I dare to point that out to him:

> –By a simple arithmetic calculation, the probabilities that. . .

> He interrupts me:

> –It's not a question of science here, but the feeling of who we are.

> –According to you, I'll have to suspect only people with no Basque blood . . . (Pinilla 2009: 110–111)

As such, there are two hegemonic discourses which Sancho Bordaberri confronts in constructing his narrative and, what amounts to the same thing, in the process of reconstructing the case: the discourse of the Francoist regime, and that of the dominant Basque nationalism. This relegates his capacity to create collective memory in the individual and the artistic realm, which perhaps may in reality be the only resource available for those who resist adopting established truths or those backed by authority.

"Sites of Memory" in the Police Narrative of Ramiro Pinilla

Ramiro Pinilla's narrative work is tied radically to space:[2] not only is his narrative universe linked inseparably to the world of Getxo, in which practically all his work takes place and in which an ample group of recurring characters coexist, but the space itself is an element full of mythical, symbolic, historical, and political meanings (Acillona 2017; Pérez Isasi 2015a). Any reading of Pinilla's work is truncated if one does not consider the meaning, therein, of Arrigunaga beach, the fields and farms of Getxo and, in contrast, the "red hills" of the mining valleys on the left bank of the Nervión River. This space implies, as Acillona contends, almost a response or resistance to the advance of "non-spaces" of postmodernity or supermodernity (Augé 1993), since they are sites in which the weight of meaning does not just not disappear, but that get denser in superimposed layers.

Throughout Pinilla's novels, a whole set of what Pièrre Nora terms "sites of memory" or Henri Lefebvre (1974) calls "lived space" emerge like this; that is, a space that goes beyond mere physical relationship (perceived space) and that is charged with collective and symbolic meaning, contrasting with (if not opposing) the representation of "conceived space" from authority and its institutions. There are abundant examples of such spaces in Pinilla's novels (beaches, trees, farms, rocks), but perhaps the best example of this resignification of space is the fig tree of the homonymous novel: a place dedicated to the permanent revisiting of trauma and guilt.

Pinilla's police novels also offer numerous examples of such spaces; in fact, one could argue that, in the three cases, the plot is based on a (sometimes obsessive) return to a precise space, the place of the crime, whose capacity to evoke, almost always traumatically, is sometimes sufficient to produce the resolution of the crime.

Solo un muerto más begins, in fact, with what will be the central point of the plot: Arrigunaga beach. "My soles crawl along the beach on the way to the sea," says the first sentence in the text (Pinilla 2009: 4).³ Shortly afterward, he adds: "I don't know why my eyes focus in on far-off rock, to the right of the beach, which the low tide has revealed. It's the rock we call Félix Apraiz. In its lower part, a ring to which someone chained the Altube twins' necks so that the high tide would drown them" (2009: 4). Two fundamental scenes are thus established (the beach and the rock) in which the memory of the crime would perpetuate: "I don't know why my eyes focus in on far-off rock, to the right of the beach, which the low tide has revealed. It's the rock we call Félix Apraiz. In its lower part, a ring to which someone chained the Altube twins' necks so that the high tide would drown them" (2009: 62); Sancho Bordaberri would return to that beach time and time again, alone or in the company of other characters: Lucio Etxe, Eladio (Leonardo) Altube, the Falangist Luciano Aguirre, or Luis Federico Larrea, as well as countless times in which he imagines or mentions the beach in conversations with other characters, above all with his assistant Koldobike.

In *Cadáveres en la playa*, this centrality of the space of the beach is even more evident, from the very title itself. In fact, the strategy of Samuel Esparta's investigation in this case consists, precisely, of exploiting the potential of the space loaded with trauma to provoke the confession of the guilty party in the crime. Thus, in the final chapters of the novel the detective returns to the beach up to four times with the four suspects (Sergio Barrondo, Jokin Arzubialde, Xabier Pagoeta, and Peru Mugarte) until one of them, overcome by the excessive weight of memory and guilt, confesses his involvement in the crime. There is, then, a broad and ambiguous meaning to the phrase pronounced by Juana Ezquiaga, who contracts Samuel Esparta to solve the crime: "A beach is not just its sand, but what it hides beneath" (2014b: 3), a phrase that is echoed close to the dénouement of the text, when Samuel Esparta affirms that "The beach guards many of our memories and sometimes it is good to regain them" (2014b: 129).

In the case of *El cementerio vacío*, for its part, the beach is not the space of memory, but the site in which Anarai was murdered, next to the chapel of San Baskardo, another significant place in Pinilla's narrative and mythical universe. The site is visited, first, by the detective and his assistant in an initial inspection in search of clues and, above all, even more importantly, by the investigators (Samuel Esparta and Cayo Fernández) with the suspect, in an attempt to get a confession out of him, as happens in *Cadáveres en la playa*. Given the nature of the crime, this place soon becomes a site of memory, with the hurried construction of a burial mound of flowers and, also significantly, a small *lauburu* (Basque symbol) which the victim wore around her neck (Pinilla 2014a: 110).

The other space destined to become a site of memory and, at the same time, its negation, is the cemetery in which Anari is buried, and in which the suspect, Pedro, also asks to be buried; in accordance with the legend that gives the book its title, coastal cemeteries are emptied, pouring the dead into the sea and giving an opportunity for lovers to reunite after death. In this way, and always in accordance with the legend, there is an emptying (both literal and of meaning) of the space of memory, whose marks (tombs, epitaphs, etc.) are preserved, but only as a spectacle without any real reference.

Final Notes
In the same way that Ramiro Pinilla's work is tied intimately to a space (a Getxo between the real and the mythical, shaped on the basis of Faulkner's Yoknapatawpha), it is also, mostly, connected to a certain chronological arc: that which stretches from the years immediately prior to the Spanish Civil War through to the final years of Francoism. This is the temporal arc traversed by his police novels and, likewise, is essential through the rest of his narrative, although occasionally his works travel to a more remote past in order to reconstruct other chapters of history or mythology in his narrative universe.

In these final notes, however, I would like to pose the question of whether Pinilla's police fiction (sometimes disregarded as a "novelist's rest" [Landaburu 2009]) opens up a possible reading of the construction of memory in other geographical contexts or in other time periods, including, too, the Basque conflict itself (on which Ramiro Pinilla barely wrote anything).

Thus, Ramiro Pinilla's novels are based, as we have seen, on the ethical impulse to make visible that which has been buried by history, "including the dinosaurs and the Neanderthals" (Pinilla 2014a: 16); that is, the demand to recover the voice of those who have been buried among the ruins of the "Angel of History." The death in *Sólo un muerto más*, like the corpse in *Cadáveres en la playa* or the corpses (supposedly) poured out into the sea by *El cementerio vacío*, are victims that demand justice, if not in a legal sense, then through the recovery and reparation of their memory.

Second, all three novels clearly warn against the danger of memory controled and manipulated by authority or by hegemonic discourses. The characters of the Falangist Luciano Aguirre and of the commissioner Cayo Fernández do not just suggest creating a narrative of the crime (an alternative novel to that of Sancho Bordaberri in the case of *Sólo un muerto más*; a supposedly neutral expert report in the case of *El cementerio vacío*). They also end up being decisive influences on the dénouement in both investigations being even more tragic. In the same way, *El cementerio vacío* demonstrates how a hegemonic discourse, even if it does not possess political or police authority, can also construct partial or distorted memories (in this case, accusing a *maketo* of the crime, based on prejudices derived from the dominant Basque nationalism in Getxo society). Thus, the only memory possible, above all (yet not only) in contexts of oppression and propaganda, is that which stems from the margins or opposition to authority, in this case the novels of Sancho Bordaberri.

Finally, the three novels recall the importance of space in the creation of memory, whether individual or collective, and its capacity to serve as an anchor for memory, justice or reparation for the guilt. This is the case of Arrigunaga beach and Félix Apraiz's rock in *Solo un muerto más*; of the open land behind the church of San Baskardo in *El cementerio vacío*, and again of the beach, which hides its secrets beneath the sand, in *Cadáveres en la playa*. They are spaces, it is worth saying, with the potential to become spaces of memory, but this potential must be activated in order to avoid, precisely, the corpses remaining buried beneath the sand.

In sum, Ramiro Pinilla's police works can, and must, be read in close tandem with the rest of his work, with which it shares preoccupations, themes, and, of course, the same geographic universe and of characters; but likewise, I believe, they can and should be read in contact with some of the most important historical, ethical, and political debates in the Basque and Spanish context during the years in which they were written: those which are related to the way of (re)constructing memory about violence, whether that of the past in the Spanish Civil War or postwar period, or the more recent variety in the Basque conflict.

References

Acillona, Mercedes (2017): "El espacio en la narrativa de Ramiro Pinilla.", in *Litterae Vasconicae*. 16: 155–172.

Augé, Marc (1993): *Los no-lugares. Espacios del anonimato: una antropología de la sobremodernidad*. Gedisa: Barcelona.

Bautista Naranjo, Esther (2011): "Sólo un muerto más, de Ramiro Pinilla, o el *Quijote* en clave detectivesca," in *Espéculo: Revista de Estudios Literarios*. 47. Retrieved June 2, 2020 from https://webs.ucm.es/info/especulo/numero47/muertomas.html.

Beti, Iñaki (2007): "La necesidad de la memoria," in *Pérgola*. April: 4.

Chacón Delgado, Pedro José (2009): "Las vergüenzas desnudas: el concepto de 'maketo' en la novelística de Ramiro Pinilla," in *Letras de Deusto* 39 (122): 167–192.

Chen Sham, Jorge (2015): "Metáforas marinas y metanovela policíaca en Sólo un muerto más," in Acillona López, Mercedes (Coord.): *Ramiro Pinilla: el mundo entero se llama Arrigunaga*. Bilbao: University of Deusto: 223–239.

Feijoo Morote, Javier (2016): "Análisis de la contextualización en la novela policiaca de Ramiro Pinilla: el Getxo de posguerra," in *Pasavento: revista de estudios hispánicos*. 4 (1): 17–37.

———. (2017): "La revisión paródica en la novela policiaca de Ramiro Pinilla," in Sánchez Zapatero, Javier, and Álex Martín Escribá (coords.): *La globalización del crimen: literatura, cine y nuevos medios*. Andavira. Santiago of Compostela: 117–124.

———. (2018a): "Libropueblo / Herriliburu: El proyecto editorial de Ramiro Pinilla y José Javier Rapha Bilbao (1977-1986)," in *Anuario de estudios filológicos*. 41: 75–93.

———. (2018b): "Metaficción e intertextualidad en la narrativa policiaca de Ramiro Pinilla," in Beltrán Almería, Luis, Dolores Thion Soriano-Mollá, and María Antonia Martín Zorraquino (eds.): *Deslindes paranovelísticos*. Fernando el Católico Institution: Zaragoza: 51–65.

———. (2020): "La figura del loco en "Verdes valles, colinas rojas", de Ramiro Pinilla," in *Anales de literatura española*. 33: 65–87.

García Mateos, Ramón (1984): "La geografía novelística de Ramiro Pinilla." *Universitas Tarraconensis. Revista de Filologia*. 7. Retrieved June 2, 2020 from https://revistes.urv.cat/index.php/utf/article/view/2237.

Ibarrola Armendariz, Aitor (2015): "Crimen y castigo en *La higuera* de Ramiro Pinilla: Del trauma y la ceguera parcial a una potencial clarividencia" in Acillona López, Mercedes (coord.): *Ramiro Pinilla: el mundo entero se llama Arrigunaga*. Bilbao: University of Deusto: 201–221.

Kortazar, Jon (2019): "*Aquella edad inolvidable*. Fútbol, nación, identidad en Ramiro Pinilla," in *Boletín Hispánico Helvético*, 33–34: 183–204.

Landaburu, Ander (2009): "Escribir una novela policiaca no ha sido un descanso del novelista. Entrevista a Ramiro Pinilla." *El País*. Jan. 30th. Retrieved June 2, 2020 from https://elpais.com/diario/2009/01/31/babelia/1233363014_850215.html.

Lefebvre, Henri (1974). *La production de l'espace*. Anthropos: Paris.

Nora, Pierre (1992). *Les lieux de mémoire*. Gallimard: Paris.

Pérez Isasi, Santiago (2015a): "*Verdes valles, colinas rojas* y la identidad vasca plural," in Acillona López, Mercedes (coord.): *Ramiro Pinilla: el mundo entero se llama Arrigunaga*. Bilbao: University of Deusto: 165–200.

———. (2015b): "El otro y la identidad vasca en la narrativa de Ramiro Pinilla," in Esparza Martín, Iratxe, and José Manuel López Gaseni (eds.): *La identidad en la literatura vasca contemporánea*. Peter Lang: Bern: 165–178.

Pinilla, Ramiro (2009): *Solo un muerto más*. Tusquets (ebook): Barcelona.

———. (2014a): *El cementerio vacío*. Tusquets (ebook): Barcelona.

———. (2014b): *Cadáveres en la playa*. Tusquets (ebook): Barcelona.

Notes

1 On the figure of the *maketo* in Pinilla's narrative, see Chacón Delgado (2009) and Pérez Isasi (2015b).

2 There are, on the other hand, several works dedicated to analyzing the space of Getxo in Ramiro Pinilla's work, clearly a fundamental axis in the world of his novels. The pioneering analysis of García Mateos (1984) stands out as does the more recent, and therefore more complete and up-to-date, work of Mercedes Acillona (2017).

3 The beach and the sea occupy a central place in the cosmogeny and mythology of Ramiro Pinilla's universe, and also in his police novels. See on this subject Chen Sham (2015).

Chapter 11

Dolores Redondo's *El guardián invisible* (*The Invisible Guardian*, 2013)

Maite Aperribay-Bermejo

Some years have passed since the character of Lizbeth Salander first captivated many of us. Following the tradition of this cosmopolitan police novel from the North, there have been many noir fiction trilogies and tetralogies published in the Basque Country which resemble Nordic sagas. In the last decade, the new category of "euskandinavo" ("Basquescandinavian"), as Ibon Martín Álvarez has baptized it (Carnero, Delgado, and García 2018), has been very successful; therein, specifically, we would include saga novels, especially Eva García Sáenz de Urturi's *Trilogia de la Ciudad Blanca* (White City Trilogy), Ricardo Alía's *Trilogia del Zodiaco* (Zodiac Trilogy), Ibon Martín Álvarez's tetralogy and Dolores Redondo's Baztan Trilogy. In the words of Martín Matos, Redondo's novels can be placed within the category of femicrime, rural noir, and the glocal:

> In the work of (...) Dolores Redondo, two current tendencies of the noir novel come together: femicrime and rural noir. The former, Nordic in origin, refers to women authors and/or protagonists in novels with a crime storyline; the latter, originating in the United States, takes place in the rural setting in which the events unfold. (...) the woman author gives form to a glocal novel, in which elements of the most immediate surroundings coexist in a natural way with concepts and ideas which globalisation has taken the noir novel all over the world. (2016: 87)

Dolores Redondo's work

Redondo (Donostia, 1969–) published her first work, titled *Los privilegios del ángel* (The Angel's Privileges), in 2009. A few years later, she achieved widespread success thanks to her Baztan trilogy: in 2013, she published *El guardián invisible* (in English, *The Invisible Guardian*, 2016), the first novel in the trilogy, as well as *Legado en los huesos* (in English, *The Legacy of the Bones*, 2018) that same year, and in 2014 *Ofrenda a la tormenta* (in English, *Offering to the Storm*, 2018). The trilogy has been translated into thirty languages, including Basque. Redondo's success has led to film; a film adaptation of her first novel was produced in 2017 and in 2018 film adaptations of the second and third novels began production, all three directed by Fernando Pérez Molina.

Thanks to the novel *El guardián invisible*, Redondo has been awarded several prizes: the 2014 Bilbao Book Fair Silver Pen award (Domingo-Aldama 2014), a 2015 CWA International Dagger awards finalist (Crime Writers' Association 2015) and the 2017 International Latino Book Award (Latino Literacy Now 2017). Likewise, her 2016 novel *Todo esto te daré* (in English, *All This I Will Give to You*, 2018), has also been very successful, winning the Planeta 2016 and Bancarella 2018 (Colpisa 2018) awards.

Among all the novels we have mentioned, the first—*El guardián invisible* (2013)—will be the focus of study in this chapter. It merits attention, as the novel has been somewhat innovative: first, because there is a female inspector in charge of the murder investigation; second, because the crimes are set in the rural environment of Baztan (Navarre); and third, because it has been incredibly successful. Although Redondo's first novel explores numerous themes (such as mythology, the presence of nature, the importance of family, the gender gap, sisterhood, etc.), in order to examine this work here, taking gender studies as the focus, I will take five steps:

First, I will turn to the gender gap. Then I will discuss sisterhood. Next, my subject will be the presence of motherhood. After, I will explore violence against women. Finally, I will consider the corporeal presence.

El guardián invisible (2013): The Predominant Gender Issues in a Novel Replete with Women

Redondo begins this novel with the corpse of the young woman Ainhoa Elizasu. Elizasu's naked body is found in a corner of a Baztan stream, but hers is not the only case, because it is the second body to be found in the same place and position recently. Both crimes are blamed on a murderer who is known by the nickname *basajaun* (lord of the woods, a Basque mythological figure). Three days later, the body of a third victim is found. Inspector Amaia Salazar of the Provincial Police is appointed to lead the investigation. Salazar lives in Iruña (Pamplona) and she must return to her hometown, Elizondo, to solve the murders of these teenagers. Besides investigating the crimes, the novel presents skilfully the conflicts Salazar suffers in the workplace, within her family, and in her personal life.

Among the thematic focal points Redondo develops in this work, perhaps the most important is her discourse on gender. In this sense, in Lasarte's words, "when it comes to constructing female protagonists, we will examine how the central themes and concepts (womanhood, motherhood, violence, etc.) in the texts are developed" (2011: 25). Redondo approaches gender from different perspectives in her novel, touching on different themes, such as the gender gap, motherhood, femininity, and violence.

One of the main examples of the aforementioned gender gap may be what Inspector Salazar has to put up with in her workplace. Salazar's workplace environment is completely male, because all of the other inspectors and deputy inspectors are men, and that does not make Salazar's career easy, but it does show her how to be resilient: "she supposed that in the three years spent surrounded by men at the police academy, and the fact that she was the first woman to reach the rank of inspector in the Homicide Division, she'd experienced enough jokes and teasing along the way to leave her with a steely inner strength and cast-iron composure" (Redondo 2017: 35). She is confident that she is capable of doing her job adeptly, and she believes she has proven herself more than enough: "she judged that her quota of 'what I must demonstrate on account of being a woman' was more than covered" (Redondo 2013: 74).

Amaia Salazar is the first female inspector in the Homicide Division of the Provincial Police, a very skilled woman who was trained, among other places, at the FBI academy in Quantico. But she is a beautiful young woman, and assigning her to a murder case has caused unrest amongst some of her colleagues: "Inspector Montes to you. Don't forget that although you might be in charge of this investigation for the moment, you're speaking to an equal (. . .) that's not up to you, even if you have begun to think so lately. Inspector Montes had already been working on the homicide team for six years when you started at the academy, chief" (Redondo 2017, 61–62). Moreover, Inspector Montes is not the only one to look down on Salazar, because some other colleagues do not trust Salazar's ability. Deputy Inspector Zabalza does not like Salazar either:

"He didn't like her, he'd heard about her, the star inspector who'd been with the FBI in the United States, and now that he knew her, he thought she was an arrogant bitch who seemed to expect everyone to bow as she passed" (Redondo 2013: 263).

Salazar will, however, work with a couple of women; namely, Judge Estébanez and Dr. Takchenko. Both Judge Estébanez and Dr. Takchenko are very successful women in the workplace. In any event, though, Salazar is the only woman in the very male police world, and she has a great responsibility, because she is in charge of the investigation of the murders that have attracted a lot of attention. The inspectors who work with her believe that such work is better suited to a man; yet as the narrative develops, they change their mind.

Having a woman inspector like Salazar as the main protagonist and being at the head of an investigation implies a subversion of gender stereotypes, because in general men tend to be at the forefront in such situations. As Losada Soler states, having a woman inspector as the main protagonist has brought changes: "The first of these would be the representation of figures of female authority, empowered women who have agency" (2015: 12). Yet Amaia's is not the only successful case of subversion presented in the novel, because Aunt Engrasi, Flora, Judge Estébanez, and Dr. Takchenko are also empowered women. Aunt Engrasi graduated in psychology from Sorbonne University in Paris, laudable for a seventy-year-old woman. Flora has also been very successful professionally, as Amaia's words make clear: "You've written books, you're going to have a television program, Mantecadas Salazar is mentioned in the media throughout Europe, and you're rich" (Redondo 2017: 122).

Bold Women and Sisterhood

Redondo's novel switches between the workplace and the family environment time and time again, interspersing murder investigations with Salazar's private life. While the workplace is surrounded by men, in the private sphere Salazar's family and support network is woven together by women. Another stereotype linked to gender is space, because in general the home is a space inhabited by women and the outside space, in contrast, by men. Even so, several women (Amaia, Flora, Judge Estébanez, and Dr. Takchenko, for example) turn this latter idea on its head, being successful in the work sphere.

On the contrary, in the home space, with some exceptions, women predominate. In the family sphere, power is in women's hands, because Redondo's is a story of the strength of women and women's networks. Indeed, instead of the matriarchal model that is so well-known in the Basque idiosyncrasy, the novel presents a matrilineal model. In the words of the anthropologist Mari Carmen Basterretxea, in Basque culture "generosity, protection, balance, communal ownership and collaboration are the basis of the matrilineal model" ("Euskal kultura, sistema matrilinealean oinarritzen zen eta gizarte eskuzabal eta orekatua zen," 2014); generosity and protection are, in particular, those which are very present in the novel. To begin with, Aunt Engrasi is the head of the Salazar family, because when the three sisters' mother falls ill, she assumes responsibility for her nieces, fulfilling the role of mother. Engrasi is the head of the family and, in that sense, she fulfils the transmission function that Lagarde associates with the mother: "the mother-woman is a transmitter, defender and custodian of the governing order in society and in culture (...) mothers are reproducers of culture, those that acculturate others" (Lagarde and de los Ríos 2005: 377). Engrasi conveys to her niece's knowledge about values, culture, tradition, mythology, gastronomy, etc.

The aunt often gets together with her friends on the pretext of playing cards. They are all elderly, and some of them have not had easy lives, but they are all full of energy and very wise. Amaia admires them greatly:

> during their stay they left an impression of vibrant energy (...) Amaia liked the girls, she liked them a lot, because they had that presence and charm of that person who is now on the way home and who has enjoyed the journey. (...) they had left behind any kind of resentment and rancour against life and they arrived every day as happy as adolescents in an open-air dance, as wise as the queens of Egypt. If with any luck she made it to be an old lady one day, she'd like to be like that, like them, independent and at the same time so rooted in their origins, energetic and full of life, giving off that sensation of triumphing over life which results from seeing one of those elderly men and women who take advantage of each day without thinking about death. Or perhaps thinking about it in order to steal another day, another hour. (...) they went about (...) leaving in the living room that black and white energy of an *aquelarre* [witches' coven]. (Redondo 2013, 117–118)

The support network created by all of those women is based on sisterhood and, as a result, thanks to mutual support several women in the novel embark on an empowerment process. As Marcela Lagarde states, "*sisterhood* is (...) an experience of women that leads to the search for positive relationships and alliance (...) with other women, in order to contribute (...) to the social elimination of all forms of oppression and mutual support in order to achieve the generic vitality of all of them and the dynamic empowerment of each woman" (Lagarde y de los Ríos 2009: 126). Sisterhood is a way of confronting oppression in a particular society: "The alliance of women in the commitment is as important as the struggle against other phenomena of oppression and to create spaces in which women may deploy new life possibilities" (Lagarde y de los Ríos 2012: 486). Somehow, the pacts that these women draw up help them fight gender discrimination and embark on the process of empowering themselves.

Motherhood or Frustration

Motherhood is another subject that is mentioned throughout the novel. In the case of the Salazar sisters, the three of them want to be mothers, but they all have problems when it comes to getting pregnant. The oldest sister, Flora, wanted to be a mother and could not conceive because her fallopian tubes were blocked. We know that she went through an in vitro fertilization procedure, did not manage to get pregnant, and had a terrible time. The middle sister Ros has not had any children either, and she also experienced the situation as a failure: "having a child became a priority for me, such an urgent need as if my life depended on it. (...) But it was not to be, (...) apparently I couldn't have children either (...) My desperation increased as the months passed without my getting pregnant" (Redondo 2013: 62).

Amaia, too, has the same problem. She is a beautiful woman, a very skilled inspector who leads a gratifying life, and her only frustration is not getting pregnant. She has been tested medically and the results clearly show that she does not have any problems in getting pregnant, yet despite that, it is recommended that she go through an in vitro fertilization procedure. Seeing how her oldest sister suffered through this at one time, Amaia is against such a procedure. That said, she cannot despair; she does not give up. She continues to try and get pregnant the natural way and every time she has her period she feels tremendous frustration and sadness: "a maternity which would just not come. A maternity which hurt." (Redondo 2013: 42). She defends the legitimacy to choose over her body and is against the in vitro fertilization procedure, but she so longs to be a mother that in the end this inspector who is so scientific gives in, puts aside her mistrust of the world of mythology, and complies with her ancestors' rites: following tradition, she takes a pebble from home to the cave of Mari, because it is said that this is how one becomes pregnant. In the final pages of the novel, we will find out if, in the end, she gets pregnant. Mari says this to Amaia: "We're living through uncertain times in the valley, and when the new solutions fail, people fall back on the old ones" (Redondo 2017: 302). As Oropesa states, "the protagonist acknowledges the existence of besajaun [sic] [lord of the woods] and the goddess Mari, the former as protector of the ecological equilibrium and the latter of motherhood" (2018: 124). In the end, as the old saying goes, "*direnik ez da sinistu bear* (sic.); *ez direla ez da esan bear* (sic.) [It should not be believed that there are, (but) it should not be said that there are not]" (Barandiarán 1984: 20) and "*izena duan guztia omen da* [everything that has a name exists]" (Barandiaran, here cited in Iñarra 1994b: 44).

Nevertheless, the custom of taking a pebble to the rock of Mari is not the only tradition that will be linked to fertility, because Redondo also presents another Christian-style rite in the novel, in this case linked to the Virgin of Uxue-Ujué: "There's a church at Ujué, in the south of Navarra, where women who want to become mothers complete a pilgrimage bringing a stone from their homes. There they leave it on a great pile of pebbles and pray to the statue of the Virgin" (2017: 103). Thus, it is clear that Christianity embraced as its own customs that were once pagan and, at the same time, women in general have always had the motherhood desire or need.

As well as the case of the Salazar sisters, the novel also discusses the yearning for motherhood in several other situations. Aunt Engrasi's case is also presented. After studying psychology at Madrid and Sorbonne Universities, she married her former professor, the Belgian Jean. They had everything, except children: "Life couldn't have been more generous to her. She lived in the most beautiful city in the world, in a university environment. Her mind was stimulated and her heart was full of that absurd security born of wanting for nothing, except children who never arrived in the five years the dream lasted" (Redondo 2017: 260). When she becomes a widow, the aunt returns to Elizondo and takes on the responsibility of her sick and unstable sister-in-law's daughters, especially the youngest, as Amaia moves in with her aunt when she is eight years old.

The book also reveals the cases of other women. The mother of the third victim, Anne Arbizu, says that her daughter was adopted. Mrs. Arbizu tells Salazar that she suffered numerous miscarriages, when they adopted Anne after the last one. Up to that point Mrs. Arbizu's main goal was to become a mother and she achieved that goal through adoption: "I was now a mother, I gave birth from the heart and carried my daughter in my arms (. . .) becoming pregnant with a child was no longer my life's goal" (Redondo 2013: 141). She then refused to get pregnant because, in her words, her uterus could not bear fruit: "my stomach was not a cradle, but my children's tomb" (Redondo 2017: 141). This situation totally affects Amaia, because she herself identifies with it: "Amaia contemplated with great sadness the immense drama of that woman, which was in part her own too; her stomach, a tomb for unborn children" (Redondo 2013: 173). In the same vein, it is worth noting that Mrs. Arbizu is not the only woman to have experienced miscarriages, as it is mentioned in the novel that more than one of Aunt Engrasi's friends also suffered miscarriages at one time or another.

The words of Inspector Iriarte's wife also make her wish to be a mother clear, and when that yearning is not fulfilled, many feel her frustration: "I don't think that any woman of child-bearing age can be complete if she doesn't have children, and I assure you that this can be an enormous, secret and dark burden. (. . .) I'd feel incomplete if I didn't have children" (Redondo 2017: 329).

In a patriarchal society, the role of women is founded on reproduction and, as a result, one of the goals of all of the women in the novel is to be a mother. As Marcela Lagarde states, the living space of women is that of social reproduction and women are only taken into account for the usefulness of their bodies: "Reproduction is the imprint which has defined the female gender up to the present" (2005: 381). Generally speaking, women have so internalized this role that having children has become a pressing need, as the above-mentioned words of Ros Salazar suggest. When they cannot reproduce, the women in the novel feel despair and pain; in their own words they feel incomplete. As Lagarde makes evident, society looks down on women who are not mothers: "those women that do not reproduce to others are considered less women, less feminine" (2005: 121).

Summarizing what we have just explained, it seems that many of the women protagonists in the novel suffer from what Jung termed "hypertrophy of the maternal": "in the daughter the mother-complex leads either to a hypertrophy of the feminine (. . .) The negative aspect is seen in the woman whose only goal is childbirth" (Jung 2003: 80).

The discourses that women in the novel construct about motherhood have been studied and, bearing in mind the presence and importance of the motherhood discourse in the novel, one can confirm that a statement in its favor is made.

Violence against Women

We explained above how many women, merely on account of being women, feel the need to be a mother. As Marcela Lagarde states:

the forms of being a woman in this society and in its cultures, constitute captivities (. . .) female happiness is constructed on a foundation of the personal realisation of the captivity which, as an expression of femininity, is assigned to every woman. Hence, beyond their consciousness, their valuation and their affectivity, and on occasion in contrast to them, all women are captives due to the mere fact of being women in the patriarchal world. (Lagarde y de los Ríos 2005: 36)

In Lagarde's words, "There are few and reduced forms of being a woman. Society is defined in such a way that women are channeled and encouraged around a reduced number of dominant cultural options" (2005: 38). She defines these dominant choices as captivity. The chief feature of those captivities is the oppression of women. A woman, for being a woman, must fulfil several roles in society: she must be a mother, she must be a wife, she must be a good woman, she must be at the service of others, and she will play the role of carer . . . All of these for the "well-being" of a patriarchal society.

It goes without saying that violence against women is structural because of the values and norms which prevail in our society. In the woman-man binomial, women bear men's oppression, and that oppression is often expressed in the form of violence. The violence that men impose on women and girls continues to be an illness in our culture, and we find clear examples of this, too, in the novel. In order to approach this theme, let us begin by defining violence against women. Article 50 of the Law of Equality of Women and Men offers this definition:

> violence against women is considered as any violent act on account of sex which results, or may result, in physical, sexual or psychological harm or in the suffering of the woman, including threats to carry out such acts, coercion or the arbitrary deprivation of liberty that may occur in public or private life. (Eusko Jaurlaritza 2005: 4).

In the novel, Redondo depicts more than one form of abuse and condemns, above all, violence in the home or in the family and in society. In this sense, she also makes it clear that abuse can be physical, emotional, sexual, economic, or social.

She first condemns the murders that make up the thread of the work *El guardián invisible*. These murders are examples of serious physical violence perpetrated by men against women. At the same time, there is also a critique of (affective) psychological violence; without forgetting, Redondo also discusses violence among women. Let us examine, then, the different types of violence denounced in the novel.

Violence in Society

The victims that die as a result of violence against women are the most serious example of the violence which takes place in society. As Echeburúa and De Corral posit, "there are still many men that consider the freedom conquered by women attacks the very essence of their identity" (2009: 139). In this sense, in the novel the teenagers who are victims of cruel physical violence ignite the aggressive instinct of the murderer who wants to exercise control. Free, independent, and sexually active girls are punished and, seeing how the murderer leaves and places their bodies, it appears that he wants to deprive the victims of everything that makes them free and active and return them to innocence. In the novel, as the psychological profile carried out on the murderer shows, the murderer sees teenagers who are playing at being grown-ups, and he does not think such behavior appropriate. He wants to punish such conduct by returning the victims to their adolescence (perhaps childhood) and innocence. Perhaps, with that objective, the murderer eliminates everything that sexualizes the victims: he removes the clothes, high-heeled shoes, make-up, pubic hair and so on from the teenagers. He erases everything related to sexual maturity in the victims and, as if they were holy virgins—the gestures of their hands recall Our Lady of Lourdes or the Immaculate Conception—places them in the corner of a stream, as if it were a cleansing ritual, perhaps so that the stream itself may cleanse the victims' souls.

As Aitxus Iñarra confirms, "the object, act and perpetrator corresponding to the victim, crime and murderer make up a complex filter. The murderer, and the victims chosen, make up a unity. The victim is often crucial for something, but the something therein are typically his aggressive needs" (Iñarra 1994b: 12). It seems that this is what motivates the novel's alleged murderer. Victor Oyarzabal, Inspector Salazar's brother-in-law, acknowledges that he has killed three teenagers, but it is explained clearly that Oyarzabal's aggressive need is nothing new, because in addition to the latest murders, he confesses that he also killed Teresa Klas two decades ago. According to him, setting out on the trail of that aggressive instinct is attributed to the consumption of alcohol: "for twenty years I remained strong, making the biggest effort a man can make, I had to drink to control it" (Redondo 2013: 429). Regarding women's social conduct,

Oyarzabal constructs the world in a binomial, and he perpetuates the binomial of the good woman (mother, wife, passive, etc.) and the bad woman (witches, prostitutes, active). But not just that, because he punishes those bad women with death: "They, they were looking for it, dressed as prostitutes, provoking men like whores, and someone had to show them what happens to bad girls" (Redondo 2013: 428).

Both Carla Huarte (the first victim) and Ainhoa Elizasu (the second victim) were sexually active. Huarte's boyfriend says that she liked rough sex: "she liked it like that (...) she was the one who liked hard-core sex" (Redondo 2017: 14-15). Furthermore, Inspector Zabalza questions Anne Arbizu's friends: "Anne lived a double life to keep her parents blissfully ignorant. According to her friends, she smoked pot, drank, and even did stronger stuff sometimes. She spent hours in online chat rooms and would publish risqué photos of herself on the net (...) She was a slut disguised as a little angel, she even had an affair with a married man" (Redondo 2017: 112). In both cases, the victims were sexually active and, because of that, looked down on. As the anthropologist Marcela Lagarde confirms, "the social image of women is devalued if it assumes any form of their own power over their sexuality" (2005: 422).

Violence in the Family or in the Home

Much of the abuse suffered by women takes place within the home. The middle sister Ros Salazar suffers this kind of violence. It seems that Ros, who has for years been under the control of a lazy idle man, is the weakest of the three sisters. When Ros decides to leave her husband Freddy, Amaia is afraid of Freddy's response, because as a police inspector she knows full well that, in situations like this, many women are at risk of suffering abuse:

> In lots of cases violence occurs at the moment when the woman announces the end of the relationship. It's not easy breaking up with those lowlifes. They tend to resist with pleading, tears, and begging, because they know perfectly well that they're nothing without their women. And if all that doesn't work, they resort to violence, which is why you shouldn't leave a woman alone when she's going to break up with the sponger of the moment. (Redondo 2017: 93).

Violence often occurs in the home environment, and, although in general women are the victims and men the perpetrators, one cannot deny that sometimes women are the perpetrators. Redondo's novel clearly reflects this reality in the case of Amaia Salazar's mother. In Losada Soler's opinion, "perhaps that reflection on the evil of women is the most novel—and most disturbing—element in these texts. Violence against women confronts us with something that is not normative and which transgresses both patriarchal stereotypes and the theoretical frame of many feminisms" (2015: 13).

Amaia's mother is possessive, authoritarian, and controlling. At first, the violence Amaia suffers at the hands of her mother seems psychological: "On the day after her first Communion, her mother made her sit on a bench in the kitchen, braided her hair, and cut it off. (...) She remembered feeling violated when she touched her head and being blinded by her boiling tears" (Redondo 2017: 95).

Throughout the novel it is explained, through the traumatic memories of Amaia's childhood, that her mother is ill, her case being the only negative example of motherhood, because she is obsessed with her daughter. She does not love her daughter and the violence she commits against her gets worse (Sánchez Díaz-Aldagalán 2015: 17). At first, although it seemed like psychological or affective violence, it would become physical when she tried to kill Amaia; her mother hit her on the head with a steel rolling pin and later she tried to suffocate her daughter Amaia in a mound of flour. In Iñarra's words, "things or implements used in everyday life will be the most typical things to kill with. This method is used above all by family and small-town code murderers" (Iñarra 1994: 53). In the case of the Salazar family, they earned a living from their confectioner's shop, and flour and the rolling pin would be, specifically, what almost ended Amaia's life. Iñarra explains the following:

> When that relationship between aggressor and victim is expressed through kinship, it is given within the functioning of family norms. (...) When instead of love hate emerges, the enclosed kinship space becomes a suitable channel to develop a murder. Within this structure, the context of blood turns a simple event into a violent and extraordinary one. Relationships developed within the family are a mirror of those produced in society; and this way if the king is the head of society, at home the father, who in most cases will be master of the house, is in charge of the family, the representative of his wife and children, and the leader of moral conduct in the house. The woman will be in charge of the children and the housework. (1994: 40)

Parents are in charge of moral conduct, in Amaia's case it is her mother who abuses her daughter and as a result she relinquishes being a leader of moral conduct. It is true that she is ill, yet Redondo makes her mother's objective clear: "Her intention was to make sure that she killed her" (2013: 233). In Lagarde's opinion, "filicide (...) is the extreme of maternal madness" (...) "it is the evidence which annuls the myth of maternal love as an instinct" (2005: 750, 755). Redondo demonstrates a case of a woman who has no maternal instinct, that of a heartless mother, that of a woman who does not match the stereotype of motherhood: "The flaws, indifference, the lack of care, and non-sanctioned beatings constitute evidence that some mothers do not belong to the correct realm of the universe. For diverse dominant ideologies, bad mothers are located in evil and in sin, in dysfunction and anomie, or in the wrong, in madness" (Lagarde y de los Ríos 2005: 733).

As a consequence of enduring serious affective-psychological and physical violence, Amaia is afraid of her mother and, understandably, would not feel safe at home: "it is frightening when someone hurts you that should be looking after you" (Redondo 2013: 371). Because of safety concerns, she goes to live with Engrasi: "a little girl who had to grow up with the weight of an attempted murder. She had to hide it by lying about it and she had to leave her own home, as if she were the one responsible for the horror she had had to go through" (Redondo 2017: 315). Salazar's trauma is so great that she identifies to some extent with the victims in the novel, because she too has been a victim (Culver 2015).

Affective Violence against Women

It is Ros who has needed everyone's help for the longest time. She is Amaia's middle sister who has been married to lazy Freddy for many years. Yet once she realised that the situation was not going to get better, she decided to leave her husband. From that moment on, she would feel free and empowered, getting away from people who treat her badly, embarking on a process of self-awareness:

> I knew that my life with him was over. (...) Making those decisions made me feel free for the first time in a long time, (...) but neither our sister nor my husband were prepared to let me go that easily. You'd be surprised by how similar their arguments, their reproaches, their tricks were ... because the two of them played tricks (...) and they used the very same words (...) Where are you going to go? Do you think you'll find something better? And the last one: Who is going to want you? They'd never believe it, but although their tricks were designed to undermine my conviction, they had just the opposite effect: I saw how small and cowardly

> they were, so inept, and everything seemed possible, easier without them dragging me down. I wasn't sure about everything, but at least I had an answer to the last question: I am. I'm going to love myself and take care of myself. (Redondo 2017: 45-46)

Once again, men are not the only ones who commit affective abuse. We have seen clearly that Amaia Salazar's mother abused her daughter psychologically and physically. But that of her mother will not be the only case, because the oldest sister Flora is also very dominating and because she will treat her two younger sisters with contempt. What is more, Flora does not believe that their mother tried to kill Amaia, and she thus denies the social recognition and justice Amaia needs as a victim. Questioning of the attack suffered by Amaia makes her a victim all over again, putting up with new suffering. In this sense, Amaia herself makes Flora's malice clear from the beginning of the novel: "Each gesture, each word that came out of her mouth were destined to wound and cause as much harm as possible" (Redondo, 2013, 52). Indeed, she emphasizes time and time again that Flora is a malicious woman: "sometimes she frightened her. Just as her mother had" (Redondo, 2013, 369).

The Corporeal Presence

As noted above, little by little the novel explains the abuse that Amaia Salazar suffered as a child and how her trauma is, still, a source of nightmares. Nevertheless, beyond the importance of psychological aspects, the physical presence of the body is also important in the novel. It seems that Inspector Salazar does not accept her body and that causes her pain:

> In her daily professional life she let her feminine side take second place and concentrtated solely on doing a good job, but outside work, her height and her slim, sinewy body, together with the rather sober clothes she usually chose, made her feel quite unfeminine when she was around other women, particularly the wives of James's colleagues, who were shorter and more petite. (Redondo 2017: 26).

References to women's bodies often appear in the novel. To begin with, the bodies of the teenage victims of the murders are described in detail. Put another way, the traces and scars left by the violence on the victims' bodies are revealed. Psychological (in the case of Amaia, for example) and physical scars are described, including those that the mother gave to Amaia when she tried to kill her:

as well as the cut on top of her head, Amaia has another strike below her right ear; two of her fingers have been fractured in a clearly defensive wound (...); in all likelihood she lost consciousness, the second blow hadn't cut her skin because it was flatter. There's no blood, but with hair that short even you can see it, your daughter has a considerable bump and a more sunken part where she was hit. (Redondo 2013: 232-233)

The scar Amaia's mother left when she attacked the nurse is also mentioned: "The nurse suffered serious injuries (...) and her life was saved because she happened to be in a hospital. She was lucky, although she'll have a scar on her neck for the rest of her life" (Redondo 2017: 316). Moreover, the brutality suffered by the corpses of the teenagers who were the murder victims is also described in great detail:

the obvious brutality of the blows to her face, the savage way in which the clothing had been almost torn into strips, the likely rape and the fury with which the killer had lost control, strangling the victim with his own hands. And then there was the matter of the trophy (...) it wasn't typical for body parts to be taken. (Redondo 2017: 203)

Besides the scars left by the violence on the victims, the corpses of the murdered teenagers would have new scars when the autopsy was performed on them:

Any self-respecting forensic pathologist will admit that the y-shaped incisions in an autopsy are brutal (....). It was when (...) the assistant closed the awful wound (...) when the evidence of the brutality that it implied became unbearable. When the body was that of a small child or a lass, as in that case, it was at that moment that they seemed more helpless and violated, more mistreated because of the large stitches that were being sewed, like the zip on the cloth of a rag doll that would no longer heal. (Redondo 2013: 74–75)

Even more, a lack of scars in the text is considered an exception. In the case of the second victim, Anne Arbizu, her skin is described as being marble-like, with no scars or marks. Her skin is so white that her aunt took her for a *belagile* (a spirit): "Anne was a *belagile*, as dark inside as she was white outside" (Redondo 2017, 142).

On the other hand, the importance of a woman's body in relation to motherhood is also significant, as noted, because many women in the novel yearn to be mothers, even though some of them will not manage to; apparently, their bodies are not so fertile.

Some Conclusions

During the last decade, there have been several innovations in the Basque police novel, especially through the influence of the crime fiction originating in Northern Europe and the United States. The main protagonist of Redondo's *El guardián invisible* [*The Invisible Guardian*] is a beautiful young female inspector, and she, too, like the teenage girls, is a victim of violence, this not being typical.

Moreover, although the novel takes place in a rural setting, global situations and problematic situations are reflected and condemned. As Redondo denounces, diseases often attributed to the degradation and alienation of the city can also be found in a rural area where everyone knows each other. Thus, among those global illnesses or problems, alcoholism, drugs, gender discrimination, violence, and murders are mentioned.

The novel's author, main protagonist, and the other principal characters (the aunt, sisters, victims, and so on) are women. In this scenario, it is hardly surprising that the main themes developed in the novel are linked to gender: as we have mentioned, the gender gap, motherhood, and violence against women are the focal points. Furthermore, Redondo reflects the captivity suffered by women as a result of patriarchal society and male chauvinist socialization. What is more still, she reflects that captivity in a fully critical way, because she does not forget that women, as well being victims, are often perpetrators, that they frequently also perpetuate gender stereotypes, captivity, and violence. In that sense, Redondo defends sisterhood; the main protagonists' affective network is woven together by women and thanks to their mutual support the women in the novel take control of their lives.

References

Barandiarán, Jose Miguel (1984): *El mundo de las divinidades en la mitología vasca*. Pamiela: Pamplona.

Carnero, S., Delgado, E., and García, M. (2018): Entrevista a Ibon Martín. Retrieved October 9, 2018 from https://sheilaentrelineas.blogspot.com/2018/03/entrevista-ibon-martin.html#.

Colpisa. (2018): Dolores Redondo, premiada con el Bancarella por los libreros italianos. Jul. 23. Retrieved July 30, 2018 from https://www.diariovasco.com/culturas/libros/dolores-redondo-bancarella-20180723165625-ntrc.html.

Crime Writers' Association (2015): CWA International Dagger Awards. Retrieved June 18, 2018 from https://thecwa.co.uk/the-invisible-guardian/.

Culver, Melissa M. (2015): "El "yo" de la detective: Dolores Redondo y Carolina Solé," in *Lectora. Revista de Dones i Textualitat*, 21. 57–71. Available at http://doi.org/10.1344/105.000002446.

Domingo-Aldama, F. (2014): Dolores Redondo dedica la Pluma de Plata a los libreros bilbaínos. May 28. Retrieved May 30, 2018 from https://elpais.com/ccaa/2014/05/28/paisvasco/1401288713_863189.html.

Echeburúa, Enrique, and De Corral, Paz (2009): "El homicidio en la relación de pareja: un análisis psicológico," in *Eguzkilore: Cuaderno del Instituto Vasco de Criminología*, 23: 139–150.

Eusko Jaurlaritza (2005): "4/2005 Legea, otsailaren 18koa, Emakumeen eta Gizonen Berdintasunerakoa," in *EHAA* 42, March 2.

Euskal kultura, sistema matrilinealean oinarritzen zen eta gizarte eskuzabal eta orekatua zen. (2014): Retrieved October 20, 2018 from http://www.kronika.eus/albisteak/erenozu/albistea/2014/03/08/fce34e74443/euskal-kultura-sistema-matrilinealean-oinarritzen-zen-eta-gizarte-eskuzabal-eta-orekatua-zen/.

Iñarra, Aitxus (1994): *Hilketa euskal herri kulturan. Hilketa Azkue eta Barandiaranen ahozko ipuin eta ele zaharretan*. Iralka: Irun.

Jung, Carl G. (2003): *Arquetipos e inconsciente colectivo*. Paidós Ibérica: Barcelona.

Lagarde y de los Ríos, Marcela (2005): *Los cautiverios de las mujeres. Madresposas, monjas, putas, presas y locas*. National Autonomous University of Mexico: Mexico City.

——— (2009): "Pacto entre mujeres: Sororidad," in *Aportes para el debate*, 25: 123–135.

——— (2012): *El Feminismo en mi vida. Hitos, claves y topías*. Institute for Women of Mexico City: Mexico City.

Lasarte Leonet, Gema (2011): *Pertsonaia protagonista femeninoen ezaugarriak eta bilakaera euskal narratiba garaikidean*. UPV/EHU: Bilbao.

Latino Literacy Now (2017): International Latino Book Awards. Retrieved October 22, 2018 from https://latino247mediagroup.app.box.com/s/agu2sbk5neg5d2yt70u5z4ogb2f479fd.

Losada Soler, Elena (2015): "Matar con un lápiz. La novela criminal escrita por mujeres," in *Lectora. Revista de Dones i Textualitat*, 21, 9–14. Available at http://doi.org/10.1344/105.000002458.

Martín Matos, Joseba A. (2016): "Glocalización en la Trilogía del Baztán. Elementos locales y globales en el universo de Dolores Redondo," in Àlex Martín Escribà, and Javier Sánchez Zapatero (eds.): *El género negro. De la marginalidd a la normalización*. Andavira: Santiago of Compostela: (87–95)

Oropesa, Salvador (2018): "Mitologia y terrorismo en la Trilogia del Baztán," in Àlex Martín Escribà, and Javier Sánchez Zapatero (eds.): *Clásicos y contemporáneos en el género negro*. Andavira: Santiago of Compostela: 121–127.

Redondo, Dolores (2013): *El guardián invisible*. Destino: Barcelona.

——— (2017): *The Invisible Guardian: A Novel*. Atria: New York.

Sánchez Díaz-Aldagalán, Carlos (2015): "La mujer como creadora y personaje de la novela negra española contemporánea," in M. Cabrera Espinosa, and J. A. López Cordero (Eds.): *VII Congreso virtual sobre Historia de las Mujeres*. Historic Diocesan Archives of Jaen: Jaen: 713–744.

Chapter 12

Unveiling the Cover: The Front Covers of Basque Detective Novels

Susana Jodra Llorente and *José Antonio Morlesín Mellado*

Who has not heard or said that one should not judge a book by its cover? This saying, which is typically used to judge people, denounces triviality or superficiality. But when numerous books are found in bookshops or shop windows, the first thing potential buyers or readers see are the covers. It is not just their titles, but the images and other elements that appear thereon that catch the eye. In order to catch our attention, they must be attractive, stimulating; something different. They must present a problem, a riddle, which we will be able to solve or guess only by reading the book. Books are stores and on their front covers, like doors or windows, we can find clues about what there is inside.

Although the general elements that appear on covers are the title, author, image, and publisher, in fact the composition is more complex and their characteristics and locations are not left to chance: colors, typographies, images, photographs as well as illustrations, positions, sizes, adornments: there is a reason for everything. We must not forget that there is not just literary, cultural, scientific interest in distributing books, economically, it is an industry that handles a large amount of money and there is a lot of competition among publishing houses. In this work, the role of graphic designers is more important than one might think, and what is more, we could say that it is essential. This is because the relationship between the content and the container, within a very limited space, must be effectively integrated.

In addition to having a commercial and communicative purpose, the basic function of book covers is that of protector; that of protecting the body of the book. In order to understand their importance and complexity, we will first immerse ourselves in the history of the book, then examine the sections that nowadays predominate in book covers and, finally, by using several chosen examples, endeavour to delve more deeply into the concrete case of the Basque police novel.

The Origin and Development of Book Covers

The development of book covers goes hand-in-hand with the history of the book itself and the techniques, materials, and tools as well as writings and themes used to implement them. Essentially, the book is formed as a content device of knowledge and wisdom with a history stretching back more than five thousand years, and as we know it down to the present, it underwent many changes. Its most direct antecedent would be the codex (*liber cuadratus*) that appeared in the third century, in which at first short papyrus and then parchment notebooks were sewn together and wooden covers were added to protect and stabilize them. In classical times, wax tablets were used as a model to take notes, and they were also reused directly for codices. Although papyrus bundles, which had been common for a long time, were in documents for centuries, the codex would be more suitable for long texts; in addition to the greater number of texts it could contain, because both sides could be written on, it was cheaper, and easier to transport and collect.

In the Middle Ages, with time, the resources for binding improved and would be adapted to the tastes of each era; ribs were inserted in the back, the wooden covers were enclosed with leather, the edges were protected with metal elements, jewelry was inserted, they were decorated with images and watermarks with gold engravings. Book covers had the function of covering and protecting, but additional decorations according to customer requirements would also be an indication of their power and wealth. Because the books were heavy and they were placed on lecterns or tables, the front cover was much more elaborate than the back cover; until the eighteenth century, when the books lay on the shelves, their backs were placed against the wall, and as they could not be seen, they were not as elaborate as the front covers.

Printing techniques had a great impact on the reproduction of books, because they would evolve from manual copying to reprinting through matrices and printers. Monks in monasteries lost their dominance of this task and the profession of printer would be established, when in the future they would come to work with binders and publishers. By means of xylography in incunabula, at first just images and then images and writing were combined; later, even more elaborate images would be obtained through chalcography. Initially, the printed book was similar to a medieval manuscript, when every effort was made to be as similar as possible: including the page order, margins, writing, adornments and illustrations. In the mid-fifteenth century, Johannes Gutenberg would invent a new metal alloy for movable metal type and promote printing. In the second half of that century, front pages would be more developed, the first page of the book, left blank for practical reasons, later incorporating writing (the summarized title, the author's and/or printer's name) and images (an expressive engraving or general adornment). As we will see, this structure would be applied to the front cover.

The aforementioned creation of paper also had a lot to do with this. Invented in China in BC 105, it would not arrive in Spain until the twelfth century and from there it spread across Europe. By the fifteenth and mid-sixteenth centuries, there were paper mills all over Europe. Printing brought with it the expansion of this medium, although until then it was interspersed with parchment, but its abundance and cheaper cost led to its dominance. Although at first the raw materials were cloths, given the need for this material in the seventeenth century, fibers from other sources would also be sought, above all from plants and trees.

In the fifteenth century, the Venetian publisher Aldo Manuzio would publish small portable books. The abovementioned new printing techniques were not just applied to the inside of books, but advances established fashions and binders introduced those novelties in the orders their received. That way, the same molds would be used in books about different themes: geometric elements, plant life, crosses, church buildings, and so on. One should note that, up to that point, any expansions, transformations, and innovations that could take place in this field were controled by guilds.

Yet as regards front covers, the eighteenth and nineteenth centuries were interesting eras, in which the mechanization of the industrial revolution and the technological advances derived therefrom brought major contributions. In eighteenth-century Europe, at the same time that the first industrial revolution and political movements improved people's social situation, so printing resources reduced the price of book production and, as well as educational texts (classical, scientific, and religious texts) being supplied to normal people, they demanded other kinds of publications. Publishing houses realized the importance that the external appearance of books could have in order to attract these new readers and luxury bookbinding was on the point of disappearing: cardboard covers surrounded by colorful fabrics, smaller books, simple and clean decorations, titles on the back cover, and so on.

From the early nineteenth century on, the mechanical techniques of both printing and those established in bookbinding, together with the industrial fabrication of cloth and paper, combined even more obviously in book publishing. The printed decorous elements, watermarks, architectural elements, and so on used on title pages were moved to the front covers and they would be related directly to the book content, thereby turning into a direct means of communicating the book's content. Visual rhetoric would be used to attract potential readers, as is the case today; because, as noted above, book covers have the ability to protect, identify, and call attention. Their attractiveness, along with the option to reproduce colorful images, initially through lithography and then through half-tone processes, was significantly enhanced.

Modernist tendencies of the time, Art Nouveau, types, images, and expressive adornments would also be established in the design and production of book covers. Poster designers and artists of the time would be commissioned to design both book covers and magazine covers. This would bring about a revolution in publishing, both in Europe and North America, leading to a massive growth in book production. Worth noting are the works of the English painter and illustrator Aubrey Beardsley. In the twentieth century, the book covers drawn up by avant-garde artists would be revolutionary, for example by Rodchenko and Lissitzky in Russia. As the book cover designer David Pearson says, books would be transformed into a part of the aesthetics and values of their era, and of course a witness to it (Pearson 2008: 41). After the World Wars, book publishing and publication would become a competitive market.

Delving into the Police Novel

The origins of the police novel genre or subject matter are located at different points in history, but when it comes to the direct antecedent of contemporary publications and book covers, Edgar Allan Poe's writings are of interest, such as *The Murders in the Rue Morgue* (a short story with the detective C. Auguste Dupin), published in *Graham's Magazine* in Philadelphia in 1841. Weeklies were publications that reached a wider readership than books, because they were cheaper. Seeing the interest created by texts of this nature, series and collections were drawn up, and stories brought together and books published as well.

At that time, woodcuts or chalcographic engravings printed in relief and black and white on the inside of the book would also be printed on the covers. Coloured lithographs would be made on additional pages, pasted on the covers or used as a cover to surround the whole book. Realist dramas full of literal scenes would arouse the interest of readers. From then on, detective characters would multiply (Holmes, Poirot, Miss Marple, Marlowe) and, following the magazine model, book series would be published, creating a collection. These books included short stories. They were reprinted over and over again and with multiple forms of book covers; pocket editions, in both hardback and paperback, with covers in color. Although cover illustrations and typographs were adapted to the tastes of the era, suggesting the time in which they were set, in many reprints the original images have been maintained. In those cases, we could say that they reveal an example of a text that has been transformed into a classic with a "retro" touch.

In the twentieth century, from the 1930s onward, under the influence of US films and following the tendency of the posters designed to publicize them, the following would be used for book covers: a strong clever man, a sexy woman in need of help, violence, guns, et cetera, with a dark setting. The image and personality of the police officer and private detective would be normalized in some way; this would come to be known as the pulp aesthetic tendency.

The end of the twentieth century, under the influence of mass media, brought with it the expansion and globalization of styles. The use of photographs on book covers would predominate, due to the speed with which they could be made and their approximation to reality. Advertising could make or ruin books to the point of turning writers into stars, not to mention when they have been adapted to film or television; for example, Swedish detective and noir fiction are known all over the world. Books which have been popular in one country are quickly translated and will be available in other countries.

In Spain, although there were published translations of stories from France and the United Kingdom, this genre would arrive very late. Readers in the Spanish state would have to wait until the end of the Francoism for their own writers. But there are special cases too, such as Emilia Pardo Bazán's stories and, as we shall see later, José Antonio Loidi's book *Hamabost egun Urgain-en* (*Fifteen Days in Urgain*).

Nowadays, we could say that there has been, to some extent, a generalization and normalization of book covers at the global level: the formats, direct photos or photomontages for images, and bright weighty large fonts for both titles and author names. Novels on the same themes look the same, both aesthetically and in regard to composition. That said, it may be the case that each publishing house follows its own "aesthetic" tendency. Finding something different will be because the publisher gives the designer or artist the freedom to create.

The Front Cover: Information about the Book and Graphic Communication

Semiotics is a discipline that studies signs and communication processes (Eco 2015) and when it comes to examining book covers, it can be an interesting point of view. Indeed, the cover design is a message aimed at the reader. In general, it is made up of two components: text and image, that which corresponds, specifically, to the *bimedia* (made up of two media) mentioned by Moles and Costa (1999). In the field of social semiotics, there is *multimedia* (Kress and van Leeuwen 2006). According to this concept, image and text would be *modes*, the media being types of support that channel messages. That way, combining more than one method, a *multimodal* message is assembled.

Cover designers work with images when it comes to bringing about a composition on the front cover that has something to do with the content of the book. However, the freedom designers have when it comes to suggestions for the front cover of a book is variable. We should not forget that it is just one step within the process itself of book publishing. Different factors may condition the design. It could be that a specific structure must be respected, in order to fit the image of the publisher's collections or identity; as noted in the previous section.

As for the components of the front cover, in the case of text, the front covers typically include the basic information (author, title, publishing house), which is used to identify the book itself. Insofar as letters are graphic signs, as well as channeling textual information, they also transmit visual data, because their appearance embodies cultural meanings. For example, in some editions of the detective Sherlock Holmes, typographies are used which recall the forms of nineteenth-century letters, with the intention of transporting the reader back to the time of the story. Sometimes, designers have chosen serif, conveying a classical nature and the tradition of letter forms. Likewise, we may also come across the features of decorative letters which were used in the nineteenth century, among other things.[1]

We noted that the front cover text is used to identify the book, but the front cover design itself can impart a specific graphic identity to the book. In order to do so, one of the designer's tasks is to determine the point of view that will guide the design work. There are multiple choices. In literary works, for example, one may favor depicting a significant passage, or choose to portray the characters, reflect the tome of the text, and so forth. Furthermore, if the text is connected to a specific literary genre, clichés of the genre may be taken from literature and included on the front cover by means of graphic interpretation, so that the reader may easily associate the book with the genre. Detectives, guns, proof of or clues to the murders, mysterious dark settings, and so on. They are codes that we share in the collective imaginary, made up of conventions. This portrayal work can be done by designers themselves, but often it is a task assigned to illustrators or photographers.

We should make it clear that the front cover of a book is not just the façade of the sleeve, but the whole sleeve. One also sees some designs used on covers on the back, adapted to its model. On others, designers use the whole space to develop the design over the full extent of the cover. For example, in Ramon Saizarbitoria's 2015 novel *Lili eta biok* (Lili and I), a photograph by Aitor Arana extends over the whole sleeve. A photo portrait of a dejected woman is situated on the front, but the photograph continues across the spine, back cover and flaps.

Besides including information about the book, we should not overlook the fact that one of the main functions of the cover is to attract the reader, by structuring the book so as to extend a striking and attractive invitation. In order to do this, designers use the resources offered by visual rhetoric time and time again. They serve to articulate graphic messages in a more unusual way instead of in the literal sense. Thanks to this procedure, the design may stand out from more commonplace ideas. However, such originality is grounded in cultural conventions. As a result of relating to the connotations in the graphic components of front covers, the spectator must be capable of understanding the concept of the front cover, or, otherwise, the effectiveness of the image used to constitute it may be called into question.

When it comes to defining visual resources, the basic model is classic rhetoric. The abundant catalog made up of traditions, metaphors, synedoches, parallelisms, and many other rhetorical functions has been adapted to visual communication. In the visual and spoken rhetoric proposed by Gui Bonsiepe (1999), he applies the abovementioned resources that we can find in one graphic message. For example, by illustrating what the title says on a book cover by means of a visual metaphor, the designer has the opportunity to combine the meanings and connotations of both text and images. Moreover, there are classifications which move away from classical models, specifically those that turn to the iconic features of visual signs or the plastic arts (Groupe μ, 2010).

The Front Covers of the Basque Police Novel

In the Basque Country, the first police novel written in Basque was Jose Antonio Loidi's *Hamabost egun Urgainen* (in English, *Fifteen Days in Urgain*, 2014), published in 1955 by the Itxaropena publishing house in Zarautz, with illustrations by José Luís Nabaskues; in the image on the front cover one can see the signature LN. In 1980, the Edili publishing house in Donostia published it, keeping the interior illustrations of course, but with a different front cover, regarding both the image and the typography used for the text. The publisher Erein published it in both 1997 and 2012 for its Auskalo series; in the latter case, the image that appears on page 31 was colored and adapted to fit the front cover. As we can see in the images, the whole composition (image, color, typography) for the front cover of each edition changes, but in all the cases the plastic language used was illustrated (not photographic).

Although in the first two volumes the images are formally very strong, in the next two we might say they are "softer." Clear forms made up of simple reduced colors predominate. Depending on the content of the images and the use of colors, the message that each volume transmits is very different. In the first two, reds and greens predominate, whereas in the next two it is blues. We can see the development of both fashion and technique on these book covers, but also in regard to the essence of the story, where the publishing house sought to focus attention; while a murdered woman is the protagonist of the first publications, thereafter it would be a group of men and a village; depicting the conspiracy and mystery created in a Basque rural setting.

Image 1. Front covers of different editions of Hamabost egun Urgainen, *written as* Amabost egun Urgain'en *in the first two editions (1955, 1980, 1997, and 2012).*

As for the typography, each publication presents different perspectives. In the first edition, the most striking thing is the inscribed title, done in lettering inspired by the Art Deco movement of the 1920s and 1930s. Geometry predominates, reflecting formal experimentation that moves away from the proportions of classical roman font; it could refer to the time when the murder took place. In the 1980 edition, however, the font used in the title, derived from the letters of a typewriter, could call to mind police reports. The connotations implied by the images of the fonts are related to the police genre in this case, so that the reader, too, may get that suggestion. On the other hand, in the later publications of Erein, the typographies are subject to the design of the series. Thus, those used are not related to the content, but instead follow the graphic identity of the publishing house.

The 1955 front cover of the book resembles the book covers of the 1920s that were produced during the same era in Europe and the United States, not just due to the typography, but the graphic language used too. It is worth bearing in mind that Spain, following the Civil War and World War II, was under the control of a dictatorship, and the economic and cultural blockade it was experiencing as a result also had a direct influence on the design of book covers. There was widespread repression in the Basque Country and, in the face of state censorship, Basque publishing houses had major problems in publishing in Basque.

Thereafter, Mariano Izeta's *Dirua galgarri* (Ruinous Money) would be published in 1962, by the Auspoa publishing house. Worth mentioning too are Xabier Gereño's 1978 *Jurgi kapitaina bretanian* (Captain Jurgi in Brittany) by the Bilbao publishing house and Gotzon Garate's 1982 *Izurri berria* (The New Plague), published by Bilboko Kutxak. Much more well-known is the 1984 volume published by Elkar, which used a work by the artist Oswaldo

Guayasamín as an illustration, a famous text that would be reprinted over the years. As we will see, as in the case of *Sasiak ere begiak baditik* (Even Brush Has Eyes), in which an old engraving was used, images taken from the field of the plastic arts would be adapted and often appeared on the front covers of books. The works of artists in the 1980s and 1990s, parts or sections of pictures, would also be used, overcoming the boundary between illustration and decoration. An illustration takes on the function of messenger, one that connects the sender to the content. When using a work of art created in a different context, the cover designer reinterprets the image in an attempt to adapt it to the content.

Image 2. Izurri berria *1982, 1984, and 1999.*

In the 1980s, there was a Basque literature series and a noir fiction series among the books of the Elkar publishing house. The importance accorded to noir fiction by the publishing house was striking, because this genre had its own fields: including the Basque-language noir fiction, Spanish-language noir fiction, and Spanish-language dark humor subsections. The series design by José Félix Igartua remained the same until it changed in the 1990s and the organization was rigid. The main components were organized between the wire-lines on the side of the front cover. The title was always at the top, followed by the name and surname of the author. Then there was an illustration referring to the content of the book. Regarding its composition, the title, author, and series title were left justified. The image and publishing house, however, were centered.

We find the main difference between them in the color. The front covers in the Basque noir fiction series have a black background, in a clearly literal direct reference to the genre of the series. Although this resource was redundant, the aforementioned series serves to distinguish it at a glance from the beige-colored Basque literature series with light backgrounds. The contrast between the two series was prominent. Furthermore, the series were also differentiated by the graphic signs. In the case of that of Basque literature, there is an image that recalls the shape of a disc-shaped gravestone in the Basque Country. In the Noir Fiction series, however, the silhouette of a cat brings to mind a mystery, as it is associated with this animal (even more so with black cats, because they imply mystery, bad luck, and evil). The designer refers to the collective imagery of our society so that the viewer can make conceptual connections between textual and graphic elements that will help them to decode the message.

Image 3. Sasiak ere begiak baditik *and* Ta Marbuta. Jerusalemen gertatua.

Although the graphic distinction was clear and sharp, insofar as content was concerned, in some cases the blurring of genre boundaries could turn the classification of titles into a complex activity. Indeed, although Aingeru Epalza's *Sasiak ere begiak baditik* (Even Brush Has Eyes) and Xabier Kintana's *Ta Marbuta. Jerusalemen gertatua* (Tā marbūṭa: What Happened in Jerusalem) express elements of the police genre, Xabier Kintana's work was the only one which fit the noir fiction series. In the cover illustration, in the foreground there is a man lying on the ground, bleeding, in a street that implies the architecture of the Middle East. Both the man and the blood come out of the picture in the illustration. This fracture emphasizes the man's dramatic satiation. He holds in his hand a piece of paper with the title "*Ta Marbuta*" written on it in Arabic, repeating it below the title above. Epalza's novel uses an old engraving which illustrates the Carlist Wars related to era in which it is set.

We will now mention another book published in the noir fiction series, namely *110. Street-eko geltokia* (110th Street Station), by Iñaki Zabaleta Urkiola. This very successful volume has gone through numerous reprints and reeditions to this day. From the first edition (that of 1985, through the Susa publishing house) to the latest, the front cover illustration has been the same on all of them: a photograph taken by the author himself and colorized by Joxemi Zumalabe. The image displays the entrance to 110th Street subway station in New York in a direct reference to the title of the novel. The added color is not connected to reality. In general, a pink ochre tone divides the space. It intensifies the presence of station graffiti through saturated pink.

The repetition of photographs, from edition to edition, has given a specific visual personality to the book, even though the position of the image and the dimensions of the front cover have changed. When Susa published it for the first time in 1985, the image took up a large space, even though the black background was maintained in the side margins and at the top, for texture. In the 1988 edition brought out by Elkar, the photograph was adapted to the design of the noir fiction series as well as making it smaller and adding an outline.

Image 4. 110. Street-eko geltokia. *The 1985, 1988, 1998, and 2003 editions.*

From the 1990s onward, José Félix Igartua once more took charge of designing the structures of book covers for series by that publishing house. The new systems put in place were similar to the previous ones. In this case, the wire-lines were eliminated but the most important graphic and textual elements were distributed within a black box, in the center of the cover. A photograph was extended on the sides and over the whole jacket, reflecting a change in texture from volume to volume.

In 2003, the latest edition of this book written by Iñaki Zabaleta was published. As regards the design, from 2001 onward, the designer Borja Goiti revamped the Literature series. What stands out in this case is the commitment was made to freeing up the structure of the cover. Since then, covers have not had a fixed lattice and images extend all over the cover. In this case, the photograph fills up the entire cover and the designer has superimposed the textual information thereon.

One should mention that the typographies used in the first edition by Susa and the latest one by Elkar do not have serif, but a font which is similar to that in the station sign in the image, connecting the two.²

Generally speaking, from the late 1990s onward, photomontages and collages predominated on book covers. Readability is essential to attract readers' attention and photographs offer straightforwardness and intelligibility. For example, Miren Gorrotxategi's *33 ezkil* (33 Bells, Elkar, 2016), Ramon Saizarbitoria's abovementioned *Lili eta biok* (Lili and Me, Erein, 2015), Alberto Ladron Arana's *Piztiaren begiak* (The Eyes of the Beast, Elkar, 2012), and Garbiñe Ubeda's *Hobe Isilik* (Best Keep Quiet, Elkar, 2013).

Image 5. 33 ezkil *(front cover: Unai Arana),* Piztiaren Begiak *(front cover: Alex Ladron Arana), and* Hobe Isilik *(front cover: Unai Arana), by the Elkar publishing house.*

Anjel Lertxundi's *Zoaz infernura laztana* (Go to Hell, Darling, Erein, 2008) and Jon Alonso's *Zintzoen saldoan* (In the Group of the Righteous, Txalaparta, 2012) are clearly of a different kind, in which, in line with noir fiction, a black background predominates. In that context, the redness of the blood, like a splash, contrasts with the whiteness of the typography or objects, achieving very dramatic effects.

Image 6. Zintzoen saldoan *and* Zoaz infernura laztana.

For the front cover of the novel *Zintzoen saldoan* (In the Group of the Righteous), the designer Esteban Montorio chose just three colors: black, white, and red. Consequently, as is the case in the cover of *Zoaz infernura, laztana* (Go to Hell, Darling), the chromatic coordination that unites the components is established. There is a photograph of a chef's hat splattered with blood, underscoring the rawness of the blood. However, the hat is isolated on a black background, without any surrounding elements, highlighting the stark contrast between the definition of the photograph and the simplicity of the background. Moreover, the image used strengthens the rhetoric. The plot of this novel begins with the death of a famous chef. Thus, the bloody hat, as it is part of the chef's murder, is a synecdochical rhetorical figure. In cases like these, one part of an element or concept replaces the same element.

It should be mentioned that police novels as well as noir fiction are part of a global money-making industry. Publishing houses bring out series by the same author or on the same theme in which book covers, in order to emphasize the personality of the series, as in the case of collections, will be made up in the same way.

Among publications in the Basque community with a detective or police officer as the protagonist, it is worth citing Ramiro Pinilla's books, in which the bookseller Sancho Bordabarri is transformed into the detective Samuel Esparta; Jon Arretxe's Black detective, Toure, an undocumented immigrant and fortune teller, whom life has treated harshly; Itxaro Borda's investigator Amaia Ezpeldoi; and the protagonist of Dolores Redondo's Baztan trilogy, the police officer Amaia Salazar. Clearly, each publishing house has its own designer and its own graphic language. As for the images on the front covers of Pinilla's and Redondo's books, we are struck by how big publishers use sources which can be found directly on the web. In Pinilla's books, there is an image of a stereotypical detective, specifically those perpetuated by police films: a raincoat, a hat which covers the face, a silhouette sculpted by contrasting lighting, and so on. In Dolores Redondo's case, the common denominator in the covers is a very mysterious setting built on forested surroundings, together with the reflection of a sole person. The person's identity is hidden, intensifying the mystery surrounding the character. Moreover, as Dolores Redondo's books have been made into films, in reeditions the film posters have been used directly; this practice has been very common in the world of novels as an influential marketing method. Photographs dominate book covers, but it is worth noting the placement of the title and the author's name too, as it is a feature which the Destino publishing house repeats.

Image 7. Examples of front covers in series by Ramiro Pinilla (photographer: Gary Isaacs) and Dolores Redondo (photographer: Stephen Carroll). Both images acquired from photographic archives. (Photonica / Getty Images and Trevillion images)

It should be said that the covers designed for Itxaro Borda's three books are very interesting for their creative aspect, because, while maintaining the same design, the images used for each story are completely different; unfortunately, the colophon or copyright page does not mention who the designer is. The image on the cover of *Bakean utzi arte* (Until They Leave Us in Peace, Susa, 1994), by Aitor Bayo and Garbiñe Ubeda, is a photograph modified and posterized with bold colors. On that of *Amorezko pena baño* (More Than Heartbreak, Susa, 1996), the image is by Asisko Urmeneta, and appears to be a part of a very expressive painting. In the case of *Bizi nizano munduan* (Until I'm Alive, Susa, 1996), the image is made up of a colorful landscape by the painter Jim Buckels, with a naïve touch. Outside settings suggest landscape environments, with the human presence in some cases transforming them in such a way as to portray a road movie, through place changes. The human presence dominates the landscape. In the first two, the effect is more violent and in the third more bucolic.

Image 8. Front covers of Itxaro Borda's books (1994, 1996, and 1996).

When it comes to design, the covers created by Cristina Fernández for the Uzta Gorria series by the Erein publishing house are interesting and rich in a plastic sense. The Detective Toure stories are part of this series. Using specific photomontages and typography for each novel, she creates different, intriguing, and very suggestive atmospheres. A common element in the series is the black space that extends from the top of the book cover, like a stain, in which the author's name and title are placed in light-colored letters; the difference between the size of the author's name and title is evident, with the title being the first element to call one's attention. While we come across a non-serif linear typography in the author's name and surname, in some of the titles there are typographies which have a decorative touch. In the novel *19 kamera* (19 Cameras), for example, there are letters that challenge the traditional font structure, recalling the geometricizing of the visual culture of science fiction or Soviet posters. On the cover of *612 euro* (612 Euros), the letters have strokes of irregular thickness which look clumsy and informal. More than choice of typography and composition, what is interesting are the cover images. Sometimes, they are photomontages (*19 kamera*, *Ez erran deus* [Don't Say Anything at All]); the photographs are always the foundation. In the book *Sator lokatzak* (Mole Mud) for example, spiked eyeballs and an ear are stacked in a bowl. In revealing objects in a situation other than their original context, the designer creates an extraordinary composition. This reinterpretation of objects recalls the same procedure carried out on several covers by the celebrated designer Daniel Gil for the Alianza publishing house in Madrid. Marcel Duchamp's readymades also stand out in the field of art.

Image 9. Designs drawn up by Cristina Fernández for the Detective Toure series (from 2012 to 2017).

In reprints, the same books published at different times may be translations published in different foreign countries or by different publishers in the same country. In the case of the Detective Toure, we might say that the same form is maintained in the Spanish-language version but that the images are more direct and explicit. Here it is worth citing Harkaitz Cano's *Pasaia Blues* (Susa 1999), published in Spanish, Galician, and German in different countries, at different times and by different publishers. Placing the volumes side-by-side, in regard to the cover images, original photomontages or illustrations, and the location and size of the title and author's name, the typography and location chosen for them are completely different.

Image 10. Publications of Paisaia Blues *in Basque 1999, German 2009, Spanish 2012, and Galician 2013.*

In the Basque version, there is a suggestive photograph by Garbiñe Ubeda. It reveals a person, whose head is slightly tilted, looking indirectly at something outside the cover. She is situated on the right-hand side, almost half out of picture. We can see that her face is partially out of focus and at the side, the photograph has been torn, emphasizing that what we are seeing is the torn-off piece of a photograph. It seems that the aim of the lack of focus and torn photo is to hide the identity of the person who appears therein, increasing the mystery surrounding the portrayal. As the composition is not centered, interesting relationships are established among the components on the cover in order to maintain the balance of the structure.

In order to conclude this short introduction to front cover design in Basque police novels, we would like to mention several points.

Formally, the design of book covers for novels offers abundant opportunities and fiction has taken over the market. Through book covers, illustrators and designers must suggest the content of the book and accentuate its uniqueness, to stand out among other publications, but the book cover is not just made up of the front part. The cover is everything that surrounds the body of the book in itself: paperback or hardback, with or without flaps, with a jacket or not, and so on. The front and back covers seem to have been forgotten. Although the front cover actually acts as an advertisement, it is the spine that can be seen when placed on shelves in libraries or in our homes. The spine is a very narrow space in which, typically, a lot of information is introduced: the title, author, the graphic personality of the series or collection and the publisher's trademark. The length or body of the book decides the size of this area. In the narrow nature of this space itself, the small size of the typography used therein makes it difficult to read this and consequently distinguish it.

It is worth noting, too, that there are also problems when it comes to terms. Terms like front cover, cover, and title page are often mixed up. Following the half title, the initial pages of the book are the frontispiece and title page respectively. The frontispiece includes just the title, while the title page includes several data points, such as the title, the author's name and surname, and the publishing house.

To finish, aesthetically, from the examples we have seen, we can conclude that the story of the Basque detective novel can be compared to that of other countries; because globalization has brought about a generalization of aesthetic trends or fashions. Difference, as noted, lies in the trust publishers place in designers and the freedom they are given. In such cases, all we may find is "something different," in which designers have the choice to reflect their own plastic and aesthetic language on front covers.

References

Bonsiepe, Gui (1999): "Retórica visual y verbal," in G. Bonsiepe, *Del objeto a la interfase. Mutaciones del diseño*. Infinito: Buenos Aires: 71–86.

Buen Unna, Jorge De (2008): *Manual de diseño editorial*. Trea: Gijon.

Dahl, Svend (1994): *Historia del libro*. Alianza Editorial: Madrid.

Eco, Umberto (2015): *La estructura ausente. Introducción a la semiótica*. Debolsillo (Penguin Random House Publishing Group): Barcelona.

Esteve Botey, Francisco (1993): *Historia del Grabado*. Clan, Técnicas artísticas: Madrid.

Fernández, Leire, Herrera, Eduardo (2016): *Diseño de cubiertas de libros. Recursos de retórica visual*. Editorial Síntesis: Madrid.

Groupe µ. (2010): *Tratado del signo visual. Para una retórica de la imagen*. Cátedra: Madrid.

Haslam, Andrew (2007): *Creación, diseño y producción de libros*. Art Blume SL: Barcelona.

Kress, Gunther, and Van Leeuwen, Theo (2006): *Reading images. The Grammar of Visual Design*. Routledge: New York.

Laplantz, Shereen (1996): *Buchbinden. Traditionelle Techniken, Experimentelle Gestaltung*. Haupt: Bern.

Llop, Rosa (2014): *Un sistema gráfico para las cubiertas de libros. Hacia un lenguaje de parámetros*. Editorial Gustavo Gili SL: Barcelona.

Moles, Abraham, and Costa, Joan (1999): *Publicidad y diseño. El nuevo reto de la comunicación*. Infinito: Buenos Aires.

Morlesín Mellado, José Antonio (2016): *Evolución, estado actual y perspectivas del diseño de la cubierta del libro: estudio particularmente orientado a la Comunidad Autónoma del País Vasco*. Doctoral dissertation. Leioa: Department of Drawing, School of Fine Arts. UPV/EHU: Bilbao.

Pearson, David (2008): *Books as History. The importance of books beyond their texts*. The British Library, Oak Knoll Press: London.

Persuy, Annie, and Evrard, Sün (1999): *Encuadernación. Técnica y proceso*. Olleros & Ramos SL: Madrid.

Pohlen, Josep (2011): *Fuente de letras*. Taschen: Colony.
Polo, Magda, and Díez, Charo (2005): *Libook. Poéticas del Libro*. Thule ediciones: Barcelona.
Ross, Tom and Marilyn (1994): *The complete guide to Self-Publishig*. Writer's digest books. 3rd Edition: Cincinnati.
Satué, Enric (1998): *El diseño de libros del pasado, del presente, y tal vez del futuro. La huella de Aldo Manuzio*. Germán Sánchez Ruipérez Foundation: Madrid.

Notes

1 Since he presented it in 1954, the typographic classification of Maximilian Vox, an expert in typography, has been very successful in teh field of graphic design. The ATypI (Association Typographique Internationale) adopted the suggested Vox-ATypI as its standard classification in 1962. Vox took into account the formal features of letter types and their historical development when he came to establish the levels.

2 According to the Vox typography, non-serif typographies (sans serif) are known as linear (Pohlen 2011). Therein, there are different subsections. The 2003 Elkar edition used Helvetica Neue, a neo-grotesque linear typography, the same style as the linear font of the station in the image.

Chapter 13

Basque Crime Fiction and World Literature Studies

Stewart King

In the revised version of his classic history of the crime genre, *Bloody Murder: From the Detective Story to the Crime Novel* (1992), the English crime writer and genre historian Julian Symons claimed that "little sparkles" in foreign crime fiction (1992: 314).[1] Admitting that his judgments are constrained by his monolingualism, thus having to read in translation, Symons is nevertheless dismissive of the crime fiction written by French, Italian, Czech, Spanish (Catalan), and Japanese writers that was starting to appear in English (1992: 314–16). Symons's judgment, however, has not stood the test of time. A year before Symons made his pronouncement, the Swedish writer Henning Mankell published the first of his Kurt Wallander series, *Mördare utan ansikte* (1991) (*Faceless Killers*, 1997), and, in so doing, within a decade Mankell had initiated the worldwide obsession with Scandi- or Nordic Noir. This, of course, was not Mankell's work alone; but he did pave the way for other writers like Stieg Larsson, Jo Nesbø, Camilla Läckberg, Yrsa Sigurðardóttir, and Ragnar Jónasson to name just a few of the Scandinavian authors who have become popular worldwide.

The question "Why is Nordic Noir so popular?" is not one that is asked about Basque crime fiction (Thomson and Stougaard-Nielsen 2017: 237). Nevertheless, there is a connection between these two fictions, as the Nordic Noir phenomenon sparked an interest in the diverse practice of crime fiction from around the world, facilitating translations from a wide range of languages as readers became increasingly fascinated by crimes set in foreign climes. Indeed, in the anglophone book industry there are publishers who cater specifically to readers' demand for international or world crime fiction. UK publisher Bitter Lemon Press, for example, publishes crime stories "for your travels real or imaginary" that offer readers the opportunity to "explore what lies just beneath the surface of the bustling life of countries" (Bitter Lemon Press), while the U.S. publisher Akashic has a catalog of over one hundred place-based noir anthologies from *Alabama Noir* (2020) to *Zagreb Noir* (2015).

The increased circulation and popularity of crime fiction from around the world has also impacted the scholarly study of the genre, with a surge of significant studies on crime fiction traditions beyond the British and American canon, including Australian, Catalan, Japanese, Mexican, Spanish, Swedish, and, including the present collection, Basque crime fictions. As these studies are focused on discrete national crime fiction traditions, they follow a general pattern, which in the case of studies on Basque crime fiction, or on crime fiction in Basque, rightly focuses on what is seen as a distinct, contained Basque literary system with its authors, publishing houses, institutional subsidies, critics, and readers. Given this national focus, it is, or should be unremarkable that the study of Basque crime fiction (or any other national literary tradition) seeks to understand its function within this literary system and within Basque society and culture more broadly. As the introduction to the present collection makes clear, the task of the Basque scholar is to historicize the genre's development in the Basque literary system, to divide it into discrete periods, and to classify it according to preexisting generic categories, such as classic detective fiction, hardboiled fiction, transgressor narratives, police procedurals, feminist crime fiction, crime thrillers, etc. The scholar of Basque crime fiction is also tasked with identifying the particular characteristics of Basque crime fiction, to mark what makes Basque crime fiction distinct from other national crime fiction traditions. The scholar of Basque crime fiction is not alone in this endeavor. It is commonplace in studies of peripheral crime fiction traditions, by which I mean crime fiction from beyond the British-American and French traditions, to narrate the progress of the national genre from (1) the translation of foreign models such as Edgar Allan Poe, Arthur Conan Doyle, Agatha Christie, Dashiell Hammett, Raymond Chandler, and Georges Simenon into the national language to (2) the initial adoption and adaptation of these models by local writers on the way to the production of what are perceived to be works of truly autochthonous crime fiction by writers in the specific national tradition that is the scholar's object of study.

Crime fiction is also a form of genre fiction and, as such, it forms part of a world literary system. Each crime writer and each work of crime fiction participate in what I have called elsewhere a "dialogue between writers and texts across national, cultural, linguistic, and temporal borders" (King 2014: 14). To explore these dialogues is to focus our critical attention beyond the national context of the novels' production and reception. When we do so, "a broader set of reflections and methodological possibilities come into view" (Etherington and Zimbler 2018: 4). With respect to Basque crime fiction, the concern is no longer—or no longer exclusively—with what is different or unique about Basque crime fiction or to consider the genre's function within the Basque literary system or to understand the way in which Basque writers use the genre to reflect on the social, political, cultural, and sexual issues that are important specifically to Basque society. Instead, another set of parameters is required. To situate Basque crime fiction within a world crime fiction literary system means engaging with the world of crime fiction beyond the initial phase of understanding the outside influences (authors and texts) that inspired Basque writers to pen their own crime fictional narratives. It means the establishment of new organizing principles that enable grounds of comparison between Basque crime fiction and crime novels from further afield. In line with the new focus, this chapter has two aims. The first is to reflect on the place of Basque crime fiction within the world of crime fiction in order to understand the specific circumstances through which Basque crime fiction came into being, and to chart the history of the development of Basque crime fiction so as to identify certain features that set the development of Basque crime fiction apart from the processes that led to the creation of other national crime fiction traditions. The second aim of the chapter is to explore several possible grounds of comparison that can hopefully facilitate fruitful transnational dialogues.

Becoming Basque: Translation and Adaptation

The global popularity of Nordic Noir and the lack of international success of Basque crime fiction is not necessarily a consequence of their respective quality. Translation and circulation beyond the originating literary and cultural context in which an individual work was produced are also important factors. Nordic Noir is translated in great numbers and thus circulates more easily in the international marketplace than does Basque crime fiction. Given their importance, it is unsurprising that translation and circulation are defining features of the new World Literature Studies, as it has been practiced since the turn of the millennium. One of the leading figures of this renewed focus on world literature, David Damrosch, for example, defines world literature as "all literary works that circulate beyond their culture of origin, either in translation or in their original language (2003: 4). While there are many crime novels that conform to Damrosch's criterion for a text being treated as a work of world literature, particularly the novels of Agatha Christie, which have been translated into more than one hundred languages, this is not the case for much Basque crime fiction, little of which is translated, or, indeed, circulates in the original Basque to other literary cultures.

If we apply Damrosch's definition to Basque crime fiction, it would be classified, instead, as the product of its engagement with works of world literature—in this case, crime fiction—produced elsewhere. Here, Damrosch's understanding of what constitutes world literature coincides with Franco Moretti's *"law of literary evolution,"* as defined in his influential article "Conjectures on World Literature" (2000: 58). For Moretti, the development of the modern novel throughout the world occurs when the novel format moves outward from the literary center to literary peripheries, where he argues a compromise takes place "between a western formal influence (usually French or English) and local materials" (2000: 58; emphasis in original). Later in the article he clarifies that this compromise consists of three elements: "foreign *plot*"; "local *characters*; and then, local *narrative voice*" (2000: 65; emphases in original). I'll return to the significance of the local materials later in the chapter.

Recent scholarship on crime fiction, world literature, and translation has identified a pattern whereby translation plays a significant, if not defining, role in the development of autochthonous crime fiction in new literary contexts (Chotiudompant 2017; Harper 2017; King 2017). In this pattern, local crime fiction traditions tend to emerge following the translation of foreign (British, American, and French) texts into the national language. These translated crime novels and stories then become models that local writers use to pen their own original texts, thus contributing to the creation of a body of works that constitute the national crime writing tradition.

In the Basque case, this is different. The first crime novels penned in Basque appeared long before canonical works of world crime fiction were translated into the language. The first work of classic detective fiction in Basque was Jose Antonio Loidi's *Amabost egun Urgain'en* (*Fifteen Days in Urgain*), which was published in 1955. Yet, when Loidi composed the novel, there had been no translations of classic detective fiction into Basque. Poe's "The Purloined

Letter" (1844) was the first translation, appearing in 1968, thirteen years after the publication of Loidi's novel.² Likewise, the first Basque-language hardboiled novel, Txomin Peillen's *Gauaz ibiltzen dana . . .* (Creature of the Night . . .) appeared in 1967, eighteen years before the first translation of a hardboiled novel into Basque: James M. Cain's *The Postman Always Rings Twice*, which was translated by Xabier Olarra as *Karteroak beti deitzen du bi aladiz* in 1985.³ The delayed translation of canonical crime fiction texts into Basque meant that Basque writers were inspired by classic detective and hardboiled novels that they had read either in the original languages or in translations into other languages, most likely French and Spanish. This is evident in the case of the author and translator Jon Mirande, who had translated several of Poe's poems and non-detective short stories in the early 1950s—"The Raven" ("Bela") in 1950, "Silence—A Fable" ("Ixiltze (Alegia)") in 1951, and "The Cask of Amontillado" ("Amontillado upela") in 1952—at the same time as he was publishing his own crime short stories. Given his work as a translator of Poe, it can be surmised that Poe's crime stories—then untranslated into Basque—were an influence on his own original stories in Basque. Whereas in other literary contexts translations provided writers with a model on which they could draw when penning crime novels in their own languages (Parcerisas 1993: 34), in the Basque case writers like Loidi, Peillen, and Mirande, among others, had to invent a crime fictional language in Basque themselves.

The delayed translation of crime fiction into Basque is significant. Apart from the few texts by Poe mentioned previously, translations of canonical texts only began to appear in the 1980s. The first Sherlock Holmes' story to be translated was "A Scandal in Bohemia" ("Eskandalua Bohemian") which was published in 1983, while the classic *The Hound of the Baskervilles* (*Baskervilletarren zakurra*) only became available to Basque readers as late as 2014. The most translated writer on the planet, Agatha Christie, has had thirteen of her eighty detective novels and short story collections translated into Basque, the first of which, *Poirot Investigates* (*Monsieur Poiroten ikerpenak*), appeared in 1989 and the most recent, *Crooked House* (*Etxe bihurria*), in 2018. As might be expected, Christie's works appear out of the order in which they were originally published. The first of her novels featuring Hercule Poirot, *The Mysterious Affair at Styles* (1920) was the tenth of her works to be translated into Basque, appearing ninety years later in 2010 as *Stylesko gertaera misteriotsua*.

The hardboiled tales of Dashiell Hammett and Raymond Chandler were also substantially delayed. Four of Hammett's novels and one short story were published in translation between 1989 and 2021, while Chandler has had only two novels—*The Long Goodbye* (*Ez adiorik*) in 1991 and *The Big Sleep* (*Betiko loa*) in 1995—and one short story—"Killer in the Rain" ("Hiltzailea euripean") in 1995—translated. Another influential American crime writer, Ross Macdonald, has had only two of his eighteen Lew Archer novels translated into Basque, in 1997 and 2006 respectively. As an historical anomaly, the Catalan writer Jaume Fuster, who named his detective Lluís Arquer after Macdonald's protagonist, had a Hammett-inspired short story collection featuring Arquer—*Les claus de vidre* (The Glass Keys)—published in Basque as *Beirazko giltzak* in 1997, the same year as Macdonald's first novel was translated and seventeen years before Hammett's own *The Glass Key* was translated into Basque as *Kristalezko giltza* in 2014. With Macdonald and Fuster published in the same year, Basque fans of crime fiction thus experienced a compressing of the genre's chronology in which influencer (Macdonald) and influenced (Fuster) were encountered simultaneously. Moreover, in the case of Hammett and Fuster, Basque readers experienced a reversal of the usual intertextual relationship, as Fuster's *The Glass Keys* was available long before Hammett's *The Glass Key*. As can be gleaned from the translation dates discussed above, a significant number of Basque writers penned hardboiled fictions long before the canonical hardboiled writers were translated into Basque, thus suggesting that Basque writers were familiar with the codes, conventions, and tropes of this subgenre through other languages.

For women writers like Laura Mintegi and Itxaro Borda, there were no examples of feminist crime writing translated into Basque that could serve as models for their own texts. Apart from Agatha Christie, none of the major pioneers of women's and feminist crime fiction have been translated. There is no P. D. James, Ruth Rendell, Sue Grafton, or Sara Paretsky available in Basque. Contemporary women writers likewise fare poorly in translation. Fred Vargas, Camilla Läckberg, Yrsa Sigurðardóttir, and the Irish international literary sensation, Tana French, have not yet been translated, while Donna Leon has had two of her novels translated, although these feature a male police detective as protagonist. The absence of feminist crime fiction translated into Basque does not mean that Mintegi or Borda were unaware of these developments. Indeed, in *Amorezko pena baño* (More than Heartbreak, 1996), Borda's detective Amaia Ezpeldoi cites Sue Grafton's work directly when she declares "I am not Miss Kinsey Millhone" (cited in Cillero Goiriastuena 2000: 301). The example of crime fiction by Basque women again underscores that Basque writers could not depend on translations to keep abreast of developments in the genre. Instead, they accessed these works in translation in languages other than Basque or in the original languages in which they were written.

While British and American writers have fared relatively well in translation, the same cannot be said of canonical crime fiction written originally in other languages. Émile Gaboriau, Maurice Leblanc, and Gaston Leroux, three important French authors in the history of the genre have not yet been translated into Basque. Georges Simenon, the Belgian author of the influential Maigret series, has only been translated twice into Basque, in 2009 and 2010 respectively. There are also significant gaps among more recent internationally popular works of Nordic Noir. Henning Mankell has two of his Kurt Wallander series translated into Basque, but the works of the founding figures of Nordic Noir, Maj Sjöwall and Per Walhöö, as well as international publishing phenomenon, Stieg Larsson, have not yet appeared in Basque. This does not mean, of course, that Basque readers are unfamiliar with the Martin Beck series or the Millennium trilogy; it's just that these works are read in a language other than Basque. While it is unlikely that there is a conscious process that determines which novelists are translated among the different publishing houses, the fact that only one or two texts per writers of the caliber of Simenon and Mankell are translated perhaps points both to the financial limitations of publishers in a small literary market and to a desire on the part of the publishers to provide readers with a taste of each writer's work, rather than to offer comprehensive coverage.

The delayed, compressed, irregular, and often incomplete translation of world crime fiction texts that we've discussed here means that Basque fans of the genre cannot rely on translations alone to gain a good understanding of the genre's historical development. Basque writers, likewise, cannot depend on the Basque literary system to provide them with the canonical texts that have shaped the genre when it comes to writing their own works. Both fans and writers must read these texts either in the original or most likely via Spanish or French translations.

The attention dedicated to circulation as a defining feature of world literature fails to give an accurate impression of the actual practice of world crime fiction. We can see this in Moretti's center-periphery model, which privileges the "foreign *plot*" over the local elements and treats the latter as though they are little more than exotica, suggesting that all a writer needs is a detective called Arretxe Irigoien who encounters a murdered *pelotari* (a person who plays Basque pelota) next to an ancient *lauburu* (Basque symbol) marker for a crime novel to become Basque. Moretti's model, moreover, implies that a power imbalance exists between the exporting and importing cultures. This assumption has been challenged by Pascale Casanova, who argues in *The World Republic of Letters* that when canonical literary texts produced at the center of the literary universe are translated in peripheral locations, like in the Basque Country, their translation is not simply a manifestation of the literary domination of the exporting culture, but "a way of gathering literary resources" that facilitates the emergence of new literary forms in the target culture (Casanova 2004: 134). Given that the international connections between works do not only manifest themselves when texts move out from their original literary context, but also when they are taken into a new context, Basque crime writers are engaging with and contributing to the development of world crime fiction even if their works have—to date—only circulated in a limited way beyond the Basque literary scene. There are exceptions to this, of course, such as the works of Bernardo Atxaga in Basque and Dolores Redondo in Castilian.

The German scholar Eva Erdmann has suggested that the focus of much contemporary crime writing worldwide is on the representation of specific places, the *"locus criminalis,"* where "the detectives and the victims live and to which they are bound by ties of attachment" (2009: 12). While in some ways the local specificities unfamiliar to international audiences should hinder potential circulation and translation, in crime fiction, such foreignizing elements do not necessarily inhibit reception elsewhere. In his analysis of the practice of translating crime fiction into English, Lawrence Venuti argues that "the specific features of the foreign culture ranging from geography, customs and cuisine to historical figures and events [. . .] don't produce a foreignizing effect because they don't question or upset values, beliefs, and representations in Anglophone culture, certainly not the canon of crime fiction" (2008: 160). Indeed, rather than inhibiting circulation and translation, these distinct local elements are, somewhat counterintuitively, what make them worldly. Their world literariness emerges through the very act of adopting and adapting the genre's narrative conventions and of creating a vocabulary for each new crime scene. In so doing, the adapted crime novel becomes a national allegory for, in the case that concerns us here, the Basque Country.[4] It is this local content that is of interest to readers, both Basque and others, for whom the crime narrative can "reveal certain aspects of a culture that otherwise remain hidden" (Cawelti 1999: 55).

Although only a few works of Basque crime fiction circulate beyond the borders of the Basque Country itself, Basque crime fiction nevertheless participates in the world crime fiction literary sphere. As Gulddal and King argue, "world crime fiction is not limited to crime narratives that benefit from international reception, but also includes texts that are never translated or read outside of their national context" (forthcoming). This is because the genre worldwide is connected "by webs of influence as well as overarching themes, shared tropes and conventions" (Gulddal and King: forthcoming). Their world literariness, their born translatability lies within them (Walkowitz 2015). It is to these shared themes, tropes and conventions we now turn.

Grounds of Comparison: Basque Crime Fiction in the World

The study of specific genres like crime fiction can facilitate the analysis of texts across different literary traditions, as the conventions that define any single genre "play a major role in the shaping of works and in forming audiences' expectations for them" (Damrosch, 2009: 47). As Damrosch suggests, "we can learn a good deal about a culture by seeing which elements a given tradition highlights, and how its writers use them" (2009 47). Franco Moretti makes a similar point, arguing that "comparative morphology is such a fascinating field" because by "studying how forms vary, you discover how symbolic power varies from place to place" (2000: 66). As I have argued elsewhere, crime narratives can function as "windows" through which readers can attempt to make sense of different societies (King 2014: 14). These "windows" also provide the grounds on which comparisons can be made across different literary traditions. So, in what ways can world literature approaches be applied to Basque crime fiction? In the following paragraphs I sketch out a few approaches that scholars might use to foster a transnational dialogue through Basque crime fiction.

As part of a worldwide genre, Basque crime fiction shares concerns with crime fiction produced elsewhere: in particular, the articulation of postcolonial identities; the investigation into the legacy of historical traumas; the interrogation of issues related to women's oppression, such as physical and psychological abuse, rape, sex work, institutional and social discrimination, as well as female agency; and the examination of the impact of globalization. Due to restrictions of space, I shall focus on just two of these concerns: the investigation into the impact of historical trauma and into one of the effects of globalization through the figure of the migrant detective. In each case, I shall draw on a single work or series, respectively Bernardo Atxaga's *Gizona bere bakardadean* (*The Lone Man*, 1993) and Jon Arretxe's Toure series.

It is not surprising that some Basque crime fiction should concern itself with the legacy of the over half a century of bombings, assassinations, kidnapping, state-sponsored paramilitary groups as well as threats, theft, and extortion that took place in the Basque Country, Spain, and France. Indeed, it is not just fiction writers who drew on the conventions of the crime thriller to make sense of this conflict. The anthropologist Begoña Aretxaga argued that these codes and conventions were used to frame the stories of real-life participants and she cites as an example the story of José Amedo and Michel Domínguez, two police officers who were convicted of organizing a anti-terrorist paramilitary group and whose story, published in the national daily, *El Mundo*, she described as a "cross between the confessional and the thriller genres [...with] the addictive quality of a soap opera, with its extravagant scenarios, secret conspiracies, spy networks and hired assassins, briefcases stuffed with public money, stolen intelligence documents charting the dirty war, and cryptic handwritten communiqués" (45).

The use of the crime thriller format to represent ongoing violence between ethnic groups is not limited to the Basque Country. In Northern Ireland, for example, there is a long tradition of what is called "Troubles Trash" or "Troubles Thrillers," generally sensationalist novels in the 1970s and 1980s that were often written by outsiders (British) and which simplistically "attribute the violence to the incurably atavistic inhabitants of the island" (Cliff 27). Like in the Basque Case, the thriller conventions are also employed by non-fiction authors like Patrick Radden Keefe, whose *Say Nothing: A True Story of Murder and Memory in Northern Ireland* (2018), is a perfectly plotted crime story while also providing a sobering account of the Troubles and its legacy.

In both the Basque and Northern Irish political contexts, competing groups claim victimhood in order to cast the other group as the criminal aggressor. Basque and Irish nationalists, for example, see themselves as the victims of state-sanctioned violence and terrorism, whereas Loyalists and Spanish nationalists position themselves as the victims of Irish and Basque nationalism (Aretxaga 2000; Keane 2018).[5] A detailed comparison of Basque and Irish crime novels representing political violence is beyond the scope of this chapter; nevertheless, I do want to gesture toward possible avenues for further analysis through a brief discussion of *The Lone Man* and Stuart Neville's *The Twelve* (2009).

Unlike many novels which take a more partisan stance, such as the justified homicide of two ETA members in *Sucedió en el AVE* (It Happened on the AVE Train, 2007) by the pseudonymous Víctor Saltero, Bernardo Atxaga's *The Lone Man* eschews the violence at the center of many novels about the conflict and attempts to circumvent this competing victimhood that only serves to perpetuate it. The novel takes place during the 1982 Football World Cup when the "lone man" of the title, the "man known to everyone as Carlos" (1996: 3), an ex-ETA member, shelters two fugitives from his former organization in a hotel outside of Barcelona that he co-owns with other ex-operatives. Carlos and his co-owners have formed a sort of family that includes a young boy called Pascal, who sees Carlos as his uncle. As a result of taking in the fugitives, Carlos again becomes caught up in the radical nationalist cause in which he no longer believes, and which has negative consequences both for himself and for his "family." While crime thrillers often privilege the perspective of the protagonist, *The Lone Man* challenges attempts to comprehend the political conflict from any single perspective. Atxaga does this through the contradictory voices that take over Carlos's thoughts at different times. These include the Rat, who pricks his conscience and mocks his motivations; Sabino, his long-dead ETA mentor, who advises Carlos on how to respond in dangerous situations; his brother, whom he betrayed; and a widow whose businessman-husband Carlos kidnapped and murdered.

The protagonist of Neville's *The Twelve*, Gerry Fegan, a former IRA hitman, is also haunted by the ghosts of the titular twelve people he murdered, including British soldiers, a member of the Royal Ulster Constabulary, a couple of Loyalist paramilitaries and four civilians. Unlike Carlos, whose voices are a consequence of his own psyche, Fegan's ghosts are real; they are seen by other characters in the novel, thus giving the novel a Gothic turn. These ghosts torment Fegan to the point that he seeks absolution by killing the IRA leaders who were also responsible for the twelve deaths even if they did not pull the trigger. With each murder Fegan commits, the ghosts' voices become quieter, but ultimately they do not provide him with the peace he seeks.

Both *The Lone Man* and *The Twelve* disrupt the nationalist discourses that attribute criminality to opposing groups and claim victimhood for themselves. *The Twelve*, for example, draws attention to the complex entanglement of police, paramilitaries, informants, and criminals across the sectarian division, thus complicating the competing claims to victimhood. The only true victims are the four civilians "who had been in the wrong place at the wrong time" and whose voices torment Fagen the loudest (2009: 4). In *The Lone Man*, Atxaga shifts victimhood away from competing nationalist groups and ascribes it to the broader community. Although Carlos believes his actions will reverberate on him alone if the police discover his involvement, it becomes clear that he is endangering the new life his "family" have built for themselves after abandoning the organization. While readers become invested in the success of Carlos's plan, the novel's conclusion does not provide the release from the emotional anxiety that the crime thriller form typically generates. The fugitives do flee, but Carlos's planned diversion to distract the police—the lighting of a forest fire—backfires; a wind changes turns it in the direction of where Carlos's "nephew" Pascal is playing, and he is killed. Although Carlos had attempted to escape ETA's influence, his renewed contact with the organization proves fatal and the community he had established with the others is destroyed.[6] By focusing on the consequences of crime through their attention to the victims of nationalist violence, *The Twelve* and *The Lone Man* offer a profound reflection on the ongoing trauma that besets Northern Ireland and the Basque Country respectively.

In the second example, on the impact of globalization, Jon Arretxe's Toure series of novels depicts a very different Basque Country from that of Atxaga. Unlike most Basque crime fiction, the protagonist of Arretxe's series is not Basque, but an undocumented migrant from Burkina Faso, Mahamoud Toure. Toure ekes out a living in the Bilbao neighborhood of San Francisco, a multicultural space in which Roma, Africans, Latin Americans, Asians, Romanians, and a few Basques coexist, although not always peacefully. In some ways, Toure resembles Eduardo Mendoza's unnamed protagonist of *El misterio de la cripta embrujada* (The Mystery of the Enchanted Crypt, 1978), with whom he shares the knack of misinterpretation and an equally humiliating series of adventures in which he tries to preserve his dignity. At the beginning of the first novel, *19 Kamera* (19 Cameras, 2012), Toure is not a private eye, but like Walter Mosley's Easy Rawlins in *Devil in a Blue Dress* (1990) he becomes one after he investigates the rape and murder of a Nigerian sex worker. Also like Rawlins, Toure uses his skills to serve his community. In *612 euro* (612 Euros, 2013) he tries to discover who murdered a fellow compatriot; while in *Hutsaren itzalak* (The Shadows of Emptiness, 2014), Toure investigates the disappearance of his daughter while she traveled on the Paris to Bilbao train. In so doing, he uncovers the sordid reality that many undocumented female migrants from Africa face: sexual slavery at the hands of white criminals. For Toure, the divisions of the whites into Basque and Spanish nationalists are irrelevant.[7] They are simply all whites who enjoy the same privileges that come from being citizens of the wealthy country in which they live.

As spaces in which alternative voices and experiences can be articulated, Arretxe's novels form part of a growing trend in European crime fiction to make visible—and, in doing so, humanize—those migrants whose individuality has been erased by the racial stereotypes often peddled by conservative politicians and media outlets. Arretxe thus stands beside the Scottish writer

Denise Mina, the Algerian-Italian novelist Amara Lakhous, the Swedish writer Henning Mankell, the German author Jakob Arjouni, and the Mauritanian French writer Karim Miské, to name just a few of the crime writers who use the genre to challenge stereotypes of threatening others and, in so doing, to counter xenophobic discourses that deny humanity to both immigrants and refugees.[8]

Like these other writers, Arretxe highlights the separation between white Europeans and the undocumented migrants who do the jobs that many Europeans consider beneath them. This disconnection is represented metaphorically through the titular security cameras of the first novel, *19 Kamera*, which subject the inhabitants of San Francisco to invasive surveillance by the police and, by extension, the broader Basque community. The cameras, however, have their limitations. They can see, but not understand. Toure's investigations overcome this disconnect by narrating the experiences, motivations, dreams, and desires of this unknown and misunderstood community for Arretxe's readers. At the end of the third novel, however, Arretxe turns the cameras' gaze metaphorically back on the white community, when a distraught and desperate Toure contemplates suicide in the Nervion River. Looking directly at the operator behind the camera, Toure challenges the operator (and, by extension, Arretxe's Basque- and Spanish-language readers) to confront his humanity:

> What do you think of me? How much is my life worth to you? Do you see a man or a shadow, an empty shadow? I am no one, a nobody for you. If I jump in the water, will you press the alarm button for someone to come and save me? Or will you just watch me slowly go under without lifting a finger? (2014: 246)[9]

Through Toure, Arretxe addresses his readers directly, challenging them to act because to remain neutral is what allows the exploitation and violence against migrants like Toure to continue. In exposing the violence that migrants like Toure and his fellow citizens of the multicultural San Francisco experience on a daily basis, Arretxe participates in a continent-wide literary movement that asks "uncomfortable but necessary questions about representations of politics in crime fiction and the marginalization of individual groups due to race/ethnicity and nationality" (Beyer 2020: 386).

Conclusion: B for . . . ?

Basque crime fiction is currently a national brand; it is not—yet—an international one. There is to date no B for Basque, Bilbao or Baztan noir, and the Basque Country is on the wrong coast for it to form part of so-called Mediterranean noir. Instead, there are individual Basque writers who have had some impact, particularly in Spanish and French translation, but not enough to constitute a recognizable brand internationally, although the success of Dolores Redondo's Baztan trilogy may change this, not just through the translation of her novels, but also via the film adaptations and worldwide distribution in multiple languages by Netflix. As I have argued in the chapter, the relative lack of circulation of Basque crime fiction does not mean, however, that it is restricted exclusively to its own national and cultural context. Indeed, the chapter has been concerned with exploring and understanding the international connections between Basque crime fiction and the world crime fiction literary system.

Although works of Basque crime fiction are little known outside the Basque Country, studies such as the present collection and Cillero Goiriastuena's PhD dissertation on Basque crime fiction (2000) make a significant contribution to world crime fiction studies. Eva Erdmann has argued that "On the map of the world there are hardly any areas uncharted by crime fiction, hardly any places that have not yet become the setting for a detective novel" (2009: 13). Yet, because few texts are translated, especially from less well-known crime fiction scenes, there are still many gaps in our understanding of the global dissemination and production of the genre. Indeed, when studies are available, they are—understandably—directed toward a national readership and therefore do not circulate easily among crime fiction scholars. This is especially the case of crime fiction written in minority languages in terms of the number of speakers, such as, in the Iberian context, Basque, Catalan, and Galician. Although the present collection focuses on a national tradition, its intended audience is not specifically Basque readers, but rather a global anglophone audience interested in developing a deeper understanding of the practice of crime writing from around the world. By writing in English for an audience beyond the discipline of Basque literary studies, the present collection and Cillero Goiriastuena's history of Basque crime fiction fill in another empty space in the map of world crime fiction studies. In so doing, they provide new insights into the transnational spread and practice of the genre.

In discussing Basque crime fiction within a world literary framework, I do not mean to suggest that there exists a hierarchy that privileges more cosmopolitan over national approaches. Instead, this chapter offers a modest contribution to the recent transnational turn in Basque Literary Studies, as evidenced through several significant publications, including *Bridge/ Zubia. Imágenes de la relación cultural entre el País Vasco y Estados Unidos* (*Bridge/Zubia. Images of the Cultural Relationship between the Basque Country and the United States*, 2019) and the monographic issue of *Ínsula* (883–884), "Harri eta berri: nuevos horizontes de la literatura vasca" (*Harri eta Berri: New Horizons of Basque Literature*, 2020), both of which are edited by Jon Kortazar. Rather than undermining or rejecting the local or the national as categories of analysis in favor of a more global approach, the two approaches can work side by side productively to understand their significance and contribution both to the specific Basque literary context and to the wider world of crime fiction studies.

References

Aretxaga, Begoña (2000): "Playing Terrorist: Ghastly Plots and the Ghostly State." *Journal of Spanish Cultural Studies*, 1,1, 43–58.

Arretxe, Jon (2012): *19 cámaras*. Trans. Cristina Fernández. Erein: Donostia.

———. (2013): *612 euros*. Trans. Cristina Fernández. Erein: Donostia.

———. (2014): *Juegos de cloaca*. Trans. Cristina Fernández. Erein: Donostia.

Atxaga, Bernardo (1996): *The Lone Man*. Trans. Margaret Jull Costa. Harvill: London.

Beyer, Charlotte (2020): "Crime Fiction and Migration," in Allan, Janice, Jesper Gulddal, Stewart King and Andrew Pepper, eds, (2020): *The Routledge Companion to Crime Fiction*. Routledge: London. 379–387.

Billig, Michael (1995): *Banal Nationalism*. Sage: London.

Bitter Lemon Press. https://www.bitterlemonpress.com/

Casanova, Pascale (2004): *The World Republic of Letters*. Trans. M. D. DeBevoise. Harvard University Press: Cambridge.

Chotiudompant, Suradech (2017): "World Detective Form and Thai Crime Fiction," in Nilsson, Louise, David Damrosch and Theo D'haen eds. (2017): *Crime Fiction as World Literature*. Bloomsbury: New York. 197–211.

Cillero Goiriastuena, Francisco Javier (2000): *The Moving Target: A History of Basque Detective and Crime Fiction*. University of Nevada: Reno.

Cliff, Brian (2018). *Irish Crime Fiction*: Palgrave Macmillan: London.

Damrosch, David (2003): *What Is World Literature?* Princeton UP: Princeton.

———. (2009): *How to Read World Literature*. Wiley-Blackwell: Malden, MA.

Erdmann, Eva (2009): "Nationality International: Detective Fiction in the Late Twentieth Century," in Marieke Krajenbrink and Kate Quinn, eds., (2009): *Investigating Identities: Questions of Identity in Contemporary International Crime Fiction*. Rodopi: Amsterdam. 11–26.

Etherington, Ben and Jarad Zimbler (2018): "Introduction," in Ben Etherington and Jarad Zimbler, eds. (2018): *The Cambridge Companion to World Literature*. Cambridge University Press: Cambridge. 1–19.

Gulddal, Jesper, and Stewart King (forthcoming): "What Is World Crime Fiction?," in Jesper Gulddal, Stewart King and Alistair Rolls, eds., (forthcoming) *The Cambridge Companion to World Crime Fiction*. Cambridge University Press: Cambridge.

Harper, Mihaela P. (2017): "'In Agatha Christie's Footstep': *The Cursed Goblet and Contemporary Bulgarian Crime Fiction*," in Nilsson, Louise, David Damrosch and Theo D'haen, eds., (2017): *Crime Fiction as World Literature*. New York: Bloomsbury. 171–185.

Keefe, Patrick Radden (2018): *Say Nothing: A True Story of Murder and Memory in Northern Ireland*. William Collins: London.

King, Stewart (2014): "Crime Fiction as World Literature." *Clues: A Journal of Detection*, 32, 2, 8–19.

———. (2017): "Making it Ours: Translation and the Circulation of Crime Fiction in Catalan," in Nilsson, Louise, David Damrosch and Theo D'haen, eds., (2017): *Crime Fiction as World Literature*. New York: Bloomsbury. 157–169.

———. (2019): *Murder in the Multinational State: Crime Fiction from Spain*. Routledge: New York.

Kortazar, Jon, ed. (2019): *Bridge/ Zubia. Imágenes de la relación cultural entre el País Vasco y Estados Unidos*. Iberoamericana: Madrid.

———, ed. (2020): *Harri eta berri: nuevos horizontes de la literatura vasca*, special issue of *Ínsula*, 883–884.

Moretti, Franco (2000): "Conjectures on World Literature." *New Left Review* 1, 54–68.

Neville, Stuart (2009): *The Twelve*. Harvill Secker: London.

Parcerisas, Francesc (1993): "La traducción en Cataluña." *Antípodas*, 5, 27–37.

Pepper, Andrew (2016): *Unwilling Executioner: Crime Fiction and the State*. Oxford University Press: Oxford.

Rolls, Alistair, Marie-Laure Vuaille-Barcan & John West-Sooby (2016): "Translating national allegories: the case of crime fiction." *The Translator*, 22, 2, 135–143.

Symons, J. (1992): *Bloody Murder: From the Detective Story to the Crime Novel*. 3rd revised edition, The Mysterious Press: New York.

Thomson, C. Claire, and Jakob Stougaard-Nielsen (2017): "'A Faithful, Attentive, Tireless Following': Cultural Mobility, Crime Fiction and Television Drama," in Rosendahl Thomsen, Mads and Dan Ringgaard, eds., *Danish Literature as World Literature* London and New York: Bloomsbury. 237–268.

Venuti, Lawrence (2008): *The Translator's Invisibility: A History of Translation*, 2nd ed. Routledge: London.

Walkowitz, Rebecca L. (2015): *Born Translated: The Contemporary Novel in an Age of World Literature*. Columbia University Press: New York.

Notes

1 I would like to thank Jon Kortazar for his generous invitation to contribute a chapter to this collection. I am also grateful to Barbara Pezzotti for reading an earlier version of this chapter and to Phillip Damon for his research assistance.

2 The translation data discussed here has been sourced from the excellent online "Euskarari ekarriak" ["Brought to Basque"] database of translations into Basque. See: https://ekarriak.armiarma.eus/?p=1.

3 Olarra's translation of *The Postman Always Rings Twice* was re-issued in 2003 with a slightly different title: *Postariak bi aldiz deitzen du beti*.

4   For a discussion of crime fiction and national allegories, see Rolls et al (2016).
5   I use the term "nationalist" here not only in its restricted application to separatist or right-wing political groups, but also to those who support the existence of established nation-states in their present form (Billig 1995: 38).
6   For an in-depth analysis of the victimhood in thrillers set in the Basque Country, see King (2019: 94-118).
7   When Toure does differentiate between Basques and Spaniards, it is associated with law enforcement. He realizes that he is in trouble when the Autonomous Basque police, the *Ertzaintza*, hand him over to the Spanish National Police for possible deportation (2012: 220).
8   Arretxe's Toure series resonates particularly with the Kayankaya series by the late German writer Jakob Arjouni, as neither Arretxe nor Arjouni shares the ethnicity of their protagonists, in the case of Arjouni, the Turkish-German private eye, Kemal Kayankaya.
9   Translation from the Spanish translation by the author.

Index

Note: Figures are indicated by *f* following the page number. End note information is indicated by n and note number following the page number.

19 kamera (19 cameras) (Arretxe), 37, 137, 234, 234*f*, 249–50
33 ezkil (33 Bells) (Gorrotxategi), 39, 230, 230*f*
100 metro (100 meters) (Saizarbitoria), 29
110.street-eko geltokia (110th Street Station) (Zabaleta Urkiola), 32, 44–61
    author of, 45
    Basque Country and language in, 49–50, 51–52, 54, 57–61
    characters in, 48–50
    fear in, 44, 54, 56, 60–61
    front cover of, 53, 229–30, 229*f*
    Genet influence on, 50–51
    homesickness in, 44–45, 57–61
    loneliness in, 44, 48, 56
    map in, 54–56, 55*f*
    narrative time in, 52–53
    as noir novel, 45–47
    overview of, 44–45
    plots and stories in, 47, 51–52
    setting or location for, 54–56, 55*f*, 59–60
    sex and gender in, 48–49
    social class separations in, 51–52, 54–57
    storytelling style in, 51–52
    structure of, 45–46, 52
    violence in, 47–48, 49, 51, 53, 54, 56–57, 59–61
612 euro (612 euros) (Arretxe), 37, 137, 234, 234*f*, 249
1280 arima (Pop. 1280) (Thompson), 21, 28

A

Acillona López, Mercedes, 189
advertising, 222, 235
Agirre, Joxean, 33–34
Agirre, Txomin, 40
Ahaztuen mendekua (The Revenge of the Forgotten) (Ladron Arana), 38
Aita gurea (Our Father) (Irasizabal), 38
Akashic (publisher), 239
Akatsbako gizonaren heriotza (The Death of an Unblemished Man) (Basterretxea), 26–27
Alarcón, Pedro, 46, 172
Alberca, Manuel, 158
Alberti, J., 172
Aldai, Xabier, 33, 175, 177–82. *See also* Lertxundi, Anjel
Aldekoa, Iñaki, 32, 34–35
Alía, Ricardo, 201
Alianza publishing house, 234
Allingham, Margery, 12
Alonso, Jon
    Beltzaren koloreak by, 23–24, 25, 129, 133
    Camembert helburu by, 35, 134
    Katebegi galdua by, 35, 38
    Zintzoen saldoan by (*see Zintzoen saldoan*)
Amabost egun Urgain'en. See Hamabost egun Urgainen
Amaia Ezpeldoi (character) novels (Borda), 35, 98–115

as ambitious literary project, 98–101
Amorezko pena baño as, 35, 99, 113, 233, 233*f*, 243
author-protagonist similarities in, 107
Bakean ützi arte as, 35, 98–99, 101, 105, 112–13, 233, 233*f*
Bizi nizano munduan as, 35, 99, 104–5, 112–13, 233, 233*f*
Boga boga as, 35, 99, 101, 105, 108, 113, 116n4
character construction in, 106–9, 112
character name in, 110
colonialism in, 101
coming out in, 111–13
in crime fiction or police novel genre, 98, 102–6
crimes in, 109–11
front covers of, 232, 233, 233*f*
guilt in, 109–10
herenerria concept in, 101
intertextualities in, 105
Jalgi hadi plazara as, 35, 99, 105, 107, 113–14
language and dialects in, 100–101, 105, 110, 115
marginalization in, 107–8
music, 105–6
normalcy commentary in, 110–11
origins and influences on, 99–100
overview of, 98
political-historical commentary in, 101, 103, 109, 111, 112–13
as popular literary form, 104–6
rurality in, 104, 112, 114
sexuality and sexual orientation in, 107, 109, 110, 111–12, 114–15
society reflected in, 102–4, 106, 109–11, 114–15
space or location in, 98–99
structure of, 102
translations of, 113
two sides of hexalogy of, 113–15
Ultimes déchets as, 35, 99, 103, 105, 108, 112–13
Amaia Salazar (character). *See El guardián invisible*
ambivalence, 5
"Ametsa" ("The Dream") (Mirande), 26

Amorezko pena baño (More than Heartbreak) (Borda), 35, 99, 113, 233, 233*f*, 243
Amuriza, Xabier, 29
antagonists, 14–15
anti-police novels, 117–18, 126
Antoñana, Pablo, 64
Antza, Mikel, 32–33, 54
Antzararen bidea (On the Trail of the Goose) (Muñoz), 148, 151
Apalategi, Ur, 88, 90, 92, 96, 98
Aperribay-Bermejo, Maite, 201
Aquella edad inolvidable (That Unforgettable Age) (Pinilla), 189
Aramotz (Irasizabal), 38
Aranbarri, Iñigo, 21
Arbina, Álvaro, 41
Aretxaga, Begoña, 247
Aristi, Maider, 79
Aristi, Pako, 31, 44, 183
Arjouni, Jakob, 24, 250, 254n8
Arotzaren eskuak (The Carpenter's Hands) (Ladron Arana), 38
Arrainak ura baino (More than Fish Water) (Etxeberria), 32
Arrastoa (Traces) (Kruz Igerabide), 186
Arretxe (Jon) noir fiction, 37–38, 137–45
19 kamera as, 37, 137, 234, 234*f*, 249–50
612 euro as, 37, 137, 234, 234*f*, 249
clichés in, 138–39, 142–43, 144
Estolda jolasak as, 38, 138, 143, 234*f*
Ez erran deus as, 38, 138, 143–44, 234
Fatum as, 37
foreigners in, 141–42, 249–50
front covers of, 232, 233–34, 234*f*
globalization impacts in, 249–50
Hutsaren itzalak as, 37–38, 138, 234*f*, 249
Kleopatra as parody of, 37
Manila konexioa as parody of, 37
marginalization and racism in, 141–42, 249–50
Mesfidatu hitzez as, 38, 138, 144
Morto vivace as, 37
narrator in, 140, 141–42
Ostegunak as, 137

place or location in, 143–44
political situations in, 249–50
protagonist in, 137–38, 139–41, 143
Sator lokatzak as, 38, 138, 234, 234*f*
as series, 137–38
social critique in, 140–42, 145
storyline in, 141, 143
structure of, 138–39
Xahmaran as, 37
Asesinato en el Comité Central (Murder in the Central Committee) (Montalbán), 147–48
Asurmendi, Mikel, 52
Atxaga, Bernardo
Behi euskaldun baten memoriak by, 86
as canonized writer, 9
Etxeak eta hilobiak by, 88
Gizona bere bakardadean by (*see Gizona bere bakardadean*)
Obabakoak by, 86–88, 100
Sara izeneko gizona by, 64
social reality not addressed by, 103
translations of works of, 245
Atzerriko eta Euskal Herriko Polizia Eleberria (The Foreign and Basque Police Novel, 2000) (Garate), 21–22
Auden, W. H., 15
"Auskalo" series, 25, 33, 225
Auspoa publishing house, 226
Auster, Paul, 120, 125
Azkargorta, Antton, 20

B

Babilonia (Babylon) (Irigoien), 44
Bakean ützi arte (Until They Leave Us in Peace) (Borda), 35, 98–99, 101, 105, 112–13, 233, 233*f*
Barambones, Josu, 25
Barandiaran, Asier, 63
Barth, John, 8
Basilika (Basilica) (Borda), 99
Basque crime fiction and world literature studies, 238–52
on Basque-language crime fiction, generally, 19–25

on comparison of Basque and world literature, 246–50
evolution of genre and, 238–39
on foreign plot and local elements, 241, 244–45
on globalization, 249–50
on historical trauma, 246–49
on investigative novels (*see* Spanish Civil War investigative novels)
overview of, 239–40, 250–52
of translations and adaptations, 240–46
Basque-language crime fiction
110.street-eko geltokia as (*see 110.street-eko geltokia*)
Amaia Ezpeldoi novels as (*see* Amaia Ezpeldoi (character) novels)
Arretxe noir fiction as (*see* Arretxe (Jon) noir fiction)
Cano novels as (*see* Cano (Harkaitz) novels)
children's and young adult (*see* children's and young adult police novels)
by Epaltza (*see* Epaltza (Aingeru) novels)
front covers of (*see* front covers)
Gizona bere bakardadean as (*see Gizona bere bakardadean*)
El guardián invisible as (*see El guardián invisible*)
history of, 25–39
Lili eta biok as (*see Lili eta biok*)
in literary system, 19–39
by Pinilla (*see* Pinilla (Ramiro) police novels)
short stories in, 32–33, 39
studies and critiques of (*see* Basque crime fiction and world literature studies)
translations in (*see* translations)
Zintzoen saldoan as (*see Zintzoen saldoan*)
Basque-language education, 27, 28, 103
Basterretxea, Jose ("Oskillaso"), 26–27
Basterretxea, Mari Carmen, 205
Baudelaire, 4
Bayo, Aitor, 233
Baztan trilogy (Redondo). *See El guardián*

invisible; Legado en los huesos; Ofrenda a la tormenta
Beardsley, Aubrey, 221
Behi euskaldun baten memoriak (Memories of a Basque Cow) (Atxaga), 86
Belarraren ahoa (Blade of Light) (Cano), 118, 119
Belternebros (Muñoz Molina), 47
Beltzaren koloreak (The Colours of Noir) (Alonso), 23–24, 25, 129, 133
Beluna Jazz (Cano), 36, 117–18, 119–22, 126–27
Bergman, Ingmar, 123
Bertsoaren ezpata (The Sword of Verse) (Zabaleta Urkiola), 45
Beti oporretan (Always on Holiday) (Cano), 118
Big Sleep, The (Betiko loa) (Chandler), 12, 243
Biguri, Koldo, 25
Bihotz bi. Gerrako kronikak (Two Hearts: War Chronicles) (Saizarbitoria), 150
Bilbao publishing house, 226
Bilboko Kutxak, 226
Billelabeitia, Miren, 146
Bioy Casares, Adolfo, 9
Bitter Lemon Press, 239
Bizi nizano munduan (Until I'm Alive) (Borda), 35, 99, 104–5, 112–13, 233, 233*f*
Bizkarrean tatuaturiko mapak (The Maps Tattooed on the Back) (Cano), 118
Bizkartzainaren lehentasunak (The Bodyguard's Priorities) (Irasizabal), 38
Bloody Murder: From the Detective Story to the Crime Novel (Symons), 238
Bloom, Harold, 7
Blyton, Enid, 12, 174–75, 176
Boga boga (Row, Row!) (Borda), 35, 99, 101, 105, 108, 113, 116n4
Bolaño, Roberto, 150
Bonsiepe, Gui, 225
book covers. *See* front covers
Borda, Itxaro
    Amaia Ezpeldoi novels by (*see* Amaia Ezpeldoi (character) novels)
    Basilika by, 99
    on *Gizona bere bakardadean*, 88, 91
    "Larrüpean ebiltzen direnak" by, 21
    police novel defined by, 102–4
    as woman author, 12, 243
Borges, Jorge Luis, 9, 46
"Bostak" series (Blyton), 175, 176
Bridge/ Zubia. Imágenes de la relación cultural entre el País Vasco y Estados Unidos (Kortazar), 251–52
Buckels, Jim, 233
La buena letra (Good Handwriting) (Chirbes), 150
Bukowski, Charles, 120
Butler, Judith, 114

C

Cabrera Infante, Guillermo, 95
Cadáveres en la playa (Corpses on the Beach) (Pinilla), 40, 189, 191, 193, 197–99
Cain, James M., 28, 242, 253n3
Callejeros (Street Guides), 151
Camembert helburu (Mission Camembert) (Alonso), 35, 134
Camilleri, Andrea, 37, 132–33, 181
Cano (Harkaitz) novels, 36, 117–27
    anti-police features in, 117–18, 126
    author's background and other works with, 118–19
    Belarraren ahoa as, 118, 119
    Beluna Jazz as, 36, 117–18, 119–22, 126–27
    in crime fiction or police novel genre, 117–18, 122–23, 126
    film noir and noir fiction influences on, 120–22, 126
    front covers of, 234–35, 235*f*
    mirror characters in, 124–25
    music in, 120
    Norbait dabil sute eskaileran as, 118, 119
    Pasaia blues as, 36, 117–18, 119, 122–27, 234–35, 235*f*
    Piano gainean gosaltzen as, 54, 118, 119
    places or locations in, 119–26
    poetry and, 118, 119
    random events in, 127
    repetition in, 127
    tangled plots in, 127

time in, 124
translations of, 119, 234–35, 235f
US influence on, 117–18, 119–21, 125–26
La cara norte del corazón (The North Face of the Heart) (Redondo), 40
Carlist Wars, 63–68, 71, 183, 229
Carlotto, Massimo, 24
Carolyn Meyer, dantzaria (The Dancer, Carolyn Meyer) (Zabaleta Urkiola), 45
Caronte aguarda (Charon Awaits) (Savater), 40
Carreteras secundarias (Secondary Roads) (Martínez de Pisón), 79
Carver, Raymond, 120
Casanova, Pascale, 245
"Cask of Amontillado, The" ("Amontillado upela") (Poe), 242
Cawelti, John G., 3
Cela, Camilo José, 31
El cementerio vacío (The Empty Cemetery) (Pinilla), 40, 189, 191–92, 194–95, 197–99
Cercas, Javier, 147–48
Cerezo, Martín, 5, 13, 19
Chandler, Raymond
  Basque-language crime fiction influence of, 31
  genre stretching by, 9–10
  realist and noir fiction by, 3, 6, 12, 20, 121, 129, 138
  on rules for crime novels, 1
  translation of works of, 239, 242–43
Chekov, Anton, 172
Chen Sham, Jorge, 189
Chesterton, G. K., 2
children's and young adult police novels, 171–86
  from 1980s onward, 175–77
  Cano novels as, 118–19
  as gained literature, 171
  Hamabost egun Urgainen as, 25, 46, 161, 171–73
  history of Basque-language, 25, 33, 34, 37, 39, 171–86
  language and terminology in, 172, 173, 174, 178–81
  late 20th century, 183
  Lili eta biok written as, 161

"Madame Kontxexi-Uribe, Brigada & Detektibe" as, 33, 176–82
  origins of, 171–75
  "Panic Attacks" series as, 184–85
  in recent years, 185–86
  translations of, 173, 176, 183, 184
Chirbes, Rafael, 150
Christie, Agatha
  Basque-language crime fiction influenced by, 31, 117, 130, 174, 183
  experimentation by, 10
  mystery novels of, 2, 5
  prominence of, 11
  protagonists influenced by, 178
  translation of works of, 28, 29, 239, 241, 242, 243
  as woman author, 12, 243
Cillero, Javi
  on *110.street-eko geltokia*, 50, 61
  on history on Basque-language crime fiction, 25–28, 29, 31–35, 37
  studies and critiques by, 22–23, 59, 251
City of Glass (Auster), 125
class. *See* social class
Les claus de vidre (The Glass Keys; Beirazko giltzak) (Fuster), 243
El clavo (The Nail) (Alarcón), 46
clichés
  in Arretxe noir fiction, 138–39, 142–43, 144
  front cover graphic interpretation of, 224
  in *Zintzoen saldoan*, 134–35
codex, 219
Collins, Wilkie, 2
Colmeiro. *See* Fernández Colmeiro, José
colonialism, 101
Coma, Javier, 20
Conan Doyle, Arthur
  Basque-language crime fiction influenced by, 31, 117, 174
  front covers of books of, 223
  mystery novels of, 2, 5
  short stories by, 11
  translations of works of, 29, 242
Corbatta, Jorgelina, 58

Costa, Joan, 223
La costumbre de morir (The Custom of Dying) (Guerra Garrido), 40
credibility, of crime fiction, 27, 132–34, 181
crime fiction. *See* detective and crime fiction
crimes
    in Amaia Ezpeldoi novels, 109–11
    in Cano novels, 121–22, 126
    as element of crime fiction, 15
    genre defined in relation to, 1–2
    in *El guardián invisible*, 202, 209
    in *Hamabost egun Urgainen*, 161
    in *Lili eta biok*, 147, 161, 164, 169–70
    in Pinilla police novels, 191–92
    in Spanish Civil War investigative novels, 147, 148, 161, 164, 169–70
    in *Zintzoen saldoan*, 130
Crooked House (Etxe bihurria) (Christie), 242
Crumley, James, 104
cynicism, 20–21, 64, 77–78, 82, 84n13, 131

D

Damrosch, David, 241, 246
Dardaren interpretazioa (The Interpretation of Tremors) (Cano), 118
de Corral, Paz, 210
Demasiado para Galvez (Too Much for Galvez) (Martinez Reverte), 59
de Pedro, Jokin, 184–85
de Quincy, Thomas, 8
"Desertuko ihizik" ("Wilds of the Desert") (Etxahun), 108
Destino publishing house, 232
detective and crime fiction
    Alonso's *Zintzoen saldoan* as (*see Zintzoen saldoan*)
    Arretxe's noir fiction as (*see* Arretxe (Jon) noir fiction)
    Atxaga's *Gizona bere bakardadean* as (*see Gizona bere bakardadean*)
    in Basque language (*see* Basque-language crime fiction)
    Borda's Amaia Ezpeldoi novels as (*see* Amaia Ezpeldoi (character) novels)
    Cano novels as (*see* Cano (Harkaitz) novels)
    in children's and young adult literature (*see* children's and young adult police novels)
    definition of, 2, 46
    Epaltza novels as (*see* Epaltza (Aingeru) novels)
    in French language (*see* French-language crime fiction)
    front covers of (*see* front covers)
    name and essence genre of, 1–4
    origins and evolution of genre of, 4–7, 238–39
    Pinilla's police novels as (*see* Pinilla (Ramiro) police novels)
    position in literary system, 7–12 (*see also* literary system)
    readers of (*see* readers)
    realist or noir (*see* noir fiction; realist novels)
    Redondo's *El guardián invisible* as (*see El guardián invisible*)
    Saizarbitoria's *Lili eta biok* as (*see Lili eta biok*)
    scholarly study of (*see* Basque crime fiction and world literature studies)
    in Spanish language (*see* Spanish-language crime fiction)
    structure and elements of, 13–15, 16 (*see also* structure of crime fiction)
    translations of (*see* translations)
    Zabaleta Urkiola's *110.street-eko geltokia* as (*see 110.street-eko geltokia*)
El detective de sonidos (The Detective of Sounds) (Etxenike), 40
Devil in a Blue Dress (Mosley), 249
Din-dan-don. . . Kanpai lapurrak non? (Ding-Dong . . . Where Are the Bell Thieves?) (Aristi), 183
dirty realism, 31, 34, 74, 81, 105, 120
Dirua galgarri (Ruinous Money) (Izeta), 26, 173, 226
domestic violence, 211–13
Dostoievsky, Fyodor, 9, 10

Doyle, Arthur Conan. *See* Conan Doyle, Arthur
Duchamp, Marcel, 234
Duhamel, Marcel, 47
Dupin (character), 5, 46, 117, 221
Dürrenmatt, Friedrich, 9

E

Echeburúa, Enrique, 210
Eco, Umberto, 2, 8, 9, 10, 15, 17
Edili publishing house, 225
Egaña, Andoni, 33
Egaña, Ibon, 34, 65, 122
Eguzki beltzaren sekretua (The Secret of the Black Sun) (Ladron Arana), 38
elements of crime fiction, 13–15
Elgeta (Agirre), 34
Elizegi, Xabier Mendiguren, 33, 175
Elkar publishing house, 32, 44, 65, 184–85, 226–27, 229–30
Elortza, Igor, 183
Elurpean (In the Snow) (de Pedro), 184–85
Elustondo, Mielanjel, 25
Emecé publishing house, 9
Epaltza (Aingeru) novels, 36, 63–82
  characteristics of, 65
  in crime fiction genre, 63, 64, 83nn1–2
  Gure Jerusalem galdua as, 72
  historical timeframe for, 63–65
  narrators in, 66, 73, 82
  overview of, 63, 81–82
  picaresque features in, 68–71, 82
  place or location in, 63–65, 71–72, 74–76, 79–81
  political situations in, 63–72, 73–76, 81
  protagonists in, 66, 72–73, 76–79, 81–82
  Rock'n'Roll as, 36, 76–81, 82
  Sasiak ere begiak baditik as, 36, 63–72, 82, 227–29
  suspense in, 66–67, 73
  Ur uherrak as, 36, 72–76, 78, 80, 81
Erdmann, Eva, 245
Erein publishing house, 25, 33, 137, 171, 185, 225–26, 233
"Eresi kantari" ("Lament Singer") (Mirande), 26

Erinias taberna (The Erinias Bar) (Ormaetxea), 175–76
Escrito en un dólar (Written on a Dollar) (Guerra Garrido), 40
Esker mila, Marlowe (Many Thanks, Marlowe) (Mintegi), 36
Eskuaren fereka (The Stroke of the Hand) (Zabaleta Urkiola), 45
Eskubeltz taldearen abenturak (The Adventures of the Black Hand Gang) (Press), 176
Espioitza (Espionage) (Gereño), 174
Estolda jolasak (Sewer Games) (Arretxe), 38, 138, 143, 234f
ETA members
  in Borda novel, 116n4
  in Cano novel, 123, 125
  in *Gizona bere bakardadean*l, 89, 92–94, 247–48
  in Martinez Reverte novel, 60
  in *Zintzoen saldoan,* 131
Etsai gordea (The Hidden Enemy) (de Pedro), 184
Etxahun, Pierre Topet, 108
Etxaniz Erle, Xabier, 34, 86, 171
Etxeak eta hilobiak (Houses and Graves) (Atxaga), 88
Etxeberria, Hasier, 32
Etxebertz, 65. *See also* Epaltza (Aingeru) novels
Etxebeste, Jon Martin, 44
Etxenike, Luisa, 40
Euliak ez dira argazkietan azaltzen (Flies Don't Appear in Photos) (Iturralde), 37
Euskal eleberriaren historia (History of Basque Novel) (Olaziregi), 23
Euskaltzaindia (the Academy of the Basque Language), 22, 171–72
Even-Zohar, Itamar, 4–5, 7–8
exile, 58–61, 157–58
Exkixu (Txillardegi), 29, 31
Ez erran deus (Don't Say Anything at All) (Arretxe), 38, 138, 143–44, 234
Ezpeldoi, Amaia. *See* Amaia Ezpeldoi (character) novels

F

La fábrica de las sombras (The Dream Factory) (Martín), 41
Fakirraren ahotsa (The Fakir's Voice) (Cano), 118
"Famous Five" series (Blyton), 174–75
El faro del silencio (The Lighthouse of Silence) (Martín), 41
Fatum (Arretxe), 37
Faulkner, William, 9, 10, 198
Faustino Iturbe (character). *See Lili eta biok*
fear
    in *110.street-eko geltokia*, 44, 54, 56, 60–61
    in children's and young adult police novels, 185
    in *Gizona bere bakardadean*, 88, 93
Feijoo Morote, Javier, 189, 190
femicrime/feminist crime fiction, 35, 201, 243–44
Fernández, Cristina, 233–34
Fernández Colmeiro, José, 5–6, 8–9, 16, 17–18, 19, 29, 135
Fernández de Gamboa Vázquez, Karla, 171
Fernández Paz, Agustín, 183
Figueroa, Antón, 87
film noir
    Cano influenced by, 120–21
    children's and young adult authors influenced by, 184
    front covers influenced by posters for, 222, 232
    Redondo novels adapted to, 202, 251
Film zaharren kluba (The Old Film Club) (Ladron Arana), 38
Las formas de la verdad. Investigación, docuficción y memoria en la novela hispánica (The Forms of Truth: Investigation, Docufiction and Memory in the Hispanic Novel) (Martínez Rubio), 146, 150
formulas, in crime fiction genre, 3–4, 5, 8–9
"Frantsesaren troka" ("Frenchman's Cliff") (Zabaleta Urkiola), 45
French, Tana, 243
French-language crime fiction

Amaia Ezpeldoi novels as, 113
    history of, 39–40
    noir fiction as, 46
    translations of, 222, 239, 241–42, 244
Friedrich, Joachim, 176
front covers, 39, 218–36
    of *33 ezkil*, 230, 230*f*
    of *110.street-eko geltokia*, 53, 229–30, 229*f*
    of Amaia Ezpeldoi novels, 232, 233, 233*f*
    of Arretxe noir fiction, 232, 233–34, 234*f*
    of Basque police novels, generally, 225–36
    of Cano novels, 234–35, 235*f*
    components of, 223
    of *Dirua galgarri*, 226
    films and posters influencing, 222, 232
    fonts or typography on, 222–23, 226, 230–31, 233–35, 237nn1–2
    global generalization and normalization of, 222–23, 236
    of *Hamabost egun Urgainen*, 225–26, 226*f*
    of *Hobe isilik*, 230, 230*f*
    information and graphic communication via, 223–25
    of *Izurri berria*, 226–27, 227*f*
    of *Jurgi kapitaina Britainian*, 226
    of *Lili eta biok*, 224, 224*f*, 230
    multimodal messages via, 223
    for noir fiction, 227–34
    origin and development of, 219–21
    overview of, 218–19, 235–36
    photographs on, 222, 224, 229–35
    of Pinilla police novels, 232, 232*f*
    of *Piztiaren begiak*, 230, 230*f*
    police novel origins and development influencing, 221–23
    of Redondo trilogy, 232, 232*f*
    of *Sasiak ere begiak baditik*, 227–29, 228*f*
    spine of, 235
    of *Ta Marbuta: Jerusalemen gertatua*, 228–29, 228*f*
    terminology for, 236
    of translations, 234–35, 235*f*
    as whole sleeve/cover, 224, 235
    of *Zintzoen saldoan*, 231, 231*f*

of *Zoaz infernura, laztana*, 231, 231f
frontispiece, 236
Funeral Rites (Genet), 50
Fuster, Jaume, 243

G

Gaboriau, Émile, 244
Gaizki ateratako argazkia (A Badly Taken Photograph) (Neuschäfer-Carlón), 176
Galarreta, Xabier, 28
Galíndez (Montalbán), 152
Garate, Gotzon, 21–22, 25, 27–28, 32, 54, 173, 226–27
García Márquez, Gabriel, 9
García Sáenz de Urturi, Eva, 40–41, 201
Garcia-Viana, Txema, 39
gastronomy, in Basque culture, 135
Gatu beltza (The Black Cat) (Peillen), 26, 173
Gauaz ibiltzen dana (Creature of the Night) (Peillen), 26, 173, 242
"Gauaz parke batean" ("In a Park at Night") (Mirande), 26
Gau ipuinak (Night Tales) (Onaindia), 31
Gauzak ez ziren sekula berdinak izango (Things Would Never Be the Same) (Irasizabal), 38
Gela debekatua (The Forbidden Room) (Onaindia), 31
gender roles. *See also* sexuality; sexual orientation
  in *110.street-eko geltokia*, 48–49
  in *Gizona bere bakardadean*, 91
  in *El guardián invisible*, 202–11 (*see also* motherhood)
Gender Trouble (Butler), 114
Genet, Jean, 50–51
Gereño, Xabier, 27–28, 37, 173–74, 226
Gezurren basoa (The Forest of Lies) (Ladron Arana), 38
Gil, Daniel, 234
Giltza publishing house, 176
Gizona bere bakardadean (The Lone Man) (Atxaga), 34–35, 86–96
  in crime fiction genre, 88–89, 96
  critique of author of, 86–88

historical trauma in, 246–49
loneliness in, 90, 92
political situations in, 91, 93–96, 246–49
protagonist and plot in, 89–96
realism in, 96
suspense in, 88, 92
time in, 91–92, 96
translations of, 87
Gizon argala (The Thin Man) (Hammett), 28
Gizon bat bilutsik pasiloan barrena (A Naked Man in the Corridor) (Agirre), 33–34
Glass Key, The (Kristalezko giltza) (Hammett), 243
Glass Keys, The (Les claus de vidre; Beirazko giltzak) (Fuster), 243
globalization, impacts of, 249–50
glocal novels, 201
Goenkale (High Street), 105
Goiti, Borja, 230
Les Gommes (Robbe-Grillet), 9
Gorria, Uzta, 233
Gorrotxategi, Miren, 25, 39, 230
Gorrotxategik, Aritz, 38
Gostin, Andres, 21
Grafton, Sue, 12, 243
Graziana (character), 67, 69–70
Greene, Graham, 7, 9
El guardián invisible (The Invisible Guardian) (Redondo), 40, 201–16
  affective violence against women in, 213–14
  awards for, 202
  corporeal presence in, 214–16
  gender gap in, 202–4
  motherhood in, 205, 206–8, 209, 212–13, 216
  overview of, 201, 216
  sisterhood in, 204–6, 216
  violence against women in, 208–10, 213–14, 216
  violence in family or home in, 211–13
  violence in society in, 210–11
Guayasamín, Oswaldo, 226–27
Gu bezalako heroiak (Heroes Like Us) (Irasizabal), 38
Guerra Garrido, Raul, 40

guilt
  in Amaia Ezpeldoi novels, 109–10
  in *Lili eta biok,* 157, 167–68, 170
  in Pinilla police novels, 196
Gulddal, Jesper, 245–46
Gure Jerusalem galdua (Our Lost Jerusalem) (Epaltza), 72
Gutenberg, Johannes, 220

H
Haitz "Rocky" Zumeta (character), 28
Hamabost egun Urgainen (Fifteen Days in Urgain) (Loidi)
  as children's and young adult police novel, 171–73
  as first Basque-language crime novel, 25, 46, 222, 225, 241
  front cover of, 225–26, 226*f*
  as noir fiction, 46
  parody of, 161
Hamaseigarrenean, aidanez (It Happened the Sixteenth Time) (Lertxundi), 30, 181
Hammett, Dashiell
  as canonized writer, 9
  realist and noir fiction by, 3, 6, 12, 129, 138
  translation of works of, 28, 239, 242–43
hard-boiled fiction. *See* noir fiction
Harrian mezua (The Message in Stone) (Ladron Arana), 38
"Harri eta berri: nuevos horizontes de la literatura vasca" (Kortazar), 252
Hauts madarikatua (The Cursed Powder) (Zaldua), 183
Hemingway, Ernest, 9, 79, 85n18
herenerria (third land), 101
Hernandez Abaitua, Mikel, 19–20, 173, 181
Herrimina (Homesickness) (Zaldua), 31
"highbrow" literature, 8–9, 18
Highsmith, Patricia, 9, 12, 92, 178
La higuera (The Fig Tree) (Pinilla), 190, 196
Hil ala bizi (Dead or Alive) (Amuriza), 29
(H)ilbeltza Grant, 25
Hillerman, Tony, 21, 104

Hilpuinak (Deadly Short Stories) (Urteaga), 39, 185
Hiltzaile baten bila (On the Trail of a Murderer) (Gereño), 27, 174
Himes, Chester, 9
Hipotesiak gordinkeriaz (On the Vulgarity of Hypotheses) (Cano), 118
Historia de la literatura vasca (History of Basque Literature) (Urkizu), 23
Hitchcock, Alfred, 120
Hobe isilik (Best Keep Quiet) (Ubeda), 39, 230, 230*f*
Hoffmann, E. T. A., 4
Holmes, Sherlock. *See* Sherlock Holmes (character)
homesickness, 44–45, 57–61
Hoppenstand, Gary C., 3–4
Hound of the Baskervilles, The (Baskervilletarren zakurra) (Conan Doyle), 242
humor. *See also* parodies
  in *110.street-eko geltokia,* 58
  in Amaia Ezpeldoi novels, 35, 106, 109
  in Arretxe noir fiction, 141, 143–44
  in children's and young adult police novels, 173, 176, 177–81, 186
  in Epaltza novels, 68–69
  in realist or noir fiction, 6, 25
  in *Zintzoen saldoan,* 135
Hunchback, The (Conan Doyle), 2
Hutsaren itzalak (The Shadows of Emptiness) (Arretxe), 37–38, 138, 234*f*, 249

I
Igartua, José Félix, 227, 229–30
Igelak benetan hiltzen dira (Frogs Really Die) (Irasizabal), 38
Igela publishing house, 28–29, 33
Iltzea (The Nail) (Alarcón), 172
Iñarra, Aitxus, 210, 212
Inork ikusi ezin duena (Second Sight) (Smith), 184
intertextualities
  in Amaia Ezpeldoi novels, 105
  in Epaltza novels, 65, 83n3

Index

in history of Basque-language crime fiction, 26, 28, 33–36, 38
"Investigación de la memoria. El olvido como crimen" ("Investigation of Memory: Forgetting as Crime") (Martínez Rubio), 146
investigative novels. *See* detective and crime fiction; Spanish Civil War investigative novels
investigators. *See* protagonists
Iraganik gabe (Without Any Past) (Juaristi), 185
Irasizabal, Iñaki, 38
Irene (Lemaitre), 10
Irene, Tempo di adagio (Aristi), 31
Irigarai, A., 172
Irigoien, J. M., 44
Irish Troubles, 247–49
Iruineako asasinatzea (The Murder in Pamplona) (Gereño), 174
Irurac bat (The Three Are One) (de Pedro), 184
Iser, Wolfgang, 15
Itsasoa etxe barruan (The Sea inside the House) (Cano), 119
Iturralde, Joxemari, 37, 175
Itxaropena publishing house, 225
Itzuliz usu begiak (Turning Usually the Gaze) (Lertxundi), 33
Izagirre, Koldo, 33
Izeta, Mariano, 26, 173, 226
Izu-izua (Terrifying Horror) (de Pedro), 184
Izurri berria (The New Plague) (Garate), 226–27, 227f
Izzo, Jean-Claude, 24

J

Jainkoen zigorra (God's Punishment) (Ladron Arana), 38
Jalgi hadi plazara (Go Forth into Public) (Borda), 35, 99, 105, 107, 113–14
James, P. D., 11, 12, 37, 243
La jaula de sal (The Salt Cage) (Martín), 41
Jimenez, Edorta, 34
Jimenez, Irati, 182
Joao Boaventura (character), 38

Jodra Llorente, Susana, 218
Johnson, Craig, 104
Jónasson, Ragnar, 238
Jon Bidart (character), 28
Jon Garai (character), 28
Joseba Telleria (character). *See 110.street-eko geltokia*
Juaristi, Felipe, 86, 88, 185
Julio Rekexo (character), 37
Jurgi Arregi (character), 27–28
Jurgi kapitaina Britainian (Captain Jurgi in Brittany) (Gereño), 174, 226

K

Kafka, Franz, 26, 31
Kafkaren labankada (Kafka's Knife Wound) (Gorrotxategik), 38
Kale gorrian (Stone Cold) (Swindell), 184
Katebegi galdua (The Missing Link) (Alonso), 35, 38
Kaxkajo bahituaren kasua (The Case of Kidnapped Kaxkajo) (Aldai), 177–78
Kcappo. Tempo di tremolo (Aristi), 31, 44
Kea behelainopean bezala (Like Smoke in Low Mist) (Cano), 118, 119
Kearen truke (In Exchange for Smoke) (Gorrotxategik), 38
Keefe, Patrick Radden, 247
"Killer in the Rain" ("Hiltzailea euripean") (Chandler), 243
King, Stewart, 238, 245–46
Kintana, Xabier, 31, 54, 228–29
Kleopatra (Cleopatra) (Arretxe), 37
Kortazar, Jon, 30, 146, 181, 189, 252
Koxme Zubia (character), 34
Krisalida, Tempo di tempo (Aristi), 31
Kruz Igerabide, Juan, 186
Kurt Wallander (character) series, 238, 244
Kusto, Cyprian, 95

L

Läckberg, Camilla, 12, 238, 243
Ladron Arana, Alberto, 38, 186, 230
Lagarde, Marcela, 205–6, 208–9, 211, 213

Lakhous, Amara, 250
"Larrüpean ebiltzen direnak" ("What Under the Skin Is") (Borda), 21
Larsson, Stieg, 238, 244
Lasarte Leonet, Gema, 203
"Lau lagun eta erdi" ("Four and a Half Friends") series (Friedrich and Valverde), 176
Lázaro Carreter, Fernando, 126
Leblanc, Maurice, 244
Le Carré, John, 7
Lefebvre, Henri, 196
Legado en los huesos (The Legacy of the Bones) (Redondo), 40, 202, 232f
Legez kanpo (Out of the Law) (Mintegi), 34
Leire Asian (character), 38
Lemaitre, Pierre, 10
Leon, Donna, 12, 243
Leroux, Gaston, 244
Lertxundi, Anjel, 9, 30–31, 33, 175, 177–82, 231
Lesterren logika (Lester's Logic) (Cano), 119
Ligeia. Izu ipuinak (Ligeia: Horror Stories) (Poe), 28
Lili eta biok (Lili and Me) (Saizarbitoria), 39, 146–70
    crimes in, 147, 161, 164, 169–70
    front cover of, 224, 224f, 230
    inspiration for investigation in, 151, 156
    memory in, 156–58, 161, 169–70
    methodological explanation of study of novels similar to, 147–52, 151f
    narrative features of, 149
    objectives of study of, 146–47
    political discourse in, 149, 163–65, 169
    storyline of, 152–56
    as thesis novel, 161–69
    truth in, 147, 152, 157, 158–61, 166–70
    writer character investigating truth in, 152, 158–61
Lissitzky, Lazar Markovich ("El"), 221
literary system, 1–41
    Basque-language crime fiction in, 19–39 (*see also* Basque-language crime fiction)

name and essence of crime fiction genre in, 1–4
origins and evolution of crime fiction genre in, 4–7
position of crime fiction in, 7–12
readers in, 15–19 (*see also* readers)
Spanish- or French-language crime fiction in, 39–41
structure and elements of crime fiction in, 13–15, 16
studies and critiques in, 19–25 (*see also* Basque crime fiction and world literature studies)
literature studies. *See* Basque crime fiction and world literature studies
Lizbeth Salander (character). *See El guardián invisible*
location. *See* space or location
Loidi, Jose Antonio, 25, 46, 161, 171–73, 222, 225–26, 241–42
loneliness
    in *110.street-eko geltokia,* 44, 48, 56
    in Amaia Ezpeldoi novels, 108
    in Epaltza novels, 73
    in *Gizona bere bakardadean,* 90, 92
Long Goodbye, The (Ez adiorik) (Chandler), 243
Lopez Adan, Emilio ("Beltza"), 21
López Gaseni, José Manuel, 1, 183
Lore erradioaktiboak (Radioactive Flowers) (Fernández Paz), 183
Lotman, Juri, 5

M

Macdonald, Ross, 243
"Madame Kontxexi-Uribe, Brigada & Detektibe" ("Madam Kontxexi-Uribe, Brigadier and Detective") (Aldai), 33, 176–82
Madrid, Juan, 37
Mahamoud Toure (character), 37–38, 137–38, 139–44, 232, 233–34, 249–50
Maiatz publishing house, 113
Maigret (character), 6, 244

"Maitarien ardoa" ("The Lovers' Wine") (Mirande), 26
Malet, Léo, 21
Malgu da gaua (The Night is Flexible) (Cano), 118
Manchette, Jean-Patrick, 24, 37
Manila konexioa (The Manila Connection) (Arretxe), 37
Mankell, Henning, 37, 238, 244, 250
Manuzio, Aldo, 220
marginalization
    in Amaia Ezpeldoi novels, 107–8
    in Arretxe noir fiction, 141–42, 249–50
Margolana (The Painting) (Elortza), 183
Márkaris, Petros, 37
Marsh, Ngaio, 12
Martin, Andreu, 88, 176, 184
Martín Álvarez, Ibon, 41, 201
Martínez de Pisón, Ignacio, 79
Martinez Reverte, Jorge, 59
Martínez Rubio, José, study by, 146–52
    methodological explanation of, 147–52, 151*f*
    objectives of, 146–47
    on writer's investigation, 152, 158
Martin Garaidi (character), 25, 172
Mas, E., 173
Matos, Martín, 201
matrilineal model, 205
Mauriac, François, 10
McCoy, Horace, 29
memory
    constructions of, 190–96, 198–99
    investigative novel focus on, 146, 147, 149, 150, 156–58, 161, 169–70
    in *Lili eta biok*, 156–58, 161, 169–70
    in Pinilla police novels, 190–99
    representation of, 161
    sites of, 190, 196–99
Mendaroko txokolatea (Chocolate from Mendaro) (Irasizabal), 38
Mendekuak (Revenges) (Izagirre), 33
Mendoza, Eduardo, 47, 152, 249–50
Menos que cero (Less than Zero) (film), 51

Mesfidatu hitzez (Mistrust through Words) (Arretxe), 38, 138, 144
Mina, Denise, 250
Mintegi, Laura, 34, 243
Mintegi, Miguel Angel, 36
Mirande Jon, 26, 242
Miské, Karim, 250
El misterio de la cripta embrujada (The Mystery of the Enchanted Crypt) (Mendoza), 47, 249–50
Modiano, Patrick, 9
Moles, Abraham, 223
Monsieur Poiroten ikerpenak (Poirot Investigates) (Christie), 28, 242
Montalbán, Manuel Vázquez
    on adaptation in genre, 9
    Asesinato en el Comité Central by, 147–48
    Galíndez by, 152
    position of writing of in literary system, 8, 24, 37
    protagonist character of, 131
    on realist or noir fiction, 5–6, 20–21
    Tatuaje by, 47
    on terrorism, 29
Montoia, Xabier, 34
Montorio, Bego, 21
Montorio, Esteban, 231
Moonstone, The (Collins), 2
Mördare utan ansikte (Faceless Killers) (Mankell), 238
Moretti, Franco, 241, 244–45, 246
Morlesín Mellado, José Antonio, 218
Morto vivace (Arretxe), 37
Moskuko gereziak (Cherries from Moscow) (Velez de Mendizabal), 34
Mosley, Walter, 249
motherhood, 205, 206–8, 209, 212–13, 216
Moving Target: A History of Basque Detective and Crime Fiction, The (Cillero), 22–23
La muerte de Amalia Sacerdote (The Death of Amalia Sacerdote) (Camilleri), 132–33
Mugetan (On the Border) (Etxeberria), 32
La mujer del reloj (The Clock Women) (Arbina), 41

Muñoz, Jokin, 148, 151
Muñoz Molina, Antonio, 47
Murder of Roger Ackroyd, The (Christie), 10
Murders in the Rue Morgue, The (Poe), 10
music, 36, 76, 105–6, 120
Mysterious Affair at Styles, The (Stylesko gertaera misteriotsua) (Christie), 242
mystery novels
    Amaia Ezpeldoi novels as, 102
    children's and young adult police novels as, 175–84
    in detective and crime fiction genre, 2–4, 5–6, 7, 12
    Epaltza novels as, 65, 66–67, 78, 83n3, 84n12
    Gizona bere bakardadean as, 88, 96
    history of Basque-language, 25, 28–29, 33
    as noir fiction, 46–47
    structure and elements of, 13–14
myth, in crime fiction genre, 3

N

Nabaskues, José Luís, 225
Naranjo, Bautista, 189
Narcejac, Thomas, 1
narrators
    in *110.street-eko geltokia*, 52–53
    in Arretxe noir fiction, 140, 141–42
    as element of crime fiction, 14
    in Epaltza novels, 66, 73, 82
    in *Lili eta biok*, 165
    in *Zintzoen saldoan*, 130, 135
Navajo Tribal Police series (Hillerman), 21, 104
Navarro, Koro, 28
La nave de los locos (The Ship of Fools) (Peri Rossi), 59
Neguko zirkua (The Winter Circus) (Cano), 118
Nesbø, Jo, 238
"Nestor Burma" (Montorio), 21
Neuschäfer-Carlón, M., 176
Neville, Stuart, 247–49
New York, New York (Garate), 54
New York Trilogy (Auster), 125
"Nobela beltza eta polizi nobela klasikoa" ("Hard-boiled Fiction and Classic Crime Fiction") (Hernandez Abaitua), 19–20
Nocturno de Chile (By Night in Chile) (Bolaño), 150
No estamos solos (We're Not Alone) (Antoñana), 64
noir fiction. *See also* realist novels
    110.street-eko geltokia as (*see 110.street-eko geltokia*)
    Alonso novels and, 129–35
    Amaia Ezpeldoi novel references to, 107, 114
    by Arretxe (*see* Arretxe (Jon) noir fiction)
    Cano influenced by, 120–22, 126
    children's and young adult police novels as, 174, 181–82, 184–85
    in detective and crime fiction genre, 2–3, 12
    by Epaltza (*see* Epaltza (Aingeru) novels)
    front covers for, 227–34
    El guardián invisible as (*see El guardián invisible*)
    hardboiled storytelling in, 46, 83n2
    history of Basque-language, 26, 28–32, 34, 36, 37–39, 46–47
    Nordic (Swedish, Scandi-), 222, 238, 240, 244
    origins of term for, 67
    parodies of, 37
    society reflected in, 18–19
    Spanish Civil War investigative novels and, 147–52
    structure and elements of, 14, 130, 138–39
    studies and critiques of Basque-language, 19–20, 23–24
"Noir Month, Basque Crime Novel Week in January, The," 24–25
Il nome della rosa (The Name of the Rose) (Eco), 17
Non dago Stalin? (Where Is Stalin?) (Montoia), 34
Nora, Pièrre, 190, 196
Norbait dabil sute eskaileran (Someone on the Fire Escape) (Cano), 118, 119

Nordic (Swedish, Scandi-) noir fiction, 222, 238, 240, 244
Novela negra con argentinos (Black Novel (with Argentines)) (Valenzuela), 59
"Novela negra y policíaca" ("Hard-boiled Fiction and Crime Fiction") (Olaziregi), 23

O

Obabakoak (Atxaga), 86–88, 100
Odolaren deia (A Call to Blood) (Irasizabal), 38
Odolaren usaina (The Smell of Blood) (Antza), 32–33, 54
Ofrenda a la tormenta (Offering to the Storm) (Redondo), 40, 202
Olariaga, Antton, 177, 182
Olarra, Xabier, 21, 28–29, 242, 253n3
Olaziregi, Mari Jose, 23, 30, 31–32, 36, 172–73
Oleza, Joan, 161
Omar dendaria (Omar the Shopkeeper) (Cano), 119
Onaindia, Mario, 31
Ordaina zor nizun (I Owed You Compensation) (Urteaga), 39
Ormaetxea, Amaia, 175–76
Osaba Gabrielen asesinatzea (The Murder of Uncle Gabriel) (Gereño), 174
Ostegunak (Thursdays) (Arretxe), 137
Otaegi, Lourdes, 50, 51, 52, 173

P

Pamiela publishing house, 45
"Panic Attacks" ("Izu-taupadak") series, 184–85
paper, invention of, 220
paratexts, 18, 39
Pardo Bazán, Emilia, 222
Paretsky, Sara, 243
Paris de la France-ko pateen kasuan (On the Case of the Paris de la France Pâtés) (Aldai), 178–80
parodies
   in *Akatsbako gizonaren heriotza*, 26–27
   Amaia Ezpeldoi novels as, 114–15
   in children's and young adult police novels, 182
   of noir fiction, 37
   in Pinilla police novels, 190
   in *Zintzoen saldoan*, 135
Pasaia blues (Cano), 36, 117–18, 119, 122–27, 234–35, 235f
Pauloven txakurrak (Pavlov's Dogs) (Cano), 118
Pearson, David, 221
Pedro Mari Arrieta (character), 65–71
Peillen, Txomin, 26, 173, 242
Pérez Isasi, Santiago, 189
Pérez Molina, Fernando, 202
Peri Rossi, Cristina, 57, 59
Persona (Bergman), 123
Pessoa, Fernando, 54
"Philip Marlowek begikeinua egin zidanean... edo porrotaren lilura" ("When Philip Marlow Winked at Me... or the Fascination of Failure") (Azkargorta), 20
Piano gainean gosaltzen (Having Breakfast on the Piano) (Cano), 54, 118, 119
picaresque features, 68–71, 82, 139
Piglia, Ricardo, 9
Pinilla (Ramiro) police novels, 40, 189–99
   Aquella edad inolvidable as, 189
   Cadáveres en la playa as, 40, 189, 191, 193, 197–99
   El cementerio vacío as, 40, 189, 191–92, 194–95, 197–99
   constructions of memory in, 190–96, 198–99
   crimes in, 191–92
   front covers of, 232, 232f
   La higuera as, 190, 196
   narrating against forgetting in, 190–92
   narrating against power in, 192–96, 198–99
   overview of, 189–90, 198–99
   political situations/commentary in, 191, 193–96, 198–99
   sites of memory or space in, 190, 196–99, 200nn2–3
   Solo un muerto más as, 40, 189, 191–99, 232f
   Verdes valles, colinas rojas as, 40, 189, 190, 194–96
Piztia otzanak (The Tamed Beasts) (Cano), 118

Piztiaren begiak (The Eyes of the Beast) (Ladron Arana), 38, 230, 230f
place. *See* space or location
Poe, Edgar Allen
    Basque-language author infuence of, 26, 46, 117, 172–73, 242
    innovation of, 5
    mystery novels of, 2, 4, 5
    short stories of, 11, 221
    translations of works of, 4–5, 26, 28, 239, 241–42
Poirot Investigates (Monsieur Poiroten ikerpenak) (Christie), 28, 242
police novels. *See* detective and crime fiction
political situations
    in *110.street-eko geltokia*, 53, 57, 61
    in Amaia Ezpeldoi novels, 101, 103, 109, 111, 112–13
    in Arretxe noir fiction, 249–50
    Basque-language crime fiction on, 38, 60
    crime fiction as reflection of, 21
    in Epaltza novels, 63–72, 73–76, 81
    front cover design influenced by, 226
    in *Gizona bere bakardadean*, 91, 93–96, 246–49
    Lili eta biok discourse on, 149, 163–65, 169
    in Pinilla police novels, 191, 193–96, 198–99
    Spanish-language crime fiction on, 40
    in *Zintzoen saldoan*, 135
Politika zikina (Dirty Politics) (Irasizabal), 38
"Polizi nobela eta irakurlea" ("Crime Fiction and Its Reader") (Olarra), 21
polysystem theory, 7–8
Portzelanazko irudiak (Porcelain Images) (Aldai), 33, 175
Postariak beti deitzen du bi aldiz (The Postman Always Rings Twice) (Cain), 28, 242, 253n3
Postariak beti deitzen du mila aldiz (The Postman Always Calls a Thousand Times) (Martín and Ribera), 176
postmodern realism, 161
poverty, 44, 47–48, 53, 69, 95
power
    in *110.street-eko geltokia*, 48–49

    Alonso on struggle for, 35
    in Arretxe noir fiction, 139, 140–44
    Borda on, 100
    in Cano novels, 121
    in literary world, 244–45
    Pinilla police novels narrating against, 192–96, 198–99
    in realist or noir fiction, 19, 47
    of sisterhood in *El guardián invisible*, 204–6
    study of crime fiction portrayal of, 21, 25
    in *Zintzoen saldoan*, 131
Press, H. Jürgen, 176
Los privilegios del ángel (The Angel's Privileges) (Redondo), 202
progressive investigative novels, 152
prostitution, 50, 67, 69–70, 83–84n6, 211
protagonists
    in *110.street-eko geltokia*, 48
    Amaia Ezpeldoi as (*see* Amaia Ezpeldoi (character) novels)
    in Arretxe noir fiction, 137–38, 139–41, 143
    as element of crime fiction, 14–15
    in Epaltza novels, 66, 72–73, 76–79, 81–82
    in *Gizona bere bakardadean*, 89–96
    in *El guardián invisible*, 202–6, 216
    as investigator, 2
    in *Lili eta biok*, 158–61
    in realist or noir novels, 6, 130, 138–39
    in Spanish Civil War investigative novels, 148, 158–61
    in *Zintzoen saldoan*, 130–32, 133, 135
psychological novels, 6–7, 96
"Public Enemy Number One" (Gostin), 21
Puig, Manuel, 8, 9
pulp aesthetic tendency, 222
"Purloined Letter, The" (Poe), 241–42

R

Radiobiografiak (Radiobiographies) (Cano), 118, 119
Ramiro Pinilla: el mundo entero se llama Arrigunaga (Ramiro Pinilla: The Whole

World Is Called Arrigunaga) (Acillona López), 189
"Raven, The" ("Bela") (Poe), 242
readers
    as characters, 124
    crime fiction genre reception by, 15–19
    as element of crime fiction, 15
    expectations of, 18
    investigation by, 13
    pact with, 15–19
    speed of, 16–17
realist novels. *See also* noir fiction
    Amaia Ezpeldoi novels as, 103–4, 105
    Cano novels and, 120–22, 127
    credibility in, 132–34
    in detective and crime fiction genre, 5–6
    dirty realism in, 31, 34, 74, 81, 105, 120
    front covers for, 222
    Gizona bere bakardadean as, 96
    postmodern realism and, 161
    readers' suspension of realism vs., 18, 134
    society reflected in, 18–19
    structure and elements of, 13–14
Redondo, Dolores
    awards of, 202
    La cara norte del corazón, 40
    front covers of works of, 232, 232f
    El guardián invisible by (*see El guardián invisible*)
    Legado en los huesos by, 40, 202, 232f
    Ofrenda a la tormenta by, 40, 202
    Los privilegios del ángel by, 202
    Todo esto te daré by, 40, 202
    translations of works of, 40, 202, 245, 251
    as woman author, 201
regressive investigative novels, 152
Relato cruento (Bloody Story) (Antoñana), 64
Rendell, Ruth, 243
repetition, 120, 127, 180, 229
Retolaza, Irztxe, 34
Ribera, Jaume, 176, 184
Los ritos del agua (The Rites of Water) (García Sáenz de Urturi), 41
Robbe-Grillet, Alain, 9

Rock'n'Roll (Epaltza), 36, 76–81, 82
Rodchenko, Alexander, 221
Rodríguez Pequeño, Francisco Javier, 15
Rojo Cobos, Javier, 53, 129, 137
romanticism, 4, 32, 64, 67, 104, 106, 131, 138
Ruiz de Alarcón. *See* Alarcón, Pedro
rurality
    in Amaia Ezpeldoi novels, 104, 112, 114
    in Arretxe noir fiction, 143–44
    front cover depiction of, 225, 233
    in Redondo novels, 201, 202, 216

S

Saizarbitoria, Ramon
    100 metro by, 29
    Bihotz bi. Gerrako kronikak by, 150
    as canonized writer, 9
    Lili eta biok by (*see Lili eta biok*)
    social class addressed by, 103
Saki, 26
Saltero, Víctor, 247
Sampedro Alegria, Aiora, 117
Samuel Esparta (character). *See* Pinilla (Ramiro) police novels
Samurai berria (The New Samurai) (Velez de Mendizabal), 34
Sancho Bordaberri (character). *See* Pinilla (Ramiro) police novels
Sara izeneko gizona (A Man Called Sara) (Atxaga), 64
Sardina Ezpain Gorriaren Kasua (The Case of the Red-lipped Sardine) (Aldai), 182
Sarrionandia, Joseba, 58, 174
Sasiak ere begiak baditik (Even Brush Has Eyes) (Epaltza), 36, 63–72
    as crime fiction, 64
    front cover of, 227–29, 228f
    historical timeframe for, 63–65
    overview of, 63–64
    picaresque features in, 68–71, 82
    place or location for, 63–65, 71–72
    suspense in, 66–67
Sator lokatzak (Mole Mud) (Arretxe), 38, 138, 234, 234f

Savater, Fernando, 19, 40
Sayers, Dorothy L., 5, 11, 12, 117
Say Nothing: A True Story of Murder and Memory in Northern Ireland (Keefe), 247
"Scandal in Bohemia, A" ("Eskandalua Bohemian") (Conan Doyle), 242
scholarly study of Basque crime fiction. *See* Basque crime fiction and world literature studies
Sciascia, Leonardo, 9, 24
Sei lore (Six Flowers) (Garcia-Viana), 39
semiotics, 223
Los señores del tiempo (The Lords of Time) (García Sáenz de Urturi), 41
"*El séptimo círculo*" series (Borges and Bioy Casares), 9
setting. *See* space or location
sexuality. *See also* gender roles; prostitution; sexual orientation
    in *110.street-eko geltokia*, 48–49
    in Amaia Ezpeldoi novels, 109, 111–12
    in Arretxe noir fiction, 139
    in Epaltza novels, 70
    violence in response to, 210–11
sexual orientation, in Amaia Ezpeldoi novels, 107, 110, 112, 114–15. *See also* gender roles
Shavit, Zohar, 5, 12
Shelley, Mary, 4
Sherlock Holmes (character), 5, 11, 29, 223, 242
short stories
    Basque-language, 32–33, 39
    in detective and crime fiction genre, 11
    front covers for, 221, 222
Sigurardóttir, Yrsa, 238, 243
"Silence-A Fable" ("Ixiltze (Alegia)") (Poe), 242
El silencio de la ciudad blanca (The Silence of the White City) (García Sáenz de Urturi), 41
Simenon, Georges, 6, 9, 172, 174, 178, 239, 244
Simple Art of Murder, The (Chandler), 10
La sinfonía del tiempo (The Symphony of Time) (Arbina), 41
sisterhood, 204–6, 216
Sjöwall, Maj, 12, 37, 244

Smith, Sinclair, 184
social class
    in *110.street-eko geltokia*, 51–52, 54–57
    in Amaia Ezpeldoi novels, 103, 109, 114
    in Arretxe noir fiction, 141
    in Epaltza novels, 81
    in *Gizona bere bakardadean*, 94–95
    in *Zintzoen saldoan*, 134
society
    Amaia Ezpeldoi novels reflecting, 102–4, 106, 109–11, 114–15
    Arretxe noir fiction as critique of, 140–42, 145
    Basque-language crime fiction as critique of, 29–31
    children's and young adult police novels reflecting, 181–82, 185, 186
    classes in (*see* social class)
    crime fiction as reflection of, 18–19, 21
    violence in, 210–11, 247
    Zintzoen saldoan clichés on, 134–35
Sokratikoek ere badute ama (The Socratics Also Have a Mother) (Egaña), 33
Soldados de Salamina (Soldiers of Salamis) (Cercas), 147–48
Soler, Losada, 212
Solo un muerto más (Only One More Death) (Pinilla), 40, 189, 191–99, 232f
Somerset Maugham, William, 9
Sorgin moderno bat (A Modern Witch) (Cano), 118–19
Sostiene Pereira (Pereira Maintains) (Tabucchi), 79
space or location
    for *110.street-eko geltokia*, 54–56, 55f, 59–60
    in Amaia Ezpeldoi (character) novels, 98–99
    in Arretxe noir fiction, 143–44
    in Cano novels, 119–26
    as element of crime fiction, 14
    in Epaltza novels, 63–65, 71–72, 74–76, 79–81
    gender linked to, 204–5, 208
    in *El guardián invisible*, 202

in noir fiction, 84–85n17
in Pinilla police novels, 190, 196–99, 200nn2–3
rural (*see* rurality)
translation and circulation limited by, 245
Spanish Civil War investigative novels, 146–70
crimes in, 147, 148, 161, 164, 169–70
Lili eta biok as (*see Lili eta biok*)
memory in, 146, 147, 149, 150, 156–58, 161, 169–70
methodological explanation of, 147–52, 151*f*
narrative features of, 149
noir fiction vs., 147–52
objectives of studying, 146–47
progressive vs. regressive, 152
as thesis novels, 161–69
truth in, 147, 148–49, 152–53, 157, 158–61, 166–70
writer characters investigating truth in, 152, 158–61
Spanish-language crime fiction
front covers of, 234, 235*f*
Gizona bere bakardadean translation into, 87
Hamabost egun Urgainen as, 173
history of, 39–41
noir fiction as, 47, 227
translations of, 242, 244
Speed gauak (Speed Nights) (Jimenez), 34
spy novels, 7, 12, 34, 38, 83n5
Stark, Richard, 6
structure of crime fiction
in *110.street-eko geltokia*, 45–46, 52
in Amaia Ezpeldoi novels, 102
in Arretxe noir fiction, 138–39
in *Gizona bere bakardadean*, 96
in *Hamabost egun Urgainen*, 172–73
overview of, 13–15, 16
in *Zintzoen saldoan*, 130
Sucedió en el AVE (It Happened on the AVE Train) (Saltero), 247
Sun Also Rises, The (Hemingway), 85n18
Susa (magazine), 20, 21, 35, 118
Susa publishing house, 44, 99, 113, 229–30

suspense
in detective and crime fiction genre, 3, 7
in Epaltza novels, 66–67, 73
in *Gizona bere bakardadean*, 88, 92
structure to create, 13
Sute handi bat ene bihotzean (A Big Fire in My Heart) (Iturralde), 37, 175
Swindell, Robert, 184
Symons, Julian, 238

T
Tabucchi, Antonio, 79
Ta Marbuta: Jerusalemen gertatua (Tā marbūṭa: What Happened in Jerusalem) (Kintana), 31, 54, 228–29, 228*f*
Tangoak ez du amaierarik (The Tango Never Ends) (Elizegi), 33, 175
Tantos inocentes (So Many innocents) (Guerra Garrido), 40
Tatuaje (Tattoo) (Montalbán), 47
Telefono kaiolatua (The Caged Telephone) (Cano), 118, 119
terrorism, 29, 60, 72, 247–48. *See also* ETA members
La testa perduta di Damasceno Monteiro (The Missing Head of Damasceno Monteiro) (Tabucchi), 79
thesis novels, 161–69
Thompson, Jim, 21, 28
Thoreau, Henry D., 104
time
in *110.street-eko geltokia*, 52–53
in Cano novels, 124
as element of crime fiction, 14
in *Gizona bere bakardadean*, 91–92, 96
Pinilla novel chronological arc of, 198
title page, 236
Tobacco Days (Lertxundi), 30
Todo esto te daré (All This I Will Give to You) (Redondo), 40, 202
Todorov, Tzvetan, 1, 3, 13, 46
Torres, Lieutenant (character), 66–68, 70–71, 83n5
translations

advertising leading to, 222
of Amaia Ezpeldoi novels, 113
of Atxaga novels, 245
broadening of, 238–39
of Cano's works, 119, 234–35, 235*f*
of children's and young adult police novels, 173, 176, 183, 184
crime fiction evolution with, 4–5
foreign and local elements influencing, 245
front covers of, 234–35, 235*f*
of *Gizona bere bakardadean*, 87
in history of Basque-language crime fiction, 26, 28–29, 33, 40
of Nordic Noir, 222, 238, 240
of Redondo novels, 40, 202, 245, 251
scholarly study of Basque, 240–46
Trial, The: Olagarroa (Onaindia), 31
"Trilogía de la Ciudad Blanca" ("White City Trilogy") (García Sáenz de Urturi), 41, 201
Trilogia del Zodiaco (Zodiac Trilogy) (Alía), 201
Troubles Trash/Troubles Thrillers, 247–49
truth, search for
  in Epaltza's realist or noir fiction, 81–82
  in Pinilla police novels, 190–92, 193–94
  in Spanish Civil War investigative novels, 147, 148–49, 152–53, 157, 158–61, 166–70
Twelve, The (Neville), 247–49
Twist: izaki intermitenteak (Twist) (Cano), 118
Txalaparta publishing house, 25
Txalorik ez, arren (No Applause, Though) (Cano), 118
Txertoa publishing house, 29
Txillardegi, 29, 31

U
Ubeda, Garbiñe, 39, 230, 233, 235
Ultimes déchets (The Final Waste) (Borda), 35, 99, 103, 105, 108, 112–13
El último Akelarre (The Last Witches' Coven) (Martín), 41
Unanua, M. A., 28
Urkizu, Patrick, 23
Urmeneta, Asisko, 233

Urola ibaian (In the River Urola) (Zaldua), 31
Urra, Óscar, 138
Urteaga, Joxemari, 39, 185
Ur uherrak (Muddy Waters) (Epaltza), 36, 72–76, 78, 80, 81
US detective and crime fiction. *See also specific authors*
  Cano influenced by, 117–18, 119–21, 125–26
  children's and young adult authors influenced by, 172–73, 174
  films adapted from, 222
  hardboiled storytelling in, 46
  rural branch of, 104, 201
  translations of, 4–5, 26, 28, 239, 241–44

V
Valenzuela, Luisa, 59
Valles Calatrava, Jose R., 2, 20–21
Valverde, Mikel, 176
Van Dine, S. S., 1, 5, 11
Vargas, Fred, 12, 243
Vascos por el mundo (Basques around the World), 151
Vázquez de Parga, Salvador, 2
Vázquez Montalbán. *See* Montalbán, Manuel Vázquez
Velez de Mendizabal, Josemari, 34
Venuti, Lawrence, 245
La verdad sobre el caso Savolta (The Truth About the Savolta Case) (Mendoza), 47, 152
Verdes valles, colinas rojas (Green Valleys, Red Hills) (Pinilla), 40, 189, 190, 194–96
Verne, Jules, 172
victims
  as element of crime fiction, 15
  in *Gizona bere bakardadean*, 247–49
  in *El guardián invisible*, 210–16
  in Spanish Civil War investigative novels, 148
violence
  in *110.street-eko geltokia*, 47–48, 49, 51, 53, 54, 56–57, 59–61
  affective, 213–14
  in Amaia Ezpeldoi novels, 114

in Arretxe noir fiction, 140, 143, 144, 250
corporeal evidence of, 214–16
in Epaltza novels, 60, 66, 72, 73–74
in family or home, 211–13
in *El guardián invisible*, 208–16
in *Lili eta biok*, 147, 155–56, 161–64
in society, 210–11, 247
against women, 208–10, 213–14, 216 (*see also* domestic violence)
by women, 210, 211–13, 214, 216
Vox, Maximilian/Vox typography, 237nn1–2

W

Walhöö, Per, 37, 244
Welles, Orson, 120
Wendyk hegan ikasi zuen gaua (The Night Wendy Learnt to Fly) (Martin), 184
Westlake, Donald, 6
Who is Killing the Great Chefs of Europe? (Christie), 130
Wilder, Billy, 120
women
  affective violence against, 213–14
  bodies of, 214–16
  as detective and crime fiction authors, 11, 201, 243–44 (*see also specific authors*)
  Epaltza novel views of, 70, 84n15
  gender roles of (*see* gender roles)
  motherhood of, 205, 206–8, 209, 212–13, 216
  sisterhood among, 204–6, 216
  violence against, 208–10, 213–14, 216 (*see also* domestic violence)
  violence by, 210, 211–13, 214, 216
Woodrell, Daniel, 104
Wright, Richard, 9

X

Xahmaran (Arretxe), 37
Xake mate (Checkmate) (Ladron Arana), 38

Xantaia kontesari (Blackmailing the Countess) (Gereño), 174

Y

Yehuda (Velez de Mendizabal), 34
young adult police novels. *See* children's and young adult police novels

Z

Zabala, Juan Luis, 86, 87
Zabaleta Urkiola, Iñaki
  110.street-eko geltokia by (*see 110.street-eko geltokia*)
  background of, 45
Zaldiak akatzen ditugu ba (They Shoot Horses, Don't They?) (McCoy), 29
Zaldua, Imanol, 31, 183
"Zazpi gizeraile" ("Seven Murders") (Mirande), 26
Zelaieta, Anjel, 86
Zelaieta, Edu, 122
Zer barkaturik ez (Nothing to Forgive) (Ladron Arana), 38
Zinea eta literatura. Begiaren ajeak (Film and Literature: The Eyes' Defect) (Cano), 118, 120–21
Zintzoen saldoan (In the Group of the Righteous) (Alonso), 36, 129–35
  clichés in, 134–35
  credibility and coherence in, 132–34
  cynicism and romanticism in, 131
  front cover of, 231, 231*f*
  as noir fiction, 130–35
  plot or story in, 130, 131–32
  protagonist in, 130–32, 133, 135
Zoaz infernura, laztana (Go to Hell, Darling) (Lertxundi), 31, 231, 231*f*
Zulaika, Joseba, 59
Zumalabe, Joxemi, 53, 229

About the Authors

Jose Manuel López-Gaseni: Graduated in Basque Philology and doctor in Psychodidactics. Senior lecturer at the University of the Basque Country (UPV/EHU) in the Department of Didactics of Language and Literature, he develops his lines of research in the areas of literary translation, children's and young people's literature and didactics of literature, disciplines on which he has published several works. He is part of the LAIDA (UPV/EHU) and LITER21 (USC) research groups. https://orcid.org/0000-0002-1743-1873

Jon Martin: He is a lecturer of language and literature at the UPV/EHU. He has a PhD on the Basque poet Xabier Lete. Graduated in Advertising and Public Relations and Graduated in Early Childhood Education. He has worked in the world of communication and education. His research focuses on oral improvisation and the popular singing. He is part of the LAIDA (UPV/EHU) research group.

Asier Barandiaran: Senior lecturer of Didactics of Language and Literature at the University of the Basque Country (Vitoria-Gasteiz). He has a PhD in Basque Philology at the same university, he has served as a lecturer at the University of Navarre from 1995 to 2011 and since 2011 at the University of the Basque Country. He is the author of *Gatazka Nafarroako Euskal Literaturan* (The Conflict in Basque Navarrese Literature) (2011), *Diasporako Bertsoak* (The Diaspora Verses) (2016), coordinator and co-author of *Egile Nafarren Euskal Literaturaren Antologia* (Navarrese Writers's Basque Literature Anthology) (I, 2017; II, 2018). He has also published chapters in collective works of the LAIDA research group on "Basque Literature and Identity", focusing his attention on the literary analysis of Navarrese authors and some aspects of the theory of polysystems. https://orcid.org/0000-0002-0249-3246

Xabier Etxaniz: Senior lecturer at the Faculty of Education and Sports of the University of the Basque Country (UPV/EHU) in the Department of Didactics of Language and Literature. His academic research focuses on children's and youth literature, highlighting studies on historiography and panoramic views of Basque children's and youth literature as well as works on the transmission of values in children's books. He has published in journals such as *OCNOS*, *Insula*, *Children's Literature in Education*, *ANILIJ* . . . as well as in popular magazines such as *CLIJ*, of which he has been a contributor since its inception. He also participates as a literary critic in Basque publications such as *Argia* or *Gara*. He is part of the LAIDA (UPV/EHU) and LITER21 (USC) research groups. https://orcid.org/0000-0002-0974-1652

About the Authors

Ur Apalategi: Born in Paris, he has a degree in Law and French Letters and a PhD in Basque Philology. He is a professor of Basque Studies at the University of Pau et des Pays de l'Adour (UPPA) and a member of the Iker (CNRS-UPPA-Bordeaux 3) and Laida (UPV/EHU) research groups. Specialist in contemporary Basque literature, he is the author of *La naissance de l'écrivain basque* (The Birth of the Basque Writer) (Paris, l'Harmattan, 2000), a book derived from his doctoral thesis devoted to the work of Bernardo Atxaga, and of *L'autre écrivain basque* (The Other Basque Writer) (Paris, L'Harmattan, 2013), work in which he studies the last period novels of Ramon Saizarbitoria. He is the promoter of the "Kritika literarioa" (Literary criticism) collection of the Utriusque Vasconiæ publishing house, which publishes books on literary criticism in Basque. He has lectured at the universities of La Plata, Oxford, Kiel, Tartu, Cork, Paris VIII, Barcelona, Santiago de Compostela, Bordeaux 3, Brest. https://orcid.org/0000-0001-8211-9168

Aiora Sampedro Alegria: She is a lecturer in the area of Basque Philology at the University of Salamanca. She graduated in Basque Studies, and completed a master's degree in Comparative Literature and Literary Studies at the UPV/EHU (2017). She has a PhD on the Basque writer Harkaitz Cano. Her lines of research are comparative literature and sociology of literatura, and she has lectured at the universities of Barcelona, Alcalá de Henares, Lisbon, and Salamanca. She collaborates in the literary criticism section of the Basque newspaper *Berria*. She belongs to the LAIDA (UPV/EHU) research group. https://orcid.org/0000-0002-5925-4959

Javier Rojo Cobos: PhD in Basque Philology from the University of the Basque Country (UPV/EHU) by means of a dissertation on the historical novel and its place within the literary production of Yon Etxaide. He has written in several journals, such as Insula. He has worked as a literary critic in the supplement "Territorios" (Territories), published by the Spanish newspaper El Correo from the beginning of this supplement in 1996 to 2021. In 2013 he was in charge of the book *Egungo euskal saiakeraren historia* (History of Contemporary Basque Essay), volume 13 of the Euskal Literatura Saila (Basque Literature Collection), published by the UPV/EHU. https://orcid.org/0000-0002-3156-5106

Jon Kortazar: Professor of Basque Literature at the University of the Basque Country (UPV/EHU). He leads the research group LAIDA (Literature and Identity) that has published *Egungo Euskal Literaturaren Historia* (History of Contemporary Basque Literature, eight volumes, 2007-2016), which has been translated into English: *Contemporary Basque Literature* (Reno, Nevada, 2016). His main works are: *Euskal Literatura XX. mendean* (Basque Literature in the 20th Century) (1990, seven reissues), *Luma eta lurra. Euskal poesia 80ko hamarkadan* (The Pen and the Earth. Basque Poetry of the 80s) (1999) and *Montañas en la niebla. Poesía vasca de los años 90* (Mountains in the Fog. Basque Poetry of the 90s) (2006). In Iberoamericana / Vervuert he has published the book *Contemporary Basque Literature: Kirmen Uribe's Proposal* (2013), and directed *Autonomía e ideología. Tensiones en el campo cultura vasco* (Autonomy and Ideology. Tensions in the Basque Cultural Field) (2016). He has coordinated several monographs on Basque literature in the Spanish journal *Ínsula*. His work has been translated into ten languages. In 2019 he held the position of visiting professor at the Luis Mitxelena Chair at the University of Chicago. https://orcid.org/0000-0003-1589-6295

Miren Billelabeitia: She has a degree in Basque Philology, and she is a teacher of Basque Language and Literature at a secondary school. She has studied the pedagogy of reading and reflected on the practice of encouraging reading. He has given lectures and training activities in Regional Renewal Centers, schools and summer courses on the teaching of Literature and the promotion of reading through literary gatherings. Her publications include: *Euskal Herriko literatura* (Literature in the Basque Country) (2003), *Esquemas de Euskera* (Schemes of Basque) (2003), *Lauaxeta. Oihartzunak* (Lauaxeta. Echoes) (2008), an anthology of the Basque poet Esteban Urkiaga Lauaxeta. As a result of a reading project, he has published *Aitita-amamen guda zibila* (Grandparents Civil War) (2019) along with the students of the Mungia secondary school. Her last book up to date is *Norberak maite duena. Hitza gogoan, irakurketa biziz* (What Everyone Loves. The Word in Mind, Living Reading (2022).

Karla Fernández de Gamboa: She is a lecturer at the University of the Basque Country (UPV/EHU). She worked as Predoctoral Fellow in GRETEL, a Research Group from the Universitat Autònoma de Barcelona (UAB), from 2013 to 2017, where she completed an international PhD in Education with her doctoral thesis on contemporary narrative for children. She is a member of the Editorial Board of *Ikastorratza e-journal on Didactics* and of *Behinola*, journal on Basque Children's Literature. Her research interests include children's literature, picturebooks and school libraries. She combines her work as researcher and teacher with children's literature outreach on newspapers in the Basque Country. https://orcid.org/0000-0002-2659-9563

Santiago Pérez Isasi: Assistant researcher at the Center for Comparative Studies of the Faculty of Arts of the University of Lisbon. His research areas include Iberian studies, literary history or the digital humanities. He is the head researcher of the exploratory project "Mapa digital das relações literárias ibéricas (1870-1930)" (Digital Map of Iberian Relations. 1870-1930) and coordinator of the IstReS (Iberian Studies Reference Site) project together with Esther Gimeno Ugalde (Universität Wien). He is the coauthor, with Antonio Sáez Delgado, of the volume *De espaldas abiertas. Relaciones literarias y culturales ibéricas (1870-1930)* (Open back. Iberian literary and cultural relations. 1870-1930) (Comares, 2018) and co-editor of the volumes *Looking at Iberia. A Comparative European Perspective* (Peter Lang, 2013), *Los límites del Hispanismo* (The Limits of Hispanism) (Peter Lang, 2017) and *Perspetivas críticas sobre os estudos ibéricos* (Critical Perspectives on the Iberian Studies) (Ca'Foscari, 2019). https://orcid.org/0000-0002-9548-4655

Maite Aperribay-Bermejo: She is a member of the Department of Language and Literature Didactics (UPV/EHU), having worked in the Department of English and German Philology and Translation and Interpretation (UPV/EHU) for a decade. She has taught foreign languages and literature and didactics of language and literature, among others, in the Bachelor's, Diploma and Undergraduate degrees. She researches in comparative literature and literary studies, especially in North American literature. Her lines of research include comparative literature, cultural studies, gender studies, and ecofeminism. In her doctoral dissertation, "Ecofeminist Perspectives on Chicano Prose of the Nineties" (2017), she combined research on gender and ecofeminism. She is the author of several chapters on these topics. She has been a member of the REWEST (Research in Western American Literature and Culture) research group since 2013. She is also a member of LAIDA research group (UPV/EHU). https://orcid.org/0000-0002-1188-1670

About the Authors

Jose Antonio Morlesín: Graduate (2008) and Doctor of Fine Arts (2016) from the UPV/EHU. He has received the extraordinary doctorate award (2018) for his doctoral thesis, entitled "Evolution, current state and perspectives of the design of the book cover: study particularly oriented to the Autonomous Community of the Basque Country". He has been a lecturer in the Department of Drawing at the UPV/EHU Faculty of Fine Arts since 2015. He lectures in the Degree in Creation and Design, as well as in the University Master's Degree in Research and Creation in Art. His lines of research focus on the fields of illustration, comics and book cover design in the Basque Country, having published articles on this area of editorial design in specialized magazines. He is currently part of the LAIDA Literature and Identity research group. https://orcid.org/0000-0001-7973-8259

Susana Jodra: Graduated in Fine Arts from the UPV/EHU, master's degree from the HDK in Berlin and a doctorate in Fine Arts from the UPV/EHU. She focuses her artistic-research and teaching activity on analogical and digital printing techniques, paying special attention to screen printing. She has participated in solo and group exhibitions nationally and internationally: Berlin, Bern, Tainan ... Together with the Swiss artist Patricia Schneider she works on the artistic project "Modulares" (Modular). She has published texts and illustrations in various publications: At present she combines her artistic and teaching activity in the Department of Drawing at the Faculty of Fine Arts of Leioa UPV/EHU, she lectures in the degrees, as well as in the Masters of Research and Creation in Art and in that of Ceramics: Art and Function. She is a member of the LAIDA research group, Literature and Identity. http://orcid.org/0000-0003-3414-1672

Stewart King: He is a senior lecturer at Monash University (Clayton, AU). His research interests focus on two broad areas: Spanish and Catalan Studies and Crime fiction as a form of world literature. His research in these interconnected fields was first established through his work on the construction of Catalan identities in literature written in both Spanish and Catalan and later on the role of crime fiction in post-Franco, democratic Spain. His book, *Escribir la catalanidad. Lenguas e identidades en la narrativa contemporánea de Cataluña* (Writing Catalanity. Languages and Identities in the Contemporary Narrative of Catalonia) (Tamesis 2005), applies post-colonial theories to develop a substantial and controversial re-evaluation of Catalan authors who write in Spanish that challenges how Catalan literature is conceived. His major contribution to the field of crime fiction from Spain has been to question the inherent Spanishness of "Spanish" crime fiction by exploring the construction of competing national and cultural identities in crime novels written in Spanish as well as Catalan, Galician and Basque. https://orcid.org/0000-0002-4663-1700